THE TAKEN

The Soul Summoner Series Book 4

ELICIA HYDER

Inkwell & Quill, LLC

GET A FREE BOOK

Robbery · Arson · Murder
And the one-night stand that just won't end.

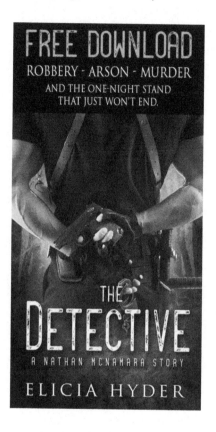

The Soul Summoner Series Order

Book 1 - **The Soul Summoner**
Book 2 - **The Siren**
Book 3 - **The Angel of Death**
Book 4 - **The Taken**
Book 5 - **The Sacrifice**
Book 6 - **The Regular Guy**
Book 7 - **The Soul Destroyer**
Book 8 - **The Guardian**
Book 9 - **The Daughter of Zion**

Standalones:
The Detective
The Mercenary
The Archangel

For Dad.
Love, Toot.

PS. The check's in the mail.

ACKNOWLEDGMENTS

Special Thanks to everyone who made this book possible:

To my badass husband…I think better when you're home.
No more deployments, m'kay?

To my kids who make me feel like a really cool mom.

To my Mom and Dad, I'm in my 30's and still can't do a thing
without you.

To Barbara Vey, sometimes you get to pick your family.
I'm glad you picked me.

TO MY AWESOME LAUNCH TEAM
THE BOOK SUMMONERS
I would be nowhere without you!

And always…thanks to the fans who love Sloan, Nathan, and Warren as much as I do.
The best is still to come.

CHAPTER ONE

"COME ON! SUCK it in!"

Adrianne jerked so hard on the gaping zipper of the gown that I floundered backward off the three-sizes-too-big heels she'd forced me into. As I sailed back into her, my life flashed before my eyes. She swore, and we both stumbled back into the full-length mirror of the dressing room.

"Is everything all right in there?" The saleslady, Marlene Peapot, gently knocked on the other side of the door.

Adrianne pushed me upright, steadied me by the shoulders, then turned me around to face her. She shook her head, her face caught somewhere between exasperation and sorrow. "I think we're going to need another bigger size, Mrs. Peapot."

"Young lady, my name is pronounced *Pay-poh*."

We'd been over this a few times since our arrival at Mountain Laurel Bridal a couple of hours before.

Adrianne ignored her again and attempted to straighten the white fluffy fur top that should have been fitted around my shoulders but instead drooped off my chest like a saggy lifesaver. Her nose wrinkled with disgust.

I turned toward the mirror. "I don't like it."

"You'll like it better when we get the right size," she said.

The right size. Ugh.

My hand slid down the bloated bulge that had overtaken my midsection. Oh, the delusions I'd had about pregnancy.

I had been certain I'd be one of those mommies who maintains their size everywhere else while growing a perfectly shaped basketball baby bump. I'd gain my expected 25–35 pounds and have nary the need for spandex or belly pouch pants until right before my blessed due date.

Lies.

Lies.

Lies.

The truth was, despite all the dehydration caused by the puking and tearfulness of my first trimester, I was promising to be an overachiever when it came to average pregnancy weight gain. Every inch of me, from my face to my feet, was swollen or fat. And it wasn't cute or acceptable baby fat either. It was your obstetrician-gives-you-a-food-diary kind of fat.

Dr. Watts started throwing around words like "gestational diabetes" and "polyhydramnios" when the scales revealed I had gained a total of twenty-three pounds at my four-month checkup. She ordered a whole new round of tests which revealed two things:

1. My body was producing too much amniotic fluid, which we needed to keep an eye on.

2. Sloan eats too much ice cream.

Enter the food diary.

It wasn't my fault, however. Demons were coming for me the first day of summer—in 139 days to be exact if not before. So what else was a girl to do but eat her feelings as the clock counts down to her demise? If I was going to go out, I intended it to be with a belly full of happiness. Besides, babies need calcium, right?

But there were others responsible for my reigning position on the pregnancy growth chart. At the top of the To Blame list was

Azrael, who cut me off from physical activity with a father-in-law-imposed house arrest for the duration of my pregnancy. I was only allowed to leave home with a supernatural escort in tow. For dress shopping that day, Reuel—my own personal Angel of Protection—waited not-so-patiently in the car. He was fully recovered from his impalement during our showdown with the angels.

I considered myself lucky. Constant security was a fair trade since Azrael didn't lock me up inside the Claymore Worldwide Security compound like he'd threatened to do "for my own protection" when we got back home. I finally consented to being chained to my townhouse on the condition that he didn't bring up me living at the security compound again.

Then there was his son, Warren, my fiancé extraordinaire. While he did provide my sole form of rigorous exercise (wink, wink), he also cooked lavish meals for me when he was home and left delivery menus for when he wasn't. And God knows this girl should never be trusted with a to-go order and a high-limit Visa.

And, of course, Nathan McNamara, a.k.a. Captain Skittles, was proving to be quite the enabler. He couldn't show up at my door without something that contained sugar like it was a cardinal sin to visit a pregnant lady without an aluminum wrapper full of calories. I was pretty sure he'd packed on a few sympathy pounds himself.

Taiya's continued milk carton status also held partial responsibility for my new habit of stress eating. In the weeks since our return from what I'd begun calling The Battle of Calfkiller River, there had been zero news, zero leads, and zero hope of finding that adorable, freaky little waif. The blurry photo showcasing her arm where I'd jokingly (sort of) written "If found, please call Sloan Jordan" originated from a phone number based in Chicago. It was disconnected by the time we tried to call it back.

While I knew she was alive and growing stronger every day, my internal GPS was scrambled when it came to locating her. Azrael said my demon mother was behind it, most likely, but he swore that wouldn't stop him from trying to find her. It was almost funny that a few months before I'd been desperate to get rid of the crazy Seramorta who frightened the bejeezus out of me; and now that she'd been taken, I'd do anything in the world to get her back.

And last, but very far from least, was the continued quest for the spirit world's Most Wanted.

My demon mother, Kasyade, and the child-possessing devil, Phenex, were still evading arrest and eternal damnation, but the intel the FBI had gathered on them was interesting, to say the least.

Photos of Phenex, posing as a pre-teen Hispanic girl, were recovered from Kasyade's home in Texas, the office of the prostitution hub in Chicago, and the law office of Abner Tuinstra. She was even the poster child for the ministry's second home in Houston. No one knew her identity, and the FBI assumed she was dead —until Calfkiller River when Phenex showed up and went full-blown Emily Rose on everyone.

Agent Sharvell Silvers had made Phenex her top priority, but so far the only leads dead-ended in more questions.

As for the young girl whose body Phenex had taken, her fate I knew for certain. She was gone. Long gone. And whoever she was, lots of cookie dough ice cream had been eaten in her honor.

But my list of excuses was lost on Adrianne Marx, my best friend and self-appointed wedding planner. She was determined to stuff me into a corseted bodice if it killed me. And it almost did when she finally worked the zipper of dress number three all the way up.

"There," she said with a deep sigh of satisfaction.

I looked at her. "I don't like it."

She scowled. "You haven't looked in a mirror yet."

My bottom lip poked out. "I can't breathe and it's itchy and poking me in the hips."

She pushed me through the door out to the mirrored platform. "You're supposed to be beautiful on your wedding day, not comfortable."

"If discomfort is the goal, I think we've found a winner," I grumbled.

In the reflection of the mirror, Marlene Peapot's head fell quizzically to the side as I stepped up on the platform. I saw why when I caught sight of my appearance. The fabric stretched taut across my belly and shoulders while it gaped around my boobs, hanging flaccid at the front of my pelvis like some kind of anatomy should have been there but wasn't. My fingertips barely extended beyond the extra-long lace sleeves and the frilly skirt engulfed my feet despite the tall shoes.

Adrianne stood so close behind me that her auburn hair brushed my cheek. I wondered if she was trying to picture herself in the gown instead of me. She must have noticed the grimace spreading across my face. "It's winter chic," she said over my shoulder.

I frowned. "I look like I'm going to freeze Narnia."

Marlene took a cautious step forward. "How formal is this wedding?"

"*Not*," I answered before Adrianne could.

"It will be glorious," Adrianne added.

I shook my head. "It will be at the courthouse."

"And the date?" Marlene asked.

"April 19th," I replied.

She winced. "May I make a suggestion then?"

I said "please" and Adrianne answered "no" in unison.

I nodded at the saleslady to indicate my go-ahead.

She sidestepped away from Adrianne and scurried toward me. "With a style so tailored to your figure, I'm afraid that you'll outgrow it again by the wedding." She tugged at the fabric around my ribs. "How far along are you?"

"Almost five months." It was a lie. I was barely four months along.

Marlene's gaping mouth was the exact reason I'd begun padding the date. She quickly snapped it shut.

I groaned.

She held up her hand. "Wait! I think I know the perfect dress for you." She squeezed my arm, then bolted from the room.

"*This* is the perfect dress for you." Adrianne's shoulders slumped in defeat. It was rare that she ever pouted. "Who does she think she is?"

My brow rose. "A salesperson. I promise this is not a personal vendetta against your sense of style. It is a lovely dress." And it was true if someone with Adrianne's figure were wearing it. On me, however, I felt like Jabba the Hutt stuffed into a sequined tube sock, and no amount of deceivingly angelic lighting or perfectly angled mirror tilt could convince me otherwise.

My left leg was still an inch shorter than the right one after our rumble with the angels, and Adrianne's shoes weren't helping my new propensity for stumbling. My ankles wobbled again in her heels as I limped off the platform.

She caught me by the elbow and frowned. "You're a liability."

"I'm aware." I hiked up the skirt and kicked off the shoes. "Help me out of this thing."

Marlene returned when I was stripped down to my cotton granny panties and support bra. She handed a bagged gown over the stall door. "Try this one."

Less than half the fabric of Adrianne's dress came off Marlene's hanger. A good sign.

Adrianne's nose scrunched as she held it up and glanced at the gap between the hem and the floor. "Where's the rest of it?"

"In the virgin bride's section where it belongs," I said.

She rolled her eyes and lifted it over my head.

The conservatively short dress stopped just above my knees, with a high-cinched waist that allowed the ivory fabric to cascade naturally over my expanding baby bulge. The sleeves were three-quarter length, and it had a deep, plunging neckline that accentuated the best byproduct of pregnancy—the boobs. But the real selling point was the material. The outside was elegant lace and tiny beading, but the inside was soft cotton and satin.

"This feels wonderful!"

Adrianne's face didn't reflect my enthusiasm, but it wasn't completely disapproving either. She tugged at the waist, smoothing the cozy fabric into place. "It isn't awful."

"I could sleep in this," I said with a wild smile.

She straightened and scowled at me. "You'd better not."

"It's a jersey cotton blend!" Marlene called out.

Adrianne smirked. "Sounds cheap."

I quivered with delight. "It sounds like pajamas."

She shook her head. "That's not a good thing."

"I promise, it's a very good thing," I argued, wiggling my hips against the satin.

Marlene clasped her hands in front of her heart when I stepped out of the dressing room. "I love it! Do *you* love it?"

My bare feet scampered up onto the platform. "I love it." For the first time in a while, I felt pretty.

Behind me in the mirror, Adrianne cracked a smile. "You do look cute."

Marlene walked a wide circle around me. "I don't even think you'll need to have it altered."

I pulled the stretch fabric away from my stomach. "And we've got some additional real estate built in for expansion." I found the price tag and made a vomiting noise.

Adrianne swatted my hand away. "Warren says you're not allowed to worry about price."

"Is Warren the groom?" Marlene asked.

I nodded. "I totally hit the fiancé jackpot."

"I'll say. Does he have an older brother?" she asked, tying a silky sash around my waist.

Adrianne caught my gaze in the mirror and smiled. "No, but he does have a father."

I pretended not to hear her. As it turned out, despite conning him into several dinners and even sleeping over at my house once while Warren and I were away, Adrianne's advances had been declined by The Angel of Death. She was still far from giving up hope, however, and she took every opportunity possible to tease me with it. I decided to let the taunting slide as long their relationship stayed platonic. Azrael had been part of our lives for months, and while I literally put my life in his care, I still didn't trust him with my best friend.

"What about a veil?" Marlene's question snapped me back to reality. She dangled a wisp of tulle from her finger.

"No veil," Adrianne and I both responded.

I pointed at her. "Hey! We agree on something!"

She brightened with hope. "I want to curl your hair and pin it up with baby's breath and miniature roses."

I deflated. "You lost me again."

"What about shoes?" Marlene asked, motioning to a glass case in the corner filled with pumps and stilettos.

Adrianne dug her fingers into my arm. "Oh, I saw the cutest pair of strappy crystal and suede Jimmy Choos!"

My head tilted in question. "Jimmy *whose?*"

She pointed to her feet. "Shoe designer."

I shook my head and shrugged.

Adrianne's face fell back toward the ceiling in anguish.

Marlene laughed. "The two of you are going to have fun with wedding plans."

Smiling to myself, I wondered if both of us would survive.

The sound of alarm bells chimed around the salon like a biohazard warning. Marlene looked up with alarm. I extended my hand toward her. "It's only my phone. Don't worry." I tapped my forehead. "Pregnancy brain is no joke. I forget everything if I don't set reminders."

"What is it this time?" Adrianne asked.

I went to retrieve the blaring phone. "I don't remember."

A notification message blinked on the screen. *Monday, February 3rd. Dinner with Dad. Nine Mile. 5:00 p.m.*

I checked the clock. "Adrianne, we've got to go!" Dinner was on the other side of town during rush hour. I yanked the gown over my head and draped it over the door. "Mrs. Peapot, can you ring this up for me?"

"*Pay-poh,*" she said again with a heavy sigh.

"Sorry!"

Adrianne wedged her tall frame through the door, taking care not to flash Marlene the sight of me in my skivvies. "What are you late for?" she asked, stooping to gather up all our stuff.

I frowned. "Dinner with Dad."

"When?"

I cringed. "In fifteen minutes."

"Sloan, it's every Monday night. How do you forget every single week?" she asked. "I have a head injury and I've never been this scatterbrained."

The memory of Adrianne's accident still made me shudder, and I refused to let her tease me with it. "Correction: I healed you from a head injury."

Her eyes widened, and she pressed her index finger over her lips. "Shush!" She pointed to the door Marlene was standing on the other side of. "You're not supposed to tell people that, remember?" she whispered.

I clamped my hand over my mouth. *Oops.*

She laughed. "Tie your shoes. We've got to go!"

If Marlene Peapot had heard my claim to supernatural abilities, she didn't make an issue of it. We paid for the dress and made it to Nine Mile at 5:06. Reuel, my Azrael-appointed bodyguard, accompanied us. He'd stayed in the car while we were in the bridal shop, but there was no way the 6'4, 309-pound angel would miss out on a meal. That guy could eat more than me...which, lately, was saying something.

Dad was seated at a high-top table near the bar when the three of us walked inside. He waved as we crossed the hardwood floor and rose to greet us. "There's my beautiful girl," he said, kissing my cheek.

"Hi, Daddy."

"You brought friends, I see." He smiled. "Hello, Adrianne, Reuel."

Reuel, who still refused to speak English, grunted with a nod.

Adrianne gave my dad a hug. "Sorry we're late."

Dad's taunting grin turned toward me as we pulled out our chairs. "I'm getting used to it."

I hoisted myself up onto the seat next to him. "Oh, hush."

"I was hoping Warren would be with you. It's been a while since I've seen him," he said.

I nodded. "Me too." And it was true. Since Christmas, Warren had been away searching for Taiya with Azrael more than he'd been home.

"Did you tell me he's in Chicago?" Dad asked.

I shook my head. "No. He's in Texas."

Dad looked up at the ceiling. "Where'd I come up with Chicago?"

"Azrael went to Chicago a few weeks ago because that's where the phone number that sent the picture of Taiya originated, but he didn't find anything. Since then, Azrael and Warren went to New York after tracing all her demon father's affairs back there, but nothing turned up there either. Now they're in Texas interrogating the two guys Warren and Nathan helped put in jail there."

"Wow, I'm behind," Dad said with a chuckle. "When will he be back?"

"He's supposed to be home sometime today, but I haven't heard from him," I replied.

"Have they found out anything about her?" he asked.

I thought for a second. "Not much."

"Her arm," Adrianne said.

"Oh yeah. You remember how my name was carved into her skin on her forearm?"

Dad frowned. "Yeah."

"The FBI brought in a handwriting analyst. Her father Ysha put it there," I said.

"What does that mean?" Dad asked.

"It means he sent her to me."

"Any idea why?"

I shook my head. "No, but I really wish somebody would send her back."

Dad's mouth dipped into a sympathetic smile. "I'm sorry they're having such trouble finding her."

I took a deep breath and let it out slowly. "Nobody's as sorry as I am."

Adrianne held her hands in the air. "If we don't stop talking about this, Sloan's going to melt into a puddle of tears right here."

She was right.

"Guess what we did today, Dr. Jordan," Adrianne said with extra enthusiasm.

"What did you do today?" Dad asked, matching her chipper tone.

The tension eased in my neck and shoulders.

"We bought a wedding dress!" Adrianne announced.

"A wedding dress?" He looked at me. "No kidding?"

"No kidding," I answered.

"Does this mean you and Warren set a date?"

"Actually, yes." I swapped a smile with Adrianne. "April 19th."

He blinked with surprise. "The day after your birthday?"

I nodded. "It was Warren's idea."

Dad smiled. "So he'll have a better chance of remembering your anniversary?"

Adrianne laughed. "So Sloan will."

Normally, I would have argued, but on Friday two weeks before, I'd actually forgotten to go into work. I just didn't go. Warren had left, entrusting my care to Reuel, who wouldn't have reminded me even if he were inclined to speak. Through groans, body language, and brooding, he'd made it perfectly clear how much he despised hanging out in my office downtown. It wasn't until my boss called at lunchtime—and we were half-way through season two of Game of Thrones—that I realized my error.

It was that night that the talks of me resigning from my job with the county began.

Azrael staged a reality-tv-worthy intervention with Warren, my dad, and even Nathan McNamara. Azrael and Warren argued I would be safer at home. Dad reasoned the change would be in the best interest of my health. But Nathan was the only one who was brutally honest. He pointed out that since all the angel nonsense had overtaken my life, I sucked at my job. And he was right. The Buncombe County office deserved better.

I handed in a tearful resignation letter to Mary Travers the following Monday. She cried, which was a shock. I cried, which was not. I trained my replacement, a bubbly intern named Emily, and the office threw me an impromptu baby shower/going away party. It was all very ceremonious and depressing. My job was the one thing I'd held onto from my "normal" life, and now it was gone.

Dress shopping was Adrianne's bright idea to cheer me up on my first official day of being unemployed. I was pretty sure Reuel would have preferred being at my office.

"I think an April wedding sounds perfect. Where will it be?" he asked.

"The courthouse," I said, studying the menu. "The magistrate said he—"

"Absolutely not," Dad interrupted.

"Thank you!" Adrianne tossed her hands up, happy to have found a like-minded cohort in her argument that a basic legal ceremony was a preposterous idea. I wanted a simple wedding. Warren wanted me to have what I wanted. Azrael thought the whole idea was stupid. And nobody asked Nathan McNamara for obvious reasons.

"What's wrong with the courthouse?" I asked.

Dad's face rumpled with disapproval. "Nothing's wrong with it, but I only have one daughter. I'd really like to give you away, Sloan."

Well, I couldn't argue with that.

Adrianne was wearing her unmistakable I-told-you-so smirk.

"We could do it at the house," he suggested. "In the garden or in front of the fireplace if it rains. Your mother would have loved that idea."

Dang.

Adrianne clapped and squealed, certain I was backed into a proverbial corner that I wouldn't try to get out of. "I'll take care of all the details!"

I sighed with a half-smile. "I'm sure you will."

Mom was the reason I didn't want a big wedding. It was too excruciating a thought for her not to be there. Some days her absence was almost tangible, like Christmas or the first time I heard my baby's heartbeat. I knew my wedding would be one of those moments. It's strange how grief can bend time. It felt like she'd been gone for an eternity, yet with each tiny reminder the sting was raw and new.

As if reading my mind, Dad gave my hand a reassuring squeeze. "It'll be a perfect day. You'll see." He winked, then sat back in his chair. "All right. What shall we have for dinner?"

I held up the new, shiny black credit card issued to me from Azrael's account. He was now supplementing my (nonexistent) income and Warren's. To make myself feel better about yet another loss of normalcy in managing my own finances, I used that card. A lot. "Order whatever you want, folks. Dinner's on The Angel of Death tonight."

The silvery winter moon was glistening off the bare Blue Ridge Mountains in the distance when Adrianne turned onto my street. From the back seat, I peeked between her and Reuel and saw cars lining the street in front of my house. Warren was home. His Dodge Challenger (that Nathan had finally recovered from impound) was parked next to mine in the driveway. Azrael's truck was at the curb behind Nathan's county-issued SUV, and there was a black sedan behind him that instantly triggered flashbacks and a severe case of PTSD the second my eyes landed on it.

It was the FBI.

My palms began to sweat.

"What the hell's going on?" Adrianne asked.

I gulped as she slid the transmission into park. "I have no idea."

Closing my eyes, I sent my evil radar into the house. Nothing sinister lurked inside my home...nothing sinister that was human, anyway. I looked at Reuel in question. He didn't answer.

"Maybe it's a party because the evil queen is dead and peace has returned to the galaxy." Adrianne's tone was sarcastic. Even she knew better.

As if anticipating my pending heart attack, Warren's tall frame appeared in the front doorway. He was in jeans and a faded red t-shirt, wearing the leather jacket I'd bought him for our late Christmas morning do-over. The few months since his military-enforced scalping had done wonders for his hair. It was the perfect finger-raking length, just long enough to fall away from his face when I dragged my nails through it. The simple sight of him in the glow of the porch light eased the tension building in my neck and shoulders. The baby fluttered in my stomach.

Bedroom eyes not included, the only time Warren's face was readable was when he was really angry. That was rare and usually directed at Nathan McNamara. On the porch, he was expressionless, but nevertheless, it made me nervous.

Adrianne parked behind my car in the driveway. Reuel got out, pushed his seat forward, and offered a hand to pull all my frumpiness out of the back seat. Warren was coming down the steps when we reached the front sidewalk.

I pointed to the convoy parked on the street. "What's this about?"

He held up his hands. "Don't freak out."

"Why would I freak out?" My unconvincing voice was a couple octaves higher than usual.

Warren's right eyebrow rose to taunt me. "Silvers came back with us. She has news."

I stopped walking so quickly Adrianne bumped into me.

"We need to install brake lights on your ass," she said.

I ignored her. "Silvers is here all the way from Texas? That can't be good."

"There's been a break in the case. A positive one."

My heart swelled with hope. "You found Taiya?"

He frowned. "Not that big of a break, unfortunately." He reached for my hand, and when our fingers touched, his warm energy flowed through my body. "Come inside. I'll let her explain." He turned back toward the house. "How was dress shopping?"

"Ugh."

Adrianne jostled the hanger of my dress causing the opaque plastic to rustle. "After much toil and tribulation, it was a success."

Warren smiled at me as we walked up the steps. "So you really are going to marry me?"

I looked up at him. "There's no going back now."

He pressed a kiss to my forehead and pushed the door open.

Nathan stood as we walked into the house. His plainclothes attire of tan tactical cargos and a black half-zip fleece didn't forewarn if he was on official police business or not. The ball cap on his head, however, signaled he was off duty; the patch on the front had a picture of a tyrannosaurus and the caption *Licensed to carry small arms.* He smiled when our eyes met.

Sharvell Silvers and Azrael were seated together on the new sofa I'd bought to replace my Taiya-stained white couch. The new one had sleek black, stain resistant leather, and a pull-out bed. It also made fart-sounds anytime someone moved on it, especially Azrael for some reason. Like it was manufactured for the sole purpose of keeping the Archangel of Death humble.

He moved to get up. *Phwaaaaawert...*

The room erupted into muffled snickers.

Azrael scowled as he stepped aside to let me have his seat.

I walked over to the couch and extended a hand to Sharvell. She shook it. "Hello, Agent Silvers."

She smiled, her lips painted a dark crimson. Her eyes were wide as she took in the sight of me. "It's good to see you, Sloan. You're looking...*healthy.*"

Healthy = Fluffy.

I sat in Azrael's spot. "It's good to see you too. What brings you all the way up here?"

"We've had some developments." Her tone was shaky. "Given the nature of our past dealings with each other—"

I lowered my voice. "Because of all the angel stuff?"

She swallowed. "Yes. Because of all the angel stuff, we all agreed this conversation should be had in person."

I looked at Azrael. "A little heads up would've been nice."

He looked at Warren for an explanation.

"It was my idea to wait till we got back here," Warren said.

"Why?" I asked.

"Because they were probably afraid you'd do something stupid," Nathan interjected.

My head whipped toward him, but his eyes met mine with a

silent dare for me to argue. I kept my mouth shut and sank back into my seat.

Agent Silvers handed me the stack of folders that was balanced on her lap. "Have a look for yourself."

When I flipped open the first one, the haunted eyes of Phenex stared lifelessly back at me. The photo was clipped to a stack of papers. The girl's name was Maria Juarez, age fifteen, and the daughter of Jorge (deceased) and Marisol Juarez of San Antonio, Texas.

Juarez. Juarez. Juarez...

I tapped the page. "I recognize this name. How?"

"Rex Parker and Tito *Juarez,* who we just visited in jail," Warren said.

My head snapped back. "Oh."

Agent Silvers thumbed through the pages until she found another paperclip. She pulled that bunch out and laid it on top. It was a federal indictment. The United States v. Marisol Juarez. *Oh boy.*

Marisol, Tito's mother, had been arrested as the head of the prostitution ring in Chicago. I looked at Warren. "I guess three's a charm and this trip was productive."

He nodded and shrugged at the same time and sat on the arm of the sofa beside me. "It answered some questions and created a lot of others."

Agent Silvers crossed her legs. "We showed Tito Juarez the photo of Phenex. He said she was his sister, but that's all we got out of him before he started making demands about a deal for release." She shook her head. "I'm not willing to do that unless I have no other choice."

"But you do have another choice," I said. "Talk to their mother."

"Exactly." The agent leaned toward me. "That's why I came to talk to you. I was wondering if you'd come with me to see her."

I touched the center of my chest. "Me?"

"No," Azrael barked, taking a reflexive step forward.

Judging from Azrael's reaction, this was not part of the originally planned conversation. Warren, however, slouched forward, balancing his elbows on his knees as he tapped his fingertips together. "I agree with her."

"What? This is ridiculous," Azrael said.

Warren looked over at his father. "Marisol Juarez isn't going to talk to us or the FBI. Sloan has a way with people. She's helped Nate get reluctant witnesses to talk before."

"He's right," Nathan added. "Not to sound too cliché, but I think it's part of Sloan's gift."

"It's too dangerous," Azrael argued.

I looked at Agent Silvers. "I'll do it."

My agreement was based partly on a desire to help, but mostly on my desperation to get out of the house and do something useful. The fact that it bugged Azrael was a bonus, regardless of whether or not he was acting in my best interest.

She looked pleased. "We can fly to Chicago tomorrow morning."

I glanced back at Warren. "You'll come with me?"

He nodded. "Of course."

Azrael walked toward us with his hands raised and a face that implied we had both lost our minds. "Hold on a second. Nobody's going to Chicago."

My mouth fell open. "Az, this woman probably knows how to find Phenex. And if we find Phenex, we could find Taiya—"

"Taiya's not in Chicago, Sloan," he interrupted. "If she was, I would have found her."

I turned my palms up. "That's beside the point. Marisol Juarez is the best lead we've had recently, and you know as well as I do that Phenex is the most direct path to Taiya *and* Kasyade."

He folded his large arms over his chest. "That doesn't mean you have to go to Chicago."

I smirked. "Yeah, it kinda does. If you and Warren walk in there, she might drop dead of a heart attack."

He scowled. "You know that's not true."

"Maybe not, but she definitely won't tell you anything."

Azrael looked at Silvers. "Can't you subpoena records on the Juarez kid? Or let me put pressure on Tito and get him to talk?"

"First, I'm afraid that whatever you might get out of Tito won't be admissible in court depending on your tactics of interrogation."

Agent Silvers had a point, but the rest of us didn't care about how all this would play out in a court of law.

She continued. "And I've started the process through my office, but we don't have time to wait for the courts to get the information about the child. She could be in danger or—"

"The child is dead, Silvers." Azrael put his hands on his hips. "She's a lost cause."

The agent visibly swallowed, then cleared her throat. "Well..." Her voice croaked. "If you want my help on this, you need to trust my judgment. I believe that the safest and most expedient route to getting the information is to go through Marisol."

"With my help," I added.

For a second, Azrael was speechless. Then after a beat, he pointed at Warren. "I'm ordering you to stay here."

This had become a common practice in our lives lately. It didn't take long to figure out what price Warren paid to come back to Earth as a full-blown angel. Free will. Similarly to the way I was able to control the souls of humans, calling them to me at will, Azrael was Warren's new puppeteer. If he so desired, he could make Warren tap-dance around the dining room table— which he did one night over drinks and homemade fajitas. While we'd all gotten a good laugh about it at first, I wasn't laughing about it anymore.

Warren had spent a lot of years in the military, so taking orders didn't bother him as much as it bothered me. It hadn't proven to be a major problem yet, but it was only a matter of time. And Azrael putting his foot down about Warren accompanying me to Chicago might be the tipping point. Next to me, the "angry muscle"—as I had taken to calling it—was working in my fiancé's jaw.

I pushed myself up off the couch and stood toe-to-toe with Azrael. "Then I guess I'll be going alone."

He blinked.

I stuck my finger in his face. "You may be able to tell him what to do, but you're not the boss of me." I considered stamping my foot for dramatic effect, but I didn't. "And if you're trying to keep me here by not letting him come with me, then I'll go without him."

The muscles around his dark eyes slowly relaxed. He knew I was right. And he knew there was nothing he could do about it. "We'll all go then."

I released the fists I hadn't realized I'd balled at my sides. "Fine."

Agent Silvers rubbed her forehead. "Forgive me if this is a stupid question, but why is Sloan any safer here than in Chicago?"

I pointed at Azrael. "Because he thinks he's the supernatural air traffic controller of Asheville."

She turned her ear toward me. "Huh?"

"I track who from my world is coming and going in this area," Azrael explained. "I've taken a lot of precautions to protect Sloan, and here in the mountains, she is a very important fish in a very small pond. Chicago is quite the opposite and is extremely dangerous for her."

"Is there anything the government and I can do to help keep her safe?" Agent Silvers asked.

"No," we all answered in unison.

Warren stood and put his arm around my shoulders. "I'll work on flights. You're good to leave in the morning?"

"Seeing as I no longer have a life, sure."

He winked at me.

I turned toward Nathan who was leaning against the back of the sofa behind us. "Are you coming with us?"

He shook his head. "I'm going to sit this adventure out. Some of us aren't on the Almighty's payroll."

I looked at Azrael. "The Almighty has a payroll?"

He rolled his eyes.

"If you're sitting this out, why are you here?" I asked Nathan.

"He was with me," Azrael answered. "He dropped by to tell me the good news."

I was surprised. "Good news?"

Nathan nodded. "Looks like I'll be headed to New Hope. Azrael made me an offer I can't refuse."

Agent Silvers crossed her arms. "Must have been quite an offer. You made it perfectly clear to the Bureau that you had no intentions of leaving Buncombe County."

Nathan glanced away with an awkward chuckle, and the rest of the room kept silent. Everyone except Agent Silvers knew exactly why Nathan's intentions had changed. His reason for staying in Asheville was twelve weeks and a pair of Jimmy Shoes (?) away from marrying someone else. And just because our relationship had been successfully wedged into a little platonic box, I still felt as guilty as a sinner in church.

Warren cleared his throat, signaling a shift in the conversation. *My hero.* "Well, I can't wait to hear all about this offer. Over dinner, perhaps? I'm starving." He patted his flat stomach and then wrapped his hand around mine. "Who's coming with us?"

Azrael nodded. "I could eat."

Reuel grunted in agreement, of course.

"We already ate," I reminded him.

Adrianne took a step closer to Az and flashed me a smile that warned me to keep my mouth shut. "So what? We can eat again."

I sighed.

"Agent Silvers?" Warren asked.

She stood, shaking her head. "I've got some paperwork to wrap up tonight, so I'm going to go back to my hotel. You have my cell number. Let me know when you finalize your travel plans. I land at O'Hare around nine in the morning."

I nodded. "We will."

Warren's head swiveled toward Nathan. "You in?"

Nathan pulled his keys from his pocket. "Nah. I'm gonna head home." He walked over and offered his hand to Warren. "But you guys be safe tomorrow. Call me if you need anything."

"Will do, brother," Warren replied.

Nathan gave me a side hug as he walked past. "You be careful," he said softly in my ear.

"Promise." I grabbed him by the sleeve as he pulled away. "Wait. When do you leave?"

He shrugged. "We haven't ironed out all the details yet. It'll be a little while."

I nodded, unsure of what else to say. It wasn't exactly *news* that Nathan was going to work for Claymore, Azrael had been talking about it for weeks, but the reality of it coming to pass was a bit jarring. Even though in a sense his acceptance of the job made him a more permanent fixture in our bizarre little family, Nathan McNamara was leaving. And it meant a whole lot more than a career change.

Warren tugged on my hand. "You ready?"

I nodded. "I'm ready."

CHAPTER TWO

*a*T THE RESTAURANT, I refrained from ordering a second dinner that I'd have to log in my food diary and sipped on a glass of chocolate milk. Adrianne rattled on about plans for my wedding. I wondered if she'd ever run out of ideas or questions.

How did I feel about hiring a caterer and bringing in tables for a garden reception?

Did I prefer roses or lilies?

Can we please, oh please, hire the McKinney String Quartet?

"I want a dark chocolate fountain," I said.

She groaned and touched her forehead. "Sloan, chocolate fountains are *so* 2004."

At that point, I gave up making suggestions. "You tell me when and where to show up, and you can take care of the rest."

She tapped the pen she was making notes with against her lips. "Whether or not you realize it, that's been the plan all along."

I slurped the last drop of chocolate through my straw. "Works for me."

"We also need to talk about the wedding shower." She pulled

out her phone and swiped across the screen to unlock it. "What do the few weeks before the wedding look like for you?"

I moved my fingers back and forth across my neck while shaking my head. "No, no, no. I don't want a shower."

She flipped her hair back over her shoulder. "Whatever. It's happening, so get over it."

I reached across the table and grabbed her hand. "I'm serious. You have to promise me, Adrianne. No shower."

She snatched her hand away. "Why the hell not?"

I sat back in my seat as tears prickled the corners of my eyes. "My mom."

Her face melted. "Oh." She put her phone down. "I didn't think about that."

"It will be hard enough to get through the wedding without her there. I don't think I can handle anything else."

She offered a gentle smile. "You're absolutely right. No shower." She looked at me seriously. "But I am taking you out and getting you terribly drunk for your bachelorette party. Absolutely no excuses."

I aimed both index fingers at my swollen baby belly.

She tossed her hands up. "Damn it!"

We both laughed.

Beside us, Azrael, Warren, and Reuel talked about Chicago. And even though I was only half-listening, it was clear Azrael was still trying to convince Warren it was a bad idea. I pulled my smartphone out of my back pocket. "I'm booking flights with Azrael's credit card before he comes up with any more excuses for us to stay home," I announced.

Azrael held up his hand and my phone sailed from my fingers across the table into his grasp. "We're not flying anywhere," he said, looking around to see if any other patrons noticed his party trick.

"Why are you so against us going to Chicago?" I asked.

At the head of the table, Reuel's body vibrated with silent

laughter that rattled the silverware against the empty plates in front of us. *"Katu de nai parakk. Azrael metum parakk."*

Warren and I exchanged a confused glance. "Azrael's what?" I asked Reuel.

Reuel mimed the next part. He pointed at Azrael. Then his eyes widened and he shook his hands like he was terrified. Then he spread out his arms and made an airplane noise.

Azrael fumed.

My mouth was gaping. "Are you afraid of airplanes?"

Now red-faced with tears of laughter threatening to spill down his cheeks, Reuel nodded.

"Is it true?" I asked Azrael again.

Azrael sat back hard in his seat and folded his arms across his chest.

Adrianne teased him with a pouty face. "Oh, is the big, badass Angel of Death afraid of flying?"

Reuel waved his hands toward us, then stretched his hand high above his head. *"Toda altuyar."*

"All heights?" Warren looked at his father. "You're afraid of heights?"

My head fell back toward the ceiling and I howled with laughter. "Oh my god. That's the funniest thing I've ever heard in my life. You know you're immortal, right?"

"I'm not afraid of dying," he snapped. "It's the plummeting from the sky bit that I don't care for."

I covered my face with my hands and laughed until I had to rest my head on top of my arms on the table. When I looked up, mascara was smudged on Adrianne's face and Warren had completely turned his back to everyone.

"I hate you all," Azrael grumbled.

"Didn't you fly home today with Silvers?" I asked.

Warren shook his head. "No, she flew here alone. We warped back." Still laughing, he put his hand on my shoulder. "Remember when NAG flew us to Claymore and you thought it was so nice that Az let Enzo take his seat on the helicopter while he drove the SUV back to the compound?"

I wiped away tears. "You've gotta stop or I'll go into labor."

Azrael stood, pushing his chair back with his legs. He slammed a fifty-dollar bill onto the table and walked outside.

Adrianne got up, trying her best to be serious. "I'd better go after him."

Warren gave Reuel a high five, then settled back in his seat. He smiled at me. "This may have been the best dinner we've ever had."

I fanned my face as the remaining giggles subsided. "Warren, tell Azrael he can warp there without us. There's no way we can drive to Chicago. It will take a week to get there with all the bathroom stops I'll have to make."

Warren draped his arm across the back of my chair. "I'll talk to him, but don't get your hopes up." He twirled a strand of my long brown hair around his fingertip. "Tell me about the dress."

I leaned an elbow on the table. "What I should really tell you about is the dress Adrianne picked out."

He grinned. "For you or for her?"

"For me." I shook my head. "But if you'd seen it, you might be convinced she was shopping for her. It was made for someone with her figure. I looked like lumpy cheese blintz covered in sequins."

He tried to suppress a chuckle but couldn't. "Babe, you'll be beautiful even if you look like a breakfast pastry."

Outside, it was clear Adrianne was using the cold as an excuse to invade Azrael's personal space. And he didn't seem to mind. "I know Adrianne's hardheaded, but do you think he's leading her on?" I asked.

Warren plucked his straw from his glass and began to chew on the end of it. "He *says* he's been straight with her."

I didn't miss his insinuation that Azrael often says one thing and does another.

Before I could ask Warren to elaborate, his spine went rigid and his head jerked toward the door. I knew what it meant.

"Azrael says we've got to go?" I asked.

He nodded.

We stood and he helped me with my coat. "He can send a text message, or hell, wave through the window. There's no need for him to be all creepy about it," I said as I pushed my arms through the sleeves.

"He's The Angel of Death," Warren said. "Creepy goes with the job title."

"Amen to that."

When we got back home, I went upstairs to take a bath while Warren finalized plans with Azrael for the next day. I was half-asleep, up to my chin in lavender bubbles, when the door creaked open. Warren trudged in and gave a heavy sigh.

"It went well, huh?" I asked, smirking.

He took a deep breath. "We're flying with Reuel. Az will meet us there."

I clapped my wet hands. "Impressive, honey."

He raked his fingers back through his hair. "The argument over the flight wasn't the worst of it."

My brow lifted in question.

"Last minute fares are ridiculous. We've really got to get better about planning these trips."

"How much?"

He cringed. "Too much."

I frowned. "That reminds me, I still owe Nathan for flying to San Antonio."

Warren walked over to the linen closet and retrieved a towel. "I already took care of it."

"You did?"

He nodded. "Of course I did. He saved our asses down there. He didn't want to accept it, but I threatened his life if he didn't."

I smiled. "That's a serious threat coming from you."

"Yep. My new credentials are coming in handy."

"Did you know Nathan took the job at Claymore?" I asked.

Warren sat on the closed toilet seat and began untying his black boots. "I knew Azrael offered it to him, but I didn't know he accepted till we got back today. I'm not surprised though. How are you feeling about it?"

"I'm happy for him. I think it will be a good opportunity, and it's probably the best thing for all of us." I sank further under the suds. "Thanks for changing the subject earlier when things got awkward downstairs with Silvers."

He grinned over at me. "I did it for Nate. Not for you. You've earned all the awkward shit karma can dish out."

"Hey!"

Laughing, he kicked his boots off and set them side-by-side next to the sink. Then he stood, and in one seamless motion, reached back between his shoulder blades and peeled his shirt off over his head. Then, because he's truly the world's most perfect boyfriend, he tossed it in the hamper rather than on the floor.

"What are you doing?" I asked when he unbuttoned his jeans.

"I'm getting in with you," he said.

My heart quickened as he pushed his pants down to his ankles. "You never take baths with me."

"That's not true," he argued.

"Once. And that's only because you wanted sex."

He had a wicked grin as he tugged off the jeans. "Who says I don't want sex now?"

I giggled as he dropped the rest of his clothes into the hamper. "You're impossible."

He stepped carefully into the tub between my legs, and the muscles across his chest and shoulders strained as he lowered himself into the water across from me. We both watched nervously as the water rose to the rim of the tub and threatened to spill over onto the floor. When the water level settled and it was clear we weren't about to flood the bathroom, he laughed. "I remember why we don't do this more often."

Even though the garden tub was huge for me, Warren's long legs were bent at an awkward angle and his knees poked out of the bubbles like mountain peaks. I pulled my feet in so he could stretch his legs around me, then I rested my legs on top of his thighs. "Better?" I asked as he relaxed against the fiberglass.

"Better, but we need a bigger one."

"Agreed."

"Sloan, we need a bigger house too."

I groaned. "I know, but can we please handle one major change at a time? I can't even think about moving right now."

His hands found my right foot under the water. He pulled it up to his chest and began massaging it with his thumbs. "OK, but when we get home, we need to start talking about it. We don't need to wait till the baby gets here and space really becomes a problem."

Water dripped off my hands as I held them a foot apart over the bubbles. "She's gonna be this big. I don't think she'll take up that much space for a while."

"Babies need a lot of stuff."

"How do you know what babies need?" I asked, raising an eyebrow.

"I've been reading."

I smiled. "Of course you have."

"I want to build her crib," he said.

"Can you do that?"

"Sure."

I sighed. "You're full of surprises."

"I'm kind of excited about starting a life with you."

I cupped a handful of suds in my hand and blew them across

the tub at him. "About shopping for baby stuff, weddings, and buying a house to grow old in together?"

He closed his eyes. "Absolutely."

When Warren died and came back without his human spirit as a full-blown angel of death, I wasn't sure where we stood on the whole "growing old together" thing. I wondered if I'd be doomed to wither and die while he stayed frozen, beautiful and flawless. But Azrael assured us that wouldn't be the case because Warren's body had been created with the flaws of humanity. He said as long as Warren stays on this side of the spirit line, his body will continue to age as it normally would. Then, at the end of his life— or mine, rather—he could cross into the spirit world with me.

It sounded like a perfect arrangement. And that scared me to death.

If I'd learned anything in the past year, it was that life could change instantly and without warning, and that the things we take most for granted are the things that hurt the worst when they're gone. But those kinds of thoughts have a tendency to impede a good night's sleep, so I pushed them away.

"Speaking of weddings, we're having ours at Dad's house," I said.

The water rippled with Warren's silent chuckles. "No courthouse, then? I guess Adrianne got her way."

"She usually does."

He smiled. "Maybe we should warn Azrael." He switched to massaging my left foot. "If they did get together, would that make Adrianne your mother-in-law?"

I groaned. "Why would you say such a thing? Let's please talk about anything else. Did you let Silvers know about the flight?"

"Yeah. She's taking a later one out of Greenville."

Lucky. "What time are we leaving in the morning?"

He glanced at his black tactical watch. "In nine hours…if Azrael doesn't think of a way to stop us from going between now and then."

I drummed my nails on the side of the tub. "Is it really that unsafe in Chicago?"

"It's a dangerous place, babe." He raked his fingertips down my calf muscle. God, it felt good. "With The Destroyer still being on the loose and Chicago being a hotbed of Kasyade's business dealings, I'm sure Az is only being cautious."

His vacant tone and the way his eyes drifted toward the window didn't add any credence to his message that Azrael was simply being protective of me. But I knew that even if Warren was having doubts about the motivations of the archangel, he would never—or could never—say as much to me about it. Not anymore, anyway. I nibbled at a hangnail on my pinky finger.

"What are you thinking about?" He was looking at me again.

"Nothing important. Are you excited about going back?"

His face soured. "Hell no. I hate Chicago."

"Really? Why?"

Again, his eyes turned toward the window. "Nothing good came out of Chicago."

I wiggled my toes in his hand. "Not true. You did."

He squeezed my foot. "And if I never go back it will be too soon."

After that, he was lost in thought for a while. My gaze followed his. Outside, the moon peeked over the top of the evergreen in my tiny backyard.

"I wonder if my mom is buried in Chicago." His voice cracked enough for me to notice. Nadine had been at the forefront of Warren's thoughts since he met Azrael. It was obvious by the number of times he brought her up in conversation.

Warren, the protector in both job and nature, had indirectly and unintentionally killed his mother. It was a fact he'd assumed his entire life, long before Azrael confirmed it. I would never know what it was like to carry that kind of guilt and grief, so I didn't probe him about it.

"We should ask Azrael if she's buried there. Maybe we could go pay our respects while we're there."

He shrugged. "We probably won't get very far. You know how he gets when she comes up."

"Deaf? Mute? PMS-y?"

That got a smile out of him.

"I'll ask Nathan and see what he can dig up," I said.

He nodded and let my foot sink back under the warm water. "That's a good idea." He stretched his arms over the rim of the bathtub. "It will be weird not having Nathan along for this adventure."

My phone buzzed on the little shelf that held my soap and bubble bath.

Warren cut his eyes across the water at me. "I thought you only did that on purpose now."

I picked it up. "We don't know that it's Nathan..."

But it was.

Before I read the text message an alarming thought occurred to me. "You're no longer human, and Nathan's not going tomorrow." I swallowed the rising lump in my throat. "If I get into trouble, I'm on my own. I can't summon any of you for help."

This news should have horrified Warren as much as it horrified me. It didn't. He should have been worried, fearful and frantic. Instead, he stared back at me like something was hanging out of my nose and he was trying to figure out a delicate way to tell me.

"What is it?" I asked, more frustrated than curious.

He grimaced. "You don't get it yet, do you?"

"Get what?"

"The entire spirit world can see you now, Sloan." He wasn't making a declaration; he was quoting what Samuel had told me months before when we battled Kasyade in Texas.

My shoulders slumped. "I *am* a homing beacon."

"What?"

"At Calfkiller River, Azrael said he was leading the demons into an ambush so we'd have the advantage. I had wondered aloud to Nathan if he was using me and the baby to lead them there. Nathan doubted it. I never did. And now it's confirmed. I was intergalactic demon bait."

"I'll always be able to find you, Sloan." Warren's tone was a good attempt at sounding reassuring.

"So will everyone else."

He cupped my face in his hands. "We'll stay together. You don't have to worry."

"Easy for you to say, angel boy."

He laughed. "What did Nate want?"

I looked back at my phone and read the text message aloud. "I wrote my resignation letter tonight to give to Davis tomorrow. I wanted you both to hear it from me. My last day with the department will be February 14th."

"We should throw him a going away party," Warren said, resting his head back and closing his eyes again.

"That's a good idea. I think we could all use a good party." I opened up the calendar app on my phone and scrolled till I found the date.

Friday, February 14th.

Oh, the irony. Saying goodbye to Nathan...on Valentine's Day.

The next morning, I woke up when the side of the bed dipped under Warren's weight. I was on my side, sprawled diagonally across my queen bed with drool forming a cold wet ring of slobber on my pillowcase. I arched my neck to look back at him. Of course, he was already clean-shaven and dressed, wearing the black sweater I'd given him for Christmas and enough cologne to send a chill down my spine. It wasn't enough, however, to coax me out from under the tangled covers. My head flopped back down, and I hugged the pillow.

He swiped a rogue strand of hair away from my mouth. "I made you breakfast."

Warren had discovered the easiest way to get me peacefully out of bed was with either bribery or sex, and bribery worked best when productivity and schedules were looming.

I yawned and stretched my arms up toward the headboard. "I smell pancakes."

He let his hand glide over the bare skin on my lower back. "I'm going to go pack the car. Will you get up?"

I nodded without protest and rolled over as my empty stomach growled loud enough for both of us to hear.

He grinned and stood up. "I'll see you downstairs."

When I finally trudged down the stairs, Azrael glanced up from where he sat on the couch, texting on his phone. His eyes drifted from my face to the sweatshirt I'd stolen out of Warren's closet, then down to my leggings and back up. "Is this a fashion statement or a fashion protest?"

"Good morning to you too," I said, walking past him to the kitchen.

Reuel grunted his usual greeting from his spot at the table where he sat with a stack of pancakes almost up to his chin. The smell of warm maple syrup and melted butter made my knees weak. My stomach growled again. Beside Reuel was a glass of chocolate milk and a plate covered with a stainless steel cover from Warren's kitchen accessory collection. I settled in front of it and lifted the lid.

"What the hell is this?" It was like my heart fell off a cliff.

Taunting me from my plate were jiggly egg whites, cheese that refused to melt, and a piece of turkey "bacon" that looked suspiciously like a big pink eraser from kindergarten.

Reuel was chuckling.

With a huff, I picked up my fork and reached over, skewering his top pancake. His nostrils flared and he blocked my fork with his. I glared. He raised a daring eyebrow. Rather than risk being stabbed through the hand in a culinary sword fight with a sentinel of Heaven, I slowly withdrew my utensil.

I sliced the "omelet" and stabbed it through with more force than necessary. It tasted like snot with salted rubber cheese.

Out of nowhere, Barry Gibbs's voice rang out through the first floor of my house with the lyrics to "Stayin' Alive."

Azrael quickly silenced his cell phone.

I spat a bite of egg across the table and laughed. Really loudly. So did Reuel. "What was that?" I asked.

Az dropped his face back toward the ceiling and sighed. "Adrianne changed my ringtone with some kind of app. Can't figure out how the hell to change it back."

Just then, Warren's heavy boots on the front porch outside announced his entrance before the front door swung open. He walked inside and wiped his boots on the welcome mat. For a second I almost forgot he tried to kill me with breakfast.

"Call Azrael's phone!"

"Shut up," Azrael grumbled.

Warren was confused. "What?"

"Call him," I insisted.

"Don't bother. It's on silent." Azrael turned on the leather couch to look at Warren. *Phwaaaaawert...*

Reuel and I burst out laughing again.

Azrael ignored us. "You ready to go?" he asked Warren.

Warren nodded. "I need to get Sloan's toiletry bag. You guys had better grab some rain gear," he said. "It's gonna be messy today."

As he crossed the room to the stairs, I snapped my fingers in his direction. "Warren Parish, we need to talk about what is and what is not appropriate to feed your pregnant girlfriend for breakfast." I frowned at my plate.

He started up the stairs two at a time and called back over his shoulder, "I love you!"

I cupped my hands around my mouth and yelled. "I'm drafting a prenup on the flight!"

I heard him laugh from our bedroom.

While he was out of sight, I bolted from my seat and retrieved the jar of peanut butter from the cabinet. I dunked my fork in, with all disregard for sanitation, and shoved it in my mouth. Reuel started chuckling again.

I sank back into my seat. "Like you'll say anything." I picked up the prenatal vitamin Warren had left on my napkin and swallowed it with the last swig of chocolate milk. I lifted the edges of my plate and looked at Reuel. "You wanna choke down the rest of my omelet?"

He shuddered.

I put my plate into the dishwasher after shoving the remaining eggs down the garbage disposal and tucked a banana into my purse. I was buttoning the only button that I could still get together on my coat when Warren came back with my bag. His bottom lip drooped with pity.

I pointed at him before he could speak. "Not one word, Warren Parish."

He closed his lips, but they spread into a tight smile.

Phwaaaaawert...

Azrael groaned and walked with us to the front door. "I'm buying another damn couch the second we get home."

Behind him, Reuel began to sing the Bee Gee's softly. "*Ha, ha, ha, ha...*"

I doubled over halfway through the doorway laughing so hard I almost had to go back in and use the bathroom.

When we walked outside, Azrael's eyes were closed like he was praying for serenity. I nudged him with my elbow. "So we'll see you when we get there?"

He nodded. "I'll check into the hotel and leave a key in Warren's name at the front desk."

My mouth dropped open. "We're sharing a room?" I looked around at Warren and Reuel. "All four of us?"

Warren locked the front door, then joined me at the top of the steps. "It's a suite," he said, like that was supposed to make me feel better.

Azrael's heavy hands rested on my shoulders. His countenance was stern, but uncharacteristically pleading. "Please don't be upset, Sloan. I'm being cautious for your own good. Chicago isn't a safe place for you. We all need to stay close."

"You should be happy. Chicago will be the perfect place for me to practice my superpowers." I flicked my fingers out a few times with corresponding "pew pew pew" sound effects as I pretended to shoot magic from my fingertips.

He forced a smile. "Yes. 'Pew pew pew.' I'm so glad you've remembered everything I taught you." He gave my neck a gentle squeeze. "Please listen very carefully and heed my words."

I raised my brow in question.

"Chicago is the last place you need to use your power. Tapping the power of the Vitamorte there will be like throwing a bucket of chum into the sea." He leveled his gaze with mine. "It will draw the sharks."

The blood drained from my face, leaving my cheeks suddenly numb against the cold.

"Come straight to the hotel when you leave the airport." Then he said something to Reuel in Katavukai before vanishing with a crack that rippled the air.

I flinched and turned to Warren. "I'll never get used to that."

He winked. "Wait till you can do it too."

"Is he serious about me not using my powers?"

"I think so."

My bottom lip poked out. "I don't want to be a chum bucket."

He laughed. "We'll take care of you." He gave me a quick peck on the lips, and when he pulled back, his dark eyes narrowed and one brow peaked in question. "Is that peanut butter?"

I held my breath and shook my head.

"*Aytim*," Reuel said with a grin as he walked past us.

"Nobody asked you, Reuel," I said sticking my tongue out at him.

Warren sighed as we walked toward his car. He tilted his head back and without him touching it, the trunk of the Challenger popped open then slowly rose into the air. "Babe, you can eat whatever you want. I'm only doing what you asked me to do. Remember?"

"Yes, I know."

He shoved the bags into the back. "Now kiss me again," he said, grabbing my collar and pulling my lips to meet his. "You taste delicious."

CHAPTER THREE

*T*HE TWO-HOUR flight from Asheville to Chicago was delayed due to an undisclosed equipment malfunction. By the time we were finally taxiing down the runway, I was beginning to think maybe Azrael was right. Flying was a bad idea. But once we were in the air, the g-force of take-off lulled me to sleep against Warren's bicep. I snoozed almost the whole trip in the middle seat between the two members of my angel entourage. As we walked off the plane and down the long terminal, we drew the attention of every other traveler at Chicago O'Hare. I felt like I should be wearing diamonds and carrying a Chihuahua in my purse.

To our left was a Goose Island Brewery restaurant crowded with patrons. Goose Island had been one of Nathan's favorite brews, and I'd fallen in love with it shortly before those two pink lines on the pregnancy test forced me into maternal prohibition. My mouth watered and my heart thumped with longing...for the beer, not Nathan McNamara, to be clear.

I snapped a picture of the sign and sent it to him.

He responded almost immediately. *I'm jealous.*

Me: *I need a favor.*

Nathan: *What did you do?*

I frowned. *Why would you assume I did something?*

Nathan: *Really? I'd make a list, but I think this text has a character limit.*

I laughed. *You're such a jerk.*

Nathan: *I know. What do you need?*

Me: *Can you find out where Warren's mom is buried?*

We got on an escalator to a lower floor.

Nathan: *Sloan, I'm not a walking 411 service.*

Me: *I know that. You're a detective. I need you to DETECT where Warren's mother is buried.*

I could almost see him rolling his eyes through the phone.

Nathan: *What's her last name?*

Me: *Umm...*

Nathan: *Are you kidding me??*

"Hey, Warren." I turned around on the step and looked up at him. "What was your mom's last name?"

"I don't know. Claymore, maybe?"

"Thanks." I looked back at my phone. *Try Claymore.*

Nathan: *You know we aren't that lucky, right? Don't get your hopes up.*

I sent back a toothy-smile emoji.

"Watch your step, babe."

I looked up as the escalator ended at the bottom in a long tunnel with a moving sidewalk highway. My eyes widened as I looked all around. The walls were a wave of colored blocks from one end of the tunnel to the other. The squares faded from red to purple to blue, green, yellow, and white the entire length of the room. The ceiling was covered with an intricate web of neon tubes that lit up like a rainbow over our heads. The light show played in time with the sound of a meditation soundtrack of chimes and soft, tinkling bells that could barely be heard over the chatter and bumbling of luggage.

We stepped onto the moving sidewalk, and I pushed the handle down on my carryon case and sat on top of it.

Warren smiled. "I guess we're riding this thing and not walking?"

"Life's too short to walk when riding is an option, Warren," I answered.

He nudged my suitcase over a few inches with his boot. "Well, it's best to keep to the side so you don't get run over."

"This place is weird," I said, watching the ceiling change colors. "It's like a scene out of *Fear and Loathing in Las Vegas* or *Willy Wonka and the Chocolate Factory*."

Warren leaned against the moving handrail. "I think it's a good show of cheerfulness to distract weary travelers from the fact that in order to get out of this place they're in for a very, very long trek."

"How long?" I asked.

He smiled. "Don't worry. Moving sidewalks almost all the way."

"Thank god."

"What did Nate say?"

"He said he'd try."

"Thank you." He pulled his phone from his pocket. "I need to call Az and let him know we'll meet him at the prison since we're running late."

The prison, I thought with a shudder.

At least the long halls of Chicago O'Hare were interesting. After the rainbow tunnel, we crossed through a finger-smudged row of glass doors into a long concrete corridor. A man on an electric guitar played blues in the corner, and as we walked by, Warren tossed a few dollars into the jar on top of his amplifier. "Thank 'ya, sir," the man said, then cut into the instrumental break of *The Thrill is Gone*.

The block walls were dotted with factoids and pictures of planets and asteroids to advertise the Adler Planetarium. Beyond them were huge, bright and colorful wall murals painted by local artists. And from my perch atop my travel bag, I counted the different flags from around the world hanging from the ceiling.

"This is us," Warren said, pointing to a sign to our left.

CTA O'HARE STATION.

"The subway?" I asked, jumping up as we neared the end of the walkway. "I've never ridden a subway."

"It's not completely a subway. It's called the "L" because most of it is above the ground." He nudged me toward the right side of the hall. "We need to get passes."

I clapped my hands together. "This is exciting!"

He laughed and shook his head as he used the touchscreen ticket machine.

When we had our tickets, we went through the turnstiles and down the escalator to the platform for the Blue Line to downtown Chicago. There were three silver trains waiting to depart the station, and not enough people to fill even a single car of one of them. "Which one do we take?" I asked.

"Whichever one is leaving first." Warren tugged me toward the left. "This way."

An odd sensation tingled my spine as we walked toward one of the trains. I looked up at my two angel companions, their searching eyes telling me they felt the same. Reuel took a protective step closer to me. We walked through the open door of a car. It was empty except for a figure near the front. It looked like a man wearing a red toboggan with a dark face hidden behind the collar of his thick black coat. But it wasn't a man at all. He had no human spirit. The three of us froze in the center aisle, and suddenly the man jumped up and slipped out the metal doors before they closed.

"What was that?" I asked, gripping my chest.

Warren put his arm around my shoulders. "I think that was a reason Azrael didn't want us to come to Chicago."

I gulped as the train lurched forward.

Only humans boarded the train at each stop after the airport. By the time we reached downtown, our car was full of mostly young business professionals dressed against the harsh Windy City weather. The Blue Line swayed and bumped over the tracks for over an hour before we reached our stop at Jackson Station downtown, another underground platform.

It was after nine in the morning when we ascended the steps toward Van Buren Street. The icy breeze off Lake Michigan was wet and sticky, the kind of cold that burns your skin and seeps into your bones. I was grateful for the skyscrapers that surrounded us and took the brunt of the wind, but I still tugged my teal scarf up over my face and ducked under Warren's arm.

The buildings overwhelmed me as I looked up, their sheer size reminding me of the literality of the word *skyscraper*. Some of their peaks disappeared completely into the clouds, like one might step into an elevator and ascend all the way to the misty heavens.

We walked to the end of the block and crossed the busy street under another "L" train bridge, avoiding the puddles of dirty slush left behind from a recent snow shower. My heart pounded harder with each step down the sidewalk, and I could have led our little group to the federal prison by the growing fear in my stomach alone.

I knew it before Warren announced our arrival. I shivered only partly from the cold.

Staring up at the tan, three-hundred-foot correctional facility, anxiety boiled up in my stomach like a soda bottle someone had given a good shake. Inside the triangular structure were nearly thirty floors of minimum to maximum security panic generators. A slow exhale puffed out my cheeks as I tried hopelessly to steady my breathing. "Why do I always wind up here?"

Warren took my hand, his touch settling my nerves almost instantly. "At least your visits are only temporary."

"Where's Silvers?" Azrael's voice behind us startled me.

I whirled around and stuck my finger in his face. "Don't sneak up on me like that!"

He pushed my hand down, then looked at his watch. "She's late. And *you're* late."

"Not our fault." I closed my eyes and reached out with my gift. "Silvers is close. She'll be here soon."

Just then, the *clop-clop-clop* of business pumps against the concrete sidewalk announced Sharvell Silvers's arrival before we saw her. Her no-nonsense, staccato gait echoed her personality, and my heart raced in time with the beat. Despite the recent turn of events—making us allies and eternally placing her in my debt—Silvers was still (like her footfalls) sharp, fast, and unstoppable... and she would forever make me nervous.

I gulped when she rounded the corner of the building, black briefcase in hand, business suit cemented in place, and FBI credentials hanging from her neck. Her shiny black bob was smoothed around her face, and her lips were painted her signature red. Blood red.

I half-waved.

She approached with her hand outstretched. "Good afternoon, Sloan. Thank you so much for coming."

I pointed at the building and sucked in a brave, deep breath. "You ready to get this over with?"

She was eyeing me cautiously. "You look pale. Are you all right?"

I nodded, but inside I was furiously shaking my head. "Let's do it."

My pulse was echoing in my ears by the time we got through security and onto the elevator. Agent Silvers and the female deputy who was escorting us were both watching me like I might collapse. I hoped I could prove them wrong but with each floor we rose, I was less and less sure. My body was shivering, yet sweat drizzled down my spine. *Breathe in. 1...2...3... Breathe out. 1...2...3...*

Warren squeezed my hand and whispered in my ear. "You'll be fine."

"He's right," Azrael said. "We'll both be with you. That should ease your anxiety."

I appreciated their confidence despite whether it was true or not.

The elevator dinged and the metal doors parted to a long tiled hallway lined with doors. The walls hummed with evil, and the farther we walked, the harder it was to inhale. When I could breathe in, the stench of antiseptic masking mold burned my sinuses.

We stopped at the end of the hallway. "This is it," the officer announced, turning the metal door knob. "Let me know when you're finished."

"Thank you," Agent Silvers said to her as we entered.

Marisol Juarez was alone, seated at the table with her eyes closed peacefully and her hands folded in her lap. Perhaps she was praying. Maybe she was asleep. Her plump face was heavily lined around her eyes and lips, and her wavy dark hair was a tad frizzy but parted neatly on the side. She didn't look like her mugshot, and she certainly didn't look like a criminal. The woman in front of us looked like she belonged behind a stove making cookies and wearing an apron, not behind bars in a federal prison wearing an orange jumpsuit.

More importantly, she didn't feel like a criminal. Quite the opposite actually. Her soul was kind and gentle, as blameless as anyone I'd ever met. For the first time ever inside a prison, my nerves calmed as the door shut behind us. I leaned toward Agent Silvers and lowered my voice. "Are you sure you've got the right person?"

Her eyes widened in question as she nodded. "Marisol Juarez?" she asked the woman.

Marisol's eyes fluttered open. "Hello."

Confused, I looked back at Warren and Azrael. Warren shrugged and Azrael's right eyebrow was arched in question.

I scratched my head and eased into the chair across from her.

Warren and Azrael stayed near the door, and Agent Silvers sat next to me.

"Mrs. Juarez, my name is Agent Silvers. I'm with the FBI." She removed a notepad and pen from her briefcase, then gestured toward me. "This is my associate, Sloan Jordan, and the two men by the door are here to observe. We'd like to ask you some questions about your daughter, Maria."

The woman pressed her lips together, possibly to keep them from quivering. "Have you seen her?" The concern in her voice was almost palpable.

Agent Silvers seemed puzzled. It was obvious that even without supernatural abilities she too had been expecting someone far more devious than the fairy-godmother-type sitting before us. "Um..." She looked to me for help.

"We saw her about a month ago under very"—I leaned forward and lowered my voice to a whisper—"unusual circumstances."

Marisol's pursed lips parted slightly, and her eyes widened enough to show the tiniest glint of guilt. Not the type of guilt that would land one deservingly in a federal holding cell, but the kind that mixes easily with remorse and heartache.

I stretched my arm across the table, offering her my hand. "It's OK, Marisol. I want to help you. Please tell me about Maria."

She stared at my open palm and her chin began to tremble. A surge of tears flooded her dark eyes and spilled down her cheeks as she grasped my hand. "I just want my baby back. I didn't mean for any of this."

I gently squeezed her fingers. "I know." And I did. There was a long list of things from the past few months that I was desperately sorry about. "What happened?" I asked. "Start at the beginning."

Agent Silvers pulled a travel-size tissue pack from her briefcase and handed it to Marisol. Marisol pulled one from the plastic and dabbed her eyes. "Thank you," she said softly.

It took a moment for Marisol to reign in her emotions enough to say more than that, but we all afforded her the time to catch her breath. Even Azrael, who often tap-danced on insensitivity, stopped and gently squeezed her shoulder as he walked to the five-inch slit window across the room.

"I'm sorry," she finally said, then paused to blow her nose.

I smiled. "Take your time. We've got all day."

She motioned around the room and snickered. "So do I."

We all laughed.

She took a deep breath. "What would you like to know?"

Agent Silvers folded her hands on the tabletop. "Mrs. Juarez, we spoke with your son, Tito, yesterday in San Antonio."

Marisol sighed. "Ah, Tito. How is he?"

"He's still awaiting trial, but he seems well, all things considered," Agent Silvers said.

"Tito was such a sweet boy." Marisol began drawing circles with her fingertip on the table. "It broke his heart when Maria got sick. I know it isn't an excuse for the things that he does"—she sighed—"for the person he's become, but he went through so much trying to be strong for her and for me. No child should have to carry that burden."

"But he isn't a child." Agent Silvers shook her head. "He's a grown man, thirty-three years old."

She nodded. "I know that. I simply wonder what his life might have been like if he'd been able to have his childhood. I lost two children, not just one." Her eyes became glassy again.

"You said Maria got sick. What happened?" I asked.

"It was Thanksgiving Day when I saw the first tumor. She was lifting the turkey out of the oven, and when she turned toward the counter to set it down, she moved her head, and I noticed a lump on her neck right here." She touched her fingers to the spot above her right clavicle. "It was a swollen lymph node. No big deal. Kids pick up germs all the time, right?"

I nodded but didn't speak.

"She'd lost some weight, but I didn't think much of it because she was becoming conscious of her looks." She smiled. "She was almost thirteen. I thought it was normal teenage stuff. But I was wrong about all of it. It wasn't until the third time she woke up drenched in so much sweat that we had to change her clothes and bedsheets that I decided to take her to the doctor. They ran some tests and cut the lymph node out of her neck. It was cancer. Stage four."

Agent Silvers passed Marisol another tissue, and I noticed she kept one for herself.

"They did another surgery, several rounds of chemotherapy, and radiation." Her eyes fell to the table and she shook her head. "She fought it for a year, but then pneumonia set in and she kept getting worse and worse. We knew it was the end."

"What happened?" Agent Silvers asked.

Marisol started to speak, then stopped. She looked around at all of it.

I touched her arm. "It's all right. You can tell us the truth. No one here will think you're crazy or lying."

She gulped.

"We'll believe you. Don't worry," I assured her.

"Ms. Smith came into the ICU that night. She came to Maria's room."

Agent Silvers was taking notes. "Abigail Smith?"

Marisol sighed. "I don't remember what name she was using then."

The agent's pen stopped. I wondered if she was trying to remember all my demon mother's aliases or if she was having a brain cramp trying to process all she'd recently learned about the world.

"Abigail Smith came to our room that night. Asked if she could pray for Maria. She asked me if I believed in healing." Marisol flattened her hands on the table. "I've been a Catholic my whole life, but believing when you're listening to your child's slowing heartbeat through life support…that's a real test. Abigail said she could save her. She asked if I was willing to believe at any cost."

Of course she had agreed. I wasn't even halfway through my pregnancy and already there wasn't anything I wouldn't do for my daughter.

"Maria's heart flat lined. God, I'll never forget the sound of that machine." She closed her eyes. "And I'll never forget the sound of when it started beating again."

"I'm sure you were relieved," I said.

She looked at me. "It wasn't only her heart. She started breathing on her own. Her color came back. Her blood pressure went back up. It was a miracle!" Her head tilted. "And then she opened her eyes. And I knew."

"What did you know?" Agent Silvers asked.

"She was different. It wasn't *my* Maria looking back at me."

I felt sick. "It was Phenex."

She nodded. "For a while, they tried to play it off, but a mother knows her child. She didn't look at me the same way or talk the same. She wasn't my little girl anymore. They made me sign her out of the hospital against medical advice, and then after we were out of the hospital, they dropped the act completely. I thought I was losing my mind."

"Did you tell anyone? Go to anyone for help?" Agent Silvers asked.

She shook her head. "I couldn't have if I'd tried."

Agent Silvers looked up. "Did they threaten you?"

"They didn't have to," Warren said behind me. I'd almost forgotten he was in the room. "Sloan, do you remember what I was like when Kasyade summoned me in San Antonio?"

Marisol gasped. "I've never heard anyone outside their group call her Kasyade."

I slowly turned back toward her. "Kasyade is my mother."

She straightened in her seat and made the sign of the cross. "Ay, Dios mio. I thought I recognized your name and face. I've seen your picture since you were a child."

She probably didn't recognize me thanks to all my recent

fluffiness.

"They call you *Praea*," she said.

I nodded. "That's correct. I hear it's my angel name."

Marisol shook her head and wagged her finger. "They are not angels. They're evil."

"Yes, I know," I agreed.

Agent Silvers tapped her pen against her pad of paper. "Hold on a second. You said you've seen pictures of Sloan since she was a child. When did Phenex take your daughter?"

"Twenty-two years ago."

The sound of breaking glass pierced the stunned silence of the interrogation room. The window Azrael had been staring out of during Marisol's story had splintered. We all whirled around toward him, and he stepped back from the wall, shocked. "Pigeon."

"Liar," I muttered.

Agent Silvers gripped her temples. "I'm sorry, Mrs. Juarez. Did you say Phenex took Maria twenty-two years ago?"

"That's right."

"And they've kept you locked up for all that time?" Agent Silvers asked.

I shook my head. "She wasn't literally locked up."

"Sometimes I was," Marisol said. "They would lock me in with the girls at the Morning Star house sometimes, but that didn't happen often. As that man said"—she pointed to Warren—"they didn't need locks. I was a puppet."

Without thinking, my eyes shot to Azrael.

I pushed back from the table. "And now you're in prison because of it."

Marisol smiled. "And since the raid, they've left me alone. This is the most peace I've had in over two decades. Don't feel sorry for me."

But I did feel sorry for her. Nothing about any of it was fair. And while I firmly believed that each of us are responsible for our own decisions, I even felt bad for Tito. I did the math in my head and realized he would have been only eleven years old when his sister was taken. After hearing the story, it was easy to see Marisol's point. I, too, wondered what his life might have been like had he not been thrust into a cesspool of evil.

Agent Silvers's voice snapped me back to the conversation. "Do you know how or where we might find Maria now?"

Marisol shook her head. "Many things are missing from my memory and many more things were kept hidden from me. I've been a prisoner for over two decades, and wardens don't share information with inmates."

"Anything at all would be helpful," Warren said. "Anything else maybe to do with the ministry. Names you may have heard, places they might have mentioned?"

She thought for a moment. "Phenex ran the home in Chicago. Kasyade was in Texas. Ysha, or Abner Tuinstra, was in charge of New York—"

"Do you know Ysha's daughter, Taiya?" I asked.

"Since she was a little girl." Marisol sighed. "Oh the hell that child suffered."

Azrael walked to the table. "What do you know about her?"

"She's spent most of her life in New York, locked in a basement and treated like a wild animal. Her father kept her close all the time when she was young. It was sickening. A few months ago, he brought her to me and left her. I was trying to teach the poor thing English."

"Why did he leave her with you?" Agent Silvers asked.

Azrael crossed his arms over his chest. "To go after Sloan. That was about the time she got pregnant."

Marisol covered her mouth with her hands and looked at me. "You're pregnant?"

"Yep," I answered, letting the 'p' pop off my lips.

Her face fell. "They're going to kill you."

My chest tightened. "I know."

"Do you know what their plan is?" Warren asked.

"No." She looked at me. "But when they talk about you, they talk about Taiya too, so she must be part of it."

Azrael shifted on his feet.

"Ysha's dead, and now Taiya is missing. Do you have any idea where she may have gone?" I asked.

She shook her head again. "I'm sorry."

Agent Silvers flipped back a page in her notes. "You talked about New York, Texas, and here. Who was in charge of the home in Los Angeles?"

"Someone named Leviathan. I've never seen him though." Her eyes dropped to the table. "Those were the times they would lock the doors and leave us there."

Her tone was more alarming than her words. It made me wonder if they were being sent away for his protection or theirs.

Azrael leaned against the table. "Do you know where they went?"

"About a year ago, they repurposed an old factory building a few miles away from the ministry. I assume they went there."

"Repurposed for what?" Warren asked.

She shrugged. "I'm not really sure. Many of the girls were taken there, some several times. When I was the one to take them, I wasn't allowed upstairs in the building."

"Do you remember where it is?" Agent Silvers asked.

She nodded. "At the corner of Lake and May, under the "L" before you get to the butcher shop. There aren't any signs, but it's the big brick building with the blue front door."

"Thank you, Marisol," I said.

She half-smiled. "Can I ask you a question?"

I straightened in my seat. "Of course."

She hesitated. "Maria…Do you know what happened to her?"

My heart sank. "She's gone. My guess is she's been gone since that night at the hospital."

Marisol's face froze. "All these years I guess I've known, but part of my heart has always held onto the hope that maybe she was just locked away somewhere."

Azrael put his hand on her shoulder again and spoke gently. "It's better this way. I promise."

She broke again. This time, shocking the hell out of all of us, The Angel of Death knelt beside her and offered his embrace. She crumpled against him and wept into his shoulder. And for the shortest of seconds, I could swear I glimpsed a tear trickle down his cheek.

We were all a little somber on the elevator ride back to the prison lobby. We walked outside and found Reuel standing with our luggage exactly where we left him. He was watching the gray sky, for what I wasn't sure.

"Well that was depressing," I said, breaking the awkward silence that had consumed us since we left the interrogation room.

"Yes, it was." Warren slipped his black sunglasses back on and zipped his coat up to his chin.

Next to me, Agent Silvers was carefully watching the cracked concrete as we walked. "I'm going to do what I can to make her sentence as comfortable as possible, but I fear it won't be much."

We formed a semi-circle around Reuel, and Azrael spoke to him in Katavukai in hushed tones. I stuck my hands in my coat pockets and scuffed the heel of my shoe against a crack in the sidewalk. "I hope at the very least she was able to take some solace in being able to talk to someone. The worst part of being me was always feeling so alone and always fearing what people would say or do if they found out who I really was."

"How old were you when you first told someone what you were?" Agent Silvers asked.

"I was in college. I told my best friend Adrianne. It was one of the scariest nights of my life," I said.

She shook her head. "I can't even imagine."

The heavy weight of sadness hung over us all like a wet blanket. "Can we go find some ice cream or something?"

Warren's head snapped back. "It's twenty-one degrees out here, Sloan."

"Well, I can't have beer. Ice cream is the next best thing," I said.

Agent Silvers checked her watch. "I would join you, but I want to get a jump on finding out what was going on in that factory building. I need to check in with the field office here."

"I'm going to look into the building as well," Azrael said, looking at her. "I hope you don't mind."

The rest of us knew it didn't matter if the agent minded or not.

She debated the request for a moment. "Please let me know what you find. You have my cell."

"Will do." He looked at Reuel. "Can you see Sloan and Warren back to the hotel?"

Reuel nodded.

"Wait, I want to come with you," Warren said.

Azrael shook his head. "This part, I need to do solo. I'll call if I need you."

Warren shifted on his feet and opened his mouth like he intended to argue.

I looped my arm through his. "Let him go and we'll grab some food. We can have some much-needed alone time."

His shoulders relaxed, and he nodded his head. Then, he pointed at Reuel. "We'll have him."

Reuel smiled.

So did I. "He doesn't talk much."

Agent Silvers offered her hand and I shook it. "Thanks again for coming all the way up here. That conversation would have been a whole lot different if I'd been on my own."

"I'm glad I came." I laughed. "I can't believe I'm saying that about a trip to jail."

Warren rubbed my back. "You handled it really well. I'm proud of you."

I squinted against the sun to smile up at him. "Thanks."

Agent Silvers took a step back. "I'm sure we'll talk again soon."

"I'm sure we will," I agreed. "Bye."

She waved, then turned on her heel toward the direction she'd come. The *clop, clop, clop, clop* of her heels was a little gentler on her departure.

Azrael checked the time on his phone. "This shouldn't take too long, but don't come looking for me if I'm not back right away. I'll meet you back at the hotel when I'm finished."

"Are you sure you don't need my help?" Warren asked.

Azrael nodded. "I'm sure, but thank you." He pointed his finger and moved it between us. "Be safe. Don't do anything stupid." He was looking at me for the latter part of his warning.

He took off toward West Van Buren, and over his head, the "L" roared by. Warren nudged my shoulder to turn me toward him. "Hey, I have an idea."

My brow lifted in question.

"Since we have some time to kill, want to drop our bags at the hotel and go see my old stomping grounds?"

Excitement bubbled up inside me. "I'd love to!"

He looked at Reuel. "You up for some sightseeing?"

Reuel bowed like an usher encouraging us to lead the way.

Warren offered me his elbow, and I hooked mine around it. I was a tourist in the Windy City on the arm of the hottest man in town. Maybe we'd stand under The Bean in Millennium Park or ride to the top of Sears Tower. For the first time in months, I felt almost normal.

And it scared me to death.

CHAPTER FOUR

*O*UR FIRST STOP was for hot dogs and chocolate eclair cake at Portillo's. (Too bad I forgot my food diary at home.) Then we went to Navy Pier so I could see Lake Michigan and ride the Ferris wheel. The Ferris wheel ride was a bust; the fog was so thick in downtown Chicago that the buildings seemed to disappear into the heavens. But the visit wasn't a total loss. Warren bought me a puffy, bright blue winter coat that actually fit from a shop on the pier.

From there we took a cab north to visit Warren's old neighborhood, reasoning we could hit Millennium Park on the way back to the hotel. As we drove, my eyes were glued to the beach off to our right. Had I not known better, I would have sworn it was the ocean.

After a few minutes, we turned onto a street to our left and after several blocks, Warren tapped his finger against his window. "Sloan, look."

I followed the direction he was pointing. Up ahead was a church, that to my architecturally untrained eye, looked like a mini cathedral made out of bricks with stone trimmings. The main entrance had a huge arched doorway at the top of a wide staircase with a stone carved picture of God or Jesus or maybe Jerry Garcia, I had no idea. Beside the main building was a huge bell tower capped with a golden cross. My brain conjured up images of The Hunchback of North Chicago.

"At the curb is fine," Warren said to the driver.

"What is this place?" I asked as the cab rolled to a stop.

Warren opened the door and stepped out, then turned to offer me his hand. "St. Peter's Parish. This is where Azrael left me when I was born."

My eyes doubled in size. "Oh, wow."

As Reuel laboriously angled out of the back of the van, I ogled the building and Warren paid the fare. When we started up the steps to the glass entry, I looked up at Warren. "How long has it been since you've been here?"

He held the front door open for me. "Probably fifteen years or more." He followed in after me, passing the open door off to Reuel. "I came by here once in high school, to check it out. Didn't stick around though."

The door eased closed behind us, and once it was sealed, we were enveloped in the stoic silence of the tidy vestibule. The room was spacious and had two hallways that branched off either side. In the center in front of us, two double doors went into the sanctuary. Water trickled down a waterfall in a large stone fountain planted in the center of the room. On one of the rocks was a bronze sign that read DO NOT THROW COINS INTO THE FOUNTAIN. Beside it was a money collection box.

I peeked through the window in one of the doors into the sanctuary. On the left side was a tall statue of Mary and a table filled with candles. At the end of the center aisle was an ornate table and Jesus was crucified on the stone wall behind it. I never understood the use of the crucifix as a decorative fixture. Maybe it was a talking point or a visual think piece; it certainly didn't serve well as a marketing vehicle for me. Surely Jesus could feed a lot of hungry children with the dollars spent on carving out his most anguished moment in alabaster or soapstone.

Near the back, in one of the pews, a man was kneeling with his head bowed. And far to his right was another figure, dark in a red hat...

"May I help you?" The woman's voice was gentle, but it scared the bejeezus out of me. I screamed, and she jumped back a few tiles, grasping her heart. The tiny old woman with a helmet-shaped white hairdo was panting in front of a sign marked 'Offices.' She wore pleated tan polyester slacks and a white shirt under a pale yellow cardigan. Her wide eyes were magnified behind the thick lenses of her silver glasses as she struggled to catch her breath.

"I'm so sorry," I apologized, then quickly checked inside the sanctuary again. The figure was gone. Or maybe it was never there to begin with. "I didn't mean to startle you."

Warren touched my arm. "Are you all right?"

"Yes." *No.*

I took a deep breath and checked through the sanctuary door again. Nothing, except the old man praying in the back.

I stepped in the woman's direction and stuck out of my hand. "Hi. My name's Sloan."

"Ruby Riddle," she said.

"We're visiting from out of town, and my fiancé wanted to show me and our friend, Reuel"—I pointed to the hulking angel standing silently by the door—"the inside of the church. I hope that's all right."

She nodded and smiled warmly. "Of course it is. The sanctuary is open for prayer, or would you like to see anything in particular?"

I turned to Warren and turned my palms up in question. It was an awkward beat of silence.

"I was actually abandoned here when I was a baby." He awkwardly shoved his hands into his pockets and shrugged. "I guess I was curious to see the place again."

The old woman's crinkled lips parted and the slightest of gasps caught in her throat. We watched the blood drain from her face. "Warren?"

His back went rigid, and we looked at each other, shocked.

"I'm sorry. Have we met?" he asked.

Ruby cleared her throat. "Well, not officially. I've worked here for almost forty years." She touched her fingers to her chest. "I'm the person who found you."

My eyes bulged. "Shut up. Are you serious?"

She nodded. "Your first foster family brought you by here a couple of times asking for prayer, but you were tiny then. You must be thirty years old or more now."

"I'll be thirty in August," he said.

She sighed. "Three decades and I remember it like it was yesterday. I came in early that Monday morning to count the Sunday offering." She pointed back behind us. "Before I even got to that door, I heard a baby screaming. Of course, I ran toward the sound. The door was unlocked when I reached it, and when I got inside, I saw a bundle of blankets on the floor. Over there." She pointed beside the fountain. "The baby was kicking and thrashing its hands. I could tell it was in awful pain, but I didn't see anything wrong with it. I scooped him up and looked around. There was nothing. No note. No bottle. No diapers. Just this screaming infant in blue footed pajamas with a sailboat on the chest." She shook her head in awe. "I'll never forget it as long as I live."

Warren looked like he might be a little dizzy. "What happened then?"

"I called Father Warren first. He lived in the parsonage behind this building." She was pointing off in the distance behind us, but my eyes were set on my stunned fiancé.

"Father Warren," he repeated to me.

I raked my fingers back through my hair. "This is crazy."

Ruby continued. "Father Warren came and we decided it best to call the police. He took the baby, and I went back to my office because we didn't have cell phones back then." She gulped. "When I returned, Father Warren was bouncing the baby up and down, trying to calm him. Suddenly, he stopped bouncing and looked at me." Her face fell. "He said my name, then tensed up, and I grabbed the baby before he collapsed onto the floor."

A chill made me shudder.

"The doctors told us later it was an aortic aneurysm. He died before the ambulance got here."

"Holy shit." One hand reached to grasp Warren's. The other flew to my mouth, mortified by the obscenity. "Sorry."

Ruby obviously didn't care, at least not under the circumstances. She was still staring at Warren, mesmerized. I was staring at him too, but for a different reason. Warren knew how many deaths he'd caused in his lifetime. All were accounted for except one. His whole life he'd assumed the one he didn't remember had been his mother. However, if the priest had died while holding him, that would mean his mother's death hadn't been his fault after all.

"The priest died," I repeated.

His Adam's apple bobbed as his eyes slowly met mine.

Ruby continued on with her story, unaware of the news bomb she'd dropped. "You screamed until the lady from the state came to take you away." She lowered her voice. "We all wondered if your mother had been on drugs or something."

Warren nodded and looked back at her. "Something like that, I think."

Azrael had once compared the effects of us being separated from the supernatural to detox.

"But you're doing all right now?" she asked, folding her tiny hands into the prayer position beneath her chin.

"Better than all right." Warren flinched and reached into his pocket. He retrieved his cell phone. "It's Az," he said to me. "Mrs. Ruby, please excuse me." He pressed the phone to his ear and walked toward the door. "Hello?"

"Thank you for taking care of him," I said to her as she watched him across the room. "I'm sure it must have been frightening."

Tears spilled down her cheeks. "It was terrifying, but I'm so thankful he's doing well."

I slipped my arm around her shoulders. "Don't cry, Ruby. He's doing great. He's about to be a *father* Warren himself." With a smile, I patted my stomach.

She swiped her fingers under her glasses and laughed through her tears. "That's wonderful news. Congratulations."

"Thank you," I said.

Warren came back to us. "We've got to go."

Ruby looked around the lobby, then walked over to a rack holding brochures and pamphlets. She brought one over and handed it to him. "This has the main phone number for the church. Call me if you ever come back to town."

"I will. Thank you." Warren gave me the brochure. I folded it and tucked it in my purse.

She hugged me first, then Warren. When she pulled away from him, she let her hand linger on his chest, over his heart. "May I say a quick blessing over you?"

Warren's eyes darted toward me. I shrugged slightly to say "I guess."

He nodded.

I expected her to close her eyes, as they do in the protestant churches I'd visited back home. She didn't. She stared Warren right in the eyes. I wondered if it creeped him out at all. Then she began to pray out loud.

"Almighty God, who has commanded thy angels to guide and protect us, entreat them to clothe his children with protection unseen, to keep them from danger and preserve them from all evil. From this day till their last, grant them wisdom and strength, and be their rock of refuge that is quick to save. May they have confidence in your loving care, through Jesus Christ our Lord. Amen."

———————

As soon as we were outside standing in the freezing cold again, I grabbed the sleeve of Warren's coat and stepped in front of him. I gripped both his forearms. "Warren, the priest died that night."

Unmistakable tears sparkled in his black eyes. "I know."

"Nadine's death wasn't your fault," I said, shaking him a bit.

He pulled me into his arms and heaved a heavy sigh of relief. "I didn't kill her," he whispered against my hair.

I could never imagine the weight that must have been lifted off him. That heartache had shaped him into the man he'd become, and in a moment he was absolved from it. I took a half-step back so I could look up at him. "See? Some good things do come out of Chicago."

He sniffed, but his tears never spilled from his eyes. "Maybe." He laughed and kissed the side of my head. "Come on. We have to go."

"Where are we headed?" I zipped my coat all the way up to my chin and tugged my scarf up around my mouth. The sky was gray with tufts of pillowy clouds that were drizzling tiny clumps of wet snow.

He offered me his hand as we neared the street. Reuel followed close behind us. "Az wants us to come to the factory building. He's found something he says we need to see."

My nose wrinkled. "I don't like the sound of that."

"Me either."

I jerked my thumb back over my shoulder toward the church behind us. "So that prayer…"

He looked at me. "Eerie, wasn't it?"

"Totally," I said. "I really wanted Reuel to bow and say something like '*Angel of Protection at your service.*'"

All three of us laughed.

"Did you catch the 'protection unseen' bit of what she said?" I asked.

"How could I miss it?" His worried tone made me nervous. He looked both ways before leading us into the crosswalk. "What did you scream about in there? You almost gave that old woman a heart attack."

"Oh!" I almost stopped walking in the middle of the street, but he tugged me forward. "I may have seen that thing again in there."

"What thing?" he asked.

I nodded. "The thing from the train."

"What? Where?" As soon as we were safely on the other side, he stopped walking.

"Inside the sanctuary."

"Reuel, did you see anything?"

He shook his head.

"I *think* I saw it in the sanctuary when we first walked in," I said.

Warren closed his eyes for a moment. "I didn't sense anything like I did this morning."

"Maybe I imagined it."

He carefully scanned the area. "Let's keep our guard up. I need to ask Azrael who, or what, that could have been."

My face was chapped from the wind by the time we reached the "L" station. We passed a group of boys hiding behind the metal stairs up to the platform, and the sweet waft of marijuana widened all of our eyes. I wondered what Nathan would have said had he been there. When we reached the empty platform above and saw it was a four-minute wait for the next Green Line train, I decided to call him. I got his voicemail, but instead of leaving a message, I sent a text. *Wanted to check in. Things are weird here, but no emergency.*

A second later, the phone buzzed in my hand. It was a reply. *No emergency? I'm shocked and a little disappointed.*

Shut up, Nathan.

Nathan: *LOL I'm on a call. Going to be awhile before I'm free to talk. Cool?*

Me: *Yeah. No rush. Everything's good here.*

Nathan: *Give my love to Warren.*

I laughed. *Will do. I'm sure he's missing you desperately.*

"Nathan says he loves you."

Warren chuckled. "As gay as it sounds, I kinda miss him being here."

I tucked my phone into the fuzzy pocket of my new coat. "I'm sure he'd come if you asked him."

He crossed his arms. "Nah. I'm sure he's got plenty of loose ends to tie up at work."

"You're right. Ooo...I thought of the perfect cake for his party," I said, clapping my hands together.

"Oh yeah?"

"Yes! And I'm going to get Adrianne to plan the rest of it."

He raised an eyebrow. "Won't that deter her from planning our wedding?"

I laughed. "God, I hope so."

The old factory was a nondescript building next to an empty grass lot on one side and an abandoned print shop with a broken sign and graffiti-covered walls on the other. Had Marisol not mentioned the blue door, we would've lost it completely in the neighborhood camouflage of faded red brick and dirty mortar. Everything about the structure discouraged visitors, from the

padlocked door to the crumbling entry step in front of it. A
window on the ground floor was broken and boarded up like
someone had tried to break in...or out.

Warren passed his hand in front of the padlock and it fell
open. He twisted it and pulled it out of the latch, dropped it in his
coat pocket, then pushed the door open. The inside of the
building certainly didn't match its disheveled exterior. Aside from
needing a thorough dusting, the office on the other side of the
door was in perfect shape. It resembled the waiting area of a
doctor's office or dentist.

I followed Warren inside and tried the light switch. Nothing
happened. A wide hallway stretched out in front of us with a
waiting area to our right and an office nook to our left. The
waiting room was lined with gray padded metal armchairs. The
white walls were bare and the only decoration was a small lamp
on a side table. The office area had a light oak, L-shaped desk with
a black rolling chair and a computer. I walked to the desk and
found the workspace untouched, aside from a doodle in the
corner of the desktop calendar. It was a child's drawing in black
ink of a rainbow that ended in a heart.

"Sloan, this way," Warren said, walking toward the hall.

We passed a door with a handwritten sign marked "BATH-
ROOM" next to a water cooler. At the end of the hall was another
door, this one made of heavy metal with a steel handle and industrial deadbolt. There was a "DO NOT ENTER" sign taped to it
with silver duct tape.

Warren waved his hand again and the lock tumbled. Reuel
walked through first, but we stayed close behind him. It was a
dark stairwell that led up to the next floor. I was latched to
Warren's sleeve as we climbed the rusted metal stairs which had
obviously been neglected during the remodel. Another metal door
was at the top. It was unlocked.

"Finally," Azrael said, looking up from where he was hunched over a cardboard box that was sitting on a long white counter. "What took you so long?"

"We took the train," Warren said. "What is this place?"

I was wondering the same thing. The room was deep, with three long white work counters complete with sinks, cabinets, and rolling chairs. On the counter tops were computers, microscopes, test tubes, and machines I couldn't identify. In the corner was a row of pharmaceutical lab freezers like the ones in my dad's building at the hospital. "It's a medical lab."

Azrael nodded toward the wall to his left. There were three evenly spaced wooden doors along it. "There are hospital beds in those rooms."

I scratched my head. "Were they treating sick people here?"

He shook his head and held out a stack of folders. "I think they may have been creating them."

I crossed the room and reached for the folders. "Creating sick people?"

He leaned his arms on the counter. "I've been trying to figure out for months why they would form a prostitution ring."

"The money," Warren said like it was an obvious answer.

Azrael smirked. "That's not why they did it."

I flipped the first folder open. It was a medical chart. I'd seen enough of them in my father's office to not be completely lost. The patient was a twelve-year-old girl named Sofia. She tested positive for chlamydia (occupational hazard) and she was treated with azithromycin (failed to cure), doxycycline (failed to cure), erythromycin (failed to cure)...the list went on and on. Sofia's condition worsened to advanced pelvic inflammatory disease, and that's where her notes stopped. I opened the next folder. Natalia was fifteen. She, too, was treated several times unsuccessfully for chlamydia. The third folder was the same for a different patient.

Warren was reading over my shoulder. "They were treating the girls for STDs?"

Azrael held out an empty vial. "I think they were infecting them."

The label on the tube said *Chlamydia Trachomatis - v29.*

"What do you know about it?" Azrael asked.

"Wear condoms," I said.

Azrael scowled. "I'm being serious."

"I don't know anything about it, but I can ask my dad."

"Find out everything you can."

I pulled my phone out and sent my father a short text message. *Need to know all you can tell me about chlamydia.*

"Why don't you Google it?" Warren asked.

"That probably would be faster than—" My phone buzzed in my hand. "Or maybe not." I tapped the answer button. "Hey, Dad."

"Sloan, are you all right?" Dad's voice was full of alarm.

"What? Oh yeah. It's not me. I'm fine."

"Are you sure? An infection could have serious consequences for the baby if—"

"Dad! I promise," I said. "We're working on something up in Chicago and it's part of the case."

He paused. "Oh. Chicago?"

I walked toward the window and looked outside. "Yeah. Sorry, I should've let you know. We'll be up here for a day or two doing some stuff with the FBI."

He sighed into the phone. "I miss the days when your biggest work dilemma was a conflict on the county event calendar."

I smiled. "Me too."

"What do you want to know?" he asked.

"Hang on. I'm going to put you on speakerphone." I turned on the phone's speaker and walked back to where the guys were still searching through the boxes Azrael had opened. "OK, Dad. Tell me what you can about chlamydia."

"It's one of the most common sexually transmitted diseases. It's a highly infectious bacteria, but it's usually treatable with antibiotics," he said.

"Hi, Dr. Jordan. It's Azrael. What would make it *not* easily treatable?"

"Well, the resistance of chlamydia to antibiotics has begun stirring alarm within the medical community in the past few months. They've identified a couple of different multidrug-resistant strains that because of their reduced treatment options could have severe complications and long-term health problems, particularly for women."

"What kind of health problems?" I asked.

"Pelvic inflammatory disease, ectopic pregnancy, and miscarriage. If left untreated, it can cause sterility in both women and men."

Azrael knocked his knuckles against the counter. "That's it."

"Pardon me?" Dad asked.

Azrael held up the empty vial again. "How would it become drug resistant?"

"Bacteria can evolve and change so the drugs become ineffective. It's usually caused by overuse or improper use of antibiotics."

Azrael looked around the room. "What about bioengineering? Could it be created in a lab?"

Dad chuckled. "That's pretty far above my pay grade, but I'm sure it's possible with the right equipment and with people a whole lot smarter than me."

I suddenly felt really warm in my cozy jacket. I pumped the front of it to force cool air inside as I began to sweat nervously.

"Thank you, Dr. Jordan. That's exactly what we needed to know," Azrael said.

"Thanks, Dad. I'll call you later, OK?"

"All right, sweetheart. Be safe."

I hung up the phone and looked at Azrael. "You're talking about biological warfare."

He shrugged and looked over the paperwork spread across the counter. "Makes a lot more sense than pimping out little girls for money."

Warren ran his hands through his hair and looked up at the ceiling.

I felt sick as I picked up the small vial. "So now we know their master plan: use my baby to destroy the spirit line, then weed out all the humans."

"But what we don't know..." Azrael said.

Warren blew out a heavy sigh. "Is if they were successful."

CHAPTER FIVE

ZRAEL CALLED SILVERS to let her know what we'd found. I continued searching through the boxes and sorted through records on sixteen different patients. The first eleven had few notes on them. It appeared the strains of bacteria didn't evolve enough to develop the drug resistance. The last five, however, were heavily documented and updated as recently as October. I set them aside. "These girls are sick. We need to find them," I said to Warren.

"Do you know where they are?" he asked.

I shook my head. "All I've got are their names and information. That's not enough for me to go on."

"You need the files from the FBI." He crossed the room and put a hand on Azrael's shoulder to interrupt him. "Tell Silvers we need to meet with her and see the list of girls who were rescued."

Azrael pulled the phone away from his mouth. "She's going to come to the hotel in the morning. They're going to process this place tonight."

"Make sure she brings the list," I called to him, "with pictures if possible!"

He gave me a thumbs up and turned his back to me.

Knowing we'd have to leave everything behind for the police, I used my phone to snap pictures of the girls' records in case the government lost the files. One of the girls, Amalia, was only eight. I had to close her folder before I fell apart completely.

Warren took the folders and put them back in the box. "That's enough for tonight, Sloan. We'll find them tomorrow." He pulled me close and put his arms around me. "Are you getting hungry?"

I rested my head against his chest. "No."

He looked at me. "Are you lying?"

"Yes."

Laughing, he pulled back and took my hand. "I know the perfect place for dinner."

Behind us, Reuel's stomach growled.

"I guess Reuel is ready to go," I said, turning toward him.

He smiled and nodded.

Azrael walked back over, stuffing his phone in his pocket. "We need to clear out. They're on their way here."

"What about our fingerprints?" I said. "Won't we get in trouble for being here?"

"Silvers will handle it. Don't worry." Azrael zipped up his coat. "Ready?"

"Pequod's for dinner?" Warren asked him.

He smiled. "Sounds good."

We walked a few blocks west, toward the golden sun that was sinking behind the buildings, before Azrael used an app on his phone to call an Uber to pick us up. Pequod's Pizza was about a twenty-minute drive, and I knew the second we stepped on the curb that the wait would be worth it. The aroma drifting from the building was intoxicating.

Warren held the door for me. "You can't come to Chicago without deep dish pizza."

"My stomach might eat itself if they don't serve us soon. This place smells so good I wanna die," I said.

The hostess showed us to a table, where we ordered drinks

and five large pizzas for the four of us. The waitress joked that she'd bring some to-go boxes when she brought our food; I bet her five bucks she wouldn't have to.

When our drinks were delivered, Azrael balanced his elbows on the table. "I need to talk to you both about something."

We needed to talk to him too.

"What's up?" Warren asked.

Azrael tapped his fingertips together, obviously trying to be careful of his words, which was very uncharacteristic. "Warren, I'd like for you to go back to Claymore."

I sat back in my seat. "Not this again."

"Hear me out. I'd at least like you to think about it. I'm not going to force you to go," he said, still not looking at me.

"Why do you want me there?" Warren asked.

"I want you to train Nathan."

Warren laughed. "What? Why? He doesn't listen to me now. He's not going to listen to me there."

"You won't be his lead instructor, but it would be beneficial for him to have a supernatural perspective on things that only you can give," he said.

"Why can't Enzo do it?" Warren asked.

"Enzo already has too many responsibilities as it is."

"What about Kane or NAG?" I asked.

"NAG is a pilot, not qualified in ground combat. And Kane's shadow has more leadership skills than he does, and he's already assigned to the Asheville detail." He looked pointedly at Warren. "I need someone I can trust."

Warren opened his mouth to speak, but Azrael stopped him.

"Take some time to think about it and you two talk it over." Azrael met my eyes. "You can always stay with me while he's gone. It's only eight weeks."

I shook my head. "No, thank you."

Warren reached over and squeezed my hand. "We'll talk about it."

Azrael seemed satisfied. "Anything interesting happen today?"

Warren nodded and lowered his voice. "At least once today, maybe twice, we've seen an angel that I don't know."

"What did he look like?" Azrael asked, leaning forward with interest.

I sipped my water. "You're such a chauvinist. Why do you assume it was a man?"

He ignored me.

"It was a male," Warren began, and Azrael held his hands up, glaring at me as if to say "*See?*"

Warren didn't stop for us to argue. "Couldn't see his face, so I can't judge his age, but he was about Nate's size. Perhaps a little smaller."

Azrael sat back in his seat. "I have no way of knowing who that could be."

I stirred the lemon around in my drink with the straw. "I'm still not sure it was him that I saw at the church."

"The church?" Azrael asked.

"I took her to St. Peter's today," Warren said.

Azrael crossed his arms. "On a little stroll down Memory Lane?"

"Something like that." Warren shifted uneasily on his chair. "Az, what happened to my mother?"

Azrael's head pulled back, then anger slowly burned away his surprise. "What brought her up?"

Warren hesitated, so I answered for him. "We met a woman at the church today who was there the day Warren was found. She said the priest died of an aneurysm while holding Warren that morning. So he accounts for the number of deaths Warren knows he's caused. Nadine can't be one of them."

"No one ever said Warren caused Nadine's death," Azrael snapped.

"I just assumed," Warren said. He held up his hands in defense.

"I'm sorry. I know you don't like talking about her, but she was my mother. I would really like to know."

Azrael tapped his index finger hard against the wooden table. "Your mother is gone for one reason, because I"—he jammed the finger against his breastbone—"wasn't strong enough to save her. That's all you need to know."

I looked around, bewildered. "On what planet is that all he needs to know? Geez, Azrael. I think you owe him the truth."

Warren was rubbing his temples like he was getting a headache. "Sloan, it's fine—"

"It's not fine." I pushed back from the table. "We didn't ask for any of this. You and Kasyade forced this life on us. The least you can do is explain. What happened to Nadine?"

"Phenex happened to her, Sloan." His face was flushed, and he barked at me through a clenched jaw, "Phenex happened to her!"

I bit the insides of my big, fat mouth.

Azrael slumped over the table, leaning on his elbows and cradling his forehead in his hands. "I went out early one morning to handle some business and came home to find her in our bed, blood soaking through the mattress. Phenex was holding Warren because she'd cut him out of Nadine's belly."

I tasted blood as my lower teeth cut into my lip.

"I had to choose between saving Warren or saving my wife." His voice was soft, and for the first time ever, weak. "I couldn't do both."

Warren swore quietly.

Without another word, Azrael rose from the table and walked out. My damp eyes were fixed on his empty chair. After a second, I stood up. "I'm going to go after him."

The door chimed when I pushed it open. My eyes scanned the streets until I spotted him walking, head down, hands stuffed in his coat pockets, half-way down the block. "Azrael, wait!" He didn't stop, so I ran and finally caught him by the arm in front of a small fitness center. There were two women riding exercise bikes in the window. Their pedals slowed as he turned around to face me.

"Azrael, I'm sorry." My nose was running from the tears and the cold. "I had no idea."

He shrugged. "You're right. You didn't know, and I should have told you and Warren sooner."

I let out a deep breath. "But that doesn't excuse the way I pushed you about it. Please forgive me."

Silently, he studied my face. "I won't forgive you."

I blinked with surprise.

He pointed his finger at my nose, stern, but no longer furious. "I won't forgive you because you didn't do anything wrong. That lurking bitch inside you is going to be the thing that saves your life someday. Don't you dare let that slip for the sake of my feelings."

My mouth fell open.

"Are we done?" he asked.

My head cocked to the side. "Did you call me a bitch?"

"Yes."

"Huh."

He offered me his arm. "Come on. Let's go back. I'm starving."

No one brought up Nadine again during dinner, and when we left, the waitress owed me five dollars. I didn't take it out of her tip, however. God knows she'd earned her pay trying to keep up with the rate Reuel could drain a glass.

We took the train back to the hotel and retired to our suite for the night. I took a bath to soak my tired legs, then joined Warren in our separate bedroom. He was bare-chested under the bed sheet watching sports commentary about the upcoming Super Bowl. He turned it off with the remote when I walked in wearing the hotel bathrobe.

"You look cozy," he said, turning onto his side and propping up on his elbow to watch me undress at my suitcase.

"I look relaxed." I smiled at him with my eyes half-mast.

I grabbed a pair of panties and one of Warren's t-shirts and laid them on the bed. Then I slipped the robe off my shoulders and let it fall to the floor around my feet.

"Sloan?"

Warren was gawking at me, but not the way I would have hoped while I stood before him stark naked. I covered my front with his shirt. "What?"

He sat up and reached for me, an unmasked frown cemented on his face. "Come here."

I held the shirt closer. "No. What's that look for? You look repulsed by me."

He shook his head. "I'm not repulsed, I'm worried. Come here."

"Worried?"

When I was close enough, he pulled the shirt away from my body and tossed it on the bed. He put his hand over my belly. "Are you feeling all right?"

"Yes. Why? What's wrong?"

"You're bigger today than you were yesterday."

Embarrassed—no, *humiliated*—I swatted his hand away. "Leave me alone. We just ate deep dish pizza."

"This isn't about the pizza and this isn't about you getting fat," he said, sitting back against the pillows as I pulled on his shirt. It *may* have fit me a tad bit closer around the middle than I expected.

"It's probably all the salt and all the walking around today," I said, moving around to my side of the bed.

The crease in his brow said he disagreed.

"The doctor said the baby's fine. She's still wiggling around in there." I folded the covers back and climbed in next to him.

"Still, I think you should go back to the doctor when we get home."

"If it will make you feel better, I will."

"Yes. It will." He leaned over and kissed me on the nose. "So, I promised Az we'd talk about the Claymore thing."

I glared.

He chuckled.

"Do you want to do it?" I asked, turning over onto my side to look at him. "Answer honestly."

He laughed harder. "Hell no."

I nodded. "All right then."

"Did you and Az make up on your little walk down the street?"

"He called me a bitch," I said.

He shrugged. "Well..."

I laughed and hit him with my pillow.

He reached his arm across my side and pulled me under the covers closer to him. I snuggled against his warm chest. "I still feel bad about how I yelled at him," I said. "I can't imagine what he must have gone through when your mom died."

"Me either."

I looked up. "He made the right decision though."

His head tilted. "What do you mean?"

"She would have wanted him to save you instead of her." I reached up and traced the line of his jaw with my fingers. "And I want you to promise me that you'll do the same if it ever comes down to me or her."

He rested his forehead against mine. "Sloan, I can't even think—"

I gently pushed him back to force him to look at me. "I'm serious, Warren. We don't know how crazy this ride is going to get before it's finished. And if things go worst-case-scenario, please know that's what I want. I want her to be the priority. Promise me."

He studied my eyes for a moment before finally nodding. "I promise." He leaned his head against mine again. "But I swear I'll never let it come to that."

"I know."

His hand slipped under my shirt to my belly. "Her life's going to be different."

I smiled. "Her life is going to be amazing." I raked my fingers through his black hair. "*Our* lives are going to be amazing."

He lowered his mouth to mine. "My life already is."

Warren didn't bother turning out the light before he expressed his gratitude *twice* for the amazing life we'd built together. After seeing stars the second time, I passed out flat on my back with one arm slung across Warren's chest beside me and the other bent sideways against the bed frame. My hair was plastered with dried sweat over my face like Cousin It and only one leg had made it under the bed sheet. At least that's how I woke up the next morning when Azrael pounded on our bedroom door.

I groaned. "Go away."

"Get up. Silvers is in the lobby," Azrael called with one final thump against the door.

I tried to brush the hair out of my face. "Why does everything have to start so early?"

Warren looked at his watch and chuckled before letting his arm fall back across his eyes. "It's almost ten."

"Seriously? Wow." I rolled toward him and rested my face against his shoulder. "I still don't wanna get up."

He raked his fingers down my bare back. "I know, but we have to. We have to fly home this afternoon."

"What time's our flight?" I asked.

"Six," he said.

I laughed and pushed myself. "We'd better leave now so we can make the pilgrimage back through O'Hare in time."

He sat up and rubbed his face. "You sound like a native Chicagoan already."

Silvers was waiting at the cafe inside the lobby when we stepped off the elevator. Her makeup was minimal, and her strangely unpainted lips dipped low in the corners. The bags under her eyes were heavy, and I was pretty sure she was wearing the same clothes as the day before. "Agent Silvers, are you all right?" I asked as we approached.

Her hands curled around the large coffee in front of her. "I had a long night and a very early morning."

I slid into the booth across from her. Warren touched my shoulder. "Would you like a drink?"

She held up a hand to stop him. "Can it wait? I'm afraid I cannot."

All of us exchanged puzzled glances.

"What happened?" Azrael asked.

She took a deep breath. "There's no easy way to say this." She looked at me. "Marisol Juarez is dead."

I turned my ear toward her and blinked. "Excuse me?"

She cradled her head in her hands, obviously needing a moment to regain her composure. "They found her this morning in her cell. She hung herself with a rope she fashioned from her mattress pad."

I covered my mouth to keep from screaming or crying out. "It can't be!"

Warren wrapped his arm around my shoulders.

I grabbed Agent Silvers's wrist. "Are you sure someone didn't—"

She shook her head. "She left a note."

I sank back in my seat and let my head fall back against the back of the booth. I closed my eyes and cried.

"Did you find anything at the factory building last night?" Azrael asked.

Reuel got up from the table and went and got me a napkin. "Thank you," I said as I dried my eyes, then blew my nose.

"We brought in a hazmat team that went through everything.

There was lots of evidence left behind in the trash and in a few of the exam rooms." She turned her palms up. "It's like they were dabbling in bioterrorism and didn't care if they got caught."

Azrael smirked. "Agent Silvers, they *didn't* care." He leaned toward her. "You need to keep in mind that you're not dealing with ordinary criminals here. They're not worried about answering to you."

For a second, I thought she might argue, but she didn't. "I'm learning that. We'll identify what was in those vials, but I think you're right. I think they tried to weaponize that bacteria."

"Honey, they didn't just try," Azrael said. "They succeeded. We need to find out if it's contained or not."

"And that starts with finding the infected girls. I need your files," I said.

She nodded and reached into the bag beside her chair. She hesitated before handing me the thick folder. "This is completely off record, Sloan. I could go to jail for this."

"I promise it won't blow back on you, and you need to trust me. I can help them."

She passed me the folder, and I took it before she could change her mind.

"When I figure out who these girls are, I may need help finding them. Do you know where they would have been taken?" I asked.

A deep breath puffed out her cheeks. "All over. These girls were picked up in three different states. Some were sent home to their families, some went into the foster program, some to private ministries…"

Azrael looked at her with smug derision. "Others were deported or turned back to the streets only to wind up in the hands of another pimp."

Her jaw dropped an inch.

I gasped. "Azrael!"

"It's true, isn't it?" He was daring her to argue. "That's what happens to most of these girls who are saved by the system."

She closed her mouth and sighed. "It does happen."

Frustrated, I raked my fingers back through my hair. "That's just great."

"Do you have connections at the CDC?" Azrael asked.

"I can get them," she said.

He nodded. "Good. We're going to need to know of any cases where this thing has spread and what kind of infection rate it has."

"I'll do my best." She pulled her coffee close. "Why would they do this?"

Azrael smiled, and it creeped me out a little. "Because they can."

When Agent Silvers was gone, I opened the folder full of information sheets with Polaroids stapled to them, and Warren got me a cup of tea. I pulled out my phone and found the photos of the reports from the factory. There were a lot of pages to sort through because the FBI had rescued over two hundred girls from the demons' operation. I divided the stack into four sections and passed them around the table. "The first girl we need to find is Sofia. She's twelve."

I flipped through my pages. Each photo of each sad little face made my stomach tighter and tighter.

Warren held up a sheet. "I've got her. Sofia Fuentes."

I snatched the sheet from his hand and studied the girl's face. "She's alive." I placed her sheet in the middle of the table and turned back to my phone. "The next one is Isabel Valenzuela. She's also twelve."

"Here," Azrael said after a minute. "She's alive."

"The next one is Ariana Padilla, age fourteen," I said. "Oh, wait. I saw her sheet, I think." I flipped back through my pages until I found her. "Yep. She's alive."

Warren was looking at my phone. "The next girl is Amalia. My god, she's only eight."

I groaned.

Reuel waved a paper in the air like he'd won a prize.

I took it and looked it over. "Good job, Reuel. We're on a roll. Amalia Acevedo is alive too. Next one is Natalia, age fifteen."

Azrael's shoulder's slumped as he stopped on a page in his stack.

"You found her?" I asked.

He nodded. "Yeah." He shook his head sadly as he handed it to me. "It says she died here in Chicago about three weeks after they picked her up."

I looked at it. "Does it say the cause of death?"

"Sepsis."

I closed my eyes. "What a depressing day."

Warren nudged me with his elbow. "Focus on the ones we can still help." He looked around the table. "Anyone else see any kids that didn't make it?"

Reuel looked sad as he gave Warren a piece of paper. I shook my head. Warren heaved a heavy sigh while he placed a paper from his stack with Reuel's. He laid those sheets on top of Natalia's.

"Save those for me," I said.

He nodded and rested his elbow on top of them.

I picked up the remaining four girls. I focused on Sofia's face first, then I closed my eyes and reached out with my gift to find her. "She's nowhere close to here." I shook my head. "South some- where. Far south."

"Texas or Mexico probably," Warren said.

I got the same feeling from Isabel and Ariana's pictures. They were far away from Chicago. But Amalia was different. "She's still here," I said, opening my eyes to read her information. "She's here in the city. Close!" Filled with excitement, I started to get up.

Azrael grabbed my arm. "Slow down. You have no idea what you're doing."

I pried his fingers off my forearm. "I'm going to go find a sick little girl and make her better."

Warren put his hand on my leg and leaned toward me. "Chum bucket."

"Oh, crap! I forgot." I sat back and slouched.

"If you heal that girl, you might as well set off a flashing beacon alarm announcing you're here," Azrael said.

I frowned. "What do we do then?"

Azrael drummed his fingers on the side of his coffee cup. "We need to get her somewhere safe. Ideally Claymore."

I groaned loudly. "This again. Are you serious right now?"

He glared at me. "You asked. I answered. You definitely can't do this here. Not now, and not without a team."

"What if I did it really fast, and we—"

From across the table, without touching me, he pinched my lips closed with his power. "I know you want to make this happen, but we need to have a better plan first. We'll come back. I promise." He was still holding my lips closed. "Are you done arguing with me?"

I tried to speak despite the force holding my mouth shut. "*Mah-wah-ma-mawa-wah—*"

"Is that a yes? You're done?" he asked.

I scowled and nodded my head.

He released my lips.

I pointed at him. "You're not allowed to do that to me!"

Warren looked at him with wide, questioning eyes. "Can you teach me?"

I smacked his arm and laughed.

Azrael tapped his watch. "We need to get our stuff together. Our late check out time is almost up and it's an hour ride to the airport."

"You go on up. I'm going to finish my tea and then we'll be

right behind you," I said.

Azrael stood. "Five minutes."

I gave him a thumbs up and started gathering up the girls' files. Warren passed me his stack and Azrael's. Reuel gave me his. I put all the pages together and jogged them against the table to line up all the edges, then I carefully placed them back into the folder.

"Oh, don't forget these." Warren handed me the three pages of the girls we'd already lost.

Natalia's picture was on top. I ran my thumb over the edge of it. *She was only fifteen.* The thought stirred all of my newfound maternal instincts. They tightened my chest, making it hard to breathe and even harder to think rationally. Across the room, I heard the elevator *ding.* I turned and watched the doors slide open and The Angel of Death step inside. They closed behind him.

"Screw it!" I pushed myself up from the table. "Come on, guys."

"Oh no. No, no, no, no!" Warren grabbed my hand and hauled me to a stop. "Sloan, you can't do this."

Reuel was arguing with me in Katavukai.

"You're either in or out, Warren, but I'm doing it." I pushed Natalia's sheet against Warren's chest. "What if Amalia is in this stack by the time we come back? She's eight, Warren. *Eight!*"

He huffed with resignation. "Damn it, Sloan. You're going to get us killed."

Ignoring him, I closed my eyes and reached out to find Amalia with my gift. "Amalia Acevedo," I whispered and pulled her to me.

I ran out of the hotel with Warren and Reuel right on my heels. Either of them could have overpowered me if they really wanted to, but I think they knew deep down this was the right thing to do. After all, with great power comes great responsibility. *Right, Spiderman?*

My moving feet knew where I was going, but I sure as hell

didn't. We ran two blocks, turned left and ran three more. We turned right and darted through a group of men in black suits. The subway entrance was beyond them. I ran down the concrete stairwell at Harrison Station.

"This is a bad idea," Warren said as he fumbled for our transit passes.

When we got to the platform, two trains were waiting. I looked at both of them. "This one!" I ran through the open doors of the train on our left. Reuel barely made it through before they closed.

Warren was red-faced and panting. "I love you, but man I could kill you sometimes."

I stretched up on my tiptoes to kiss him. "Think how good you'll sleep tonight knowing that little girl is safe and healthy."

My phone buzzed in my pocket. I pulled it out and looked at the text message from Azrael. *Five minutes is up. Where are you??*

I powered my phone down.

Suddenly, next to me, Warren's spine went rigid. Azrael was calling him too, *not* on the phone. He twisted his neck in pain and swore.

I gripped his arm. "We're almost there. Hang on!"

The train stopped again. This time at Jackson Station. The doors slid open, and I ran out onto the platform. Commuters crowded the platform. Some were boarding, some were heading toward the exit. My brain was spinning. I didn't know which way to go.

Someone bumped into me with a strong elbow. I spun toward the blow and saw the man in the red toboggan standing at my side.

Before I could react, the piercing squeal of metal scraping metal ricocheted off the concrete block walls and floor of the station, igniting the horrified screams of the waiting passengers around us. I looked in time to see the front car of the train from the opposite direction coming right for us.

CHAPTER SIX

I CLAPPED MY hands over my ears at the same time Reuel's heavy hand slammed against my back and grasped my shirt, ripping me off the ground. He threw me forward and sideways away from the train with so much force that I sailed through the air and crashed against the corner of the attendant's station with my left hip. I landed hard on my stomach, followed by my cheek and forehead smacking the cold cement.

Pain, unlike any I'd ever felt, ripped through my abdomen. My body twisted as it gripped me, and I uncontrollably spewed the Earl Grey that was still warm in my stomach.

A solid boot connected with the back of my head and spun me around enough to see the sparks showering the landing as the wheels of the derailed train scraped across the concrete. The noise blistered my eardrums. People stampeded through the station and dived across the platform. In the blur and through the haze of dust and smoke, I watched the train fall back onto the tracks and slow in a firework show of wild electricity and bright flashes down the dark tunnel ahead.

Warren suddenly appeared over the top of me with a crack that echoed off the walls. He shielded me with his body from the people running off the train we'd arrived on. It had never left the station. Some passengers fled to the street above, others to the transfer tunnel below. We were caught in the middle of the two stairwells, and feet pounded all around us. I brought my hands up to cover my skull, and I closed my eyes and prayed we wouldn't be trampled to death in the stampede.

Another razor-sharp pain tore through my stomach, and I may have blacked out for a second. It all happened so fast I couldn't tell. Nothing made sense. Then I felt the familiar tingle of Warren's hand as it clasped my arm and hauled me to my feet. He gripped both of my elbows as my stance wavered. Someone bumped into us as they ran past, and he pulled me close, curling his strong arm around my body.

"Are you OK?" he shouted above the noise of the mob.

I clenched the fabric of his shirt and bent at the waist, forcing him a step back. "The baby" was all I could choke out before my knees buckled under me.

Warren caught me before I hit the cement again, and he scooped me up into his arms and carried me across the platform away from the direction the fleeing passengers were moving. The crowd thinned, and the noise had decreased so that it no longer rattled my brain. I saw the last car of the train that almost killed us poking out of the tunnel.

He laid me on an empty waiting bench and knelt beside me, gently resting his hand on my forehead. "Talk to me, Sloan."

"It hurts. Something's wrong." Then I screamed out with a massive contraction.

"Breathe," he said as he gently lifted my shirt up over my belly. "What hurts?"

My teeth clenched, and tears leaked back into my hair. "Everything."

I felt his hand slide between my thighs and when he raised it back into the air, his fingers and palm were tinged with red blood. His eyes widened. "We need to get you to a hospital."

I tried to sit up, but it hurt too much.

"Lie still. I'm going to get help."

Before he could move, a frantic woman in a blue uniform bent over me. "Paramedics are on the way." She began blowing a whistle and pushing the surrounding people toward the stairs. "If you are able to move, I need you out of the station! Move it, people!"

Another contraction ripped through me and a burning pain seared through my stomach below my belly button. I gripped Warren's hand and pulled it against my broken face as I screamed. Before the contraction subsided, another one began. This time a gush of warm blood spread through my jeans.

"Help me," I said, gasping for air.

Terror was etched all over Warren's pale face. He slipped an arm under my legs, the other behind my back, and lifted me again. "Everybody, move!" He pushed his way out of the subway tunnel. I heard sirens in the distance.

Then I was gone.

Beep...beep...beep...beep...

"I'd hate to say I told you so."

My eyes fluttered open, or at least the right one did. The left was too swollen to flutter. Backed by the halogen glow from the overhead lights, Azrael was leaning over me. I smelled antiseptic. And blood.

I coughed. "Then don't." My voice was rough and slight. "Just keep your mouth shut for once."

A heavy weight lifted from my hand. It was Warren's head. Tears streaked his dirty face. There was a swash of blood across his forehead where he'd wiped it with his hand. "Oh my god." He panted as he collapsed over me, cradling my head in his arms. "I thought you were going to die."

My weak hand tangled in his hair. "I'm not that easy to kill, remember?"

He pulled back and wiped his eyes before pressing his mouth against mine. "Are you OK?" he whispered.

I nodded. "The baby?"

He straightened. "She's fine. It was close. Something about a uterine rupture. I don't know. They said there was scar tissue on the ultrasound. They didn't understand why there was so much blood because the tear was closed."

The rupture had closed on its own before they ever even saw it. If anyone needed a medical identification bracelet labeled "Mystery," it was me.

"What happened down there?" I asked. "I don't remember much."

"The train left the tracks, and Reuel tackled it and pushed it back off the platform."

"Where is he now?"

Warren shook his head. "I haven't seen him since he disappeared into the tunnel ahead of the train."

The curtain around my triage room pulled back, and a stout man in a white lab coat walked in carrying a clipboard. His face was wide and round with spots from the sun and heavy wrinkles around his eyes. And he had a short beard that was now more gray than brown that faded into an overgrown tapered haircut with a high receding hairline at the side part. The breast of his coat pocket said DR. DANIEL JOHNSON, M.D. OB/GYN, but he looked more like a deep-sea fisherman.

"Ms. Jordan?"

I gave a little wave.

"How are you feeling?"

"Sore. Tired."

He nodded. "I'm sure. You appear to have lost quite a bit of blood."

"But the baby's OK?" I asked.

He squeezed my foot under the blanket. "The baby is fine. Strong heartbeat and doing somersaults." He put the clipboard on top of my legs and moved over beside my head. He pried my swollen eye all the way open. I winced. "You have some ruptured blood vessels here. How's your vision?"

"It's fine."

"Not blurry? No spots?"

"No, but my head hurts."

"We did a head CT, and it looked fine. You have a hairline fracture below this eye, but it's nothing time won't heal. You were extraordinarily lucky today."

"Did anyone die?" I asked, afraid to hear the answer.

"No casualties so far. A few broken bones, but mostly bumps and bruises."

I exhaled slowly, my chin quivering as I tried to hold back my emotions.

He picked up his clipboard again. "Your uterus is a bit of a puzzle. There has been a significant tear at some point. Do you know what caused it?"

Being thrown out of the path of a train.

I shook my sore head.

He put his hand on my shoulder. "Make sure your regular obstetrician keeps an eye on it during delivery."

I nodded. "I will."

"Also, we saw an excess buildup of amniotic fluid. Have you noticed?"

"I've noticed," Warren said, squeezing my hand and flashing me an apologetic smile.

"Well, it may have saved your baby's life today," the doctor said. "It's a condition you need to keep an eye on, but the extra padding in there did nothing but good things for both of you today."

I gently rested my hands on my sore belly and silently promised to never curse my weight gain again. I didn't understand it at all, but I knew it wasn't a coincidence. "Thank you. Can I leave?"

He read over his notes. "I'd really like to keep you overnight for observation."

"I really have no desire to stay here," I said.

He studied my face. "Well, I can't legally keep you here, and your vitals have been fine since you arrived, so I won't object too much if you want to leave. Please take it easy the rest of the day."

"We're supposed to fly home to North Carolina," Warren said.

The doctor shook his head. "No flying today."

Warren stood and shook his hand. "Thank you, Dr. Johnson."

When he was gone, Azrael folded his arms over his chest and scowled at me. "What were you thinking, Sloan?"

"I was thinking about a little girl who's spent the past two years being raped by grown men. I was thinking that without my help she could develop sepsis and die, or best case scenario never be able to have children."

"A lot of innocent lives could have been lost today because of your selfishness."

"Well, they weren't."

"No thanks to you."

I thought about shooting him the bird, but I didn't because I knew he was right. Maybe it was my selfishness, coupled with my insanity-inducing hormones, that almost killed a lot of people that day. It was only because of Reuel that no one died. Without him, the story would be quite different, and I would be responsible. As if the universe was making my point, at that very moment an elderly woman on a gurney was wheeled past the foot of my bed. The man who held her hand had white tousled hair and dirt on his face that matched the dirt on Warren's.

I let out a deep sigh. "Is this really my fault?"

Azrael's face was non-committal as he bent to take a closer look at my swollen eye. "I wouldn't go so far as to say it's your fault, but yeah. It's your fault."

"Who did this then?" Warren asked.

Azrael shrugged. "I don't know. Could be The Destroyer, could be the Morning Star or one of his lackeys. Hell, it could be your mother."

I shook my head. "Don't call her that."

"Is the Morning Star here in Chicago?" Warren asked.

Azrael shrugged again. "It's possible."

Acid churned in my stomach. "Right before the train hit, the man in the red toboggan was standing right next to me."

Warren looked at me, then at Azrael. "I didn't see him."

"Interesting," Azrael said. "I'll look for him when I go try to find Reuel. You say he went into the tunnel and never came back out?"

Warren nodded. "A lot of people would have died if it weren't for him. He forced the train back onto the tracks."

I sat up a little in the bed, and it hurt like hell. "Should I come too? What if he needs my help?"

Azrael gave my head a patronizing pat. "We've survived more years without you than your weak human brain can calculate. I'm sure we'll manage."

"Do you always have to be such a jerk?"

He grinned. "Yes."

A young nurse came in to discharge me. She brought a pair of pants from what she called the hospital's "Blessing Closet" because my jeans were soaked with blood. I thanked her and signed myself out. Azrael waited outside the curtain as Warren helped me get dressed. The bruising on my stomach was alarming. If I'd drawn on two eyes, my belly button could've been a nose and the pooled blood beneath it, a smile.

Warren led me by the hand out of the room to where Azrael waited with a wheelchair. "They said I could push you out," he said with a wicked smile.

I frowned and gently sat down. "Are you going to run me into walls and doors?"

"Perhaps."

They walked and I rolled through the large emergency room triage area that was filled with patients I'd put there. And for what? I never found Amalia. Maybe Azrael was right. Maybe I was selfish.

Warren grabbed the arm of my wheelchair, stopping me so fast I almost fell forward onto the floor. He turned the chair to the right. In a bed, half-way hidden by a partially closed curtain, was a little girl with ashen tan skin. She was lying on her side, curled in the fetal position because I knew her stomach hurt. She was all alone, and she was crying.

I looked up at Azrael, my eyes pleading with him. His shoulders sank in resignation, and he slightly bowed his head to give his permission.

Warren hooked his arm under mine and helped me out of the chair. I hobbled over to her bedside as Azrael checked the medical chart that was resting in a slot on the footboard. I didn't need to know what it said. I knew who she was.

I sank onto the bed beside her. "Amalia?"

She turned to look up at me, her eyes terrified and leaking the biggest tears I'd ever seen come from anyone. I rested my hand on her beaded forehead. She was burning up.

"I'm going to help you," I whispered. "Don't be afraid. Can I touch your tummy?"

Her head bobbed nervously as I gently rested my palm on her tiny stomach. My fingers began to tingle and heat rose in my skin as my power flowed into her. She began to tremble and cry harder but so quietly only I could hear her ragged breaths.

My hand cooled as the last drops of my power left my body. She suddenly relaxed, and her wide eyes blinked up at me. I slowly shook my head as I wrapped my hand around hers. "It's all over now. You're going to feel so much better."

With tears streaming down my cheeks, I started to pull my hand away, but she grabbed it and pulled herself up to wrap her little arms around my neck. She didn't say anything. She didn't have to. It was finished.

Even Azrael smiled.

None of us spoke as we walked out of the emergency room, but the sun was brighter, the air wasn't quite as chilly, and another miracle was sitting on a bench by the door. Reuel stood when he saw us and waved with the one arm he could obviously move. The other was limp and looked strange at his side, hidden beneath a dark blanket. He was covered in black dust and his shirt was torn at the neckline, halfway to his bellybutton.

"Is it me or does he look like a ghost?" Warren asked.

"He's lost a lot of blood." Azrael slipped on his sunglasses. "Warren, call us a cab, please. A big one."

Azrael wheeled me across the sidewalk to Reuel. "How did he find us?" I asked, looking up at Az.

He kept his eyes on Reuel. "Chum bucket."

I slouched in my chair.

When we were close enough, Azrael put the brakes on my wheelchair and helped me up. He spoke to Reuel in Katavukai, then Reuel shook his head furiously as he sat back down.

"She can help you," Azrael said in English.

Reuel looked like he might cry.

I took a step over in front of him. "Come on. Let me see it."

Reuel flinched away from where my fingers were trying to grasp the edge of the blanket he'd commandeered. I didn't have to see his arm to know it was bad. I could smell the blood from where I stood.

"*En ai fuknam,*" he said, "*nakal vis videre.*"

I looked at Azrael. "Did he just cuss me out?"

Azrael smiled.

Reuel shook his head.

"I know it's bad, Reuel, but you need to let me see it." I held my hands up. "I promise, I'll be gentle."

He finally let out a reluctant sigh and nodded his huge head. He cautiously looked around, then spoke to Azrael.

"He says you should probably sit down," Az translated.

I sat down, facing him on the bench. Reuel braced himself as I carefully pulled the blanket back enough to see under it.

"SWEET MOTHER OF GOD!" Warren yelled beside Azrael, staggering backward.

Sour bile filled my mouth. I turned my head and gagged toward the ground.

"*Eshta!*" Reuel hissed, looking around.

Azrael chuckled to himself.

I'd seen my share of horrific injuries. During our last battle alone, I'd fought a demon who'd lost half his skull to a gun blast; I reached inside a man's torso and held his guts together long enough to heal him; and hell, even Reuel (honest-to-god) had been impaled by a tree. None of those compared to what was hidden under that blanket.

I had to take several deep breaths to keep from passing out again.

To be honest, if it weren't for the thumb and index finger that were still somehow attached, I wouldn't have known I was looking at an arm. From what used to be his bicep all the way to the tip of his missing fingers, the arm was splayed open down to the splintered bones like a butterflied and shredded filet being held together by broken kabob sticks. Skin and tendons dangled around shredded muscles and ripped veins. A human would have already bled to death. Reuel, however, had barely broken a sweat.

"I hope he's right handed," Warren said.

Reuel cracked a smile. A small one. Then he gently tucked the arm back underneath the blanket.

Azrael crossed his arms. "How did you do that?"

Reuel gave a long monologue in Katavukai. Azrael did a lot of cringing, some swearing and knuckle biting, but zero translating. I nudged him with the toe of my shoe. "Hello? Want to subtitle this story for us?"

"Sorry." He pointed at Reuel. "His arm was crushed by the train."

I shook my head, dumbfounded. "Good to know my deductive reasoning skills are still sharp. Thanks a lot, Az."

"How did it happen?" Warren asked.

"Yeah. It looks like he tried to chew it free," I said.

"Maybe he did. I'll ask him." Azrael looked at Reuel. "*Nankai meltuum ta kai llavacal?*"

Reuel smiled. "*Nich, illai nan oru multo temporcik paci vantatu esurit!*"

The answer evoked a rare, hearty laugh from Az. He looked at me. "He said no. He was stuck there so long he got hungry."

Warren and I laughed.

Azrael jerked his thumb toward the street. "We need to get a cab."

"We need to stay right here at the hospital. He's got a wet and bloody, busted red piñata for an arm," I said. "He needs help."

"He needs a hacksaw," Warren added. "That thing needs to be amputated."

I shuddered.

"They can't do anything for him here. We'll bandage it up enough to travel, then Sloan can work on setting it right."

I cut him off. "Azrael, there's nothing left to set right anymore."

He turned to face me and used his finger to trace the deep scar down the center of his face. "There wasn't when this happened either, but we're built to recover. Have some faith. You'll have plenty of time on the trip home tonight."

"Tonight?" Warren asked. "The doctor said she can't fly."

Azrael slapped him on the back. "That's right. Cancel your flight and book us a car. We're driving."

CHAPTER SEVEN

O N OUR INCREDIBLY long drive back to North Carolina, I called Agent Silvers to update her on what had happened. I told her I'd found and healed Amalia, but there were three other girls I hadn't yet found. She promised to look for them and keep me updated.

Thirteen hours, thirty-six minutes, and nine stops later, we pulled into my driveway as the sun came up in Asheville. I went straight to my room and slept all day. When I woke up, I was alone in my bed and there were stars outside my window. I could hear voices downstairs.

My body protested movement with a blistering pain when I rolled to sit up. My face throbbed once I was vertical, and I sat on the edge of the bed until the dizziness passed before I dared to stand. When the room stopped spinning, I pushed myself off the bed and trudged to the bathroom.

I flipped the light switch on, and when I caught sight of my reflection I almost shut it back off. "Oh boy."

The entire left side of my face was swollen and bright blue with purple splotches. I gently pried my eye open to find blood where the whites should have been.

"Knock, knock!" I heard Adrianne call from my bedroom door.

"In here," I replied. "Prepare yourself before you walk in this bathroom. I look like I should be dead."

I heard the *click-clack* of her heels against my bedroom floor.

"Don't be such a drama qu—*whoa*! Oh my god! What happened to your face?" She froze halfway through the bathroom door behind me.

I turned to face her. "I told you to be prepared."

She covered her gaping mouth with her hands, the newly plastered pink acrylic tips on her nails nearly gouging her eyes. "Sloan," she whimpered.

"It's not the worst of it," I said.

"I don't know how that's possible."

I pulled up the front of my shirt, and Adrianne stumbled back into the doorframe. "Is she OK?" Her voice squeaked with concern as she stepped forward and gingerly touched the sides of my belly.

"She's fine. The doctor said my ice cream addiction saved her."

"I'm so glad you're OK." She straightened and put her arms around me.

I winced when she squeezed. "Ouch."

She let go. "I'm sorry."

"It's OK. I'm going to be sore for a while I'm afraid." I turned toward the mirror. "Can you put my hair up? It hurts to raise my arms."

She raked my hair up with her hands and leaned next to my ear. "I will always do your hair," she said and kissed my cheek.

"Did you go home and change after work?"

She had on designer jeans and a fuzzy, blue cowl neck sweater that matched her blue three-inch heels.

"Maybe."

"Are you here to see me or my father-in-law?"

She finished tying my hair in a messy bun on the top of my head. "Do you want the truth?"

I rolled my eyes.

"Hey, it's not my fault. I didn't even know you went to Chicago, much less that you were hurt. Warren never tells me anything." She eyed me in the mirror. "You really should fix that. What if something serious happened?"

"More serious than being hit by a train?"

We both laughed.

"Come on. Let's go downstairs," she said. "Nathan's here."

Halfway down the staircase, I decided changing floors was a very bad idea. Even with Adrianne on one side for support and the hand rail on the other, I wasn't sure I'd make it to the living room. Each step felt like it was ripping my torso in half, and if going down hurt that bad, I didn't even want to imagine what going back up was going to feel like. We were almost at the bottom when Warren saw us and jumped up to help. Nathan and Azrael were seated at the dining table with beers in front of them, and Reuel was on the couch.

"I've got you," Warren said, stepping into Adrianne's spot.

Two more steps.

One more.

I almost cried when we reached the floor. My forehead was prickled with sweat. "That wasn't the smartest thing I've ever done."

He put his hand under my chin and tilted my face up. "You need an ice pack, babe."

"There are some in the freezer," I said.

"I got it," Adrianne announced, crossing the room ahead of us.

Nathan stood when we were most of the way to the dining area. He had come from work, a night job. I knew by his dark green pants and black pullover. His badge dangled from a chain around his neck. "Sloan." His voice cracked with emotion.

"Do I look that bad?" I asked.

Everyone else answered a resounding "yes" in unison, except for Reuel, who said "*aytim.*"

Nathan cleared his throat, then cupped the normal side of my face in his hand and examined the bruising. "You're a train wreck. *Literally.*"

I laughed and pushed his chest. "Shut up."

"Here," Adrianne said, handing me an ice pack she'd wrapped in a kitchen towel.

"Thank you."

"Come sit down," Nathan said. "You look like you're going to black out...or puke." He made a dramatic sour face. He'd had to deal with my vomit a lot.

"Stop making me laugh. It hurts."

Warren helped me into the chair at the head of the table. "Are you hungry? Nathan brought over dinner."

I shook my head.

"What?" Nathan asked. "Sloan's not hungry? No way."

I chuckled again. "Thanks for bringing dinner."

"You need to eat," he said. "There's steak and spinach salad. Both are high in iron. I heard you lost a lot of blood."

"I did. Thank you." I looked at Warren who was standing beside me. "Maybe I should eat a little."

He nodded. "Coming right up. Nate, you want another beer?"

"Nah, I'm good. Thanks." Nathan stretched his legs out, crossing one boot over the other, and laced his fingers behind his head. "I hear you saved a little girl."

"She did, and derailed a train while she was at it," Azrael said.

Nathan scowled across the table at him. "Oh, lay off, Az. If God didn't want her to use that power, I don't guess he would've given it to her. Nobody died."

Adrianne was sitting next to Azrael, and she pinched her lips together to stop the smile that was trying to tip up the corners over her mouth.

Nathan looked back at me and winked.

Warren returned with my plate of food. He'd even cut my steak. "Eat what you can."

"Thank you."

He kissed the top of my head, then brought a chair in from the kitchen to sit beside me.

"Tell me what you found out at the prison," Nathan said, not directing the question at a specific person.

That one, I didn't want to answer, so I chewed a piece of steak slowly. Warren told him everything we'd learned from Marisol. How she'd basically been held prisoner for twenty years after signing a deal with the devil to keep her daughter alive. Nathan's face fell when Warren told him she'd killed herself during the night. Across the table, Adrianne's eyes got a little misty.

"She did help us find the demons' second hideout where it looks like they may have been dabbling in bioweapons," Warren said.

Nathan's eyes widened. "No shit?"

"They were testing drug resistant STDs on those kids," Warren said sadly.

Nathan rubbed a hand over his mouth. "Wow."

"Azrael thinks they may have been trying to thin out the human race for when they take over the world," I added.

"Seriously?" Adrianne asked.

"Yep. There's no better time than now to be practicing safe sex," I said.

I didn't miss the pink that rose in my best friend's cheeks.

"What does all that have to do with the train though?" Nathan asked.

I shook my head. "It doesn't have anything to do with the train. The wreck happened because I left to go find the sick little girl." I gestured toward Azrael. "He told me the risks, and I did it anyway."

Nathan sat up straight in his chair and leaned his elbows on the table. "But that doesn't make any sense. These demons worked like hell to set all this in motion, right? They've busted their asses for thirty years to make sure Warren and Sloan have this kid." He lifted his hands in question. "So why do they keep trying to kill her?"

Adrianne nudged Azrael's arm. "That's a good point."

Azrael was peeling the label on the bottle in front of him. "You assume that all the angels are aligned under the same plan, Detective. There are plenty of angels who don't want the spirit line destroyed, and they certainly have no desire for a being with the power to destroy them."

"There was a demon on the platform," I said to Nathan. "He'd been following us all day."

"Or maybe we were following him," Warren said. "He seemed to be wherever we showed up."

I nodded. "I think he was behind the train. It was too big of a coincidence that he was there."

"Who is he?" Warren asked Azrael.

Az shrugged. "I'm not sure, but I intend to find out. His behavior is curious."

"He reminds me of Taiya," Warren said.

I pointed my fork at him. "I got the same vibe, but he's not Seramorta, right?"

"Definitely not," Warren answered.

"Tomorrow, perhaps, I'll go back and look for him," Azrael said. "I want to find out who he is and what part he plays in all this."

"You're going back?" Warren asked, surprised. "Am I going with you?"

"You'll stay here. Sloan and Reuel will need your help for a couple of days."

I looked at Nathan. "Have you seen Reuel's arm?"

Nathan made a gagging noise.

"You should have seen it yesterday. It's worlds better now than it was," I said.

"So I hear," Nathan said. "That's pretty badass that he tackled the train."

"I'd be dead if it weren't for him," I said.

"A lot of people would be," Warren agreed.

"What about Taiya?" Nathan asked. "Any new leads on her."

My shoulders slumped. "Nothing. Marisol knew her but had no idea where she might have gone."

"I'll call around tomorrow and see if she's turned up at any of the local departments," Nathan offered.

"Thanks." I turned to Warren. "Speaking of calling people, did you call my dad?"

He shook his head. "No. Sorry, babe." He picked up his phone. "Want me to?"

"No, don't. It will probably scare the hell out of him. Maybe the bruising will fade before I see him."

"Or maybe he'll think Warren's a wife beater," Nathan said with a grin.

Warren sat back and crossed his arms over his chest, smiling. "Man, I'm going to be glad when you're gone."

"That reminds me," I said, putting my fork down. "I want to have a going away party. We need to celebrate."

Nathan laughed. "I've been with the department for six months. That's nothing to celebrate."

"Well, we should celebrate the new job," I said. "It's a big deal, and I think we all need something to be happy about."

"I think it's a great idea," Adrianne said. "We should have it here."

"Here?" I asked.

I recognized the eyes-glossed-over gaze that she had as her eyes swept around my house. I'd seen it many times since she started planning my wedding. "Oh yeah. I could do a lot with this space. You handle the food and drinks. I'll take care of the rest."

Nathan shook his head. "Sloan doesn't need to handle the food."

I laughed. "Warren can do it. I'll order the cake."

"Thank god. We don't need a Thanksgiving do-over," Nathan said.

"Amen to that," Adrianne agreed. "Nathan, are you excited about the job?"

Nathan's face was inscrutable. "I am. It's going to be really different from what I'm used to."

"What exactly *is* the job?" I asked.

Azrael drained what was left of his beer. "I want to become more hands-off with the business, so I need someone I can trust to take over."

My brow lifted. "You want Nathan to take over Claymore?"

"Eventually." Azrael draped his arm around the back of Adrianne's chair. "Warren and I will have a lot of work to do once the baby is born to—"

I interrupted him and tapped my chest. "You mean Warren and I will have a lot to do. We're the parents."

Azrael's lips parted, but no sound came out.

"Azrael, I'm not going to just hand this kid over to you once it pops out," I said with an incredulous laugh. "If that's what you think, then you need to do a reality check really quick."

He sighed. "Of course not. I only mean that our number one focus is going to be keeping you all safe."

I relaxed, but only slightly.

Azrael got up and carried his beer bottle to the kitchen. He returned with a fresh one from the refrigerator. "Claymore is a worldwide, billion-dollar company."

"Billion?" Adrianne asked, turning fully sideways in her chair as he sat.

He nodded. "Yes. There's no way I can keep it going and prepare for what is to come. I need help, and Detective McNamara is the logical choice to train as my successor."

I held up my hand. "No offense, Nathan, but there's nothing logical about it. He's a really excellent cop, but I don't see how that translates into running a billion-dollar mercenary firm."

Warren groaned.

Azrael held up a finger. "First of all, you *have* to stop using the word mercenary. It does nothing for the company image. Second, I can train a soldier, but I can't teach anyone what Nathan has learned this past year. He fits in well in my world without being part of it."

The sound of ripping Velcro caught my attention. I looked over to see Nathan remove the American flag on his hat and replace it with his "Regular Guy" patch. Warren chuckled.

Nathan winked at me. "Besides, it has one hell of a benefits package."

I looked back at Azrael. "You're going to get him killed."

Az pointed at me. "No, that's your department."

"Oh, burn!" Nathan yelled, biting his fist.

Warren shoved back from the table laughing.

Adrianne hid her face behind her hands.

Even Reuel laughed from the couch.

"You all suck," I said, pushing my plate away.

Nathan nudged my leg with the toe of his boot. "It's all good, buttercup. You did make me a little bit invincible."

I groaned.

Warren knocked his knuckles against the table and looked at Nathan. "Az wants me to go to Claymore to train you."

Nathan laughed loudly. "Right."

"Why is that so funny?" Azrael asked. "Warren's one of the most qualified soldiers we've ever had."

Nathan made a sour face. "Because it's him. You know we can only handle each other in small doses, right?"

"He has a point," Adrianne said.

Warren tilted his head toward me. "Besides, Sloan and I already agreed not to go."

I smiled. "I guess you'll have to find somebody else."

Azrael looked at Warren. "Maybe I'll bring in Fury."

Warren's head whipped toward him, then he smirked. "Good luck with that."

Nathan got up and pulled his keys from his pocket. "While you guys decide my future, I'm going to go home and get some sleep." He looked at me. "When is my party?"

I thought for a second. "Your last day. Friday the 14th. Seven o'clock sound good?"

He nodded. "Seven is great."

"Can you invite your family?" I asked him. "I'd really love to see them again."

"Sure. I'll see if they can make it," he said.

Adrianne raised her hand. "Wait. Friday the 14th is Valentine's Day."

"Yep," I said.

Her bottom lip poked out. "What if some of us already have plans?"

My head tilted in question. "Do you have plans?"

She looked at Azrael, who wasn't saying anything. "Well, not yet..."

"Then don't make any." I laughed and waggled my brows teasingly at her. "Look who's killing two birds with one stone now."

She stuck her tongue out at me.

I reached for Nathan. "Help me. I'll walk you out."

"You don't have to do that," he argued.

"I want to. Help me up."

He took my hand and bent to hook his other arm behind my back. God, he smelled good. "Warren, come with us," I said.

Warren stood and Nathan passed me off to him. Arm in arm, we followed Nathan to the front door.

"Goodnight, everybody," Nathan called over his shoulder. "Reuel, take it easy."

Reuel grunted.

"Bye, Nate!" Adrianne replied.

"See ya, man," Azrael said.

Nathan waved and opened the front door. Cold wind rushed inside and took my breath away.

"Holy smokes," I said, gasping.

Warren grabbed my coat and draped it around my shoulders before helping me out to the porch.

"Go back inside," Nathan said. "It's freezing out here."

"No. I want to ask you something. Shut the door."

He closed the door behind us. "What's up?"

I lowered my voice to a whisper. "Did you find out anything about Warren's mom?"

He shook his head. "Nothing. I don't think her last name was Claymore."

My nose scrunched up. "Yeah, I figured we weren't that lucky."

"Why don't you ask Az?"

Warren grimaced. "It's a sensitive subject."

I sighed. "I made the mistake of bringing it up again in Chicago."

"Well, I'll see if I can dig anything up when I get out to New Hope."

I pulled my coat tighter around my shoulders. "I know this really isn't any of my business, but are you sure you want to take this job? It doesn't sound like you."

Nathan looked out at the night sky. The moon was almost full, a pale yellow against a clear black canvas. After a second, he nodded. "I'm sure. It's going to be a good thing for me." He turned his gray eyes back to me. "It's going to be a good thing for all of us."

Warren offered him his hand. "I think you're right, brother."

Nathan shook it. "Thank you." He released Warren's hand and gently touched my elbow. "Keep ice on your face and get some rest. I'll check on you soon."

"Thanks again for bringing dinner," I said as he headed down the stairs.

He looked back at us and winked. "It's the least I could do for not being in Chicago to save your asses."

Warren laughed. "Goodnight, Nate."

Suddenly, Nathan stopped at his door and turned back around. "I almost forgot." He reached into his pocket, then tossed whatever he retrieved up to me on the porch.

I looked in my hands and saw a Milky Way.

"Have a good night, guys," he said. He got into his SUV and drove away.

CHAPTER EIGHT

$\mathcal{I}$T TOOK FOUR more days, but the swelling and pain in my aching body finally dissipated. The bruises, however, were promising to linger for a while. I decided to face my father at dinner on Monday night. Warren and I took him to his favorite place to eat, The Red Stag Grill, and I prayed the ambient lighting would be dim enough to minimize the gawking at my battered face.

I felt bad for Warren. "Maybe you should wear a sign," I suggested as he stood in his underwear beside me at the bathroom sink, brushing his teeth while I applied another layer of concealer. "I could make you a t-shirt with puff paint that says, 'I did not do this' and have an arrow pointing at me."

He spat out his toothpaste and laughed. "I appreciate the thought, but I can handle a few hateful glares better than I can handle puff paint. Your dad's going to be pissed."

I shook my head. "No, he's going to be terrified and that's far worse."

"You're right." He walked to the closet. "What should I wear?"

I smiled at his bare back in the mirror. "Absolutely nothing. You're perfect just like that."

"That would take the focus off your face," he said, flipping on the closet light. "What are you wearing?"

"A dress," I answered. "This place is fancy-schmancy, like Bram Stoker could have put it in his castle if Dracula served seasoned elk to the villagers of Transylvania."

"Elk?"

I swiped on a layer of mascara. "Yeah. All their plates are very manly. I think they infuse the meat with extra testosterone."

He laughed. "You should write their marketing copy."

"I know, right?"

"Do I need to wear a tie?"

"Do you own a tie?"

"No."

I smiled. "A button up shirt and jeans will be fine."

He pulled a pair of dark jeans off the shelf and grabbed a black shirt that was on a hanger. "Which dress do you want?"

I stood up and untied my robe. "Hand me the one that looks like a garbage bag. That sack will fit anybody."

"Adrianne would be so proud of you." He turned around as I shrugged out of my robe. Unable to look anywhere else, his eyes fell to my discolored stomach. "Did you call the doctor?"

I sighed. "Yeah. I have an appointment next week before Nathan's party. I'm hoping the splotches will be completely gone by then."

He hung his shirt on the bathroom doorknob and put his jeans on the counter before removing the dress from its hanger and lifting it over my head. Being careful to not dishevel my updo, he eased it down past my face and over my shoulders. "You're going to need a sweater," he said as I straightened the sleeveless top.

"I know."

"What if the bruises aren't gone when she sees you?" He stepped into his jeans and tugged them up over his black boxer briefs.

"Then she's going to ask a lot of questions," I said as I smoothed the front of my dress.

"That doesn't have to be a bad thing."

I walked to the closet to look for a pair of shoes. "And how do you propose I answer those questions?"

"Truthfully?"

I grabbed a pair of black ballet flats. "I can only imagine the look on her face when I tell her my baby is a super angel."

When I came back out of the closet, he was hiding his perfect abs behind the buttons of his shirt. "If she's going to deliver this baby, she needs to know it's not going to be a typical day in the OB ward."

"I'll think about it," I said as I slipped on my shoes. "Have you heard from Az today?"

He shook his head and walked into the bedroom. "No. He didn't call me back last night either."

"I wonder what's taking him so long."

Warren sat on the edge of the bed and bent to put on his boots. "I'm not sure, but I won't argue with another day of him out of our house. It's been so peaceful around here."

I laughed and fastened a silver chain around my neck. "I know."

The Red Stag Grill was busy for a Monday night in Asheville, but Dad had secured a table with high-back, cushioned chairs by the fireplace. Warren's eyes were everywhere except where he was walking as he followed me to the table, stepping on the backs of my heels twice.

"Sorry," he said the second time. "I'm looking out for elk hunting vampires."

I laughed. "Well, look out for feet before you make me fall and blacken my other eye."

"Ouch."

Speaking of black eyes, my father saw mine as we approached. He rose from the table and stepped around it in our direction, then grasped both of my shoulders. "Sloan Jordan, what on Earth happened to you?"

I patted one of his hands. "I'm all right, Daddy. I didn't want to worry you."

"H-how? I mean, what?" He looked at Warren. "What the hell happened?"

For the second time in our relationship, Warren held his hands up in surrender to my dad. "I didn't do it this time either."

I motioned toward the square, candlelit table. "Can we sit?"

Dad didn't move for a second as if he was having trouble remembering how to move his feet. He rubbed his hands down his face. "Why do you always show up with bruises?"

I put my hand on his arm and gently pushed him toward the table. "Dad, sit."

He sank into his chair, then Warren pulled one out for me. I kissed him quickly as I sat.

Dad leaned on his elbow, then braced his forehead with his white-knuckled fingers. "Please explain."

I reached over and touched his arm. "There was an accident while we were in Chicago. We were in the subway and a train derailed—"

"A train!" My father's voice caused the patrons at the surrounding tables to turn and look.

I leveled my gaze with his. "Dad, no screaming."

He took off his glasses and placed them on his napkin, then he pinched the bridge of his nose and pressed his eyes closed.

"Reuel pushed me out of the way of the train and I hit the concrete pretty hard, but they took me to the hospital and I'm fine. My uterus ruptured—"

He gasped.

I gripped his sleeve. "But you know me, I heal really fast. The baby and I are both fine. I'm not even sore now."

Dad sat back in his chair and looked up at the ceiling. "You're going to put me in an early grave."

I squeezed his hand. "Then I'll have to bring you back."

He smirked. "Not funny." He looked around. "Where is Reuel? I assumed he'd be here."

"He was pretty mangled by the train incident. He's laying low while his arm heals," I said.

"Did you see it today?" Warren asked.

I nodded. "I put my voodoo on it over breakfast. The muscle tissue has closed all the way around the bones now."

Dad's hand stopped midway to the bread basket. "Do I want to know?"

I shook my head. "Nope."

The waiter came to take our drink order, but as soon as he saw my face, he froze. I smiled. "Can I get a glass of water, please? No lemon." I winked my eye that was still bloody. "I'm fine, by the way."

"I, uh..."

"It's OK. Just bring my water," I said.

"I'll have a sweet tea," Warren added.

The waiter scurried away without so much as a nod. I smiled at Warren. "This is fun. We should have left the house days ago."

He laughed softly, shaking his head as he looked over the menu.

"Sloan, a uterine tear is very serious. It can cause a lot of complications during your delivery," Dad said.

"Dad, my life is one big complication right now, but don't worry. The doctor in Chicago already advised me to discuss this with Dr. Watts."

"Are you going to?"

"Warren and I were talking about it earlier. I have an appointment soon. If I don't cancel it, she's going to see the bruises on my stomach. What do you think I should do?"

He slipped his glasses back onto his face. New lines I'd never noticed before creased the corners of his eyes. "I think the more your doctor knows, the better."

"Dad, she's going to think I'm nuts."

He chuckled softly. "Sweetheart, you are nuts."

I laughed, grateful that he was lightening up.

"You should tell her," he said. "She's bound by patient confidentiality, and she's a good person. She won't tell anyone."

"What if she doesn't believe me?" I asked.

He smiled. "Then heal half her caseload like you did at my office to prove it to her." He looked at Warren. "She almost put me out of business while you were gone, son."

"And since when is making people better a bad thing?" I asked.

Dad picked up his menu. "When I have to come live with you because I can't pay my mortgage, you'll know."

"Well, I don't think I can heal people from having babies, so we'll cross our fingers and hope she doesn't have me committed."

"Have you talked about what kind of delivery you'll have? I'm hoping it's a traditional hospital delivery in case you need a cesarean or emergency surgery," Dad said.

"I really don't know." I cringed and looked at Warren. "A hospital delivery sounds nuts to me. We don't want demons descending on Mission Hospital."

"You're right," he agreed. "We'll need to think about that one."

"All the more reason to talk to Dr. Watts," Dad said.

I groaned. "I know."

The waiter returned with our glasses, then hurriedly took our order. I ordered the short ribs and grits, hold the horseradish. Dad chose the lamb. And Warren ordered the elk because how could he not? He even asked for extra testosterone.

"I love you," I said with a laugh as the waiter left our table, hopelessly confused.

Warren leaned over and kissed my lips.

Dad looked pleased when Warren sat back in his seat. "How are the wedding plans coming along?"

I nodded. "They're good. We reserved chairs and tables this week, and we booked the caterer and cake lady."

"And by 'we' she means Adrianne," Warren added.

"That is true, but she did use my credit card."

"How is she? I haven't seen her in a while," Dad said.

I sipped my water. "She's doing well. Still pining over Azrael, I'm afraid."

"You don't want her to be with Azrael?" Dad asked.

"No. It's creepy."

He smiled. "What about Nathan?"

"I don't want her to be with Nathan either," I said without thinking it through.

Warren's head pulled back in surprise. "Oh, really?"

"She's not interested in Nathan," I said.

He folded his arms on top of the table. "But it's good to know you're pretty interested in the prospect of his relationships."

"That's not what I said."

"I meant, how is Nathan doing?" Dad asked, attempting to defer an argument.

Warren looked at me.

I shrugged and picked up a piece of bread. "I'm not sure. I haven't talked to him in a few days. Dad, did you know he's leaving the sheriff's office to go and work for Claymore?"

"I had no idea."

"Yep. We're having a going away party for him on Valentine's Day. You should come. It's at seven at my house. You can finally meet Nathan's parents."

"They are coming?" Warren asked.

I nodded. "I think his sister and her family are coming too."

"That sounds like fun. I should be able to make it," Dad said.

The rest of dinner was filled with pleasant conversation, mostly between me and my father. Warren didn't say much through the meal, nor on our ride home after. We pulled into the driveway at home, and I grabbed his sleeve when he moved to get out of the car.

"Hang on."

He turned with an expression that said, *"What do you want?"*

"Are you mad at me?"

"I'm not *mad* at you."

"Then what's going on here?"

He turned his palm up on the steering wheel. "I don't like how you got all defensive about the idea of Adrianne dating Nathan. It bothers me that you're still holding on to feelings for him."

"That's not fair," I said. "I'm not holding on to anything."

"You were pretty quick to voice an opinion back there."

"It was only a reaction. It didn't mean anything."

His brow wrinkled with scornful doubt.

I put my hands in my lap. "OK. It *would* bother me if they got together. Would you believe me if I lied and said I'd be happy about it?"

He sighed and shook his head.

"It certainly doesn't mean I'm holding on to my feelings for him." I put my hand on his arm. "It's just going to take me a little while to completely not feel them anymore. I know I don't deserve it, but can you please be patient with me?"

He took a deep breath and squeezed my hand. "Of course. I'm sorry." He leaned over and kissed me. "Let's forget about it."

"Or..." I bit my lip. "I don't know if we should." I leaned toward him and lowered my voice. "Because you know, our makeup sex is really, *really* hot."

The lines across his forehead relaxed as his frown slowly bent into a smile. "I could stay mad for a bit longer, I guess." He slid his hand up my jaw and pulled my lips to meet his.

"Want to get a little crazy?" I asked, moving my mouth against his.

A low growl came from deep inside him. "What'd you have in mind?"

I stretched across his lap, but couldn't reach the buttons on the side of his seat, so I disconnected the kiss and my seatbelt so I could stretch a few more inches until I found the knob to move his seat back. Slowly, with my head pressed against his shoulder, the seat moved back away from the steering wheel.

"Are you doing what I think you're doing?" he asked, his chest rising and falling quickly as anticipation sent his breathing into overdrive.

I flashed him a sultry smile. To spare the leather of his Dodge Challenger, I kicked off my shoes before getting on my knees to crawl across the center console. It was more difficult than it had played out in my head. I got my left knee up on the armrest without too much trouble, then tried to stretch my right leg across his lap. With nowhere to put my foot, I jammed it in the painfully small space between the seat buckle and the door. Then I pushed with my left knee a little too hard and toppled forward, smacking my forehead against the driver side window.

"Are you OK?" he asked.

"I'm fine, I'm fine."

I pushed again, this time putting all my weight on my pinned right ankle. I straddled his lap, but when I tried to settle my right foot between the armrest and the seat, I slipped backward right on the horn.

HEAARRRRRRRRRRRRRRRN!

Startled, I thumped my forehead against Warren's.

He threw his head back and laughed. "Oh my god! This is the funniest shit I've ever seen!"

I plopped onto his lap. "It's sexy," I whined.

He had tears in his eyes and he was starting to hyperventilate. "It's the least sexy thing *ever*, but oh man. So damn funny." His whole body convulsed with laughter.

I scrunched up my face and poked out my bottom lip.

He jerked his thumb toward the house. "Can I please take you inside and try this again in our bed?"

I huffed. "I guess."

When he opened the car door, my foot slipped out, and I was officially doing a split across his lap. He cackled again.

"Warren, I can't move."

He couldn't either because he couldn't catch his breath.

In order for me to get up, he had to lay his seat all the way back. Then I could move my left leg across his face and slide out of the car onto the gravel. "Just shut up," I said, straightening my twisted skirt.

"This was officially the best night of my life." He was still panting as he got out of the car.

"I'm going to write a letter to Dodge," I grumbled.

He clicked the lock button on his key chain, then took my hand and led me up the sidewalk. "You make my life so interesting, Sloan."

"What is this?" I asked, pointing to a silver sedan parked at the curb.

"No idea."

All the lights in my downstairs were on, and when we reached the front door, we found it unlocked. Warren went in ahead of me.

The man with the red toboggan was sitting on my sofa.

CHAPTER NINE

*O*UT OF HABIT, Warren reached for the gun he no longer kept tucked in his waistband, then used his arm to keep me corralled behind his back. But I wasn't moving. The last time I'd gotten close to that strange man, a train had been thrown at me. Who knows what might happen indoors. I kinda liked my house and didn't need it collapsing on top of me.

"Who are you?" Warren barked.

"Hey, you're home!" It was Azrael in the kitchen.

Warren looked around, confused. "What the hell?"

The man on the couch still hadn't moved or even glanced in our direction. He was staring at the fireplace. I wasn't even sure that he was breathing.

Azrael was wiping his hands with a dishtowel when he came into the living room. "Hi, guys!" He was downright chipper, and it freaked me out.

Warren pointed toward the man. "What's going on? What's he doing here?"

"I found him," Azrael said.

I stepped around to Warren's side. "And? Is this a lock-in at the

Jordan residence? Am I running a halfway house for fallen angels now?"

Azrael shook his head. "He's not an angel. Well, not all of him, anyway."

I put my hands on my hips. "Explain, please."

"He's human."

"Then why can't I see a human spirit?" I asked.

"Go look at him. Really look at him," he said.

I stepped behind Warren again. "I don't wanna."

Sighing heavily, Azrael grabbed my arm and dragged me into the living room. "He won't bite."

"No, he'll just chuck a train at my face."

"I don't think that was his doing." Azrael rounded the couch and walked in front of the man.

He was a lot younger than I'd originally thought. Maybe in his early forties, judging from the salt and pepper scruff on his jaw. It appeared to be there from neglect, not because it was trendy. His clothes weren't a fashion choice either. He wore a Chicago Cubs pullover with worn elbows, and acid washed jeans that were a couple of sizes too big and still sporting the color-coded tags of a secondhand store.

But his brown eyes were what captivated my attention. They were hollow and empty, except deep in the pupils where I caught tiny shimmers of life, like rays of a golden sunset trapped on a speck of glitter.

Suddenly, his eyes focused on mine.

My spine tingled, and I took a step back.

"*Eh ta kahl morteira,*" he said.

Azrael looked at me. "He says he thought you were dead."

"I thought he was too." My hands were trembling slightly. "He's a human that speaks your language. Does that mean..." I gulped.

"He was taken."

I fanned my face, suddenly feeling very warm.

"Right now you're talking to Lamal, an Angel of Prophecy. I haven't yet figured out who the gentleman is."

"Is his head going to start spinning around?" I asked.

Azrael reached out and jostled the man's head gently. "It feels pretty sturdy to me."

The man glared at Azrael and spoke to him again in Katavukai. It gave me chills.

Azrael ignored him.

"Why did you bring him here?" Warren asked, walking over to us.

"For Sloan."

My head bobbed a little frantically. "Thanks, but next time a t-shirt is a good option for a souvenir."

Azrael rubbed his palms together with excitement. "He's your next lesson."

I shook my head. "I don't like where this is going."

Azrael smiled like he'd awarded me a prize. "You're going to learn to separate the angel from the human!"

"Exorcism?" Warren crossed his arms. "Are you serious?"

"Yes!"

"No." I was adamantly shaking my head.

Azrael began to pace the living room. "Sloan, this is what you want. You want to help people." He pointed to the man on the couch. "This man needs your help."

"Then you should help him," I said, turning and stomping off toward the kitchen.

Warren followed me, and Azrael walked in behind him. "Sloan, this isn't a request. You need to learn how to do this," Azrael said.

I spun around on my heel, throwing my arms up into the air. "Why? Why do I need to learn to do this?"

Azrael put his hands on my shoulders. "For the sake of argument, let's assume this angel did try to kill you in the train station. Now, you have the power to destroy the angel. How would you feel knowing you destroyed an innocent man as well?" His eyes were pleading. "There's a person locked away inside that body. Would you really sentence him to die simply because you're afraid to learn how to save him?"

I hated it when Azrael was right. I looked over his shoulder at the man sitting on my sofa, and I couldn't help but wonder if he had a family back in Chicago somewhere. What had his life been like before it was taken from him? Could he have a life again if I could set him free?

Azrael knew he was winning, and he took a step closer. "What if you'd been there the night Phenex took Marisol's daughter Maria? Would you have saved her if you knew you could?"

I shoved him in the shoulders. "I really hate you sometimes."

Warren's face was screwed up with doubt. "Why is he being so compliant if he knows you brought him here to destroy him?"

With that, the man jumped from the couch and stormed toward the kitchen. I ducked behind Warren as the man shouted in Katavukai. "*Keshta kor te lateva. Ninkai velita ventum—*"

Azrael waved him off. "Calm down. She's not going to destroy you."

The man's glare shot to me.

I held up my hands in defense. "I'm not doing anything."

Azrael pulled out a chair at the dinette table in the kitchen and slid it toward me. "Can we sit and discuss this?"

I sighed and sat in the chair. Warren sat next to me, and Lamal retreated to the living room. Azrael carried a sandwich he'd been preparing on the counter over to the table with us.

"In 2008, Lamal did something very stupid," Azrael began. "And recently, it put him on the shit list of some very dangerous angels."

"What did he do?" Warren asked.

Azrael shook his head and took a bite of his sandwich. "That's not relevant here," he said around a mouthful before swallowing. "What is important is that for the past several months, Lamal has been in hiding. He sought you out in Chicago because he knows that without your help, he's worse off than dead."

I dropped my elbows on the table and cradled my skull in my hands. "I don't understand. What do I have to do with anything?"

"When an angel takes a human as a host, they can go dormant and hide behind the host's spirit. They disappear off the radar of angels and are almost completely undetectable by us," he said.

"I don't understand," I admitted.

Azrael looked at Warren. "Where's Reuel right now?"

Warren pointed toward the ceiling. "Upstairs in the guest room."

Azrael moved his finger between himself and Warren. "You and I know Reuel is upstairs because we can feel him there. He's not of this world, so his presence in it makes waves that our senses can detect."

Warren gave a slight nod.

Azrael looked at me. "The same goes for Lamal. Right now, we can *feel* him sitting in the other room."

"Hey, don't leave me out of this. I can feel him sitting in the other room too, you know," I said.

Azrael's head pulled back. "You can?"

I nodded. "Now I can. I couldn't when we first got here."

He slowly clapped his hands. "I'm so proud of you, Sloan. That's really amazing."

I felt like a circus monkey who'd just figured out its first set of tambourines. "Yay me," I said with a smirk.

"That's really good though. It means you're getting stronger. Remember, your power will grow as the baby does," he said.

"So you're really not proud of me at all," I said. "You're proud of your granddaughter."

He smiled like he suddenly realized I was right. "Exactly."

"Ugh."

Warren snapped his fingers. "Let's stay focused, please. Are you saying we couldn't *feel* Lamal here when we came into the house because he was dormant?"

Azrael smiled; he really was proud of Warren. "That's correct. Imagine a really long game of 1, 2, 3 Quiet and Still." He pointed his turkey on wheat toward the sofa. "That's what Lamal has been doing for many months now. Staying very small and very still, hiding in the darkness of that dude's body."

"If he doesn't want to be there anymore, why doesn't he leave?" I asked.

"Yeah," Warren said. "Why does he need Sloan?"

Azrael shook his head. "For starters, he can't leave on his own until the host dies. Not without the help of the Vitamorte."

"Why can't you help him?" I asked.

Azrael grinned and aimed his voice toward the living room. "Well, mostly because I don't want to."

The angel in the other room muttered something that carried a smart-ass tone.

Azrael didn't respond. "And I would have to kill the host to free him. The host needs you."

"Where did he get the host?" I asked.

"I have no idea. He was probably a bum with a drug problem, living on the streets somewhere in Chicago. They make easy targets."

I huffed. "You're so insensitive."

He nodded. "Yes, I'm aware. But the guy being a bum doesn't mean he deserves to live subject to the whims of a babbling, self-serving angel with elaborate daydreams."

"You just said Lamal has been quiet and still," I reminded him.

"He has been. Most of the time. A few days ago, however, he decided to take his host to Jackson Station and wound up in the flight path of a train."

"You think Lamal caused the wreck?" I asked.

Azrael shook his head. "I think the train was intended for him. Not you."

I shoved him in the shoulder. "So it wasn't my fault?"

"I don't think so. Once I found out who the man in the red toboggan was harboring, I changed my mind."

"I think you owe me an apology," I said.

"Think all you want; it obviously doesn't do you much good."

I *thought* about kicking him under the table.

Warren sat back and folded his arms across his chest. The slant of his eyes told me that he knew, like I did, that information was being withheld from us. "Why don't you want to help Lamal?"

"Let's say he was a very powerful catalyst in our entire situation. We might not be in our current predicament if he were better at keeping his mouth shut," Azrael said.

Lamal began to speak again, but Azrael continued talking over him. "But he claims he wants to make amends and help us, so the first thing he can do to help is to be a learning aid. Then when he's been freed, I'll think about protecting him."

"Is he a demon?" I asked.

Azrael chewed another bite of his sandwich, looking up at my ceiling as he pondered the question. That was never a good sign. "You use the word 'demon' like we make a choice and suddenly become a completely different entity. That we morph into something wicked with a tail and scales that are somehow hidden from mortal eyes like yours."

He was mocking me. Again.

"Do you trust him?" Warren asked.

Azrael laughed. "Hell no." He put the crust of his sandwich back on the paper towel and wadded it all up into a ball. "But just because I don't trust him doesn't mean I'm not willing to use him for my greater purpose."

I cocked an eyebrow. "Which is?"

He tossed the paper towel across the kitchen toward the garbage can with perfect free throw follow-through. It was a slam dunk. Then he turned back to answer my question.

"To save the world, my dear. Of course." He settled back in his chair and folded his hands behind his head. "That begins with teaching you how to destroy an angel without getting anyone killed."

Lamal jumped up again, babbling like he had before when the word 'destroy' came up in the conversation. Azrael stood and walked into the other room, this time to physically subdue him back to his couch cushion.

It was hard to argue with the logic of me learning anything that would keep people safe, but the thought of getting Lamal out of that man conjured up images of levitating little girls and projectile pea soup. I ran my hands down my face, pulling my mouth into an exaggerated frown. "This is too much," I said to Warren.

He reached over and squeezed my arm. "I'm not going to force you to do anything that makes you uncomfortable."

"You might not, but he will," I said, pointing to Azrael.

"Maybe you're making this worse in your mind than it actually is. It's probably easier than you think." He leaned toward me. "And it's definitely not going to be like Hollywood."

"How do you know?" I asked. "Because the last six months of my life would make one hell of a blockbuster."

He slid his hand up to my neck and pulled me close till our foreheads touched. "You can do this, Sloan. I know you can."

"I'm glad you have so much faith in me. I'm not sure anyone else does, me included." Suddenly, I straightened and cut my eyes at him. "Wait a second. Did Azrael command you to convince me to do this?"

Warren's eyes widened just enough.

I gasped and pointed at him. "No! No. No." I got up, pushing my chair backward so that it slid across the tiles with a long squeak. "You can't do that to me!"

He stood and reached for me. "Sloan, come on. Don't get upset—"

I marched into the living room and around to where Azrael

was talking to Lamal. I shoved him back a step, and he sat when his legs hit the couch. "You're not allowed to manipulate mine and Warren's relationship. You stay out of it!"

Spinning on my heel, I stormed off toward the stairs. Azrael moved to come after me and the couch farted.

Phwaaaaawert...

I was so mad I couldn't even laugh.

I'd washed my face, brushed my teeth, and changed into my pajamas by the time Warren finally came upstairs. I was crawling under the covers when he walked in and eased the door closed behind him. "Can we talk?"

"You can talk," I said, pulling the blanket up to my chin and then tucking it in under my thighs to make it clear that our unfinished business from the car would not be revisited. "I may or may not listen."

He came over and sat beside me. "You have that choice. I don't anymore. Not with him."

I slammed my fists against the mattress. "Sometimes I really, really hate him, Warren."

"I can tell." He stretched one arm across my lap and leaned toward me. "Please don't start hating me too."

My head flopped back against the headboard with a thud. "I'm not, but this isn't fair. He can't interfere with us."

He touched his chest. "You know I agree, right?"

I nodded. "I know, but it's going to cause really big problems for us if I can't trust you," I said. "And that's exactly what this is."

The angry muscle twitched.

I touched his face. "I don't want to ever question if you're telling me the truth or you're telling me what he's making you tell me."

He sighed. "I didn't think about it that way. I'm really sorry."

"We have to talk to him about this."

"We will." He pushed my hair behind my ear. "Tomorrow. We'll sit and talk to him tomorrow."

I put my arms around his neck and hugged him. If there were a contest for staying mad at Warren Parish, I'd be sent home without even a participation ribbon.

"Can I ask you an honest question?" I asked with my chin still resting on his shoulder.

He pulled back to look at me. "Of course."

"Leaving Azrael out of this for a second, do you believe I should help that man?" I dropped my hands to his forearms. "Because if you didn't immediately get defensive about Azrael forcing you to talk to me, then you must have agreed with him on some level."

He took a deep breath and let it out slowly. "Yes. I think you should help anyone that's in your power to help."

"But you know as well as I do that's not what this is about. That's Azrael's con line to get me to do it," I said.

He nodded. "Yes, but that doesn't make it untrue. That man doesn't deserve to have Lamal in control of him whenever he wants."

I sighed. "I know. It just freaks me out."

"Any more than healing Reuel's filleted arm or bringing Nate back from the dead?"

He had a point, and I immediately felt bad about it. Would I have been more willing to overcome my fear had the man been a friend? Or even a cute little stranger like Amalia?

"I'll do it, but don't tell Azrael tonight. I need one more good night's sleep without bad dreams."

Smiling, he stood and unbuttoned his shirt. "Who the hell says you're getting any sleep?"

I pushed up my sleeves and shook out my hands to loosen them up. Then I jogged in place for a second and bounced a couple of times up onto the balls of my feet.

Azrael bit his lower lip and crossed his arms. "Are you about done?"

I planted my feet, sucked in a deep breath, and rubbed my palms together. "Now I'm done. I'm ready. Let's do this."

Across my living room, Lamal was sweating nervously through his host. His eyes darted back and forth between me and Azrael. "*Nan itea ceyai vitaluyar.*"

I wasn't sure what he said, but his shaky tone did nothing for my confidence. On the couch that was pushed back against the back door out of the way, Reuel chuckled to himself.

"You've got this, babe," Warren said from his perch atop the back of the love seat. He caught my eye and winked.

Azrael grasped the front of my hoodie and pulled me forward across the living room until I was almost nose to nose with Lamal. "I want you to focus on the man. Lamal, what's your host's name?"

Lamal was still staring at me, terrified.

Azrael thumped him on the forehead. "Hello? What's your host's name?"

"Jesse."

It was startling to hear the angel say something I could understand.

"Sloan, can you see Jesse?" Azrael asked.

I looked for the glint of life in his eye again. For a fraction of a second, I thought I saw something, but it flickered out so quickly I couldn't be sure.

Azrael nudged the man's arm. "Help her out, Lamal."

A low squeak came from the man's throat. His eyes were even wider now.

"This was your choice, Lamal. Time to grow a pair," Azrael said, nudging him harder the second time.

The man's eyes closed. When they slowly reopened, I jolted upright. "Hi, Jesse."

Jesse looked around bewildered. "Where am I?"

The fear in Jesse's eyes was different from when I was looking at Lamal. It was coupled with confusion, which broke my heart. The poor guy had no idea where he was or who we all were. If Azrael knew me at all, he would've started his appeal like this the night before.

I put a hand on Jesse's shoulder. "Jesse, you're OK. My name is Sloan, and you're at my house. I'm going to help you get home."

His eyes landed on Azrael and he panicked. Clambering backward, he tripped into the mantle and knocked the framed photo of my parents off, shattering the glass all over the floor. Without thinking, I gripped him with my power before he stuck his leg into the crackling blaze in the fireplace and set himself on fire.

I gently pulled him toward me, back to safety.

"Jesse, I need you to listen to me," I said. "No one here is going to hurt you."

Azrael leaned in my direction and lowered his voice. "Nothing says that more than holding him immobile against his will."

I put my hands up. "I don't want you to hurt yourself. Can I let you go?"

He nodded slightly.

Slowly, I eased my grip around his body. Without a word, he took off running. He grabbed the front door handle, threw it back, and jumped off the porch before sprinting down the sidewalk out of view.

The room erupted in laughter.

Azrael turned toward me with both thumbs up. "Good job. That was impressive."

"She did get Lamal out of here," Warren pointed out.

Reuel slapped Warren on the chest using his good arm. "*Peyotum, utaiyar. Enai se, kor?*"

Azrael doubled over laughing. "*Bona.*" He looked at me. "Reuel says Exorcise, exercise…same thing, right?

I crossed my arms with a huff. "How do we get him back?"

Outside, heavy footfalls on the porch turned our heads. Jesse—or Lamal, rather—trudged back inside and slammed the door closed. "*Tivira?*" he asked.

I didn't need a translator to know that meant 'are you kidding me?' or something similar in Katavukai.

Azrael chuckled again. "It's her first time. Cut her some slack."

Warren walked to the kitchen and returned with a broom and dust pan. He cleaned up the glass while Azrael squared Lamal's shoulders again in front of me.

"Can you see Jesse now without us having to put him at the helm?" Azrael asked me, taking a step back by my side.

"Yes." It was much easier to find Jesse's spirit once I knew exactly what I was looking for.

He gripped my shoulder. "I want you to focus on sending life into Jesse. Send all your healing power into him, and only him."

"How will I know if I'm doing it correctly?" I asked.

"Lamal won't feel it," he said.

I nodded and closed my eyes. I placed my hands on the man's chest and focused on Jesse in my mind. On cue, my palm came alive with power and warmed against his torso.

"*Nan. Akai kiren.*"

I opened my eyes. Lamal was shaking his head.

With my gaze locked on his, I found Jesse in his eyes and sent my power again.

"*Nan,*" Lamal said after only a few seconds.

I took a deep breath and let it out slowly. I focused. I healed. Lamal said, "*Nan.*"

Actually, he threw my hand back at me and shouted, "*Nan! Akai toda kiren!*" He walked away from me, furiously shaking his head. "*Eshta. Nakal ceyren!*"

"No one promised you this was going to be easy," Azrael told him.

"*Naru entam nakal nurir ep tai kuri!*"

Azrael fired back at him in Katavukai so I tuned him out and looked at Warren. "Do you think we need to be here while they fight about this? I'm starving."

He stood. "Sounds good to me. Reuel?"

Reuel got up and patted his stomach with a smile. I walked over to him. "Before we go, let me see your hand."

Warren cringed. "You sure you want to do that right before we eat?"

I nodded and began unwrapping his bandages. "It will be fine."

Just then, a loud crack of thunder from an angel crossing the spirit line rattled the windows of my house.

"Oh my god." I was panting, trying to breathe.

Azrael moved to the window with the precision of a jungle cat. "Reuel, take the back. Warren, kitchen window. Now."

The only person left for me to hide behind was Jesse-Lamal, and I did.

We all watched and waited. The sudden silence was deafening. Until...

The song "Stayin' Alive" played through my house.

Azrael began fumbling for his cell phone.

"What the hell is that?" Warren asked from his post at the kitchen window.

The music continued.

Reuel was slumped over the back of the couch with his face buried in his good arm, laughing loudly.

Azrael finally found the phone in his back pocket and stopped the song by answering the call. "What?" he barked into the speaker.

I could only see Warren's back in the kitchen, but he was shaking with silent laughter. Had I not been scared out of my mind, I would have been laughing too. Or perhaps I was laughing on the inside and that was part of the reason I was trembling so much.

"We have movement here. Where are you?" Azrael asked whoever was on the phone. He paused. "OK. Wait for my signal."

"What do you see, Az?" Warren asked. "Oh, wait, I see him. Is that…?"

"The Destroyer."

CHAPTER TEN

*E*VEN FROM ACROSS the room, I felt Abaddon's solid fist pound against my front door. The door clattered against its hinges with each blow. "*Tiranta, Azrael!*" His booming voice made me jump despite the wall and the space between us.

Warren returned from the living room, and I ran into his arms.

"Abaddon, I know The Morning Star sent you, but this isn't even your fight. Stay out of it!"

"You stay out of my way. Open the door!"

Azrael pulled the door open, and Abaddon walked in without an invitation, bending and turning slightly to the side to inch past the six-and-a-half-foot door frame. My jaw plunged. The only time I'd seen him before was in the woods with the backdrop of fully-grown pines as his only comparable measure.

"Since when are you the hired help?" Azrael asked. "Is the pit not exciting enough for you anymore?"

Abaddon paid him no attention as his eyes swept the room before locking on mine. Warren's grasp tightened around me. I expected Abaddon to charge us and take me like I was Ann Darrow being plucked from the streets of New York by King Kong.

But he didn't.

Instead, he crossed the living room toward Lamal in three strides. "We've been looking for you." He grabbed a fistful of Lamal's jacket and backed him up against the wall. Then he lifted the man at least six inches off the floor before slamming him back so hard that he cracked the drywall.

Lamal began pleading with him in Katavukai.

Abaddon snarled to shut him up. "You were a fool to show your face, Lamal. Did you not think I would be watching? Waiting for you?"

"Abaddon!" Azrael bellowed.

"What?" The demon spun around.

The front door was wide open. Azrael motioned to it. "Put him down and get out. I'm not going to say it again."

Abaddon laughed, sounding a bit like Santa Claus. Only instead of "*Ho! Ho! Ho!*" it was "*Ha! Ha! Ha!*" He held up a hand. "Azrael, you know I love a good fight with you, but I have no time to humor you today."

"All right. Have it your way," Azrael said with an annoyed sigh. "No fight it is."

Azrael quickly twisted, throwing his hand forward in the direction of Abaddon's unsuspecting face. An invisible blow sent The Destroyer flying backward. He crashed through the living room wall, then took out the railing of the back porch before landing in a pile on the lawn. Through the gaping Abaddon-sized hole left in my living room, I could see an army in my backyard with assault rifles trained on the stunned fallen angel.

Abaddon pushed himself up and stood. He pointed at Az. "I'm going to break you," he threatened.

Azrael shook his head and walked through the hole out into the cold. We cautiously followed him. "Not today you won't."

Abaddon dismissed the group of at least fifteen soldiers with a wave of his huge hand. "You know they can't kill me."

Azrael shrugged. "True, but they can slow you down long enough so *she* can kill you." He pointed at me.

I gulped and gripped Warren's arm.

Abaddon did his Santa laugh again, but he didn't argue. He also didn't come after any of us. "This isn't finished, Azrael."

"I'd be disappointed if it was," Azrael said.

With a loud crack, Abaddon vanished, and the force shook the broken wall behind us so hard that a large damaged piece of the framing splintered and snapped in half. When it did, several boards came clanging down behind us. Warren moved me out of the way to spare my bare feet from impact.

"Well, if we ever wondered why they call him *The Destroyer*, now we know," Warren said, draping an arm around my shoulders.

I let out a heavy sigh.

Next door, my neighbor, Wilda Gillespie, was peeking through her blinds. When she caught my eye, the slats snapped shut.

"I'm going to hear from my HOA about this," I said, shaking my head.

"You're going to hear from the police about this," Warren corrected.

Azrael's men lowered their weapons, and he walked out into the yard to talk to them. They were all dressed for war in multi-cam fatigues and combat boots. I recognized Kane from the Calfkiller River battle. He was a member of SF-12, Azrael's personal combat team made up of angels and humans, including a few humans with the ability to see the supernatural. Kane was one of those.

"How'd they get here so fast?" I asked.

Warren turned my shoulders to the left and pointed. "Az bought that house with the tan siding. He didn't want to tell you because he was afraid you might freak out."

I whirled around toward him. "I don't freak out!" As soon as the words left my mouth at the volume they did, I closed my lips and nodded my head. "OK, I might have freaked out."

He smiled and kissed my forehead. "He's done a lot more than you know around here to keep you safe. Half of Claymore is stationed in different places around this city now, I think."

"Under what direction?" I asked. "I doubt the real reason is printed in the company newsletter."

He shook his head. "They don't have a company newsletter."

I rolled my eyes.

"You're labeled as a low profile, high value asset."

"I feel so special." I turned back to my broken house. "What are we going to do? How am I going to explain this to the insurance company?"

"We'll figure it out. Maybe it's time to start looking for that bigger place," he said.

My phone vibrated in my back pocket. I pulled it out and saw Nathan's picture on the screen. He was sticking his tongue out at the camera. "Hello?"

"Why is your address coming over my radio?"

My nose wrinkled. "It's bad that you don't even sound worried or surprised anymore."

"You're telling me. What happened? People are calling in an explosion."

"Azrael threw Abaddon, The Destroyer, through my living room wall."

"Everyone OK?"

I sighed. "Yeah. We're fine. Nobody was hurt this time."

"Well, that's an improvement at least. I'll be there soon," he said.

"Nathan, what do I tell the police?"

He laughed. "I have no idea."

I heard the sirens before I even got my phone tucked back in my pocket. Azrael's men cut through the neighbor's yard and returned to the tan house. The three of us went back inside to greet the police.

Lamal was sitting against the wall by the fireplace with his knees pulled up to his chin. I walked over to him. "Are you all right?"

He nodded but didn't meet my eyes.

The doorbell rang.

"Let me do the talking," Azrael said.

"Gladly."

Azrael opened the door. Two uniformed sheriff's deputies stood on my porch. I recognized both of them, but nothing in me wanted to go over and say hello. The only thing that would come out of my interaction with them would be for my bruised face to put Warren on some sort of domestic violence watch list.

Instead, I sat next to Lamal. "Why are they after you? What did you do that would make them send Abaddon after you?"

He looked over his shoulder at me. "*Nakai lleshta.*"

My shoulders slumped. "That's right. You can't tell me, can you?"

He shook his head. "*Et akai vishta, Praea.*" Then he grabbed my hand and the world swirled away.

Suddenly, I was no longer sitting in my living room. I was walking down a long, crowded corridor that stretched out in front of me. It was an airport terminal with hurried travelers dragging suitcases behind them. A man passed by me, gesturing wildly as he shouted into a cell phone. A janitor near the bathroom was shaking out a trash bag. A woman was holding a red-faced, screaming toddler.

I wondered where I was going.

My legs were moving, though I didn't seem to be controlling

them. I'd never seen the shoes on my feet before. I checked the paper ticket in my hand.

American Airlines Flight 209.

From: Charlotte. To: San Antonio.

Passenger Name: Abigail Smith.

Abigail Smith?

I blinked, and when I reopened my eyes the scene had changed.

The sun beat down on my business suit as I followed a sidewalk. A bead of sweat trickled down my spine, and I knew immediately I was in Texas. I turned a corner and saw a brick church with a tall, black steeple. I'd seen it before but couldn't remember when or where.

The chatter of young girls caught my attention to the left, and I followed the sound. In the grass was a tall sign with bright green letters. *Morning Star Ministries.*

I wanted to run away, but once again my legs were on auto-pilot.

Three teenage girls were being led into the ministry through the glass front entry doors. The blonde ushering them inside, I'd met her before. She smiled when she saw me and held the door until I approached. "Good morning, Ms. Smith."

Wait? Could I be...? No, it's not possible, I thought.

I blinked, and the scene changed again.

Larry Mendez, the most evil man I'd ever met, stormed into the room where I sat at a cherry wood desk. The nameplate on the door he threw open said *Abigail Smith.*

He pulled a teenage girl by the arm behind him. Her face was red and streaked with tears. He shoved her toward the floor by my chair. She crumpled onto the carpet and pulled her knees up to her chin so she could hide behind them.

Part of me desperately wanted to grab her and pull her into my arms. Another part, feelings that felt foreign and wrong, was absolutely indifferent to the child. I simply didn't care.

I reached toward a heavy ceramic planter that held a hearty fern. I wished I could hurl it at Larry's head. I didn't. I pulled a dead leaf off and dropped it in the wastebasket at my feet.

I blinked.

Marisol Juarez was sitting on a sofa cradling a young girl in her arms. The girl's face was swollen with a large cut across her cheek that had been closed with a butterfly bandage. My gratitude for Marisol's kindness was quickly met with a surge of unfamiliar rage. I watched helplessly as the hand that was attached to the body that carried me, reached out and backhanded the woman across the face.

I blinked again.

A young girl walked beside me up the staircase of the abandoned factory we had visited in downtown Chicago. It took me a second to realize the girl was Phenex. She was speaking quickly in Katavukai and gesturing wildly with her hands.

We walked into the lab where several people in scrubs and lab coats were working. Phenex pulled me toward one of the exam rooms, and when she opened the door, I saw a dead girl on the bed.

It was Natalia. And I felt happy...

"What do you think you're doing?" Azrael shouted over my head.

I rubbed my face. I was back in my demolished living room, sitting on the floor with Lamal. "What happened?"

"What did he show you?" Azrael demanded.

Remembering what I'd seen, I covered my mouth and gasped. I scurried away from Lamal. "You caused all this!"

He began a passionate rebuttal in Katavukai, but Azrael silenced him with a hand. "Save it, Lamal."

Warren steadied me by the shoulders. I'd started to cry

without realizing it. "Sloan, what's the matter?" he asked, carefully studying my face.

I looked at Azrael. "You said he's an Angel of Prophecy, right?"

Azrael nodded and cast his eyes at the floor.

"He showed the future to Kasyade. I saw it. I saw it all through her eyes," I said to Warren. "He set this whole plan in motion. The ministry in Texas. The sex slavery. The biological weapons…all of it. That's why they want to kill him now, isn't it? Because it all fell apart and he didn't warn them!"

Lamal took a step toward us, but Azrael used his power to pin the angel against the wall.

"And you!" I shouted, stepping around Warren toward Azrael. "You wanted me to save him! Are you serious? No wonder you tried to keep it from us!"

Azrael put up his hands. "I did try to keep it from you because I didn't want what he did to overshadow the truth that Jesse deserves to be free." He pointed at Lamal. "*Jesse* deserves your help. Not Lamal."

Lamal stalked to the kitchen and sat with his back to us at the kitchen table.

Warren pulled me close, and I felt my body trembling against his. "Take a minute and catch your breath." He stroked my hair. "Breathe."

But my minute was cut short by a knock at the open front door. We all looked over as Nathan walked in with wide eyes. "I hear someone's been disturbing the peace around here."

I had completely forgotten about the police force that had gathered outside. "What did you tell them?" I asked, looking up at Warren.

Nathan walked over with a grin. "A DIY home remodeling project, was it?"

Warren shrugged. "It could happen."

"What about the 'army men with guns' that your neighbor next door reported?" Nathan asked.

"We don't know what she's talking about. That old bird is crazy," Azrael replied.

Nathan folded his arms and nodded. "Yeah, the whole department thinks she's nuts. She calls and complains about all sorts of insane stuff around here: men coming and going at all hours, the police showing up all the time." He lowered his voice to a whisper. "She even called one time and said she saw a man disappear into thin air."

He was making fun of me.

"Do they believe her?" I asked.

He shook his head. "No, I'm serious. They all think she's a loon." He crossed the room and surveyed the hole in the wall. "Az, you really threw the big guy through this?"

"I did."

"I'm impressed." Nathan turned back to us. "What was he doing here? Did he come after Sloan?"

I shook my head and pointed at Lamal. "He came after Lamal."

Nathan followed my finger. "And who is he?"

"The guy from Chicago who we thought caused the train accident," Warren said. "He didn't."

Lamal looked back over his shoulder and his eyes doubled when they landed on Nathan. He jumped up from the table and ran toward him.

"Whoa!" Nathan shouted, stepping sideways to dodge him.

Lamal grabbed Nathan's arm, then reached wildly for me. Warren moved me away from him and deflected Lamal with his arm.

Azrael spoke to Reuel, then Reuel walked over and used his good hand to grasp Lamal by the back of his jacket. He carried him out through the hole in the back wall and tossed him off the porch. I couldn't help but smile.

Nathan held his hands up. "What the hell was that about?"

Warren sighed. "It's a long story."

"Is he dangerous?" Nathan asked.

"Not physically," Azrael answered.

Nathan scratched his head. "Well, there's been a train accident and now a house demolition involving him. I'd say he's bad luck either way. Not to mention he's freaking creepy."

"I agree," I said.

"Angel or human?" Nathan asked.

"Both," Warren and I said at the same time.

Nathan laughed and shook his head. "I don't even want to know." He walked toward the door. "If you guys need a place to crash while the wall is being fixed, you're welcome to stay with me."

"You don't even have a couch to sleep on," I reminded him.

He nodded. "True, but I'll be gone after Friday and won't need my bed for a while."

The thought of sleeping in Nathan's bed with Warren was weird, to say the least. "Thanks, but we can stay with my dad if we need to."

He walked to the door. "All right. If you need anything, let me know. We still on for Friday?"

"Yep. Seven o'clock," I replied.

"See you there."

We met with a contractor that afternoon about fixing the wall. He said it would take about a week to repair all the damage. In the meantime, he boarded it up with plywood so we didn't have to leave home. It was cold in the house, but I was thankful we could stay.

For the rest of the day, Azrael locked Lamal in the guest room. He didn't mention him to me again either, which I was thankful for. The charity and goodness of my heart were still overridden by the desire to see Lamal punished, and with that kind of attitude, I could be no help to Jesse.

The central heat in my house couldn't keep up with the rate at which the warmth from the vents was hemorrhaging out the back wall downstairs. I snuggled as close to Warren as possible under all the blankets I owned.

"You've been quiet today," he said softly in my ear.

I nodded. "I know. That vision with Lamal screwed me up a little."

He tightened his arm around me. "Do you want to talk about it?"

"I honestly don't even know where to begin."

"Well, what was it like?" he asked. "Was it like a dream? A hallucination?"

"Maybe. Sort of." I thought about it for a second. "Did you ever have a View-Master as a kid?"

"A what?"

"It was a toy. It looked like a red pair of binoculars, and it had a cardboard wheel with tiny pictures on it that you could insert in the top of it. When you pulled the handle on the side, it would change the picture," I explained.

"Yeah, I know what you're talking about. I never had one though," he said.

"It was kind of like that. It seemed that every time I blinked my eyes, the scene would change." I hesitated for a second. "Only, I wasn't simply watching. It was like I was trapped inside Kasyade's body. It was like I *was* her."

"But you're not her."

"I know, but I felt what she felt." I hugged my pillow. "Warren, I saw the girl who died in the lab, Natalia. I saw her lying there. Gray skin, hollow eyes. And I was glad."

He gently jostled my shoulders. "You weren't glad. Those weren't your feelings, Sloan."

"It felt like my feelings," I said. "It was like a nightmare that I couldn't control."

He rested his cheek against the back of my head. "That's exactly what it was. It wasn't real."

"Oh, but it was."

He sighed. "But your involvement in it wasn't real. You had nothing to do with it."

"I keep trying to tell myself that," I said. "I just want to go to sleep."

"I can help with that."

I frowned. "Warren, don't take this the wrong way, but I'm really not in the mood tonight."

He laughed. "That's not what I meant."

"Then what did you mean?" I asked.

"Close your eyes," he whispered.

I did, and I immediately fell asleep.

<hr />

Stark white walls. A cheap wooden desk made out of particle board. A large corkboard mounted in front of me with photos. Photos of dead girls. I recognized their faces. Ashley McNamara, Melissa Jennings, Angela Kearn, Leslie Bryson...

All of Billy Stewart's victims.

A hand reached toward the mouse for the computer on the desk. A man's hand. I clicked a notification on the desktop and an email window popped open.

Nate, this came through our office this morning. Might want to add it to your list. Rachel Smith, missing since 11–27. See attached. - Mike.

I clicked open the attached document, a standard missing person's report. There was a photo of Kasyade in the top left corner. Name: Rachel Smith. 24. Reported missing by co-workers at Child Protective Services in Greensboro, NC...

I blinked.

"Welcome to the department, Detective McNamara." Sheriff

Davis handed me a badge and shook my hand. His grip was stronger than I remembered.

Over his shoulder, a woman in the back row looked like she might pass out. *Whoa.* It was me. *Why is my face so pale?* Right, we were inside the jail at Nathan's swearing-in ceremony.

I blinked.

I pressed the doorbell. *My* doorbell at *my* front door. It opened. My heart was pounding inside my chest. Then I was standing there, looking at myself in the doorway, wearing Nathan's black S.W.A.T. team hoodie. I had a bag of my favorite food in one hand and a folder full of dead girls in the other. I realized I felt hopeful—terrified—as I walked through the door.

The scene skipped ahead and we were in the living room. I was looking at myself from the love seat, holding a picture of Ashley. I'd spewed grits all over Nathan's lap. I reached over and put my hand on his, and when I did, I realized that Nathan forgot to breathe.

I blinked and we were in his office. I was looking over my own shoulder at the desk. I showed me a photo of Kasyade, then leaned close to my head. The scent of my lavender shampoo was making Nathan dizzy.

I blinked.

We were on a path in the woods. Nathan was following me and Warren; we were holding hands. It was Butner Falls. The vision flashed forward and suddenly we were somewhere else. Warren was up ahead, and dangling off his finger was a jawbone. Ashley's jawbone. Nathan threw up a little in his mouth.

I blinked.

The room was dark, but I knew exactly where we were. Nathan's old bedroom at his parents' house in Durham. I also knew that the heavy weight I felt on Nathan's chest was my own head. His fingers were tangled in my hair. "Please, don't. Please, don't say it." It was like I was saying the words and hearing them again at the same time.

So much emotion was surging through Nathan that it was hard to tell where my thoughts ended and his began. "I can handle being shot at and having my body broken in half by a demon," he was saying, "but I can't stand hearing you tell me you love me."

I closed my eyes and began to cry.

When I opened my eyes again, I was staring at a campfire. Azrael was there with his feet propped up on a rock talking to Enzo. Across the Calfkiller clearing there was a trailer that I knew I was inside with Warren. Nathan sucked in a painfully deep breath in an attempt to quell the anxiety churning in his chest. He was turning something over in his fingers. He looked at it.

My silver angel pin sparkled up at him. I thought I'd lost it in our accident the night we almost drowned in the river.

I blinked.

The barrel of the rifle Agent Silvers was holding was pointed right at my face. *BOOM!* Warren dove in front of me.

"No!"

Warren was shaking me. "Sloan! Sloan, wake up!"

I bolted upright in the bed. Sweat poured down my face. In a sliver of moonlight through the room, I could see Lamal panting in the corner. Warren dove across the bed in his direction.

"Warren, stop!" I screamed.

Mid-lunge, Warren froze. I grabbed the back of his t-shirt and pulled him back.

Azrael threw the door open and turned on the light. It scalded my eyeballs. "You again!" He picked Lamal up off the ground with his power.

"Azrael, put him down!" I jumped off the bed and jumped between Azrael and Lamal. "I know why he did it!"

Azrael still held Lamal, but his eyes fell to me. "What are you talking about?"

I held my hands up. "I know why he showed the demons the vision." I glanced toward the ceiling where Lamal was suspended. "Please, put him down."

Azrael dropped his hand, and Lamal crashed to the ground.

I rushed over to help him. "Are you all right?"

He nodded and pushed himself up.

"I'm sorry we didn't give you a chance to explain," I said.

"*Gratalis.*" I didn't need to understand him to recognize the relief in his countenance.

"What happened, Sloan?" Warren asked, swinging his legs off the bed.

I stepped back and sank down on the edge of the bed next to Warren. "He showed them the vision to send Kasyade to Texas at the right time. He knew Nathan was looking for Billy Stewart's victims. When she left, it put her on his radar. He knew Nathan would find me and that we could stop all this." I looked at Lamal. "And now you're being hunted by The Destroyer to pay for it, correct?"

He bowed his head in affirmation.

I don't think I'd ever seen Azrael so shocked. He looked at Lamal. "*Verta?*"

"*Verta.*"

"Why didn't you say anything?" Azrael asked.

It was Lamal's turn to be shocked. His mouth dropped open with disbelief.

"Probably because you don't listen," I said.

Lamal gestured to me and nodded.

"You saw this for yourself?" Azrael asked. "This isn't just something he told you?"

"She was screaming in her sleep," Warren said. "She definitely saw something."

Azrael stared at the floor for a moment, then walked over to Lamal and offered his hand. "I'm sorry. I should have listened."

I wondered if Azrael's head might explode. I doubted that remorse was an emotion his brain was used to.

I looked at Lamal. "I'm going to help you, I promise."

He smiled for the first time since he got to my house.

"But not tonight." I pointed to my door. "Everyone out of my room. Humans need their sleep, remember?"

When they were gone, Warren settled back in the bed beside me. "Are you OK?"

I nodded. "I will be."

He snaked an arm around my waist. "I'm here if you want to talk."

I covered his arm with mine. "I know. Thank you."

But I didn't want to talk to Warren about what I'd seen, not most of it anyway. It wasn't fair to keep rehashing everything with Nathan, especially when we were so close to getting a clean break from him.

Unfortunately, I couldn't get my brain to shut off the replay. Every time I closed my eyes, all I saw was Nathan's fingers turning my angel pin over and over. I'd thought it was lost forever; and Nathan had it the whole time.

CHAPTER ELEVEN

*L*AMAL WAS BRACING for impact, with squinty eyes like a kid waiting to have his face hosed with spray-on sunscreen. "Remember," Azrael said. "Keep Jesse alive. It's a one-two punch."

"One-two punch?" I asked. "Who are you talking to? Don't use boxing analogies with me."

"Use beer analogies if you can," Adrianne teased from where she sat, sipping a mimosa on the couch between Reuel and Warren.

"You're not helping," I said.

She shook her head. "I'm not here to help. I'm here to taunt." She'd taken the day off to help me get ready for Nathan's party, or so she said. I knew she'd also taken the day off in hopes of spending Valentine's Day with Azrael.

"Well, knock it off. You're making me nervous. Do you want me to kill him?"

Azrael and Warren laughed. Reuel shoveled a handful of popcorn into his mouth. And Lamal was visibly shaking. I'd been trying to free him all week without any success at all, and everyone was starting to feel it was a joke. But no one's faith in me had dropped lower than mine, except maybe Lamal. He looked like he might cry each time I got close to him.

I put my hand on his shoulder. "Don't worry. Look at it this way: I haven't been able to free you yet, but I also haven't killed you either. And if anything, I *am* getting better, right?"

He didn't respond. Neither did anyone else.

"One-two punch," Azrael said again. "Send life in, but hit Jesse with enough killing force to knock Lamal out of him."

I dropped my hands. "What if I can't do this, Azrael? Worst case scenario, what happens to Jesse and Lamal?"

Azrael sat on the arm of the couch. "Absolutely nothing. They're stuck like this."

That made me feel better. At least nothing catastrophic would happen…

"That is, until Abaddon finally does get to him," Azrael continued. "He'll murder Jesse and take Lamal to the pit where he'll spend eternity enduring torment you can't even fathom."

I sucked in a deep breath. "OK, great."

Lamal was trying to smile at me confidently, but he was failing.

"What happens if she succeeds?" Adrianne asked. "Is he going to float around the ceiling or what?"

That was a good question.

"If she succeeds, Jesse can go back to Chicago and Lamal can go back across the spirit line," Azrael said.

"Why didn't he do that to begin with?" Warren asked.

If I wasn't mistaken, Azrael looked a little guilty. "He wasn't allowed."

I pointed at him. "Because of you?"

He gave a slight nod.

I held up my hand with a question. "Does this mean I'm cleaning up your mess this time?"

Azrael rolled his eyes. "Save this guy, please."

I focused on Jesse; he was in there, probably shaking as bad as the angel stuck inside him. I blasted him with so much life it knocked him backward into the wall.

"You forgot the second punch," Azrael said.

The alarm bells chimed on my phone. "Oh, thank god." I ran to the dining table to pick it up. *Friday, February 14th. Pick up Nathan's cake. Southside Sweets closes at noon.* "Uh oh."

"What did you forget?" Adrianne asked.

"The cake."

"Cake?" Warren asked.

I nodded. "I ordered a cake for the party tonight. The bakery closes at noon."

Warren looked at his watch. "Where is it?"

"Biltmore Village," I said.

His head shook with surprise. "Biltmore? We've got to go."

Relief washed over Lamal's face.

Adrianne stood and carried her drink to the kitchen. "You guys go get the cake. Azrael and I will stay here and start decorating."

Azrael scowled. "I'm The Angel of Death. I don't decorate."

"You do today," she said with a sweet smile.

He rolled his eyes.

Reuel went and stood by the door.

"You're coming with us?" Warren asked him.

He smiled and nodded his head enthusiastically.

I nudged him with my elbow. "You want to go to the bakery, don't you?"

He nodded again.

"Come on, let's go."

We pulled into the parking lot at Southside Sweets at 12:06. Warren stayed in the car, but Reuel was right on my heels as we went inside. The bells on the door chimed as we ran in and skidded to a stop on the black and white checkerboard tile. "I'm here! I'm here! I'm sorry I'm late!" The smell of caramelized sugar and carbs made my mouth water. Reuel went straight for the jar of free cookie samples on the top of the counter.

Brienne Casey, the shop owner and a girl I went to high school with, came out from the open kitchen, wiping flour from her hands on her apron. She was laughing and shaking her head. "I knew you'd come, Sloan. Calm down."

Reuel stuck an entire chocolate chip cookie inside his mouth.

Her nose scrunched up when she saw my face. "The bruising isn't much better, I see."

I shook my head. "Nope. I'm afraid my fiancé is going to have to deal with the dirty looks a little bit longer."

"That's unfortunate." She disappeared into the walk-in cooler and came out with a large, flat yellow box. She looked at the sticky note on top. "Chocolate cake with buttercream icing, right?"

My stomach growled at the mention of sugary goodness. "Yes."

She put the box on the counter and spun it around so I could see it through the plastic window top. I covered my mouth and laughed. "It's perfect. He's going to love it."

Her eyes were wide as she accepted my credit card. "I think it's the most unusual request for a cake I've ever received."

"It's a joke," I said with a smile.

"When's the party?" she asked.

I glanced up at the cupcake-decorated clock on the wall behind her. "At seven." I let out a sigh as I signed the transaction slip. "I'll probably be late for it too and it's at my house."

"Speaking of being late," she said. "I need your wedding cake order soon. Brides who wait until the last minute make me nervous, and the date is in April, right?"

"Yes. I'll get it done soon. I promise."

She smiled and handed me my receipt. "Give the detective my best."

"You know Nathan?" I asked.

"Sure. He comes by here for lunch sometimes," she answered.

I looked at the glass cases full of cakes and cookies and laughed. "Of course he does. Thanks so much, Brienne."

Reuel shoved the rest of his second or third cookie into his mouth and picked up the cake. We walked out to Warren's Challenger. I climbed in the back seat and Reuel handed me the box. Warren looked back as Reuel got inside. "Do we need to stop anywhere else that you forgot about?"

"Shut up," I said, pulling on my seatbelt.

He put the car in reverse.

"Oh! We have to get the balloons from the dollar store!"

Laughing, he shook his head and pulled out of the lot.

———

We had to wait for the balloons to be blown up, so it was after two when we made it back to my house. Carrying the cake, I followed Warren and his two fistfuls of gold and white balloons inside. I froze when we walked through the door. "Whoa!"

Adrianne was pushing a long, white tapered candle into a beer bottle. "You like it?" she asked, motioning around the room.

"I can't believe it's the same house!" I looked at the clock on my phone. "How long have we been gone?"

The couch and love seat were still pushed back against the wall, but behind them, over the plywood hole, she'd hung a long curtain rod with opaque shimmery gold curtains. I recognized them from her bedroom.

The dining room table was sitting in the center of the living room with another table of similar size parallel to it. Both were draped with white tablecloths and both had centerpieces made out of beer bottles, flowers, and candles.

"Azrael, can you tie these balloons behind the food table in the kitchen?" Adrianne called over her shoulder.

Without argument, Azrael came and took the balloons from Warren.

"Adrianne, I'm not sure what impresses me more: the fact that you've pulled off this stunning setting that's both manly and elegant in a living room that's missing a wall, or that you've got Azrael taking orders about party decor."

Adrianne placed the beer bottle candle in the center of the table. "Thank you. Both tasks were equally challenging." She walked over and took the cake from my arms. "Wait." She turned the box around in her arms and looked through the window. Her eyes widened. "Sloan!" Her voice was clearly caught between amusement and alarm. "Does this say what I think it says?"

"What does it say?" Warren looked over her shoulder.

She angled the box so he could see it.

My nose scrunched up. "Is it tacky?"

Warren laughed. "It's hilarious, but you know Nate's mom is coming, right?"

I cringed and sucked in a sharp breath through my teeth. "I didn't think about that."

"Clearly," Adrianne said.

Azrael looked over from where he was arranging balloons in the kitchen. "What is it?"

"It's made to look like a patch for his hat," Warren said. "It says 'GTFO' in big letters on it."

Azrael shook his head. "I don't get it."

Adrianne walked over and whispered in his ear. He immediately started chuckling. "That's funny."

"And inappropriate." Adrianne looked over at me. "Didn't you tell me his sister is bringing her kids?"

I covered my face with my hands. "Oh man. What did I do?"

Adrianne rolled her eyes. "You're going to be such a good mother."

Warren kissed my cheek, still laughing as he walked by. "I love you so much."

I followed him to the kitchen. "Leave it in the box, Adrianne, and put it on top of the refrigerator. Maybe we can cut and serve it before anyone sees it."

"You've got to at least let Nate see it. He's going to love it," Warren said.

When I came downstairs at a quarter till seven, the house smelled amazing from whatever Warren was spooning out of the huge pan on the stove in the kitchen. I stood on the bottom step and admired everything. Adrianne was lighting the candles on all the tables. Reuel added wood to the fireplace from a stack of logs in Lamal's arms, and Azrael sat on the leather couch drinking whiskey.

"This place looks wonderful," I said.

Adrianne walked over. She'd changed into a black dress and low heels. "You really like it?"

I nodded. "I really do. It makes me excited to see what you do with my wedding."

With my added height from the step, we were almost eye to eye. She leaned close to me and winked. "You ain't seen nothin' yet." She tugged on my sleeve. "You look adorable. Is that the sweater I picked out?"

I nodded and ran my hand over the light cream, cashmere sleeve. "Of course."

"And your hair," she said, nodding with approval. "You did it all by yourself."

I'd done nothing except flat iron it down my back. "I think it's time for a cut. It's getting really long."

"Prenatal vitamins make it grow faster," she said. "Come by the shop and I'll cut it this week."

"Need any help with anything?" I asked.

She shook her head. "Nope. Might want to check with Warren though."

I walked to the kitchen and put my arms around Warren's waist from behind. "I think this is what heaven smells like."

He turned around in my arms. "I hope you're hungry."

I stretched up on my tip-toes. "I'm always hungry." I kissed his lips. He tasted like red wine. "What's for dinner?"

"Grillades with gouda grits," he answered.

I whimpered. "You made me grits?"

"I did."

I kissed him again. "I love you."

He smiled. "You'd better."

"Need any help?"

The doorbell rang and he looked toward it. "Yes. Answer the door."

But before I could turn to leave the kitchen, we all heard Azrael get up off the couch. *Phwaaaaaawert...*

I chuckled. "It never gets old."

He pulled the door open as I walked into the living room. It was Nathan, carrying his nephew Carter who was passed out over his shoulder. His parents and his sister Lara were right behind him. His mother was gawking at the bruises on my face, and Nathan was mesmerized by the transformation of my living room. "Wow," he mouthed, so as not to wake the little boy.

Silently, I waved to James, Kathy, and Lara before tugging on Nathan's sleeve. "Let's put him upstairs on my bed."

Nathan nodded toward the stairs for me to lead the way. When we reached my bedroom, he bent over the bed and gently laid Carter on top of the comforter. I pulled the fleece throw off the chair in the corner and carefully draped it over him as Nathan pulled off Carter's tennis shoes. Nathan caught my eye and smiled.

When we were outside the door with it closed behind us, Nathan opened his arms. "Hello. Good to see you."

I hugged him and laughed softly. "When did he fall asleep?"

"Right before we turned off the highway, of course. He might be out for a while." We walked down the stairs. "Did you buy a new house?" he asked when we reached the living room.

I pointed at Adrianne. "She's secretly moonlighting as Martha Stewart, I think."

"It's incredible. Thank you." He walked over and gave Adrianne a side hug.

"Kathy!" I cheered, walking over to where Nathan's family was talking to Azrael.

"Oh, Sloan, I've missed you," she said, pulling me into a tight hug. She squeezed till I felt lightheaded. When she stepped back, she grabbed my chin to examine my face. "What happened to you?"

"Nathan didn't tell you? I was in a train accident up in Chicago. I'm fine though, really."

She looked skeptical. "No, he didn't tell me." Then she put her hands on my belly and smiled. "He did tell me about this, however. Look at you. No hiding it now, huh?"

My nose wrinkled. "Definitely no more hiding it. I'm eating for two now and it shows."

She laughed and patted her round hips. "At least you have an excuse. Not all of us do!"

Lara was waiting behind her mother for her turn to say hello. I hugged her. "Hey, Lara! I'm so glad you made it." I stepped back and looked around. "Where's your husband?"

"He's at home with Rachel. She had her very first dance at school tonight for Valentine's Day."

"Rachel?" I asked. The only Rachel I knew was my demon mother.

She thought for a second. "I guess you didn't meet my daughter at Thanksgiving because she was with her dad. She's ten."

I shook my head. "No. I guess I only met Carter." I pointed up the stairs. "We put him on the bed in my room."

"Thank you. He's been a pill this evening." She looked at her mom. "No nap and grandma brought him cookies."

Kathy waved her off. "That's what grandmas are for."

"Hey, Sloan," Nathan's dad, James McNamara, said as he wrapped his arm around my shoulders. "Thanks for having us."

"Are you kidding? Thanks so much for coming!"

In the kitchen, Warren was wiping his hands on a towel. I motioned him forward. "I want you all to meet my fiancé, Warren Parish."

They turned and looked up at him as he approached. Kathy did a double take, then looked at Azrael. "Brothers?" she asked.

"Not brothers," I said, "but they are related."

Warren offered his hand to her, but she pushed it away and put her arms around his neck. "I don't shake hands, son," she said. "I'm a hugger."

Warren patted her on the back. "It's nice to finally meet you, Mrs. McNamara."

"Shush. Call me Kathy. And it's lovely to meet you," she said, pulling away from him. "I've heard so much about you, I feel like we've been family for years."

"Warren," I said, "this is Nathan's sister, Lara."

Lara had that dewy-eyed stare that most women got when looking at Warren for the first time. She must have realized it because she blinked and shook her head. "I'm sorry." She offered her hand. "It's nice to meet you. Nathan told us about your engagement. Congratulations to you both."

Warren smiled at me. "I'm a lucky guy."

Kathy nodded. "Yes, you certainly are."

"Sloan, you're supposed to show her your ring," Adrianne said.

My lower lip poked out as I held up my bare hand. "My fingers are too swollen to wear it."

Kathy laughed and squeezed my hand. "Same thing happened to me with Lara. Perfectly normal. Maybe you're having a girl!"

Warren and I exchanged a smile. "Maybe we are," he said.

"This is my best friend, Adrianne," I said to Kathy and Lara. "She did all the decorating tonight." I looked around the room and pointed to the angels in the corner. "And those are our friends,

Reuel and Lamal. They don't talk much. And I'm guessing you already met Azrael." I pointed at him.

Kathy's head tilted. "Azrael? I thought your name was—"

Azrael cut her off. "Yes, Damon Claymore. Azrael is a family nickname." He cut his eyes toward me.

"Oh, OK." Kathy still looked confused.

I felt stupid.

The front door opened, and my dad walked in, saving me from further embarrassment. "Dad!" I scurried over and grabbed his arm. He was carrying a bottle of wine. "Everyone, this is my father, Dr. Robert Jordan."

"Hello," Dad said. "I hope I'm not late."

I kissed his cheek. "You are right on time."

The meal was incredible, and after we finished, Warren stood up with a beer. "Excuse me for a second, I'd like to say something."

"Uh oh." Nathan was grinning at the head of the table.

Warren pointed the bottle at him. "You should *always* be very nervous around me."

"Oh, I am," Nathan replied, laughing.

Warren turned to all of us. "The first time I met Nate, he pointed a gun at my face."

"That's not true," Nathan argued. "I had my gun out, but I didn't point at you."

"He wanted to," I said.

"True," Nathan admitted. Everyone laughed.

Warren continued. "Whatever the details, the first time he saw me, he wanted to kill me."

Nathan laughed and raised his beer. "Some days I still do."

Warren clinked his bottle with Nathan's. "Likewise." He looked back around at all of us. "The truth is, Nate and I are supposed to hate each other. We were certainly never meant to be friends. And while our friendship is rocky at best sometimes, there's no one in this world I trust more."

"Hey!" Azrael and I shouted at the same time with a pitch of offense in our voices.

"You two shut up. It's not your party," Nathan said.

Warren turned toward him. "So, brother, I wish you the best of luck on this new part of your journey. And I hope that where ever you end up"—he held up his beer toward Nathan—"that it's far, *far* away from me and my wife."

The room howled with laughter. I dropped my red face into my hands. Everyone clapped and cheered. Nathan got up and hugged Warren, then they both sat back down at the table. A moment later, a sleepy little boy appeared on the stairs rubbing his eyes.

"Oh," I said. "We woke him up. Hi, Carter."

He stuck his thumb in his mouth and trudged the rest of the way down the stairs. He ran to his mother, and Lara scooped him up in her arms.

"Who wants cake?" Adrianne announced, standing up while several people shouted "me" in response.

Warren looked at me. "You'd better hurry and show him."

I grabbed Nathan's sleeve. "Come with me a second."

He stood and followed me to the kitchen. Adrianne was pulling the cake off the refrigerator. "What's going on?" he asked.

I pointed to the cake as she opened it on the counter. "Go look at it. Hurry, before anyone else sees it."

Nathan walked over and immediately laughed. "Oh man, is that a patch?"

"Yeah."

He looked at me, still chuckling. "GTFO. You really want to get rid of me that bad?"

I jerked my thumb over my shoulder. "Obviously Warren does."

"Obviously." He smiled. "I love it. Thank you. Why are you hiding it?"

I sucked in a sharp breath and pointed to the living room. "I didn't think about your mom being here."

"Pshh, Mom won't care. Hell, she probably won't get it," he said. "Lara, come look at this cake."

Lara carried Carter into the kitchen. He turned the cake toward her on the counter. "Oh, that's hilarious," she said.

Kathy walked in. "I want to see!"

My heart dropped into my stomach.

Kathy's eyes squinted. "GTFO. What does that mean?"

Nathan looked at me. "See?"

I smiled.

Kathy crossed her arms. "What is it?"

Nathan pointed to the cake. "It means Get The Fu—"

"Nathan!" I shouted, slapping him on the arm.

Kathy's face turned as red as mine felt. "Oh mercy. Never mind. I understand."

I winced. "I'm sorry, Kathy."

She laughed and put her hand on my arm. "It's not my party, honey. It's perfect for Nathan."

Adrianne nudged me with her elbow. She was holding a butcher knife. "Is this all you have to cut the cake?"

I shrugged.

"That's sad, Sloan."

Adrianne cut the cake and passed out slices at the table. Warren brewed a pot of coffee and I got clean forks for everyone. The cake may have been offensive, but it was delicious. Nathan ate two pieces. So did I, but when no one was looking.

Carter had icing all over his face. "More," he said to his mother.

She shook her head. "Not till you eat some dinner. Do you want some real food?"

He nodded and Lara led him to the kitchen.

When Kathy finished her cake, she curled her hands around the coffee mug in front of her. She looked at Azrael. "Nathan hasn't told us very much. What exactly is he going to do for you, Mr. Claymore?"

Be the liaison between the supernatural leader and the mortal employees, I answered in my mind as I swiped a bit of frosting off Warren's plate with my finger.

"He's going to train to be the head of operations. In a few years, I'd like to see him overseeing all the day-to-day affairs of the company," he said. "And please, call me Damon."

She folded her arms on the table. "But Nathan doesn't have any military experience."

Azrael smiled. "He will when we're finished with him."

I knew he meant the statement to be positive, but Kathy's head pulled back in fear. I reached across the table and put my hand on hers. "He means Nathan will be well trained before he's given any major responsibility."

Her shoulders relaxed.

"He leaves for boot camp tomorrow," Azrael said.

I was surprised. "Boot camp?"

Warren nodded. "It's every bit as intense as the Marine Corps boot camp, too." He looked at Nathan. "I don't envy you at all."

"How long is it?" I asked.

"Eight weeks," Nathan said.

Warren looked over at Azrael, who was sitting at the other table. "Are you going to let him have his phone? Or only write letters?"

"He may not even get to write," Azrael said. "He sure as hell won't get any special treatment except the pleasure of working directly with me."

"You're going to Claymore?" I perked up in my seat.

Azrael nodded. "Sometime next week. I'll be there about a month."

My wide eyes turned back to Nathan. "Working with Azrael for a whole month?" I asked, looking at Nathan. "Better be one hell of a benefits package."

He laughed. "You have no idea. Don't forget to send me your address so I can—"

Just then, a blood-chilling scream came from the kitchen. It was Carter.

"Nathan!" Lara shrieked over the cries of her son.

Nathan jumped up, toppling his chair as he ran to the kitchen. Kathy was right after him. I ran to the doorway as Nathan yelled. "Lara, don't touch it!"

"Dr. Jordan, we need help!" Kathy screamed.

Dad moved to go, but Azrael blocked him with his arm. He pointed at me. "Sloan, get in there." His voice was commanding.

"Sloan, help!" It was Nathan.

I swallowed hard and pushed by James into the kitchen. The butcher knife Adrianne had used for the cake was buried in Carter's tiny foot. Blood was darkening his sock around the blade. Carter's face was turning purple as his piercing screams echoed around the kitchen. Lara was holding his arms still, and Nathan held his legs.

"Mom, move!" Nathan yelled.

James grabbed the back of his wife's shirt and yanked her out of my way.

"Nathan, get the doctor!" Lara cried.

Nathan's terrified gaze locked with mine. "Fix this. Tell me what to do."

"Azrael! I need you!" I called out.

A second later, he pushed his way into the room. "Let me have him," he said to Lara. She shook her head, tears streaming down her face. "Let me have him," he said again, this time prying her son from her arms.

He pushed her back a few steps, and she pounded his back with her fists. Of course it didn't faze him. "Sloan, pull out the knife."

"No!" Lara screamed.

Warren broke through Kathy and James and grabbed Lara from behind.

"Sloan, do it!" Azrael yelled again.

I gripped the handle of the knife, closed my eyes, and pulled. It clanged against the tiles when I dropped it on the floor, far under the table away from everyone. Then I grabbed Carter's foot and blasted all my power into it.

"Carter, look at me," I said.

His eyes looked like they might fall out of his head. Huge tears poured from his eyes and watery snot ran from his nose.

"Carter, breathe with me," Azrael said, pulling Carter against his own chest and taking exaggerated slow breaths. "That's good. Keep breathing. Miss Sloan is going to make your foot feel better. Just breathe."

After a few deep breaths with Azrael, Carter started breathing more normally on his own. His screaming subsided as the heat left my hands. I pulled off his bloody sock, then used it to wipe his foot. A two-inch mark was in line parallel to the bones on the top, and there was a smaller puncture mark on the bottom where the tip of the blade had gone clean through.

Azrael released Carter back to Lara who was still crying, but too shocked to make any sound.

Kathy grabbed my shoulder. "What did you do?"

"She healed him," Nathan said, reaching over and grabbing my hand.

"Healed him?" Kathy asked.

Nathan stood and pulled me to my feet. He hooked his arm around my neck and pulled me in for a tight hug. "Thank you," he whispered against the side of my face. "Thank you."

"But how...?" Kathy's voice faded away.

"God, who cares how?" Lara grabbed me around the neck and hugged me with the arm that wasn't holding Carter. "Thank you, Sloan."

"You're welcome."

No one pressed further about how I was able to heal Carter's foot, but we all knew the secret was out and that an explanation would have to be given sooner or later. To my great surprise though, none of Nathan's family treated me any different after the accident. If anything, they seemed to love me even more, which was evident in the long embraces I received from each of them on the porch when it was time for them to leave.

Kathy teared up. "I don't know why I'm so weepy. I'll see you again," she said.

"You're coming to the wedding, right?" Warren asked.

"I'd love to. When is it?"

"April 19th." I looked at Lara. "You're all invited."

Lara smiled.

"April 19th," Kathy repeated to her husband. "Make it happen, James."

He saluted his wife. "Yes, ma'am."

Kathy hugged me one more time. "Take care of yourself and that baby."

"I will."

She hugged Warren, then they left the porch, leaving us with Nathan.

"Any last-minute advice?" Nathan asked Warren.

Warren laughed. "Yeah, don't go."

"I appreciate that," Nathan said with an eye roll.

"All I can tell you is to keep your head down and your mouth shut. Don't be an overachiever or an underachiever. Try to blend in."

Nathan nodded and offered him his hand. "Thanks, man."

Warren pulled him into a hug. "Good luck and take care of yourself. Keep us posted on how things are going."

"I will. Remind Sloan to text me your full address here."

"I won't let her forget." Warren took a step backward toward the front door. "I'll give you two some privacy."

When he left, Nathan laughed and shook his head with disbelief. "He's either very confident or *seriously* stupid. There's no way in hell I'd leave you alone with me."

"He's not stupid. He trusts you," I said.

Nathan closed his eyes and took a deep breath, then blew it out very slowly. "I'm not so sure that he should," he finally said quietly.

His tone disrupted the butterflies in my stomach.

"You're *certain* you want to leave?" I asked again.

He kicked his boot against my welcome mat. "Yeah. I need to get out of here for a while."

I shook my head. "That's not what I asked."

"That's the only answer I can give you," he said.

"I'm going to miss you, Nathan."

He forced a smile. "I miss you every single day."

I put my arms around his neck and hugged him. Burying my face between my arms and his neck, I began to cry.

He shook his head against mine. "Don't do that." He pulled back and cradled my face in his hands, brushing my cheeks with his thumbs. "No more tears."

I sniffed. "Please be safe."

He chuckled. "*You* be safe. You're the one getting trains thrown at you. Not me."

For a moment, he studied my eyes, then his gaze fell to my lips. But instead of moving closer, he took a deep breath and a step back. He grabbed my hand and squeezed.

"Goodbye, Nathan."

He smiled and walked away.

CHAPTER TWELVE

"TAKE A DEEP breath, Sloan," Warren said as we sat in the waiting room of Dr. Watts' office the next Friday for my twenty-week checkup.

My knee wouldn't stop bouncing.

The front door of the practice swung into the waiting room and my dad walked in. "Did I miss it?"

I shook my head, tapping my nails against the side of my chair. "Nope. Still waiting. She's a little behind today."

He looked around. "Is it just the three of us?"

I clicked my heels together. "Yep. Az and Lamal drove to Claymore yesterday for the next few weeks. Reuel is in the car."

"They're both gone for a few weeks?" Dad asked, surprised.

My toes were tap dancing under my seat. "Yep. Azrael wanted to be there for something with Nathan's training, and he took Lamal with him so that The Destroyer wouldn't be tempted to crash through my house again. They're going to be gone almost a whole month. It's glorious."

Dad seemed a little puzzled as he sat next to me. "Is that safe? He's been such a close guard all this time."

Warren nodded. "She's well protected, Dr. Jordan."

"Of course she is. No offense intended, son," Dad said.

Warren smiled. "None taken, but really, you shouldn't worry. There's always a team nearby, even if you don't see them."

Dad let out a sigh. "That does make me feel better. Thank you."

I drummed my nails on the armrests of my chair until Dad put his hand on top of mine to stop it. "Sloan, why are you so jittery?"

"She's going to have a lot of explaining to do today with the bruising on her stomach and the scar on her uterus," Warren answered for me.

Dad curled his arm around my shoulders. "Tell her the truth. Or a watery version of the truth."

I raked my fingers through my hair. "Too many people are finding out about me. Nathan's whole family, now the doctor..."

"And nothing bad has happened. Right, Warren?" Dad asked.

Warren put pressure on my bouncing knee. "Nothing at all."

"Sloan Jordan?" the nurse called out as she entered from the hallway.

I popped up out of my chair so quickly I got a head rush. "Here!"

She looked twice when she saw the fading bruises on my face, but she didn't say anything. "C...Come on back." She stuttered slightly.

"Can they come too?" I asked.

She looked at Warren with wide eyes and finally nodded. "Of course."

"She thinks I'm a wife beater," he whispered.

"What did you expect?"

Our first stop was the scales. Shockingly, I'd only gained about five pounds that month and I'd lost the food diary right after Chicago. She scribbled the number down, then led us to the exam room where she took all my vitals and asked all the routine questions.

Have you had any nausea? Only when I thought about demons coming to take my baby.

Are you feeling the baby move? All the time, like she was training to be a gymnast.

Have you noticed any fluid or vaginal bleeding? Not since my uterus was ripped open.

Have you had any contractions? See previous question.

Of course I didn't say those answers out loud.

"Dr. Watts will be in shortly," she said and left the room.

Warren offered me a high five. "Only five pounds this month. Congratulations."

I shot him the bird instead of slapping his hand. He laughed and kissed my forehead. My father sighed and shook his head.

There was a light knock on the door, then Dr. Watts walked inside. "Hello, Sloan."

I waved. "Hello."

She froze. "My stars. Are those bruises? What happened to you?"

My nose wrinkled. "I was in an accident a couple of weeks ago." I pointed at Warren. "I promise, he didn't do it."

She gripped my chin and turned my face to the side. "No one is assuming he did, but what kind of accident?"

"Train."

Her mouth fell open. "You were in a train accident?"

I nodded. "Well, not so much an accident as an incident, but a subway train derailed in Chicago."

"Oh. I heard about that, I think. It happened downtown?" she asked.

"That's the one." I pointed to my dad, hoping to lighten the mood. "Look who's here."

It worked. Her face brightened when she saw my father. "Hi, Dr. Jordan. This is a pleasant surprise."

He gave her a one-armed hug. "It's good to see you," he said. "I hope you don't mind a proud grandpa crashing an ultrasound."

She smiled. "I'm honored. Have a seat. Sloan, how have you been feeling? Any belly trauma in that accident?" she asked.

"Maybe a little."

"Well, I wouldn't be surprised. Let's check you out." She flipped on the machine by the exam table. "Go ahead and pull your shirt up for me."

I sucked in a deep breath. "About that."

Her brow lifted in question.

"I don't want you to freak out," I said. "But it was pretty intense belly trauma."

"And you didn't call me?"

"I went to the hospital in Chicago. They said the baby's fine," I said.

"What kind of belly trauma?"

"The worst kind."

She stared at me.

"You should prepare yourself. If you think my face is bad, I'm afraid my stomach is much worse," I said.

I slowly pulled my shirt up to my ribs. The smile-shaped bruise that stretched from beneath my bellybutton to well below my panty line had faded to lighter shades of brown and green, but it was still horrifying to behold. That was obvious from the doctor's gasp, which was a pitchy note well above middle-C. "Sloan!"

I threw my hands up. "I warned you it was bad, but I'm fine."

She looked like she might cry. "What happened?"

My dad took a step toward the ultrasound machine. "Emily, maybe we should start with the ultrasound so you can see for yourself that the baby is fine. That will make it a little easier to stomach when you hear the whole story."

Dr. Watts was visibly shaking, but she nodded and moved over in front of the machine. She cleared her throat as she squeezed warm blue jelly on my stomach. "Try to relax."

I wasn't sure if she was talking to me or herself.

She took the ultrasound wand and pressed it into the jelly, then she moved it a few inches below my bellybutton. The computer screen filled with black blobs and gray fuzz. She moved it around.

"There she is!" I pointed excitedly at the screen when the shape of the baby filled the black space.

Dr. Watts breathed an audible sigh of relief.

I covered my mouth with my hand. "I can actually see her without being shown this time," I said with a laugh. "She really looks like a baby now."

Dad chuckled. "What did she look like before?"

Warren answered "an alien" and I answered "a bobblehead" at the same time.

"Is that her hand up by her head?" Warren asked.

"It is." Dr. Watts pointed to a flashing black spot. "And there's the heart. Let's see if we can get some sound." She flipped a switch, and the glorious sound of her heartbeat filled the room. Warren squeezed my hand.

"Are you two still sure it's a girl?" she asked.

I nodded. "Pretty confident."

"Will you be disappointed if it's a boy?"

Warren laughed. "We're pretty sure it's not a boy."

Dr. Watts looked at my dad. "It's like these two have a crystal ball or something. I've never heard two parents more certain. Let's try to get a different angle here." She moved the wand around some more. "Ah, OK. See these three little white lines?" She clicked a button and the screen froze.

I strained my eyes. "Yeah."

Warren nodded. "What's that?"

She smiled. "That's your confirmation. You were right. It's a girl."

Warren kissed my lips. He had tears in his eyes.

"It's a girl!" Dad cheered, clapping his hands together.

I smiled at Dr. Watts. "I told you so."

She nodded. "Yes, you did. Congratulations."

I sat up on my elbows. "I also told you she was fine."

She nodded again.

I pointed to the screen. "Now I want you to look for the source of all that blood under my skin. Look around a bit and you should see a scar on my uterus."

She unfroze the screen and moved the wand again. "Huh." She pointed to the screen and traced a faint gray streak with her finger. "I don't understand."

I moved to sit up, and jelly got all over my pants and shirt. "Eww." Dad pulled some tissues out of a box and handed them to me. I cleaned off my clothes, then tossed it in the wastebasket.

Dr. Watts pulled a pen from her jacket pocket.

I held up my hand to stop her. "I need you to *not* write this down."

"Uh…"

I took a deep breath. "I'm about to tell you something you're going to think is nuts. I can assure you, I'm not crazy, but I need you to know a few things if you're going to deliver our daughter."

Dad put his hand on my arm. "I encouraged Sloan to talk to you so that you'll know all the facts before she goes into labor."

She crossed one leg over the other. "OK?" It sounded like a question.

My hands were sweaty. I sucked in another deep breath. "I'm sorry, this is hard."

She rolled her chair closer and put her hand on my knee. "I'm sure it's not as bad as you think it is."

Dad chuckled. "No, it probably is."

"Thanks, Dad."

"When the train left the tracks and came up on the platform of the train station, I was thrown through the air. I collided with a metal structure before landing hard on my stomach. My uterus ruptured. That's what you saw on the ultrasound," I said.

Her gaze was fixed, like she was staring right through me. "That's not possible. If your uterus had ruptured at this stage in the pregnancy, the fetus would have been lost. It would have required major surgery, possibly a full hysterectomy, and you could have died."

"I warned you it sounded crazy, but I'm telling you that's what happened. Did you ever see that scar there before?" I asked.

She thought for a moment. "No, but—"

"You didn't see it because it wasn't there," I said slowly.

I pulled up my shirt and touched the bruising. "That's why there's so much blood. The wound healed, but the bruises fade normally, unfortunately."

She touched her temples. "This isn't medically possible."

I nodded. "I know."

"Emily," Dad said, causing her to look up. "I'm a doctor, too, remember. I know we're not trained to accept things for which we can't see a reason, but Sloan is telling you the truth."

"Dr. Watts, I understand if you don't want to be my doctor anymore, but whoever delivers her needs to know at least this much of the truth. I don't know what may happen when she's born, but as I understand it, these kinds of ruptures can be quite serious."

She nodded. "Uterine ruptures can be fatal for you and your baby."

I smiled. "Well, I'm not that easy to kill, if it makes you feel any better."

She didn't laugh, and she didn't speak for what felt like an eternity. She simply stared at the tiled floor like she was doing a calculus problem in her head. Maybe she was trying to come up with a nice way to tell us to get the hell out of her office.

"Dr. Watts?" I asked, drawing her attention back to us.

She took a deep breath and let it out quickly. Then she leaned to put her hand on mine. "You're right. This all sounds nuts to me, but"—she squeezed my fingers—"I've known your family for a decade. You're not crazy and you're not a liar. I'll still be your doctor."

I fully exhaled for the first time all day. "Thank you."

"Now, I need you to lie back so I can get some measurements," she said.

"Well that turned out better than you expected," Warren said, taking my hand as we left her office and walked down the hallway.

My father slapped him on the back. "And you're having a very healthy baby girl."

"Yes, we are." Warren pulled me against his side and wrapped his arm around my waist.

When we reached the elevator, Warren pressed the down button and my father pressed the up one. "Are you two headed home?" Dad asked.

I nodded. "I think I'm going to go home and take a hot bath, then pass out till it's time for Warren to feed me."

Dad laughed. "That sounds like a great idea. I wish I could do the same. Alas, I must go back to work and try to heal people the old-fashioned way."

I smiled up at my dad. "I can go with you if you'd like and cut your day short."

"As tempting as that sounds, I'm going to let you go home and take your bath." He gave me a hug. "Thanks for letting me come to your appointment."

"Of course. I'm so glad you wanted to." I gave him a hug as the elevator doors slid open.

"I love you, sweetheart."

"I love you too, Dad."

On our drive home, Reuel sat in the front and I wedged my only-five-pounds-bigger frame into the tiny back seat of the Challenger. Warren looked at me in the rearview and smiled. "Since it's official, can we finally pick out a name for her?"

"Of course we can," I said. "Although, I need to warn you that someone, I won't name any names, is insisting that if it's a girl we call her Adrianne and if it's a boy, then Adrian, without the last *n* and *e*."

He laughed. "Why would we name our baby anything else?"

"Do you mind if we swing by her shop since we're so close? She said she'd cut my hair if I came by," I said.

"Sure." He glanced at his watch. "I might actually let Reuel stay with you. I need to run a quick errand." He looked at Reuel. "Is that OK?"

Reuel grunted and nodded his head.

"Where are you going?" I asked.

"No being nosy," he said. "Not this close to the wedding."

I rubbed my palms together. "I love your surprises."

He laughed. "I hope so."

I leaned against the back of his seat and traced my finger along the seam of his shirt. "So, did you have any baby names in mind?"

He glanced back at me again. "I was thinking maybe we could name her Audrey, after your mother."

I clasped my hands over my heart. "That's so sweet. You would really do that?"

"Absolutely. I loved your mother," he said.

I leaned my head back against the seat. "Man, I miss her."

He reached back and patted the side of my knee. "I know you do."

"What about your mom? What if we named her Audrey Nadine?" I suggested.

He shook his head. "I'd rather not. I never knew her, so I don't feel like it would be honoring her life as much as it would be memorializing her absence."

"I guess that makes sense," I said. "I wonder if Nathan's had any luck with finding out more about it."

He shifted in his seat and reached into his back jeans pocket. "That reminds me. You got a letter in the mail." He handed me a white envelope over his shoulder.

"Really?"

I recognized Nathan's handwriting on the address at once. I slipped my finger under the flap and ripped it open.

Sloan,

Azrael wasn't joking. I'm not allowed to have a phone. I'm not sure why I thought he might be because we all know he wasn't born with a sense of humor. This place sucks balls. I'm not sure what I was thinking. I had a good job with a good department, and I gave it up to be yelled at while doing pushups. I've got my fingers crossed that this will all be worth it in the end, but I'm doubtful after the last couple of days. He's supposed to get here tomorrow. That should be interesting.

I feel like Azrael runs a shady operation here. There are places that are completely restricted, even from me, and yet he wants me to take over someday. How much sense does that make? I hope he's not doing anything illegal. You know I can't be party to that. Ask Warren and see if he knows anything about a building they call Echo-10. I'm going to do some digging and see what I can find out on my own. If I ever get any free time, that is.

It's almost lights out. Write back if you get a chance. I hope you and the baby are doing OK.

-Nate

P.S. Tell Warren my mom called after I left your house and asked if he beats you. That should make him feel good about himself.

I decided not to tell Warren about what Kathy had said.

"How's he doing?" Warren asked as he pulled into a parking space on the street near Adrianne's salon.

"He says it sucks," I said, folding up the letter and sticking it back in the envelope.

He nodded and put the car in park. "It does suck."

"Are you coming in?" I asked.

"Yeah, I'm going to go say hello," he said.

Reuel got out of the car and pushed the front passenger's seat up for me. He offered a hand and pulled me out as Warren came over and met us on the sidewalk. "So you had to go through Claymore's boot camp too?"

"Everyone goes through it," Warren said.

"Why, if you've already been through the military?"

He shrugged and slipped on his black sunglasses. "I think it's so they know we're all trained the same way."

"Makes sense, I guess."

"It's tough though. As hard as RECON school."

"Nathan wants to know if you've ever heard of a building called Echo-10," I said.

He took my hand as we walked down the street. "Yeah, everyone's heard of it. Did he get to go inside?"

"No. I think it's making him nervous. He's wondering if Az might be doing illegal stuff in there."

Warren nodded. "The rumor when I worked there was that there are ten torture chambers in that building. They say it's called Echo-10 because all you can hear inside of it are the echoes of your own screams."

"Geez. Do you believe that?" I stopped walking and Reuel caught my shoulders before bumping into me.

He laughed. "I wouldn't be at all surprised."

The welcome bells chimed when we walked through the door of the Merrimon Avenue Salon. Reuel stayed outside by the window. There were two other stylists working, and Adrianne was painting color onto an older woman's hair near the window.

"Hey! What are you guys doing here?" she asked, wrapping the hair in her hands in a square of tin foil.

I twirled a long brown strand of my hair around my finger. "You said you'd cut it, remember? Do you have time?"

"I will in about two minutes, as soon as I put Mrs. Antley under the dryer."

I held up a warning finger. "Only a trim. I don't want you to go all 'Adrianne' on my hair and chop it off. Got it?"

She smiled. "Of course. How was your appointment today?"

Warren walked over and handed her the ultrasound photo he'd stuck in his pocket. "She's perfect. And the doctor confirmed today that she is a girl."

"Yay! I'm so happy for you…and for me because I'll get to braid her hair and take her shopping!"

He looked back at me. "Our kid's not even born yet and she's already creating a monster."

I pointed at her. "If she's half as bad of an influence on her as she was on me, we'd better start saving up bail money now."

He nodded. "I can believe that." He tucked the picture back in his pocket, came over, and pushed my hair behind my ear. "You sure you're all right if I take off for a little bit?"

"Yeah, I'm good."

"Hey, Adrianne. About how long will this take?" he asked.

She thought for a second, then shook her head. "Not long. Half an hour, maybe."

"Perfect." He kissed my lips. "I'll be back."

Warren left, and Adrianne helped Mrs. Antley over to the stationary hair dryer in the corner, then lowered the dryer over the woman's head and twisted the dial on the timer. "Where's he going?" she asked.

I shrugged. "I have no idea."

She flipped on the television that was mounted in the corner of the room before walking back to her station. "All right, girl-friend. Get your butt over here before my next client shows up."

I walked to her chair while she retrieved a clean, long black smock from the linen closet in the corner. When I sat, she fastened the smock around my neck. I stared at her in the mirror. "I mean it, Adrianne. Don't you dare whack all my hair off without asking. I want to be able to wear it up for the wedding."

She spun me around to face her. "Don't play the wedding card with me. We both know you want it long enough to yank it up in a ponytail when you don't feel like washing your hair."

I smiled. "And that is why you're my best friend."

"Speaking of wedding stuff, what are your plans next week?" She hosed my hair with water from her spray bottle. "We've got work to do."

I crossed my arms. "So now that Azrael is out of town, you want to make time for me?"

She combed my long bangs over my face. "Something like that. We need to visit the florist and the caterer."

"Yeah," I said. "Brienne needs the order for the cake too. I promised her I would get it done."

"How are you doing with the guest list?" she asked.

"The what?"

She sliced my bangs off below my chin. "Sloan!"

I held my hands up. "You didn't tell me to make a list."

Exasperated, she put a hand on her hip. "Do I have to tell you everything?"

"Yes!"

She leaned in my face, bracing her hands on the armrests of my chair. "I need you to make a list of everyone you're inviting to the wedding. We need names and addresses."

"What about emails?"

She thumped me on the head with her comb. "We're not sending email invitations." She moved to the left side of my head. "And you need to finish the list tonight and tomorrow so we can put the invitations together on Sunday and mail them on Monday."

I raised an eyebrow. "Do we have invitations?"

She sighed. "One of my clients does them and we ordered fifty from her. You paid for them, remember?"

I squished my mouth over to one side.

She groaned.

"Do I have them?" I asked.

"No. I have them. I don't trust you." Adrianne shook my shoulders. "All I need you to do is create a guest list with addresses. It's not that hard."

"OK. I can handle it," I said.

"Yes, you can," she said, combing out another section of my hair.

On the television to my right, I heard the familiar syrupy-sweet and over-rehearsed voice of my arch-nemesis. My head whipped toward the television. "This is WKNC news at noon! Hello and welcome, I'm Shannon Green and this is your—"

"Oh my god!" Adrianne shrieked.

I threw my hands toward the television. "I know! Can you believe they let her—"

"No, Sloan! Your hair!"

I looked up to see the horrified countenance of my best friend. "What? What happened?"

She covered her mouth with her hand and squealed. "Her voice...and then you looked, and I looked and your head moved..." She picked up a huge chunk of hair at the back of my head. "I was cutting the side, and when you moved your head, I caught this back piece between the blades."

My mouth fell open as she lifted the severed bunch that was at least a half an inch thick.

"There's no way I can blend this." Adrianne looked like she was about to burst into tears. "Sloan, I'm so sorry."

I looked at Adrianne. I looked at the television. I looked at the clump of hair in Adrianne's hand, then I looked back at Shannon

Green's bouncy blond head on the TV screen. "Oh my god!" Instead of crying, I erupted in giggles.

Adrianne exchanged a nervous glance with one of her coworkers as I went into a fit of uncontrollable laughter.

"Shannon Green butchered my hair!" I covered my face and howled into my hand. "Of course she did! It's like her ongoing revenge!"

After a second, Adrianne started to relax. I spun around in the chair and took the hair from her hand. "It's not your fault, Adrianne." I pointed the hair at the screen.

"It's Shannon's fault!" We both screamed and laughed together.

Warren's eyes were huge when he walked back into the salon a half an hour later. "Whoa."

"Do you like it?" I asked.

He nodded as he walked over. "I really like it."

Adrianne ended up cutting it all short in the back and layering it longer toward the front, creating an angled bob with long bangs that framed my face. I kind of looked like Posh Spice, but when was that ever a bad thing?

His head fell to the side. "I don't think you'll be putting it up in a ponytail anytime soon."

I sighed. "Nope, but Adrianne promised it will be easy to manage."

"It will be," she said behind me.

"What changed your mind?" he asked.

"Shannon Green."

His head snapped back. "What?"

We told him the whole story and he laughed, shaking his head in disbelief.

"I still can't believe it happened," Adrianne said,

"Me either," I agreed. "I can't wait to tell Nathan."

CHAPTER THIRTEEN

*A*DRIANNE HAD AN armful of colorful flowers when I opened the front door to her on Sunday morning. She offered them to me as she stepped inside. "If you weren't pregnant, I would've brought you beer instead."

"What are these for?" I asked.

"They're I'm-sorry-I-screwed-up-your-hair flowers." she said, slipping off her coat and hanging it by the door.

I touched the back of my short neckline. "Honestly, I love it. My hair has been long my whole life. If I'd known how easy this was to take care of, I'd have told you to chop it off years ago."

She forced a hesitant smile. "Really?"

"Absolutely. Besides, we got a great story out of it." I chuckled all the way to the kitchen.

"Yes, we did," she said.

"Thanks for the flowers though. They're beautiful."

"You're welcome. Oh! I didn't even notice the back wall. When did they get it finished?" she called from the living room.

"Uh, Thursday," I said, pulling out a vase I kept hidden under the sink. "We still need to paint it, and Warren has to fix the back deck, but other than that, the house is almost as good as new." She walked into the kitchen and I pointed at her. "You should have come over last week. One of the construction guys was *hot.*"

"Too bad I missed that."

I thought of Azrael. "I know. Too bad."

"How did you do with the list this weekend?" she asked.

When the vase was full, I stuck the flowers into it, then carried the vase to the table. I put them in the center and picked up the notepad that was resting at my place. "Thirty-eight names and addresses. *Voilà!*"

She slowly clapped her hands. "I'm so proud of you," she said, taking the notebook from me. "We can knock these out and get them in the mailbox today."

"I'm sure I'll have a few more that I've forgotten about as we go through them."

Adrianne held up the small boutique paper bag. "We'll have extras."

She sat at the table and began pulling papers out of the bag.

Warren came downstairs wearing navy jogging pants with a stripe down the side and a fitted white thermal long-sleeve shirt. "Hey, Adrianne."

"Good morning," she replied.

"Nice flowers," he said, kissing me on the cheek. "From your other boyfriend?"

"Yep. He loves me more than you do." I sat next to Adrianne and picked up a pen. "Where are you off to?"

"Going for a run."

I frowned. "Gross. Have fun."

He nodded and jogged to the front door. "Hey, I told your dad we'd come by for lunch today at noon. Hope that's OK."

"That's fine, but why?"

"Beats me. Adrianne, you're invited too."

"Thanks!" she said.

He looked at his watch. "I'll be back in an hour or so."

"Don't freeze, and watch for cars!"

He closed the door behind him.

"Does he usually run?" Adrianne asked as she filled out the front of an envelope with my Aunt Joan's mailing address.

"Every day almost," I said.

She looked over at me. "Do you ever go with him?"

"Ha! You know that's a dumb question." I pointed to the stack of envelopes. "Hand me one."

"Does Azrael run?" she asked.

"Occasionally when he needs to talk to Warren and doesn't want me eavesdropping," I said. "He says he doesn't have to, though, to stay in shape."

She made a sour face. "I wish I didn't have to."

"You don't."

She laughed. "And I'm not in shape."

"Whatever. You look great."

With a little more flair than was probably necessary, she flipped the envelope over when she finished with it. "You know what? You're right. I *do* look great." She flattened her palms on the table. "And I'm perky and funny, and guys like me. A lot. Always."

"I agree."

"Then what's wrong with him?" she whined, dropping her forehead on top of her hands.

"Who? Azrael?"

"Ugh. Yes, of course Azrael. Who else would I be talking about?" She straightened and grabbed another blank envelope. "I know he's interested in me. Why won't he make a move?"

I'd seen her throwing herself at him, but I didn't see much reciprocation. "Not to be rude, but what makes you so sure he's interested?"

"When you and Warren aren't around, he's different with me. He's...I dunno, lighter, or something." Her eyes drifted to the side. "He smiles more. And he laughs a lot."

My face must have conveyed my doubt because she shoved me in the shoulder.

"I mean it. You don't see him when it's just the two of us. I *know* he's interested, but he won't admit it, and I can't understand why."

"You've got to stop trying to figure him out like he's a normal guy. There's no use in trying to make sense of anything he does because he's *not human*." I over-enunciated the last part slowly.

She clenched her fist around the pen and raised it in the air. "I know. He's so frustrating!"

"He's had a bazillion years to practice patience, Adrianne. You're not going to wait him out on this. Maybe you should take the next few weeks that he's gone to focus on other things. Focus on other people. Trust me, you don't want this life if you can help it."

"Are you saying you're not happy?"

"No, I'm very happy," I said, "but it's been so nice the past week with some peace and quiet. Azrael took Lamal with him to Claymore to hopefully give Abaddon and the others one less reason to rain down hell on this place, and it's almost been normal around here." I sighed and looked out the window. "I was beginning to forget what normal feels like."

A flash of Nathan holding my angel pin flickered through my mind, but I quickly dismissed the thought and turned back to Adrianne. Her face was sad.

I put my hand on her arm. "You deserve better." I wanted to shake her. "You always deserve better."

Her bottom lip poked out. "Why couldn't you have been born a man, Sloan? You're my soulmate. You know that?"

I smiled. "I know. I always will be."

She faked a cry. "Then why are you marrying some stupid boy?"

I laughed. "Two days ago you were jumping all over me for not doing enough wedding planning. Now you're mad because I'm getting married at all."

She sighed. "I'm gonna miss you, that's all."

"I'm not going anywhere," I said. "I may be marrying Warren, but you"—I pointed at her—"are stuck with me *forever.*"

"Sloan, let's take your car," Warren suggested as he put on his coat.

I grabbed my keys off the hook by the door and handed them to him. "OK. How come?"

"The back seat is bigger. We don't need Adrianne's legs getting cramped," he said.

I wound my scarf around my neck. "You don't ever worry about my legs getting cramped."

Adrianne patted me on the top of the head. "That's because you're a wee little one," she said in a munchkin voice.

We walked out to my car, and Adrianne and I climbed into the back seat. Warren and Reuel got in the front. Adrianne surveyed our small space. "You're going to be driving a minivan before you know it."

"Bite your tongue!"

Warren laughed and backed out of my driveway.

It was a nice day in Asheville for February. It was cold, but the sun was bright and the skies were blue. The drive up the mountain toward my dad's house was beautiful, as always. Maybe Warren was distracted by the scenery too because he drove right past my dad's driveway.

"Uhh, you missed it," I said.

"Oh, you're right. I did."

Something in his voice caught my attention. "What's going on?"

Adrianne was trying to hide her smile by focusing out the side window.

"You guys are being weird. Something's up," I said.

Up the street, Warren put on the blinker and turned left into a wide driveway of a house that was built into the side of a small slope. It had a three-car garage on the lower level and a pathway that wound up to the front door. A black, luxury sedan was parked in the driveway.

"Warren, this isn't my dad's house."

He turned around in his seat and smiled at me. "I know. It's *our* house."

I blinked. "What?"

"Well, it's our house if you want it, anyway."

"Wait. What?" I asked again.

He laughed. "Get out of the car."

Adrianne got out first, then pulled me out of the back seat. A woman with auburn hair in a sharp business suit was getting out of the sedan. Warren walked over with his hand outstretched. "Thanks for meeting us, Linda," he said.

The two of them walked back to the rest of us. The woman smiled and reached to shake my hand. "You must be Sloan."

"Uh...Hello?" It sounded more like a question than a greeting.

"Sloan, this is Linda Cagle. She's our real estate agent," Warren said.

I shook her hand. "Um, I didn't know we had a real estate agent."

Warren winked. "Surprise."

I laughed a little nervously.

"Linda, these are our friends, Adrianne and Reuel," Warren said.

Linda shook their hands as well. Then she looked back at me. "Would you like to see inside?"

I looked at Adrianne who was nodding excitedly. "Sure," I said.

Warren took my hand. "I hope you're not mad."

"Mad?" I shook my head. "No. I'm shocked though. I didn't realize we were this serious about moving yet."

We started up the steps on the bank. "Well, I drove by it the other day and saw the sign. Turns out they'd just put it up that afternoon. I was the first person to call about it."

"Did you buy it?" I asked as we approached the front door.

He shook his head. "No, but I did make an offer. Contingent upon your liking it, of course." He leaned close and lowered his voice to a whisper. "You're going to like it. I promise."

I already liked the outside, and I really liked how close it was to my dad. But looking up at the two-story, like-new structure, I wondered how on Earth we would afford it. Neither of us had jobs with paychecks anymore, and this wasn't a cheap part of town. As sick as it made me, Azrael had set up a direct deposit to my bank account to pay the bills, but it certainly wouldn't cover anything like this. My stomach was flip-flopping between excitement and nausea.

But all that fizzled away when Linda stuck the key in the front door and pushed it open. I swear, trumpets from Heaven sounded as we stepped into the bright, massive living space. Two couches were centered on the shiny hardwood floor, angled around a massive stone fireplace that stretched all the way up to the wooden beam rafters of the high ceiling. Three of my living rooms could have fit between the fireplace and where we stood at the door. My silent, awestruck lips parted.

"I told you," Warren whispered in my ear.

"Is this what you were doing yesterday?" I asked.

"Yeah. I went by Linda's office to sign the contract."

"What did Azrael say?"

He cringed. "He has no idea. I haven't told anyone."

I laughed, really hard. "I've never been more proud of you."

He touched my arm. "Come on. I want you to see all of it."

The kitchen and dining area were in the same room, on the very far side of it. A heavy chandelier with tall pillar lights hung over a table large enough to seat everyone in our growing clan. Reuel went to inspect the kitchen closer, or to look for unsecured snacks. Beyond the kitchen, two French doors opened to the back deck that was screened in with rocking chairs and a built-in gas fire pit.

"The master bedroom is through here," Linda said, leading us through a large, dark wooden door.

The bedroom was massive, making the king size bed look like a double. And the bathroom...oh, the bathroom. It had a glass shower big enough to share and a separate tub that could have easily held two of mine from the townhouse.

I looked at Warren. "Where do we sign?"

He laughed and draped his arms over my shoulders, linking his hands behind my neck. "Yeah?"

"Absolutely." I took a step closer to him. "But can we afford this place?" I whispered.

"Yes."

"How?"

"I've got the down payment in savings, and we're on the Almighty's payroll now, remember?" he said with a grin.

He meant it to be funny, but it made me sad instead. Aside from our upcoming wedding, buying our first house was the most normal thing we'd ever done as a couple. The thought of it ultimately coming from Azrael's bottom line tainted the moment for me just a bit. Fortunately, those reservations were quickly squelched by the excited grin on Warren's face as he grabbed my hand and pulled me through a second door in the bedroom.

"This is supposed to be an office." He put his hand on my stomach. "But I was thinking it could be the nursery."

I put my hands on the sides of his face and kissed him. "I love you."

"I love you too."

On the same floor were two other bedrooms. The last one overlooked the mountains that were beginning to pop with the green of springtime. I stood in the doorway and looked out the window.

Warren slipped his arms around me from behind. "What are you thinking about?"

"My mom would have loved this place."

"Your dad said the same thing."

I smiled. "I want this to be Taiya's room whenever we get her back."

"I think that's a great idea."

I turned around in his arms. "We are going to get her back, aren't we?"

His face was serious. "I promise. If it's the last thing I ever do."

On our way home, we stopped at my dad's for lunch and told him the good news about the house. His eyes teared up when I said that in three weeks we'd almost be neighbors. It was then I realized that being so close to him would be the biggest perk of all, even above the giant bathtub and the fire pit.

When we got back to the townhouse, Adrianne came inside so we could plan out all our wedding planning stops for the next day. She picked up the stack of invitations that were still sitting on the table. "Hey, Warren. Can you put these out in the mailbox before we forget?"

"Sure."

He carried them out the front door, and Adrianne began making a list. "We've got the caterer at nine, and the flower shop said we can stop by whenever we have time."

"Put Brienne on the list too," I said. "I can't forget to go place the order for the cake."

Reuel spun toward me.

I laughed. "Yes, you can come."

"What kind of cake are you going to order?"

"Chocolate. Duh."

Warren came back in, carrying a stack of mail with him. He handed it to me. "This was in the box. Guess we didn't check it yesterday."

"Thank you." I thumbed through the stack until a simple, printed white envelope took my breath. "Uh oh."

"What is it?" he asked.

I held it up to read the return seal out loud. "U.S. Department of Justice, Federal Bureau of Investigations." It was addressed to me. "I wonder what it is."

"You won't know until you read it," Adrianne said.

I gulped and tore it open. There was a white folded piece of paper with a small yellow sheet of paper inside it. The white page was typed.

Dear Sloan,

This letter was sent to Marisol Juarez's public defender the day before she died. It was written to you. I'm not sure what she is talking about. Hoping you will. Let me know.

Regards,
Agent S. Silvers

I opened the yellow sheet and saw Marisol's flowing cursive. She had the penmanship of a fairy godmother. "It's a letter from Marisol."

Warren looked over my shoulder.

"The woman who killed herself in the prison?" Adrianne asked.

"Yes."

"What does it say?"

I read it aloud.

. . .

Dear Sloan,

By the time this letter finds you, I'll be gone. I hope you don't feel responsible in any way for the decision I made. It is simply time for me to face whatever sentence awaits me from the only judge who truly matters. Perhaps, He will be merciful and reunite me with my Maria. That is my prayer. Either way, my heart is at peace knowing my little girl hasn't been in torment all these years, and I will be eternally grateful to you for sharing that with me.

After you left, I thought of a few more things you might find useful or interesting. Taiya's mother might be a woman named Melinda Harmon, or maybe it's Hamilton, I can't really remember. Several years ago there was talk of her being a problem, but I don't recall the details.

And finally, Phenex had a child before she took my daughter's body. I'm not sure what happened to her, but if she's alive, maybe she can help you. All I know is her name was Alice.

I sincerely hope I've helped you come closer to putting a stop to their evil. I only wish there was more I could do.

Yours truly,
Marisol

When I looked up at Warren, he was as pale as I'd ever seen him, including the day he died at Calfkiller River. "What is it? You look like you've seen a ghost."

His eyes slowly turned to meet mine. "Maybe I did. Sloan, I think Phenex's daughter was *my* Alice."

It took a moment for my brain to process the name, and when it did, I'm pretty sure my face turned as white as his. I covered my mouth with my hand. "Oh my god. Alice, the girl you were in the foster system with."

He sat back in his seat and stared up at the ceiling.

Alice, the little girl who had been abused by the child molester Warren killed when he was eight.

Alice, the teenager who had overdosed in Warren's arms.

Alice, the only family Warren had ever had.

I crumpled forward and buried my face in my hands. "I don't believe it. How can this even be possible?"

When I looked back at him, it was clear he was searching his thoughts. "Phenex took Maria's body because Azrael destroyed her first body."

I pointed at him. "And Azrael said Phenex was pregnant when he destroyed her and the baby lived."

"Alice would have been your age, Sloan."

I gulped.

He bolted up out of his seat. "We need to go."

"Go where?"

"I need to talk to Azrael."

"Azrael's not here," I reminded him. "You're going to go to Claymore?"

He didn't answer, but I could tell he was considering it.

I grabbed the tail of his shirt and pulled him beside me at the table. "Calm down and let's talk this through."

"I don't understand. What's going on?" Adrianne asked.

"Your pseudo-boyfriend is a big fat liar," I said.

"What did he do?"

"He likes withholding information." I pointed at her. "Which is another very good reason you should give up and move on." I turned back to Warren. "We're jumping straight to the certainty that it's the same Alice. Maybe it's a coincidence."

His loud laughter mocked me. "You, of all people. Did you use the word *coincidence*?"

I sighed. "OK, but why wouldn't he tell us this? Maybe he didn't know."

Warren shook his head. "He knew. How could he not know?"

"Who is Alice?" Adrianne asked.

Warren pushed his chair back. "You explain. I need to go think for a while." He walked through the living room and out the front door, slamming it closed behind him. He hadn't even bothered to put on a coat over his black t-shirt.

Adrianne nudged me. "Explain."

"She's a girl who was in the foster system with Warren when they were kids. She was horribly abused and then got mixed up in drugs when she was older. She died, Adrianne," I said.

Adrianne turned her palms up on the table. "Did Azrael kill her?"

"No."

"So why are you mad at him?"

"Because he knew and he didn't help her," I said.

Her brow crumpled with doubt. "I've noticed he's not the kind of person who decides to act or not act without a good reason."

"He's not a person at all. You keep forgetting that," I reminded her.

"It's a matter of semantics."

I brushed my new angled bangs out of my face to more effectively glare at her. "It's a matter of *biology*."

She ignored me. "You know what I think is really going on here? He didn't help Warren when he was a kid, and that's what you're really mad about."

I tossed my hands up. "Well, yeah! That's definitely part of it. Who abandons their kid and lets them grow up like that?"

Adrianne leaned toward me. "I don't know if you've noticed this or not, but Warren's a pretty spectacular guy."

"I know that."

"Maybe that's because of how he grew up. Did you ever consider that?"

I hadn't, to be honest.

"Maybe Warren turned out so great because Azrael did abandon him."

I let out a deep sigh. "I don't trust him, Adrianne." It was the first time I'd admitted it out loud. "I want to. I know that I should. I just don't trust Azrael."

She paused and studied the table for a minute before finally speaking. "Sloan, you're a very open-book kind of person. And you distrust anyone who isn't the type to throw all their business out on the table. You've got to get over that. Not everyone is like you. It doesn't automatically disqualify them from being a good person."

Dang.

"Why don't you tell me how you really feel?" I said with a smirk.

"I love you, and sometimes you need a bit of verbal bitch-slapping. Today is that day."

"Thank you?" I was more confused than truly grateful. But maybe she was right. I was the type to throw all my feelings out for the world to sort through, and it wasn't easy for me to trust others who didn't do the same. However, the man wearing a path on the sidewalk in front of my house with his frantic pacing was of the closed-book sort, and his anger superseded my own.

Warren didn't trust Azrael either, and that worried me more than anything else.

Warren came back in after a few minutes and went straight upstairs without a word. Adrianne got up from the table and picked up my notebook. "I'm going to let you go handle that." She nodded toward the stairs. "Shall I pick you up at eight in the morning? Maybe we can squeeze in breakfast at Sunny Point."

I walked her to the door. "Sounds good."

Her face twisted with confusion as she put on her jacket. "8 a.m. sounds good? You must be worried."

I laughed and shook my head. "I'll see you in the morning."

"Love you, freak." She pulled the front door open and walked outside.

"Love you too."

At the bottom of the steps, I took a few deep breaths. Then I took the stairs two at a time up to my bedroom. I heard Reuel's television on in the guest room as I passed by to my door which was closed. I knocked lightly, which felt strange in my own house. I didn't wait for a response before I eased it open.

"Warren?"

The shower was running in the bathroom.

I slipped off my shoes by the bed and walked to the bathroom. I pushed the door open and a wall of steam rolled over me. "Warren?" I called out softly into the cloud.

He still didn't answer.

When enough of the haze cleared, I saw his silhouette through the obscured shower door. I crossed the room and silently slipped out of my clothes. He didn't move when I slowly slid the door back. He was facing the shower with his arms braced against the wall, and his head was down so that water streamed all around his face. I could tell by the subtle shudder of his shoulders that he was crying.

Silently, I crept up behind him and wrapped my arms around him. He wept harder, and I tightened my grip around his middle. I rested my cheek against his spine and held him without the need to inquire what was wrong. When I was eight, my greatest trauma was being pelted with a rock; when Warren was eight, he killed a man to save his best friend. And years later it destroyed her anyway.

Even though he never said it, I suspected he may have been in love with Alice. It was in the watery far-off look that betrayed him whenever her name was said out loud. And it was in the slight hitch in his voice when he called her "*my* Alice."

"I should have saved her," he said loud enough for me to hear over the shower.

"There was nothing you could have done."

"Maybe if I hadn't been there. Maybe she wouldn't have gotten worse."

"Warren, if you hadn't been there, she would have died alone."

He heaved in a deep breath. "Do you ever stop and think about how sick all this is?"

"I try not to," I admitted.

He turned his face to look over his shoulder. "They did this to us, Sloan. They made me into a—"

"Shhh." I pulled on his arm to force him to turn and look at me. He did and pushed his wet hair back out of his face. I put my hands on his chest. "You listen to me. What you've lived through, most people can't even imagine in their scariest nightmares. And not only did you survive, but you became the strongest, bravest, and most selfless man I've ever met. Don't you ever, *ever* forget that."

He searched my eyes. "You know there's nothing I wouldn't do for you."

I touched his cheek. "I know."

He bent and when his lips touched mine, a hot swell of his power flowed into me. The nerves in my spine prickled with energy as his fingers slipped back through my hair and held my mouth firmly in sync with his. My knees wobbled, but his right arm snaked around my waist, pulling me against his hard, wet body as he moved me back against the shower wall.

The tips of his fingers dug into my hip while his other hand took mine and pulled it up in the air between us. Pushing gently against my side, he spun me under his arm till my back was against his chest and my breasts were pressed against the cool, slick tiles. He flattened his palm on top of mine against the wall as he buried himself in me from behind.

Arching against him, I reached back for his neck as he bit my shoulder, and the world spun in and out of focus.

CHAPTER FOURTEEN

*S*EX DOESN'T ALWAYS fix everything, but it damn sure doesn't make things worse...not with Warren, anyway. Our post-coital pillow talk was also productive because I convinced him to wait till Azrael came home to inquire about Alice. I knew that confrontation was coming soon enough, and when it did, we needed to have all the facts.

After Warren fell asleep, and while I could still hold my eyes open, I emailed Agent Silvers to ask her to dig into Alice's background. I hoped I was wrong and that Az would turn up as blameless as Adrianne believed he was, but Warren had once told me to "hope for the best, but have your guns locked and loaded for the worst," so that's what I was doing.

It took over a week, but I finally got a call from Silvers's private cell phone number.

"Hello?"

"Hi, Sloan."

"Hey, Agent Silvers. Hang on. Let me grab Warren." I ran through the house out to where Warren and Reuel were staining the deck they'd rebuilt. "Silvers is on the phone."

Warren handed his paintbrush to Reuel and followed me back inside.

We walked to the kitchen, and I pulled a pen and notepad from the junk drawer before sitting next to Warren at the kitchen table. "Please tell me you've got something useful." I clicked the speakerphone button and laid the phone in the center of the table.

"A few things, I hope," she said. "Again, this is all strictly off the record."

"I understand."

She cleared her throat and I heard papers shuffling in the background. "OK, first. Let's talk about Alice Delaney."

I started scribbling notes, and Warren leaned on his elbow.

"Alice Delaney was found at a fire station on Foster Avenue in Northern Chicago on March 19th, 1985. The doctors said she was only a few hours old when she was brought to the hospital. Her first set of foster parents were Fred and Maxine Delaney. The Delaneys adopted her, but Alice was eventually removed by Child Protective Services in 1990 after reports of physical abuse were filed. I found some medical reports saying she was developmentally delayed and was referred to speech therapy.

"Fast forward to two foster families later, and she was placed along with Warren into the home of Ellen Burke, a nurse at Caldwell Memorial Hospital. Both children were removed from the home following the death of Burke's boyfriend, Charlie Lockett."

I glanced at Warren to make sure he was OK. His eyes were fixed on the table. "Does it say anything more about her being found at the fire station? Was there a note or another person involved?" he asked without looking up.

"I'm sorry. There's nothing like that. It only says she was found," Silvers said.

I tapped my pen against the pad of paper. This wasn't the conclusive evidence I'd hoped for.

"On a different subject, I did find some information on the other woman mentioned in Marisol Juarez's letter to you. She mentioned that a woman named Melinda Harmon, or Hamilton, could be your friend Taiya's mother."

I perked up in my seat. "Go on."

"Well, there are no records of Taiya's birth, but Melinda Harmon, age 45 from Brooklyn, pressed charges against Abner Tuinstra for domestic abuse back in the mid-eighties. The charges were dismissed. There's not a lot on her except for two minor drug possession charges over the years and a recent court-appointed stint at Wards Island Adult Psychiatric Center. I was able to find a cell phone registered in her name, but that's the extent of personal property or accounts tied to her. I've subpoenaed the phone company for the call history, but that may take a while to get back."

"Can you get me a picture of her? Do you have one?" I asked.

"Sure. I can email you an old mug shot if you think it will help," she said.

"Yeah, old or new, it doesn't matter."

"I'll send it over when we get off the phone."

"Thank you." I looked at Warren. "Do you have more questions?"

He shook his head. "Not right now. Thanks for your help, Agent Silvers."

"You're welcome. I'll let you know when I get the phone records."

I disconnected the call and sat back in my chair. "So, essentially, we know nothing more than we did."

He blew out a sigh. "Not a damn thing."

My phone beeped with and incoming email. It was from a private, generic email address.

See attached photo. -S.S.

. . .

I tapped the file and a woman's face popped up on the screen. She had over-processed, bleached blond hair that was cut in uneven layers that flipped out all around her face. Heavy bags sagged beneath her pale blue eyes and her upper lip was cocked in a quizzical snarl.

"Well, she's alive," Warren said. "Know where she is?"

I focused on her for a few seconds, but finally huffed and shook my head. "I've got nothing."

Warren drummed his finger on the table. "It's times like this that I wish Nate was still around. He's better at linking facts together than I am."

"Me too."

"Have you heard from him lately?" he asked.

I shook my head. "Not since that first letter. I wonder how he's doing."

"Maybe you should try to summon him."

I pressed my lips together. "Hmm. You really think I should?"

He shrugged. "What could it hurt?"

"What if he gets in trouble with Az?"

"Screw Azrael," Warren barked.

"OK." I closed my eyes and reached out with my gift to find Nathan out in the universe. I pulled him to me, and for the first time ever...nothing happened.

After a week, I was really beginning to worry. After two weeks, I was ready to drive myself to Claymore. We heard nothing from Nathan—no calls, no letters, nada. For the first time ever, I realized how dependent I'd become on my powers, and despite how many times I'd wished them away during my life, I was now completely lost without them.

We also heard nothing from Azrael, which was equally disconcerting given his permanent placement up my ass since the day he arrived. Warren kept reminding me they were training together, and that Azrael probably had safeguards against powers such as mine, but it was obvious even he was anxious to make contact with them.

My nerves weren't helped at all by the surge of thunderstorms that had taken residence over the state of North Carolina. Each time thunder boomed, I wondered if it was The Destroyer, returning to finish the demo job on my house, or worse.

Warren kept me busy by constantly replenishing my stack of moving boxes to fill. As small as my place was, we'd acquired a lot of crap since everyone else had moved in, and after almost two weeks of cramming stuff into boxes, we still had a long way to go.

Adrianne had also written me a wedding to-do list as long as my arm. In between packing sessions, I hand painted wooden signs directing guests from Dad's driveway, around the side of the house, to the backyard—because the flowered arbor marked "WEDDING ENTRANCE" over the path around back might not be enough to keep our friends and family from wandering off the side of the mountain. I also had to cover about a thousand tea light votives with gold glitter, which had since ended up all over my side of Asheville.

Monday night was our regularly scheduled dinner date with Dad, and I was grateful for a reason to leave the house. The baby was craving some Shoo Mercy Sweet Potato Pancakes and goat cheese grits, so we picked Dad up at his office and drove to Tupelo Honey in South Asheville.

Reuel got out of the passenger's seat of my car and Dad closed his umbrella and climbed into the back seat with me. "Hey, Dad."

"Hi, sweetheart." He moved his legs to the side when Reuel straightened his seat back into place. "Goodness, Sloan. You're going to have to get a bigger car."

I sighed. "I know."

"I'm sorry if I'm tracking mud onto the floor mats," he said, looking down at his wet shoes.

"Don't worry about it. I've decided to not even bother cleaning my car till this rain finally goes away."

Up front, Warren laughed. "That's your excuse now?"

"Shut up."

"Look at me," Dad said after he clicked his seatbelt into place.

I locked eyes with his.

He grabbed my chin and turned my face from side to side. "All the bruises are completely gone. That's wonderful!"

"I know. It's great," I said.

"I'll bet Warren's happy," Dad teased.

"Oh, I am," Warren said. "How was work today, Dr. Jordan?"

He nodded. "It was quite well, *Mr. Parish*," Dad answered with an exaggerated, formal tone.

Warren smiled in the rearview.

Dad turned to me. "Do you remember Otis Cash? A patient of mine that you cured of stage four lung cancer back in November?"

"Yes."

"I saw him today. He asked about you."

"How is he?" I asked.

"He's doing great. He still doesn't realize he doesn't have cancer anymore, but he doesn't care," Dad said with a chuckle.

"How does he not know?" I asked.

Dad waved his hand. "He stopped letting anyone do tests on him when they diagnosed it as terminal. Said it stressed him out too much to know, and he wanted to enjoy every second he had left."

For the first time in a while, I thought of the first day of summer—the day Kasyade and her crew were planning to kill me and take my baby. It was a pity I was too stressed out to be able to enjoy my last days, if in fact that's what they were.

Dad put his hand on mine. "You feeling all right?"

I took a deep breath as Warren pulled onto the highway. "Yeah, just a lot on my mind."

"Stressed about the move?" he asked.

"That's part of it, I guess. It feels like we've been packing forever. Who knew we had so much stuff?"

He smiled. "You've lived there a long time."

"Four years," I said. "It's kind of hard to believe."

"You're excited, though, about the new place?"

I reached up and squeezed Warren's shoulder. "Very excited."

"When do you move in?" he asked.

"We close and get the keys one week from today," Warren answered.

"So Monday dinner next week, we'll have takeout at your new place?" Dad asked.

I nodded. "That sounds good. Can you bring pizza from Marcos?"

"You'll have to remind me. Are you hiring movers?" he asked.

Reuel turned around and raised his hand.

Dad pointed at him. "They're hiring you?"

"I already put a down payment on his services in the form of a cake from Brienne Casey," I said. "Right, Reuel?"

He held up two fingers.

I nodded. "Yes. You get another one upon completion."

Dad laughed. "Sounds like a fair payment method to me. Is she doing your wedding cake?"

"She is."

"I like Brienne. She's a nice girl," he said.

"Me too. I invited her to the wedding."

Dad looked surprised. "I didn't realize you were that close."

I shook my head. "We aren't, but Adrianne said it would be polite. Besides, I could use some more normal humans in my life, no offense to the supes in the car."

"None taken. Couldn't agree more," Warren said as he changed lanes.

"Speaking of normal humans, have you heard how the detective is fairing during his training?" Dad asked.

My heart sank into my stomach. "I got a letter from him a

couple of weeks ago, but I haven't heard from him since. It's another thing on the list of current stressors in Sloan's world."

Dad bumped his shoulder gently against mine. "I'm sure he's fine. It's not like he's at summer camp, you know?"

"I know."

"When does Azrael come back?" he asked.

"Supposed to be next week," Warren said. "But we haven't talked to him recently either."

The mention of Nathan's name had made me sad and worried. The mention of Azrael's ticked me off. I folded my arms. "I think he's avoiding us so he doesn't have to come home in time to help us move."

"Smart man," Dad said.

My phone buzzed in my pocket, but there was no way I could bend around my belly in the tiny back seat to pull it out, so I waited till we reached the restaurant to check it. When we got out of the car, I ducked under the outdoor seating's black awning to read the screen. It was a missed call from Agent Silvers.

"Dad, you and Reuel go on in. I need to make a quick call." I showed the phone to Warren. "Silvers."

He crossed his arms. "Ooo, call her back."

The rain was too loud to put it on speaker, so I called her number and pressed the phone to my ear. She answered on the third ring. "Sloan?"

"Hi, sorry I missed you. What's up?" I asked, plugging my free ear with my finger.

"I got the call log from Melinda Harmon's phone," she said. "Most of the calls originated in New York, but the last call was placed from somewhere around Hertford, North Carolina."

I looked at Warren. "Hertford, North Carolina?"

"What about it?" Warren asked, his eyes narrowing.

"The map shows it near the coast," Agent Silvers said in my ear.

"She says that's where the last call on Melinda's phone record was made from. It's somewhere near the coast."

Warren's jaw was grinding. "I know exactly where Hertford is."

"You do? Where?"

"It's about ten miles east of Claymore."

"Shut up. Seriously?"

He nodded and leaned close to the phone. "Who did she call?"

I turned on the speaker and we both leaned close enough to hear.

"She dialed 911."

A chill ran through me, but it wasn't from the cool mountain air.

"I followed up with the emergency call center, but their records show no active conversation was taped. That means before she spoke to an operator, she hung up."

Warren looked at me. "Or someone hung up for her."

I swallowed hard.

"Anything else?" Warren asked.

"No. That's all I have. What are you thinking?" Silvers asked.

Warren looked up at the darkening sky. "I'm thinking we know where our missing friend is."

"And where our friend has been this whole freaking time," I added.

"Where's that?" she asked.

Warren and I answered her together. "Claymore."

We ordered our food to go and profusely apologized to my father for cutting the evening short. Then we drove home and did some more packing, this time in a suitcase rather than cardboard boxes. After realizing there was no way either of us would get any sleep that night, we decided to leave as soon as the bags were in the back of the Challenger. We got on the road by eight o'clock and Warren drove all night in the rain with my not-so-secret security detail following the whole way.

I prayed the entire trip across the state that we were wrong. For the first time since she disappeared, I prayed we wouldn't find Taiya. Not like this. Not at this price. But I knew she was there. It was the same feeling, the same certainty I'd had when I found the bond receipt for Rex Parker and Tito Juarez in Kasyade's home office in Texas. Azrael was behind this. I knew it in my soul.

The sky was only drizzling when we pulled up to the front gate at the Claymore compound at three in the morning. The hefty guard at the gate didn't look happy as he approached Warren's window. "We're closed, buddy, and this is private property."

"Call Damon and tell him Warren is here," Warren said, eyeing the metal gate like he was thinking of driving his beloved car right through it.

"I ain't callin' nobody," the man replied, shifting the utility belt around his massive midsection.

"Fine." Warren jerked the gear shift into park and flung his door open. "Have it your way."

"Uh-oh," I said to Reuel, who was watching as intently as I was.

The guard stepped out of his shack toward Warren. The name patch sewn onto his camouflaged chest pocket said *V. Blankenship*. "Sir, I'm going to have to ask you to get back in your car before I have you arrested for trespassing."

Warren didn't even look at him before slowly raising his arms toward the gate. All he did was open his fingers and the heavy steel door was blasted from its hinges, sent spinning through the air before it landed on top of a parked Humvee.

I gasped and covered my mouth as sirens blared all over the compound. Cool and collected, Warren got back into the driver's and waved to the stunned guard as he rolled by him. I squealed with excitement. "Oh my god, that was awesome!"

His stern face didn't break. "Don't be too happy. Shit's about to get ugly."

Warren obviously knew where he was going as the car spun up

gravel on the loosely paved roads. I braced myself against the side wall to keep from being slung off my middle seat. Armed soldiers poured out of almost all the buildings we sped past.

I ducked my head in case bullets started flying. They didn't.

Warren took a sharp left to stop in front of a housing unit I recognized from the last time we were there, and rocks sprayed the side of a black SUV in the parking lot. When he pushed his driver's side door open again, I heard Azrael swearing. "Damn it, Warren. What are you doing here?"

I got out after Reuel and stayed behind him in case there was violence.

Azrael was shirtless and bleary-eyed, something I'd never seen before. We must have woken him from sleeping, which rarely ever happened. Azrael's torso was heavily scarred from years of abuse, but it looked like it had been sculpted by God himself. I was glad we'd left Adrianne at home.

"Where is she?" Warren demanded.

Azrael put his hands up. "Where is who?"

Warren grabbed his father by the throat and backed him up against the wall. "Don't feed me that bullshit, Az."

Around us, a few of Azrael's men closed in. One of them, I recognized. It was Enzo, wearing tactical pants and a twisted t-shirt because he'd clearly dressed in a hurry. Azrael halted their advance with a hand signal. He looked almost amused as he studied Warren's eyes like he was trying to decide if Warren was bluffing or holding a winning hand.

"Enzo," Azrael said. "Bring me the girl."

I almost passed out there in the driveway.

Enzo turned his ear toward his boss. "Excuse me, sir?"

"Bring Taiya to me." He was glaring at Warren. "My *son* wants to see her."

Something was off. Maybe it was how the word 'son' dripped off his tongue like a curse. Or maybe it was the ominous ridicule in his tone. Whatever it was in Azrael's voice... it twisted my insides into knots.

"Yes, sir," Enzo said. He took off in a jog toward a building a little farther down the road we'd torn up on our way in.

Azrael's eyes narrowed at Warren. "Now, take your hands off me before I take them off of *you*."

This time, Reuel took a protective stride in their direction. I couldn't see his face, but his good fist was clenched at his side, ready to swing—at Azrael, I hoped.

Warren withdrew his hand, leaving impressions of his fingers behind on Azrael's flushed skin.

"Where's Nathan?" I asked.

Azrael laughed with heavy sarcasm. "Imagine that." He cut his eyes at Warren. "Your wife is worried about Nathan McNamara."

"Where is he?" Warren asked.

"He's in training. Exactly where he's supposed to be!" Azrael's raised voice was terrifying. He pointed at another man who looked vaguely familiar. "Go get him."

I shrank back behind Reuel again.

The squeak from the door to our right caught my ear. It was accompanied by the desperately angry pleas of a woman with a sharp Brooklyn accent. I looked over in time to see Enzo step out into the moonlight with a body cradled in his arms. It was Taiya. Right behind him, Melinda Harmon pounded his shoulder. She was wearing nothing but a nightgown, not even shoes.

"She needs to be in the bed! What'ah ya' doin'?" Melinda was crying as she pulled on Enzo's arm.

His face was set. "I'm following orders, ma'am."

"Screw his ordahs! Take her back to her room! She can't be out here in this wet, freezin' cold!"

I sprinted across the lawn until I reached them. Taiya was even thinner than she had been before, if that was possible, and her pallid skin was translucent, showcasing her small veins and the bones of her tiny arms. She had a disconnected I.V. in her hand and a nasogastric tube taped up her nose.

"What did you do to her?" I cried out.

"I saved her pathetic, miserable life," Azrael hissed as he stalked toward us, followed by Warren and Reuel.

"Enzo, put her down. Gently," I said. He eased her onto the grass. Using my fingers, I pulled her left eyelid open. Her wide pupil tightened slightly against the light from the streetlamp. A good sign.

Melinda knelt beside me. Her hair was wild and her eyes bloodshot from being woken up. "Who are you?" she asked.

"I'm a friend of your daughter's," I said. "My name is Sloan."

Her head pulled back. "Sloan? *The Sloan?*"

I sighed. "Probably so." I looked up at where Azrael and Warren were now standing over me. "You lied to me, Azrael. You've lied to all of us for months!"

"I tried to get you to come here," he barked. "Remember those conversations that you wouldn't have any part of?"

"But you didn't tell me she was here. Why didn't you bring her to me?" I asked.

"Because she's going to kill you!"

I blinked and sank back onto the ground.

Azrael put his hands on his hips and looked up at the stars. "The Destroyer told me at the camp that Taiya was programmed to kill you. That's not something to take lightly. I had to find her before you in order to keep you safe."

I touched her cold face. "Azrael, look at her. She couldn't kill a houseplant!"

He pointed at me. "And that's exactly what's going to get you killed. Any human too close to you is dangerous, and much more so one you underestimate as much as Taiya."

I picked up her limp arm and dropped it onto the grass. "Are you kidding me?"

"She's a robot, Sloan. Her whole life she's been brainwashed to do what they tell her to do. Don't forget who sent her in the first place. Do you think Ysha thought you were lonely and needed a new friend?"

Just then, Nathan came stumbling out the door of a large building across the yard in front of us. When he got closer, I saw his hair was standing straight up in the back, and he was rubbing his eyes. He wore black gym shorts and a zip-up gray hoodie with CLAYMORE WORLDWIDE embroidered across the front. He had one white tube sock and one white ankle sock with a pair of black flip-flops. "What the hell's going on out here?" he asked through a yawn. "Sloan? Warren? What are you guys doing here?" He noticed Taiya lying on the ground. "Holy shit...is that Taiya?"

I pressed the heels of my palms against my eyes as dots of information connected in my brain. "Oh my god. This is why you sent Nathan here! This is why you gave him this crazy job he's not qualified for, isn't it?"

Azrael didn't respond.

Warren looked at me. "Nathan's a liability because he's human."

"Yes, I've told you that for months!" Azrael shouted. He pointed at Nathan. "You didn't believe me even after he tried to kill you. I thought for sure *that* would teach you a lesson!"

"Teach me a lesson?" My mind was spinning on his words as I turned over onto my knees and pushed myself up. "You thought it would teach me a lesson?"

Images flashed through my mind. Nathan and I in my bed. His hands clenched around my throat. My killing power blasting into him. Warren's fists pounding Nathan's skull while Azrael sat by the campfire and laughed. The guilt I'd felt every day since...

Anger inside me was about to boil over. "How did I not see this before?"

"I know I'm half asleep right now, but what's she talking about?" Nathan asked, stepping over beside Warren.

My jaw was clenched as I slowly closed the space between Azrael and myself. "It was you. The night Nathan and I...in my room. The night I almost destroyed him!" I jammed my finger into the center of his chest. "It was you!"

Azrael took a few steps backward and put his hands up between. "Sloan, listen to me. Everything I've done, I've done to—"

"I'm going to kill you." I was shaking my head, trying to keep my sanity and failing. "I'm going to kill you!" I lunged for him, but with a loud *crack*, Azrael vanished into the night sky.

CHAPTER FIFTEEN

"WHEA' THE HELL did that guy go?" Melinda's nasal voice pierced the stunned silence left by Azrael's sudden departure.

Warren looked at me. "He warped somewhere safer than here."

"Warped? What is this—Star Trek?" Melinda asked, curling her lip up on one side.

Nathan laughed.

Everyone else seemed too shocked to move. Some of the guys were looking around the grounds, a few others were searching the sky. Enzo finally pointed toward the building he'd come from with Taiya. "We need to get her back inside." He slipped his arms underneath Taiya's knees and behind her back. "Follow me."

Nathan fell in step between me and Warren. "I'm really confused. When did Taiya get here?"

My teeth were still clenched with rage. "I don't know," I said. "How long has she been gone?"

Nathan looked at me. "You think she's been here all this time?"

I nodded. "Looks like it."

"I got here Christmas night," Melinda called over her shoulder to us. "Taiya was brought in a few days before me."

"Yep. Then she's been here the whole time then," I said with a sigh. "Why would he do this?"

"I have no idea," Warren answered.

Nathan looked over at me. "Did you cut your hair?"

"Adrianne did."

"I like it."

We crossed the lot to the building he'd come out of, an unremarkable structure that was five or six stories high and made out of concrete. There were no windows and only one door in and out.

"Cooper, get the door," Enzo said to the guy I'd seen earlier.

I suddenly realized why he looked familiar. I'd saved him from being tossed off a cliff at Calfkiller River.

"I can do it," Warren said, moving his hand past the lock.

Nothing happened.

Enzo shook his head. "That won't work at Echo-10, sir. You have to be scanned into the building."

Cooper used a retina scanner to unlock the door.

"This is Echo-10?" I asked.

"Yes, ma'am." Enzo carried Taiya inside, then we followed him and Melinda with Reuel and Nathan on our heels.

Nathan paused at the doorway. "I'm not sure of protocol now. Am I allowed in here?"

Warren waved him forward. "Protocol left the planet, man."

A little bewildered and still very sleepy, Nathan scratched his head and walked inside.

Compared to the outside, and considering its bland and simple shape, the interior was remarkable. The doorway led into an L-shaped lobby with an elevator to our left. To the right of it, two glass sliding doors appeared to lead into some kind of living space with a loft. Straight down the long tiled hall in front of us were a series of open doors off to the right.

We followed Enzo down the hall. The first couple of doors led to large office rooms, but the third door was marked with a medical cross. Melinda opened it to what looked like a commercial urgent care facility.

There was a nurses' station that faced two square rooms with glass doors. Enzo went into the one on the right and settled Taiya onto the hospital bed. A plump nurse in black scrubs reconnected the I.V. to Taiya's hand and then checked the pulse in her wrist. She was grumbling about moving patients in the middle of the night and not being paid enough.

"What's happening with her?" I asked the nurse as I watched from the door.

"We're slowly weaning her off life support," she answered, checking one of the machines. "She's been off the ventilator for a few weeks now. We're hoping she wakes up soon so they can take out the feeding tube. Her vitals look good."

Melinda shot a hateful glare across Taiya's bed at Enzo. "At least her vitals *did* look good before people started yankin' her out into the dead of winter!"

I looked back at Nathan. "You really didn't know she was here?"

He shook his head. "I had no idea, and I've literally been right next door. How did you know where to find her?"

"It's a long story," I said.

"Where have you been?" Warren asked him. "Sloan's been trying to call you for a week."

Nathan patted his empty pockets. "No phone, remember?"

"I wasn't using the phone. I tried to summon you but I couldn't, like the same way I couldn't find Taiya."

"It's in the walls," Enzo said, joining us outside Taiya's room. He pointed over to what I assumed was an external wall. "It's the way they're designed. A half an inch lead plate with two layers of a composite metal foam called high-Z, and then concrete and steel."

"High-Z?" Warren asked.

"It's a new material that was recently developed for the military by a research team at NC State," Enzo said. "They discovered that it blocks radiation, so we started testing to see what else it might block." He shot us a knowing glance. "This place is a fortress. Your powers bounce right off."

"But Nathan's never been in this building before," I said.

Enzo nodded. "Most of the structures have been modified in the last year. If he was indoors, he was off the grid."

"I've been indoors a lot lately with the bad weather," Nathan said.

"Wow," I said. "Why is it called Echo-10?"

He pointed up at the ceiling. "There are four floors above this one. The top is the private owner's floor, and the other three are comprised of ten separate four-man housing units."

"And the *Echo* part?" I asked.

"Like I said, nothing gets through these walls," he said.

Warren looked at me and winked. "So, no one to hear the screams."

Reuel chuckled.

Enzo smiled. "Come with me, please." He led us all back to the lobby. "The elevators go up to the living quarters, and these doors are for the common area."

The glass doors slid open and we walked inside. There was a large living area with two sectional sofas facing a flat screen television. A huge open kitchen to its left had an industrial size refrigerator and cereal dispensers on the counter. And up the center staircase was a workout room, judging from the two ellipticals and two treadmills that lined the glass loft wall. Enzo motioned to the large table near the kitchen. "Have a seat."

We all sat. "Do you know where your boss went?" Warren asked.

Enzo shook his head. "No."

"Do you think he'll come back?" I asked.

He shrugged.

"I say good riddance!" Melinda was suddenly standing beside

my chair, pointing an acrylic nail that was in desperate need of a fill-in at Enzo's face. "Your boss is as crazy as Abner."

"Abner Tuinstra?" I asked.

Her eyes cut to me. "You know him?"

"I killed him two months ago."

She beckoned me with her fingers. "Get up, honey, and let me kiss your feet."

I didn't move, but it was hard to suppress a smile.

"Two months, you say?" she asked, walking around the table and pulling a chair out next to Nathan.

"About that long," I said.

"That makes a lotta sense."

"Why?" Warren asked.

"Because that's when they locked me up. For years they said I was nuts. That I imagined the whole thing." She tapped her temple. "But I knew. And it musta been when that son of a bitch died that I really remembered everything. Nah, I wasn't nuts."

"How did you get here?" I asked her.

She gestured toward Enzo again. "Crazy bastahd had me kidnapped."

Enzo sighed. "You were *not* kidnapped."

Melinda put her thumb to her ear and her pinky to her mouth like a telephone. "This guy calls me up at the hospital in New York and says they've got my girl down here. Asks if I want to see her for the holidays. I say yes and they send me a bus ticket. I get to the bus station in Podunk B.F.E. and what happens? This whole damn army picks me up and brings me here. And they won't let me leave!" She looked at me. "Don't that sound like kidnappin' to you?"

I nodded. "A little."

Reuel nodded as well and held up two fingers millimeters apart.

Enzo crossed his arms. "We told her she could stay or she could leave on her own. Those were the terms."

"They expect me to leave here without my girl. Can you believe that? It's been years since they let me see her, now they want me to just leave. Don't tell nobody, he says. This guy," she muttered and flicked her hand toward him.

I liked Melinda.

Nathan leaned his elbows on the table. "Does this mean I'm out of a job?"

"The company isn't built around Azrael," Enzo said.

"Great," I said with a smirk. "Who *is* it built around?"

Enzo pointed at Warren.

"Me?" Warren asked.

"Yes, sir," Enzo said. "Our orders are clear. In Azrael's absence, you're in charge."

I found that hard to believe.

Warren looked at Nathan. "Nate, you're fired."

Nathan shot him the bird.

I looked around. "Seriously, what happens now? I mean, we can't drop everything and come here to live. What the hell? We have a house to close on this week."

"A house?" Nathan asked.

"We're buying a bigger house over by her dad," Warren said.

Nathan was surprised. "That was fast."

"Yeah, and we can't miss it!" My words were coming out a little more frantic than I would have liked, but I realized this may have been the stupid archangel's plan all along to lock me up in his compound. "Enzo, we can't stay here and run Claymore. That's insane."

Enzo held up his hand, chuckling—no, he was straight-up laughing at me. "No one says you have to stay here. We'll be fine."

Warren put his hand on mine. "It's a big company. There's a whole corporate office that runs this place, remember?"

I nodded, still not completely convinced this wasn't some sort of trick.

Warren looked around the room. "Enzo, is there a place we can crash here tonight? Sloan needs to rest."

"Or maybe a couple of days," I said. "I'd like to stay with Taiya for a little while."

"Absolutely," Warren said.

Enzo stood. "The top floor is all yours, sir. The door has a fingerprint lock, and yours is in the system."

Warren shook his head. "The suite is really not necessary. Just a bed is fine."

Enzo seemed a little confused. "Sir, the room is yours and Sloan's. That's what it's there for."

Warren and I exchanged a puzzled glance before he looked back at Enzo and nodded. "If you insist," Warren said. "Sloan, are you ready to go to bed?"

No. I was still way too keyed up for sleep, but I got up and nodded my head.

Nathan stood and looked at his watch. "I guess I'll go take a shower."

"Five a.m. roll call?" Warren asked.

"You know it," Nathan said.

We all walked back out to the lobby. "If you need anything, I'm on the third floor, unit one," Enzo said. "Reuel? I'm assuming you'll take your bed in unit three?"

Reuel grunted in confirmation.

Warren shook Enzo's hand. "Thanks for everything."

Enzo smiled. "It's good to have you back here, sir."

"I'd like to say the same, but I'm not going to," Warren said with a laugh.

"Roger that, sir." Enzo waved to the rest of us as he opened the door to the stairwell. "Goodnight."

"Goodnight," we replied.

The elevator doors dinged and slid open. Melinda stepped inside. "You guys goin' up?"

I held up a finger. "One sec." I turned back to Nathan. "We'll see you tomorrow?"

He tapped his watch. "You'll see me again today, hopefully."

I nodded. "It's hard to keep the days straight when you haven't slept."

"You both need to try to get some rest. I have a feeling this isn't over," he said.

I walked over and gave him a hug. "For now, I'm glad you're OK. It's good to see you."

"It's good to see you too." He stepped back and offered Warren his hand.

Warren shook it. "See you later, man."

Nathan pulled Warren back when he tried to withdraw his hand. "Hang on, I have a question." Nathan jerked his head toward me. "So, since Azrael orchestrated the whole me almost hooking up with Sloan thing, does this mean you'll finally forgive me?"

Warren laughed and shook head. "Not a chance, man. Not a chance."

Nathan hung his head and sighed. "Damn."

"You guys in or out?" Melinda barked from the elevator. "It's way past my bedtime."

"Bye, Nathan," I said.

He waved at the door before pushing it open. "See you after a while."

We said goodnight to Melinda on the fourth floor, then took the elevator up to the top. The doors slid open into a short, empty hallway with one door at the end of it. There was a nameplate on the door marked PRIVATE, nothing else.

Warren placed his index finger on the digital scanner above the handle, and after a quiet beep, the lock tumbled. He opened the door and I followed him inside. "Holy smokes," I said out loud.

The top floor was actually two floors. It was an open concept on the bottom with a living area and a huge eat-in kitchen centered around a bi-level staircase in the center up to a loft. It was minimally, but elegantly, decorated with off-white walls around the perimeter and dark charcoal walls around the stairs and in the kitchen. The living room had simple black tables and a large white sofa with oversized pillows.

It was like something Adrianne would have forced me to watch on a home improvement reality show on cable. A show that could have been called *Extreme Home Makeover: Warehouse Edition.*

"This place is insane," I said, running my hand along the dark walnut dining table.

He was checking out the biggest flat screen television I'd ever seen that was mounted on the wall. "Insane." Warren shook his head. "None of this makes any sense, Sloan."

"I know it doesn't. And, honestly, not understanding is the most terrifying thing about it to me." I walked over to him. "I'm afraid of Azrael, but I'm even more afraid of not having him around."

"I know what you mean."

"Warren, what if he makes you leave me?" I asked.

He gently gripped my arms and bent to look me in the eye. "That's not going to happen."

"You don't know that." I swallowed. "We don't know anything anymore."

"Come here." He pulled me against his chest as I started to cry.

It felt like we were being forced to the edge of a great precipice with nowhere else to go but to jump. And jump into what, I wasn't sure. All I could see looking off our proverbial cliff was darkness.

"You have to try to get some sleep," he said softly against my hair. "This will all be clearer tomorrow."

I sniffed. "There's no way I'm falling asleep now."

Smiling, he pulled away and took my hand. "Let's see if we can find a bed."

He led me up the stairs to a loft that overlooked the living space and two bedrooms, one on each side. The one on the left had a crib. The one on the right, a king bed with a fluffy white comforter like mine at home. I scratched my head. "This is so weird."

Warren pulled a dresser drawer open. "There's not much," he said, moving its contents around, "but here's a clean t-shirt and some Claymore sweatpants."

I changed into the outfit that was too big for me, but not quite big enough for Warren. The t-shirt fit snugly around my middle. Warren pulled the comforter back for me and I slid underneath it. The bed sunk under his weight when he sat beside me.

"Are you going to sleep?" I asked, knowing for him it was an option rather than a need.

He shook his head. "No, but I'll stay right here."

"You won't leave me?" I asked.

He tugged the blanket up around my chest and bent to kiss my forehead. "I'll never leave you, Sloan."

And in an instant, I was fast asleep.

CHAPTER SIXTEEN

*W*ARREN WAS BESIDE me, as promised, when I opened my eyes the next morning. I assumed it was morning, anyhow, since there were no windows in the apartment. Lights were on downstairs and Warren was reading by a bedside lamp. "What time is it?" I asked, stretching my arms up over my head.

He pressed the button on the side of his tactical watch and it lit up in lime green. "Just after nine. How did you sleep?"

I rolled onto my side toward him and hugged my pillow. "Like the dead. What's this new voodoo trick of yours to get me to sleep?"

He grinned. "Pretty nifty, isn't it?"

I nodded. "Nifty, yes, but I worry it's habit forming. Have you been here all morning or did you go out?"

"I went out for coffee earlier and poked around in Azrael's office for a while." He held up his index finger. "Apparently, I have access to everything now."

"Is it just me or do you feel like he's one step ahead of us?" I asked.

He closed the manila folder in his hand and turned it around so I could see. The tab at the top said FOR WARREN. "He definitely knew this was coming."

I pulled down the edge of the file folder. "What is it?"

"I'll read it to you." He opened the folder again. *"Dear Warren, if you're reading this, then I'm already gone. If you've happened upon this letter on your own, I can only assume my exit was hasty. No matter the circumstances precluding my departure, I trust you know I would not leave were it not absolutely essential—"*

I snorted and flopped back on my pillow. "Essential because he knew I was going to kill him."

He continued. *"I cannot tell you where I am going, nor when or if I will return. This is what I can tell you: The Morning Star is your greatest enemy. Not Phenex. Not Kasyade, even. The Morning Star is behind everything, and he is as smart as he is dangerous."*

"Great," I mumbled, draping my arm over my eyes.

"Echo-10 at Claymore is the safest place for Sloan and the baby, but it is far from absolutely impenetrable. In the event you are driven underground, safe houses have been strategically placed around the world that only you and Sloan have access to. And should this come to war, which I pray it doesn't, you have an army at your disposal. Enzo can fill you in on all the details, but my special ops team, SF-12, has been trained to execute a number of scenarios.

"Depending on when you find this letter, you should have a small window of time to prepare. The Morning Star will not attack before the baby can survive outside the womb, sometime around the end of March."

I shot straight up in bed. "The end of March? That's in a couple of weeks!"

He put his hand on the back of my neck to help calm me and kept reading. *"Thanks to Taiya, we know their original plan was to wait till the kotailis, but you should exercise extreme caution any time after the fetus is viable. Sloan will know when that is. You likely will as well."*

I held up both hands. "How the hell am I supposed to know?"

He shook his head. "It doesn't say."

"Continue," I said, willing my lower lip not to quiver. I was determined to not start crying before I even got out of bed.

"Remember, angels who are not tied to this world can move across time and space freely. They are your biggest threat. This includes The Destroyer, should he still be at large.

Finally, it is imperative that Sloan continues her training. She must free Lamal. His freedom is the key to unlocking the next phase of my plan. Warren, you must help her. Reuel and Enzo are great resources as well. Use them. Until I see you again, my son. Azrael."

I grabbed my cell phone off the nightstand.

"What are you doing?" he asked.

"Googling fetus viability outside the womb," I said.

"I already did." He looked over at me. "Some sources say as early as twenty-two weeks with intensive neonatal care. The standard age of viability is twenty-four weeks."

The tears were hard to keep at bay. "I'm almost twenty-four weeks now."

It was in Warren's nature to uncork a geyser of bullshit to make me feel better when I was sad or worried, but in that moment, he silently stared at the letter on his lap as lost in fear as I was.

I pushed myself off the bed.

"Where are you going?" he asked.

"Well, first, I'm going to look for a toothbrush. Then we've got work to do." I pointed back to the bed. "I figure I can lie here all day feeling sorry for myself, or I can get to work and maybe try to learn something before Satan comes to kill me."

He nodded and stood up to follow me to the bathroom. "That's a plan I can get on board with."

"And I want to see Taiya this morning before we do anything else."

"Definitely."

In one of the drawers I found a toothbrush and my brand of

toothpaste. Staring at the tube of Colgate Total Whitening (paste not gel), it suddenly became impossible to hate Azrael.

I sighed and shook my head. "I hope he knows what the hell he's doing."

Maybe it was the cold of the night before that had made Taiya so pale, or maybe it was her proximity to me that brought color back to her cheeks—whatever the reason, there was a marked difference in the pallor of my freaky little friend when we got to the medical clinic. Melinda was sitting in a chair by the bed, playing what sounded like a slot machine on her cell phone.

"How is she this morning?" I asked, sinking down carefully on the edge of the mattress.

Melinda's phone chimed with a jackpot tally as the sound of digital coins falling echoed around the stale triage room. She silenced the phone and laid it on the bedside table. "Ah, she looks good today considerin' the hell they put her through last night. The nurse says her vitals are better than they have been since she got here."

Warren squeezed my shoulder from behind.

I took Taiya's hand and focused on sending my healing power into her. I wasn't sure if her condition was something I could fix, but it couldn't hurt to try. I looked over at Melinda. "Can I ask you a question?"

She sat back in her chair and crossed one leg over the other. "Sure."

"What happened with you and Abner Tuinstra?" I asked.

She made a vomiting noise.

"We don't have to talk about it if you don't want to," I said.

"Nonsense. I wouldn't mind talkin' about the bastahd to someone who doesn't think I'm crazy. Whatd'ya wanna know?" She flipped her hair back over her shoulder.

Taiya's hand was warm in mine. "How did you meet him?" I asked.

She laughed. "Where you meet all the good men, honey. At a bar in Brooklyn. I was nineteen, flauntin' around my fake I.D. for the first time." Her eyes drifted toward the corner of the room. "And Abner slid onto that damn barstool next to me like he was Humphrey-Freakin-Bogart, or somethin'." With a huff and an eye roll, she shook her head. "The moves that guy had."

"You were in a relationship with him?" Warren asked.

"Ha, if you can call it that," she said. "He's a weird one, Abner."

"How so?" I asked, knowing why I thought Abner (Ysha) was weird. And terrifying. And hopefully burning in hell, or something.

"I thought he liked me, certainly put on a good front like he did. Asked about my friends and my family, like he was real interested." Her gaze drifted off again. "And I was a smitten kitten from the word *go*. Like he hung the damn moon or somethin'." She sighed. "I couldn't get enough of him, even when he was so hateful to me. I guess that's why I got pregnant so fast. Found out a couple of weeks after that night at the bar."

"What did he do when you told him you were pregnant?" I asked.

She laughed. "He *told me* I was pregnant like he had some kind of crystal ball stashed away in the back of his damn Mercedes. He kept me at his house, locked up in the damn bedroom till I went into labor. Made me deliver her in that bed like we were on Little House on the Prairie, or somethin'."

"Didn't someone report you missing?" Warren asked.

"Nope. My dumb ass told everyone I was in love, and I was an adult so I was movin' out. What's funny is, I didn't even really want to, but I did it anyway."

I didn't think it was funny. I knew what that kind of control was like. "What happened after Taiya was born?"

"When Taiya was born, he took her from me and kicked my ass to the curb," she said. "I went to the police, even filed charges against him. But that Abner was crafty. Convinced everyone I was a nut job!"

I shook my head. "You're not nuts."

She jammed her fingers into her breastbone. "I know that. Try tellin' those doctors. You know, they didn't even believe I'd had a baby? Called it pseudocyesis, a 'hysterical' pregnancy." She used air quotes around the word *hysterical*. "But God as my witness, I never stopped lookin' for my girl. No matter how many times they called me crazy."

"You couldn't find her?" I asked.

"No. And I wasn't the only one lookin'. That's how I first met Azrael—called himself Damon Claymore back then. He's the one that told me Abner was a devil." She smirked. "Hell, I didn't need to be told that one."

Warren sat on the other side of Taiya's bed. "When did he come find you?"

"A few weeks after Taiya was born. He was hopin' to find me still pregnant, I think, but he'd just missed it."

I looked at Warren. "I think she's pretty fortunate he didn't find her still pregnant, don't you?"

Warren stared back at me.

"You think he would've killed me, right?" she asked, tapping her nail on the table. "Because I think he would have too."

"You don't trust Azrael, then?" I asked as the last of my power flowed from my hand into Taiya's.

Melinda laughed, really loudly. Then she leaned forward and pointed at my face. "Sloan Jordan, I don't trust you neither."

Warren jingled a set of keys in front of my face as we walked out of the clinic. "Enzo gave me a HOK to use while we're here. If we hurry, we can get a hot breakfast in the dining hall. I think they stop serving at ten."

"We can't take the car?" I asked.

He shrugged. "We could, but this way I don't have to pay for gas."

"Is the food in the dining hall like school cafeteria food?"

He shook his head. "No, it's pretty good actually."

"OK. I'd like to talk to Enzo about training."

Warren raised an eyebrow. "Like Azrael suggested?"

I sighed. "Yes."

He nodded and pulled his phone out of his pocket. "I'll call him when we get outside. There's no service in this building at all."

"Makes sense, I guess."

He dialed the number when we walked through the double doors at the end of the hall into the chilly sunlight. As he talked, I followed him toward a high occupancy ATV, commonly known as a HOK in the Claymore world. We got in and Warren ended the phone call. "Enzo's going to meet us at the galley."

I nodded. "Cool."

We drove a few minutes up the road to a large, single-story, brick building. Inside it looked like a school cafeteria, except that it was speckled with soldiers wearing camouflage. The woman behind the cash register reminded me of Virginia Claybrooks, if Ms. Claybrooks was a lunch lady in a hairnet instead of a jail guard with a Taser.

The woman looked up at the clock on the wall. It read 9:43 a.m. "Skating in under the wire, aren't we?"

"Yes, ma'am," Warren said politely as he pulled out his wallet.

She rested her fingers on the keyboard of the computer in front of her. "Name or ID number?"

"Warren Parish," he answered.

She straightened as she typed. Whatever she saw on the screen made her do a double-take. "Oh, I guess you can come eat breakfast anytime you want, Mr. Parish," she said with a smile as she looked up at him, then at me. Turning sideways in her chair, she gestured toward the trays that were stacked behind her. "Help yourself."

"Was that weird?" I asked as we walked to pick up our trays.

He didn't look at me. "Yep."

Warren was right. The food was delicious. Certainly not the powdered eggs and limp bacon I remembered from my elementary school. I had an egg fried over hard, two sausage links, a bowl of grits, and a glass of chocolate milk the size of my head. Maybe an awesome breakfast was a sign of good things to come. Then again, maybe the need to parlay grits into my greatest hope for survival was sadly indicative of how dire the situation really was.

"I want to go see Taiya when we're finished," I announced, changing the subject that I wasn't actually verbalizing.

He skewered a piece of pineapple with his fork. "That's a good idea."

I looked around the room as Enzo walked in the door and removed his cap. He waved from the door and came over. Warren stood and shook his hand. "Morning, sir," Enzo said.

Warren shook his head. "Don't start with that 'sir' bullshit with me."

Enzo laughed as he sat. "Yes, sir."

"Good morning, Enzo," I said.

He smiled, his mismatched blue and green eyes were blood-shot and tired from the night before. "Good morning, ma'am."

I pointed at his face. "Definitely don't call me 'ma'am.' We've been over this. My name is Sloan. That's an order."

Warren cut his eyes at me and smiled. "You're not allowed to give orders."

I stuck out my tongue.

"Did you rest well?" Enzo asked.

I nodded. "Azrael put a lot of thought into that apartment, didn't he?"

"He did. He's been working on it steadily since he's been here the past few weeks." He gestured toward us. "While your arrival was certainly unexpected, it actually came at a pretty good time."

Warren pushed his plate back and leaned his elbows on the table. "How unexpected were we? I found a letter from him this morning in his office, so he knew we were coming at some point."

Enzo looked like he wanted to answer but was hesitant to, like a Secret Service agent the breakfast after inauguration day.

Warren leveled his gaze at him. "I need to know what you know."

Enzo took a deep breath. "He was supposed to call me toward the end of this month to move Taiya into the Claymore trauma center across the compound." He split a glance between me and Warren. "The trauma center isn't equipped with high-Z in the walls."

I straightened. "Azrael was going to let me find her? He was using her to lure me here?"

He nodded. "I believe so."

"Why?"

"Because once you fully come into your power, The Morning Star will come looking for you, and we're in the best defensive position here."

Warren reached across the table and put his hand on mine. "We're early, so don't freak out just yet."

"We're early," I whispered to myself, pressing my eyes closed.

Warren turned to Enzo. "In his letter, he said SF-12 was trained for a number of scenarios should there be a war. He said you could fill me in on the details."

Enzo looked around the room. It was mostly empty, but he lowered his voice anyway. "We are ready, sir. Azrael intends to take the fight away from Claymore, to catch the enemy by surprise, rather than wait here for them to prepare and come to us. So SF-12 has orders to be one hundred percent mobile at a moment's notice. We have a plane and helicopters at our disposal, as well as safe houses all over the map."

"Did he say where he intends to have this fight?" Warren asked.

"No, sir, but he was planning to leave at some point. I assume to do recon work. That's why you've been put in charge of everything."

Warren rubbed his chin. "He's scouting out a venue for war?"

Enzo shrugged. "I think he's looking for The Morning Star. But"—his tone was hopeful as he looked at me—"I was told when the time comes, you'll be quite an asset."

I paused with my milk glass midway to my mouth and laughed sarcastically. "So it's certainly not now."

He didn't join my laughter. "He was very clear about it, Sloan." He pointed at me. "He said when the time is near for war, we'll know because you'll be ready."

I shook my head. "That makes no sense."

He turned his palms up. "Perhaps not, but he's never been wrong."

I wasn't sure if that made me feel better or worse.

"Sloan needs a training plan," Warren announced, diverting the conversation. "She's having some trouble with focus and directing her power."

"I've heard," Enzo said. "Have you thought about taking her to the range? Focus, aim…both fundamentals of shooting."

Warren shook his head. "I've thought about it, but she can't shoot. Most doctors advise against it during pregnancy. Too loud and recoil risks."

I looked at Enzo. "I can't shoot when I'm not pregnant either, and it has nothing to do with a doctor's recommendation. I suck."

Enzo laughed, then sat back in his chair and looked at the ceiling. "What about a bow?" He turned to Warren. "It's silent and there's no recoil."

Warren considered it.

I held up a hand. "Hold up. You want to what?"

Enzo pulled back a fake bow and released a fake arrow across the cafeteria.

My head snapped back. "You're serious?"

He nodded. "Why not?"

"I think it's a great idea," Warren said.

"Really?" I asked, still in disbelief.

Warren grinned. "We're not talking about turning you into Katniss Everdeen or anything, but I think Enzo is onto something. It could really help you focus, to visualize where you want to send your power, and of course, how to aim."

"My aim isn't that bad. Not with my powers, anyway. I did pretty good on the battlefield, didn't I?"

"You did," Warren agreed, nodding emphatically. "You're a completely different person when your adrenaline is pumping. Maybe learning something still and quiet like the bow could help you wield your gift through focus rather than frenzy."

"I'm not so good with target practice." I cocked my head to the side. "Do you remember how terrible I was at the gun range?"

Enzo shook his head. "Guns and bows are very different. Like I said, bows don't have recoil or loud bangs."

Warren pointed at me. "And even with the gun, once you got past those things, you weren't terrible."

I crossed my arms and stared at him.

He laughed. "You could improve with practice."

They both stared at me expectantly.

After a moment, I nodded my head. "All right. Let's do it."

Enzo knocked his knuckles against the table. "Awesome."

"Sloan, I'm proud of you." Warren was unable to hide the surprise in his deep voice.

I pointed at him. "Don't be too impressed yet. I may shoot somebody before it's over with."

Enzo laughed. "At least you can heal them if you do."

"Good point," I said.

Warren looked at Enzo. "Do we have bows in the armory?"

Enzo shook his head. "No, but Walmart sells some basic ones. We have guys that buy them there for bow season."

Warren rubbed his palms together. "We'll go get one today. Where can we set up?"

"You should be fine setting up anywhere near the interior fence line," Enzo said.

Warren offered him his hand. Enzo shook it. "You're brilliant, man. Whatever we're paying you, it isn't enough."

Enzo smiled and pushed himself up from the table. "Just doing my job. Let me know if I can help with anything else."

We said our goodbyes and when he was gone, Warren pointed to my plate. "Finish your breakfast. We've got weapons to buy."

Warren took the long way back to Echo-10 to pick up the Challenger so he could give me a tour of the compound. "How big is Claymore?" I asked as we passed what looked like a television station with satellite dishes on the lawn.

"Around two thousand acres."

"Two thousand? Wow."

I pointed to the roof of the building. "What are those white whirlybird things spinning around up there?"

He leaned across the cab to look up through the opening in my side door. "Those are radar towers."

"A weather forecaster?"

He shook his head. "No. Aircraft radar."

"That makes more sense."

He smiled over at me. "I think we should start calling them 'whirlybirds' though."

A group of people in uniform were running alongside the road up ahead of us. Warren slowed as we passed. "Think that's Nate's group?" I asked.

"Could be," he said.

I didn't see him.

"This is the Kill House."

I followed the direction of his finger over the steering wheel. In the center of a dead field was a run-down concrete structure with a couple of simple doors and windows. It didn't appear to have a roof but a metal catwalk instead. "Do I want to know why it's called the Kill House?"

"We use it to train soldiers how to clear buildings," he said. "Nothing too sinister."

"What is that big square tower behind it?"

"That's the rappel tower."

"Why does it have windows on the side?" I asked.

"To practice window entry and how to shoot through windows," he said.

I blinked with surprise. "You do that?"

He nodded but didn't elaborate.

We took a right turn by a huge asphalt lot where an armored Humvee was driving around a maze of cones and barriers. On top, a soldier was holding onto the biggest gun I'd ever seen. I didn't need to ask what they were doing. It was pretty obvious.

"Tactical pursuit driving," Warren said.

"I can tell. That's a big gun."

"It's called a 50-Cal." He looked at his watch. "Want to see something really cool?"

"Of course."

He pointed toward a tree line up ahead to our right. "Watch the top of the trees for a red flag. I'm hoping we didn't miss it."

"Miss what?"

"You'll see."

My side of the road was a forest blocked by a ten-foot fence with coiled barbed wire across the top. It was marked every few feet with big red signs that said "WARNING: DO NOT ENTER. UNEXPLODED ORDINANCES."

"What's an ordinance?" I asked.

"Bombs," he said. "It's alarming how many unexploded mine-fields we have in America."

A red flag rippled by the winter wind caught my attention up above the trees. I pointed. "Red flag. There it is."

He drove on until the trees opened up to a huge clearing the size of a few football fields. It was littered with old cars, Humvees, and at least one helicopter laying on its side. Some were scorched till they were unrecognizable, and all were shot up and in pieces. "What is this place? Claymore's transportation graveyard?"

He laughed as he parked on the shoulder. "You could call it that."

BOOM!

I jumped in my seat.

Out in the field, the front passenger door of a sedan and part of its roof was blown into the air in a spray of metal and dirt. "Sweet Jesus!" I yelled, grasping onto the door handle of the HOK.

Warren laughed. "Isn't that awesome?"

"What are they doing?" I asked, still panting.

"This is the M203 range." He pointed to a small group of men beyond the fence. "M203s are grenade launchers."

The group launched another grenade toward the helicopter. Before it struck near the nose, I had the good sense to wrap my arms around my head to muffle the blast. Warren looked over at me. "Cool, huh?"

I smiled and nodded. "I can't deny that it's pretty cool."

"That's one of the top reasons I joined the Marines right there. It's one of the best parts of the job. Next to the armory, this is my favorite spot on the compound," he said, pulling back onto the road.

"Do I get to see the armory too?" I asked.

He reached over and squeezed my thigh. "That's my girl."

The armory was as nondescript as Echo-10. Concrete walls, no windows, and one door as far as I could tell from the parking lot. Warren parked next to a few other HOKs and got out. There was a fingerprint reader on the wall outside the door. He laid his index finger across it and the locks tumbled.

A stocky man with a fair complexion and strawberry blond hair looked up from behind the counter when we walked into the room. It was a large open room with the Claymore emblem painted in the center of the smooth cement floor. The walls were lined with metal cages, each holding different styles of weapons. As we crossed the floor toward the counter, the man's head snapped back when he recognized Warren. "Parish?"

Warren laughed. "Hey, Huffman."

"The Shadow has returned," Huffman said as he came around to meet us. "Wow, long time no see. What are you doing here?"

Warren welcomed him with a hearty handshake. "Just visiting for a couple of days. This is my fiancée, Sloan."

The man smiled at me. "Nice to meet you." He turned back to Warren. "Rumor has it you're coming back on board."

Warren's brow wrinkled and he shook his head. "Don't believe everything you hear." He jerked his head toward me. "We're engaged and getting ready to have a baby."

"I heard." Huffman shook his hand again. "Congratulations." He pointed off to the side. "We've got some new shotguns in if you need to borrow one for the wedding."

Warren shoved him in the shoulder and Huffman laughed.

"I'm kidding," he said to both of us. Suddenly, he looked past us to the other side of the room. "Hey, Fury, look who's back!"

Warren's spine went rigid, and I immediately looked around for Azrael. Instead of finding The Angel of Death, I saw something much, much worse.

A woman.

CHAPTER SEVENTEEN

I'D OFTEN WONDERED about the women in Warren's life before me. He was too skilled in bed to have been a complete loner all his life. But unlike some people who need to know all the gory details of their lovers' pasts, I was always too afraid to ask him. The reason? The vision of the woman standing in the doorway of a cage filled with assault rifles. She was *exactly* everything I'd feared. Lara Croft meets Jessica Rabbit. A brunette Barbie doll in tactical gear.

She was tall with a tan face, plump lips, and shiny chocolate brown hair loosely braided over her shoulder. She wore fitted olive green cargos and a long-sleeve black t-shirt that looked like it had been melted to form to her bulging rack and tiny waistline.

I muttered a swear word.

She stared back, but she wasn't looking at me.

Warren still hadn't turned around. He hadn't budged. Nor was he breathing, I realized, when I went to nudge him. This wasn't good.

"Warren Parish." It was like she was making a declaration to the universe, her voice as smooth as the way she glided across the room toward us—or him, rather. I wasn't even sure she'd noticed me standing there.

He turned slowly to face her. She nearly matched his height, towering over me (still the invisible bystander of their reunion).

"Hello, Allison." His greeting wasn't welcoming, at least. He even folded his arms across his chest and took a step back. The problem was, despite his abrasiveness, one thing was painfully obvious: there was unfinished business between these two. Dirty business. Sexy business. If the tension had been nerve gas, we'd all be dead.

I cleared my throat and stepped in between them, jutting my hand out in her direction. "Hi, I'm Sloan."

Her dark eyes sliced toward me; one was almost black, the other a dark emerald. "I know who you are."

Still preoccupied with her mismatched eyes and what that could mean, I slowly lowered my unaccepted hand when she turned back to my fiancé.

Redness rose in his cheeks; the angry muscle was in overdrive. "Glad to see nothing's changed, Fury, and that you're still a hateful bitch."

Whoa! I didn't think Warren had it in him to talk to anyone that way, much less a woman.

He looked at me and shook his head. "Ignore her."

That was kind of hard to do since she was standing so close that the holster strapped to her thigh kept brushing against my rejected hand.

Fury's lips spread into a thin smile. "Is that what you've been doing for the past year, Parish? Ignoring me?"

He smirked. "Yeah. What are you even doing here? Is there a shortage of insurgent-fueled exhilaration in the world right now, or did you need to drop by to pack some fresh underwear?"

Her mouth laughed, but her eyes did not. "I was recalled to train the latest recruits and then it looks like I'm going back to Afghanistan. So yeah, it's the panties thing. Why? Do you miss them?" She fiddled with the zipper on the front of his coat and he quickly swatted her hand away.

My mouth hung open. I couldn't believe this was actually happening right in front of me. "Oh my god. Seriously? Who the hell do you think you are?"

Warren spoke to her through clenched teeth. "You know, I think you're the only woman I've ever wanted to kill."

She leaned toward him. "I consider that an honor."

Behind us, Huffman chuckled.

Fury pushed through us toward him. "I'll be back later"—she glanced back over her shoulder at Warren—"when it's not so crowded in here. Parish, you know where to find me."

"Bye, Fury," Huffman said, his eyes glued on her ass as she walked out.

I whirled toward Warren, unable to formulate a complete sentence. "What the—? Who...huh...*what*?" Giving up, I gripped the sides of my skull.

Huffman mimicked warning tones as he walked back behind the counter. "*Dun, dun, dunnn...*"

I pointed to the door. "What the hell was that about? Who is she?"

Warren's face dropped and he stared at the floor. "She's a long story."

"It's a good story," Huffman added.

Warren looked back at him. "Can you give us a minute?"

Huffman laughed. "Hell no."

Rolling his eyes, Warren grabbed my hand and pulled me outside. Fury was driving out of the parking lot in a black ATV. Warren growled up at the sky as he put on his sunglasses.

I folded my arms. "Well?"

"I'm sorry. There's no excuse for her. She's an *awful* person," he said.

"An awful person that you've clearly slept with."

He nodded. "I'm not proud of it, but I'm not going to deny it either. I haven't seen or talked to her since long before I met you. She called me a few times last summer, but I didn't answer. That's it, I swear."

I raked my hands through my hair. "Warren, I'm not mad at you, but dang, a little heads up might have been nice."

He shook his head. "I had no idea she was here. The last I heard, she took a contract in Saudi Arabia with another company. I didn't even know she worked for Claymore anymore."

A memory from a conversation with Azrael popped into my mind. "Oh my god! Azrael told you he was going to do this the night you told him you wouldn't."

"I know, but I never dreamed she would accept."

"Does she have powers? Is she part of Azrael's little super group, SF-12?" I asked.

"What?"

I used my fingers to pry my eyelids open wide. "Her eyes, Warren. Can she see angels?"

His head pulled back and he looked around, genuinely perplexed. "I don't know." He rubbed his hands over his face and was frustratingly quiet, looking everywhere but at me. "Geez, I really don't know."

I put my hands on my hips. "So you know nothing about this woman. It was just blowing shit up and sex with you two, huh?"

He scrunched his nose. "Pretty much."

I swore again, this time not under breath. I groaned and walked off across the gravel lot.

He quickly came after me, took hold of my arms, and bent to look me in the eye. "Don't freak out about this, babe. It's nothing."

"What if it's not nothing? What if Azrael brought her here to split me and you up?" I asked.

He laughed with heavy sarcasm. "Then he's in for a huge disappointment. I let that ship sail years ago. There was a time, long before I met you, when she wanted to come back, and I wouldn't even return her calls. You have nothing to worry about, Sloan."

My bottom lip poked out. "But she's gorgeous."

He smiled gently. "Gorgeous isn't everything, babe. She's only attractive till she opens her mouth."

I sighed. "That's the truth." There were so many things I wanted to ask and didn't want to ask at the same time. "Why would Azrael bring her here if not to hurt us?"

"Because she's good," he said seriously. "She's damn good."

Of course she is, I thought. "You met her here?"

"No. I met her in Iraq in 2008 when I was still in the Marines. She was with Claymore even back then."

"How?" I asked.

He led me over to a picnic table by the building and we sat. "It was outside Baghdad. My unit was following a lead to a village west of the city, and we stopped to rest and rehydrate in an area that seemed to be abandoned. We cleared this old building and found a crew from Claymore bunkered down inside. They were doing an escort and had stopped for a break there like we had.

"Our guys set up a perimeter, and I was off in position away from everyone, watching through my scope. Some time later, one of my guys inside took a sniper round from out of nowhere. I heard the echo, but couldn't find where it came from. I guess either our team or theirs had been tracked by an insurgent cell. Then the ground fire started. Our unit and the Claymore team returned fire.

"I was doing my job, picking off who I could from my position, but I didn't realize there was a second, smaller group that was flanking me. Fury saw them before they engaged and took out two of them." His eyes drifted away from mine. "I'd be dead if it weren't for her."

I swallowed hard. Warren had died *because of me.*

"I saw her again a few weeks later before I came home. We exchanged information, but I didn't see her again until she recruited me to Claymore."

My face fell. "And then what happened?"

He bit the insides of his lips for a second. "I finished training and we had a couple of weeks together before she decided she wanted other things. She took an assignment in Somalia, and I haven't seen her since."

"Ugh."

He laughed. "It's a bad thing I haven't seen her?"

"She left you. It explains the angry muscle when you saw her."

He blinked. "The what?"

"Nothing. Never mind."

With a finger, he turned my face toward his. "Even if she hadn't left, it never would have worked. I'm exactly where I'm supposed to be."

"You're the boss now. You can fire her," I suggested.

He kissed my forehead and laughed. "I'll let her finish training Nate, and then she's gone."

Snuggled against the cold into his chest, I thought of how tolerant Warren had always been about Nathan. Suddenly, the Allison Fury bombshell (pun intended) felt an awful lot like the business end of what goes around, comes around. And I knew one thing was certain:

We hadn't seen the last of Fury.

On our drive to Walmart, I did what any girl in my situation would do: I alerted my best friend to the situation at hand. I sent a text message to Adrianne. *OMG. I need to talk to you.*

When she didn't answer immediately, I did the only other thing that came naturally: I Googled Allison Fury until we pulled into the store's parking lot. Of course, I found nothing on her. I wasn't even sure what her actual name was, and I wasn't about to ask Warren. While we went shopping for archery equipment and dinner (two things sold a few aisles apart at any major department store in North Carolina), my phone finally buzzed in my hand. It was Adrianne.

Sorry.

I'm not ignoring you.

Crazy day at work.

What's up?

I always wondered why she felt the need to split up her sentences. One long text message would suffice, but Adrianne was a 'more-the-merrier' personality in all aspects of life, digital communication included.

I must have groaned or sighed loud enough for Warren to notice because he asked, "Everything OK?"

"Yeah. I don't understand why Adrianne can't send one text message. She has to send every line separately like she wins a prize at the end of the month for meeting a quota of messages sent."

He chuckled. "I've noticed that."

I tapped out a response as he led the way toward the fresh meat section. *What do you get if you cross GI Joe and Miss America?*

Her reply came faster than I expected. *Wonder Woman?*

Me: *Good guess, but no.*

Adrianne: *?*

Me: *Warren's last girlfriend. :(*

Warren was looking at a sale sign over a massive pile of ribeye steaks. "What do you think about having some of the guys over for dinner tonight?"

I nodded. "Whatever you want to do is fine with me."

He started loading steaks into our cart beside the bow and arrows he'd picked out.

My phone buzzed again.

Adrianne: *How did you find that out?*

Me: *I just met her.*

Adrianne: *Shut up.*

Me: :'(

Adrianne: *That sucks so hard.*

Me: *She's perfect.*

Adrianne: *I'm sure that's not true.*

Adrianne: *If she were perfect, Warren wouldn't have dumped her.*

Adrianne: *I'm sure you have nothing to worry about.*

Me: *She dumped him.*

Adrianne: *Oh. :(*

Adrianne: *Still.*

Adrianne: *You have nothing to worry about.*

Adrianne: *Warren loves you.*

Adrianne: *Where did you meet her?*

My eyes drifted down the long aisle of blood red meat, realizing I hadn't even told Adrianne we were at Claymore, much less what we'd found out about the supernatural love of her life. "Warren, she doesn't know we're here, does she?"

He shook his head and pushed the cart toward the marinades and spices. "I haven't told her. See if she's heard from Az."

Me: *We're at Claymore. We drove up here for a couple of days. Have you heard from Azrael?*

Adrianne: *No. Isn't he there?*

Adrianne: *I've left messages.*

Adrianne: *I feel like he's ignoring me.*

Me: *He may not have cell reception. He's out in the field.*

It wasn't a complete lie. 'The field' could be anywhere, and I wasn't even sure Azrael had a phone when he vanished or if it would work wherever he was going. The last thing I wanted to do was explain everything that happened to Adrianne using only my thumbs, and there weren't adequate angel emojis to properly explain our current predicament. "She hasn't heard from him."

"No surprise there," he said.

Me: *Let's have dinner when I get back.*

Adrianne: *When will that be?*

Me: *Not sure yet, but I'll let you know. Sometime this weekend because we close on the house on Monday. I'll call you later.*

Adrianne: *XOXO*

I dropped the phone onto my lap. "She's going to be crushed."

"Don't worry about it till you have to." He nudged me with his elbow. "There are pressing matters at hand. Sweet potatoes or white?"

"Knock, knock," a familiar voice said as we sat down to dinner in the downstairs common kitchen of Echo-10. I turned as Nathan walked into the room, holding up his index finger. "Guess who has a magic fingerprint and retinas with security clearance now." He was in civilian clothes and smiling from ear to ear.

"Guess who's had it all along and only found out about it today?" Warren asked with a grin as Nathan pulled out the chair next to Reuel at the end of the table.

"Really?" Nathan asked.

Warren nodded. "Enzo told me this afternoon."

"You talked to the boss man about me, huh? Checking my report card?"

I pointed at Warren who was carrying a slab of butter to the table. "He talked to him so he could break you out of boot camp for dinner."

"Thank you. You have no idea how much I appreciate it."

Warren laughed. "Yeah, I do."

"It smells amazing in here." Nathan looked over the table that was filled with fresh grilled ribeyes, a pile of baked potatoes I almost couldn't see over, and a salad bowl big enough to feed the rest of Claymore.

"We did some shopping in town today, and Warren picked up food while we were there." I picked up a potato with a set of tongs and put it on a plate with a steak before offering it to Lamal.

"*Gratalis*," he said as he accepted it.

"I've never felt so manly in my life," I said. "We walked out of there with a bow, twenty-four arrows, and ten pounds of ribeye."

Nathan looked confused. "Do you feel manly often, Sloan?"

I smoothed my shirt over my belly. "Not lately." I picked up a fresh plate and pointed the tongs at Reuel. "Do you want one steak or two?"

Reuel held up five fingers.

I laughed and put two steaks and two potatoes on his plate. "You can have more after everyone else has eaten. Warren, did Enzo ever say how many guys to expect?"

Warren cringed as he poured honey mustard over his salad. "I decided not to tell him."

I moved my hand wide and almost smacked Melinda in the head with the juicy tongs.

"Hey! Watch it!" she bellowed.

"Sorry." I put another steak on a plate. "Warren, why did you do that?"

He cut his eyes over at me. "After talking with Enzo this afternoon, I decided if we couldn't invite all of the team, we probably shouldn't invite any."

I'd almost forgotten about Fury. But not quite. My stomach turned in a knot. "Oh." He'd confirmed it. She was a member of SF-12. "What else did you find out?"

"He got a call. Said we'd talk more later," Warren answered.

Nathan was too concentrated on his plate of food I was holding to notice the shift in the conversation. He reached over the table and took it from my hands. "Warren, why did you buy a bow? Bow season has been over for months."

"I'm going to teach Sloan how to shoot," Warren said.

"Oh my god," Melinda whined. "You can't serve dinner without almost killin' somebody. Keep me the hell outta wherever you're gonna be handlin' weapons."

Nathan perked in his seat. "I have to come watch."

I spun toward him. "You'd better not. I'm nervous enough without an audience."

Nathan looked at Warren. "What is it? A thirty pound draw weight?"

Warren smirked and shook his head. "If that. Maybe less. It's a basic compound bow, might even be for a kid."

I smiled. "It's purple."

Nathan laughed. "Of course it is."

"I'm hoping it will help her direct her powers easier," Warren said, sitting at the table's head.

I tried to discreetly nod toward Melinda. "We have company tonight for dinner, darling."

Melinda made a sputtering noise with her lips. "Powers, shmowers. Bet I've seen Abner do worse. No need to mind your tongue around me, cupcake."

"Good to know," Warren said.

"How's Taiya doing?" Nathan asked, splitting open his potato and slathering it with sour cream and butter.

Melinda nodded. "All her numbers are better. Doc says we're just waitin' on the lightbulb to flip back on."

Unfortunately, Taiya's lightbulb had never been all that bright to begin with. "There's no telling when that could be, I guess?" I asked.

"I wish there was. Me and my girl have a lot of time to make up for," she said.

"What are your plans?" Warren asked.

She pointed at her own face. "Do I look like a planner to you, Mr. Parish?"

He grinned.

Nathan moaned with satisfaction as he chewed a bit of steak. "Oh man, real food. This is so good."

"They don't feed you real food?" I asked. "The cafeteria isn't bad."

He shook his head. "We have a separate mess hall, and we eat a lot of MREs." He looked at Warren. "That shit's gross."

Warren laughed. "Yep."

"What do you think about your instructors?" I asked.

Nathan stopped mid-chew, looked around, then slowly finished chewing the bite in his mouth before swallowing with a lot of effort. The corners of his mouth were bending upwards.

"I met Fury today," I added.

He coughed and covered his mouth with his fist.

I rolled my eyes as he started laughing.

He looked at Warren. "Dude."

"Did you know Warren used to date her?" I asked.

Nathan's eyes doubled. He clearly didn't know. "Seriously?"

Warren wiped his mouth with a napkin. "*Date* isn't the word I would use."

"That's lovely," I said, suddenly nauseated.

Nathan slowly clapped his hands. "Bravo."

I stabbed a piece of steak so hard that my fork tines chimed against the plate. "She's a nightmare."

Nathan's head tilted. "She's certainly made an appearance in my dreams a time or two."

I thought about chucking a potato at his head. "Do you know if she has any kind of abilities?"

He smiled. "I'm sure she does."

"Nathan, be serious," I said. "Does she have any supernatural powers?"

He shrugged. "Don't know. Her eyes are crazy though. Is that what you're talking about?"

"Yeah," I said.

"She might have. Az told me before he disappeared that someone would be training me on the supe stuff but didn't say who." He looked up toward the ceiling and folded his hands in the prayer position beneath his chin. "God, I hope it's her."

I sighed. "Men."

"How long are you guys staying?" he asked.

"I have a doctor's appointment on Thursday," I said to Warren.

"We'll leave tomorrow," Warren said.

"So no shooting tomorrow?"

"We can practice for a while in the morning before we head out, or we can shoot when we get home. Set up a target in the backyard at the new house."

"Please practice tomorrow," Nathan said with a laugh.

I looked at Warren. "We can practice tomorrow, but Nathan can't come."

"Nathan has work tomorrow, anyway," Warren reminded him. "When do you graduate boot camp?"

Nathan thought for a second. "The week before your wedding."

Warren made a sour face.

Nathan held up his hands. "You don't want me at the wedding?"

Warren put his fork down. "Of course I do. That's not what I was thinking about. I was hoping you'd be done sooner."

"Why?" He sat back and scowled. "Need me and my truck to help you move?"

I groaned. "I wish it was that."

My grim response stirred Nathan's curiosity. "What's going on?" he asked, balancing his elbows on the table.

"I found a letter from Azrael this morning." Warren took a deep breath. "We may have problems in the spirit world sooner than we expected."

"What happened to the first day of summer?" Nathan asked.

"It looks like that could have been a tentative plan," Warren answered.

No longer hungry, I dropped my napkin onto my plate. "I could have a week left on the planet, boys."

Nathan rolled his eyes, clearly unsusceptible to my melodrama. "Are you going to come back and stay here?"

I sighed. "I really don't want to, but it does beat the hell out of Asheville when it comes to security."

"Also, Taiya is here, and we can't move her like she is right now," Warren added. I knew he was trying to make me feel better about it.

I nodded. "I know."

Warren caught my eye across the table. "This is only a temporary solution, Sloan. We're buying that house and I intend for our daughter to grow up in it."

"You're right. It's only temporary." I forced a smile. "Let's do it."

Warren looked satisfied, but my brain was turning on all the reasons I hated the thought of living at Claymore. My dad and Adrianne being first among them. The list had only gotten longer since we arrived, and Allison Fury was now racing toward the top. But the thing that irked me the most was Azrael. We'd discovered the truth of his lies and manipulation, and here he was, still the master puppeteer.

Only now, it was me dangling at the end of his strings—*exactly* where he wanted me to be.

CHAPTER EIGHTEEN

"*P*LANT YOUR FEET and pull."

I planted. I pulled. With the arrow aimed up at the sky, I prayed for the help of gravity to get the string back. It didn't move more than a couple of inches no matter how hard I strained.

Warren was trying not to laugh and failing. "Stop. Stop. Are you hunting for doves? Bring it down out of the sky, babe."

I huffed and lowered the bow in the direction of the foam box target he'd set up against the fence line.

He covered my fingers with his over the release and helped me pull. "Once you get it about three-quarters of the way back, you'll feel the pressure let off and it will be easier to pull."

Just as he'd said, there was a break in the pressure and I could pull the string back, but still only with his help. Carefully, he eased the string forward. "Now you try."

I pulled and pulled. The arrow flopped around on the rest and then fell off.

Warren bit the inside of his lips when I looked at him.

"This is the dumbest idea ever," I said.

He massaged my shoulders. "Don't overthink this. Breathe. You can do it."

I took a deep breath and Warren moved back. Inhaling, I moved the bow up into position, then I pulled and the string moved back into place. I was so shocked, I released it. The string slapped against my inner elbow and the arrow flew wildly over the fence. I screamed and dropped the bow. Crumpling over in pain, I gripped my arm. "Holy hellfire! That hurt!"

My arm was already bright red.

"Everybody does that when they first start." Warren slapped my back. "Shake it off."

"Shake it off," I mimicked, full snark. "You're such a guy."

He pointed at the target. "Again. This time don't release till I tell you to."

When the throbbing eased in my arm, I picked the bow back up, pulled the string back, and aimed it at the bullseye. "Now what?" I asked.

"Anchor your index finger against your cheek."

I touched my knuckle to my cheek. "Like this?" I asked.

"Good. Line up your peep site with the front site and put the bullseye in the middle of it."

"My what?"

"The peep site" He pointed to a black circle in the string. "Look through that and line up with this site here." He touched his finger to another ring that was mounted on the side of the bow.

"OK." I matched up the circles toward the red circle on the target. "Got it."

"Pull the trigger to release the arrow."

Pain still burned in my arm. "I don't want to."

"Your elbow is bent and out of the way. Release the arrow."

I pressed the trigger and dropped the bow to watch the arrow sail about two feet over the target and through the fence, narrowly missing the "WARNING: DO NOT ENTER" sign. I frowned. "I didn't come anywhere close."

"But you didn't kill anyone or hurt yourself, so I call it a win," he said, squeezing the back of my neck. "Try again."

In a half an hour, we lost nine of the two dozen arrows we'd bought, and I hadn't landed any anywhere near the bullseye. I had hit the box a couple of times, even touching the outer blue ring twice, and I hadn't slapped my arm with the bow string again, but I was far from being a natural archery talent.

"Draw, anchor, release," Warren said again.

I released another arrow and it sailed through the fence. I dropped the bow at my side and turned to Warren. "Can I quit now?"

Before he could argue, a black fifteen passenger van with dark tinted windows pulled off the road onto the grass by our ATV. The side door slid back and Nathan stepped out, all smiles as usual.

I frowned. "Why are you here?"

He turned up his palms. "I thought you could use some encouragement."

"You lie," I said.

He nodded. "Yeah, I do." He pointed at the target. "Go on. Let's see what you can do."

"Does it look like I can do much?" I asked with a frustrated huff.

He laughed. "Nope."

Warren gestured toward the van. "Who is with you?"

Nathan shrugged. "Just the guys from my unit. Come on, Sloan. I haven't got all day."

I scowled at him, and he folded his arms across his chest. I nocked an arrow. With my eyes fixed on the target, I pulled the string back, touched my thumb to cheek, and shot toward the target. By all the mercies of the universe, I pierced the red ring of the target. Nathan clapped his hands. "Nicely done. Maybe I'm a good luck charm."

"I doubt it."

"Do it again," he said. "This time, level out your back elbow."

I nocked another arrow, drew it back, leveled my elbow, and released the arrow. This time I watched it sail up through the fence again. I scowled at Nathan. "Why do I listen to you?"

"Because I'm smart." He walked over to me. "And irresistibly charming." He looked at Warren. "Can I help her?"

Warren nodded, only mildly reluctant.

Nathan stood behind me and held his arms alongside mine, covering my hands with his. He pulled the string back. "Sloan?" His voice snapped me out of a daze, and I opened my eyes that I hadn't realized I'd closed. *Damn pheromones.*

"Yeah?"

"Did you know you have a *lot* of glitter in your hair?"

"I'm not surprised."

Behind us, Warren cleared his throat.

Nathan coughed and adjusted the bow. "See how our arms are level?"

I nodded. "Yes."

"Keep your arms in this position. Don't move." He took a step back. "Now line up the sites with the yellow inner circle of the bullseye and fire."

I did and looked up to watch the arrow hit the white shell of the target. I groaned.

The front passenger door of the van flew open. "God, you're a bunch of morons." It was Fury, dressed in all black, fitted tactical wear. Her hair was pulled back and she was wearing black aviator sunglasses.

In a few long strides, she was on top of me. "Your anchor point is different every time you shoot, but the biggest problem is you drop the bow the same second you release. You have no follow through and it's pushing your angle up." She snatched the bow out of my hand, nocked an arrow, and drew it back without hindrance. She aimed and released the arrow, landing it almost dead center in the yellow eye of the target.

She stayed frozen in place. "You never lower your weapon till you strike your mark. After the strike, then drop your weapon." She lowered it, and then she pressed the bow back into my arms. "Do it again. This time, don't move your ass till you hear the thud."

I thought I might throw up. She even smelled amazing.

My hands were shaking so much I almost dropped the arrow as I tried to nock it. It took me two attempts to pull the string back. When I got the string back, she stepped up next to me and touched the side of my face. "Your anchor point is wherever you feel comfortable. Just do it the same way every single time."

I nodded and rested my index finger against my cheekbone.

"Breathe in and as you slowly exhale, pull the trigger. Then don't move till after the arrow is in the target." She stepped back beside Nathan and Warren.

I sucked in a deep breath, and as I blew it out slowly I released the arrow. I watched—this time through the sights—the arrow strike almost the bullseye.

"Holy shit," I whispered, finally dropping the bow.

Warren and Nathan clapped. Fury walked back to the van and slammed the door shut before I could say anything to her.

"Again," Warren said.

I drew another arrow, anchored along my cheek, breathed in deep, slowly exhaled...and sunk another arrow right beside the last. No one was more shocked than me.

"McNamara, get in the damn van!" Fury yelled from her open window.

Nathan paused beside me and squeezed my arm. "Nicely done, Sloan."

"Thank you."

"You guys are still heading out today?" he asked.

I nodded. "Yeah. Pretty soon."

He studied my face for a second. "Stay alive, all right?"

"I'm doing my best. We'll see you in a few days."

He waved to Warren and took off in a jog toward the van. It

started rolling away and he jumped through the door to get inside. As they drove back onto the pavement and around the curve, I shook my head and sighed. Warren walked up behind me. "I told you she's a damn good teacher."

I groaned up toward the sky. "But I hate her so very much."

He laughed and turned me around to face the target again. "Then picture her face and aim right between the eyes."

"What do you think I was doing?"

We spent another half hour shooting until I hit the inner two rings of the target three times in a row. Then he took the bow from me and stood at my back. "Using your power is no different. You need the same focus, the same steady hand, and the same aim. Breathe and fire the same way." He pointed over my shoulder at the target. "Hit it this time without the arrow."

I frowned. "But I've been able to do that for a long time. That's not what I need to learn."

"Do it anyway."

With one swift thrust of my hand, the target flew backward, striking the fence before flipping up into the air. I turned toward Warren with my hands raised as if to say "See?"

"Good. Now, lift the target and hold it steady with one hand and blow it up with the other."

I raised an eyebrow. "Really?"

"Really."

"Blow it up?"

He made an explosion sound with his mouth and splayed out his fingers.

I sighed. "OK."

I turned toward the target and used my right hand to lift it into the air against the fence. I pumped my left fist a few times. Then released the power from my left hand, but moved my right enough so the target flipped up and somersaulted over the fence into the forbidden territory. My nose wrinkled as I looked at Warren and shrugged.

He pointed. "Get it back over here."

Using my power, I picked up the target and gently lifted it back over to our side of the fence.

"Again."

I held it up and focused on it for a moment. My left hand rose to meet my right and I heard Fury's voice in my head. *Breathe in and as you slowly exhale, pull the trigger.*

The target exploded into a million pieces.

Warren looked at me when we pulled into Echo-10. "I'm really proud of you, babe."

I smiled. "Thank you. I'm kinda proud of me too."

His head tilted in question. "Are you proud enough to attempt it on Lamal?"

I sucked in a sharp breath through my teeth. "Not quite. I think I need a few more days of practice before I start testing it on humans."

He nodded. "Fair enough." We got out and walked toward the building. "I think he should stay here then till we get back."

"I agree."

He used the retina scanner to get us inside, and when we reached the lobby he pointed to the elevator. "I'm going to check to make sure we didn't leave anything in our room. Do you want to sit with Taiya till we're ready to go?"

"Yes. Thank you." I squeezed his hand before he walked to the elevator.

"Oh my god, you're back!" Melinda's voice carried down the hallway from the clinic. "Girl, I need your number!"

I looked around with alarm. "What's going on?"

"She's awake. My girl's awake!" She motioned for me to hurry up. "C'mon. Geez, you're slow."

"When did she wake up?" I asked, doubling my pace toward the hall.

"Just now, but she ain't real lucid yet." She grabbed my sleeve when I was close enough and pulled me into the clinic. We walked into Taiya's cubicle where the nurse was adjusting the tube on one of Taiya's I.V. bags. When I got close enough to the bed, my hopes deflated.

Taiya's eyes were closed.

"What happened?" Melinda asked the nurse.

The nurse scribbled some notes on a clipboard. "I told you this is a process and to not get too excited yet."

Melinda looked at me. "She was awake. I swear she was."

I smiled and put my hand on Melinda's arm. "I believe you."

Tears pooled in Melinda's eyes. "I thought she'd turned a corner, ya know?"

"I know, but she is getting better," I said.

"She certainly is," the nurse agreed. "All her vitals are holding at normal." She patted Melinda's shoulder. "It's only a matter of time now."

Melinda wiped her nose on the back of her hand and sniffed. "I know." She looked at me. "Quick. Tell me somethin' funny. Did you shoot anyone today with that purple bow and arrow of yours?"

I grinned. "No, but I did blow up the target."

She laughed. "Of course you did."

"We're heading home today," I said.

She slumped onto the edge of her daughter's bed. "But you are comin' back, right?"

I crossed my arms. "That almost sounds like you *want* me to come back."

"I may not trust you, but you're not half bad," she said. "As long as I can keep my eye on you."

"We'll only be gone a few days. Sometime next week, I think. Can I bring you back anything from the real world?" I asked.

She smiled and put her hand on Taiya's arm. "Nah. I got every-thing I need right here."

I left my cell number with Melinda, and then I rode back to Ashe-ville with Warren and Reuel. The next morning, we went to my appointment with Dr. Watts. I'd gained a low record of only three pounds that month. I told her we'd be traveling for a few weeks and that I'd schedule my next appointment when I got back into town. I didn't tell her I might die between now and then because I was pretty sure I'd stressed my doctor out enough at my last checkup.

We spent the weekend packing, and on Monday we went to the bank where Warren signed all the documents to buy the house. We left with the keys and immediately drove the first truckload of boxes to the new house. Warren wouldn't let me lift a thing, not using my arms, anyhow. I was able to use my power, however, inside the house to put things where I wanted them. Outside the privacy of the house, Warren enlisted the help of our security detail. While the men moved furniture, Adrianne showed up around noon to help me unpack.

She was wearing a ball cap and zero makeup. This wasn't a good sign. "You OK?" I asked as she walked through my new front door.

"Yeah."

I raised an eyebrow. "You don't look OK. What's going on?"

She groaned and dropped her purse on the kitchen counter.

"Is it Azrael?" I asked.

Her head snapped up. "Have you heard from him?"

I pointed toward the sofa. "Sit. We need to talk. Do you want some coffee? Breakfast?"

She frowned. "Do you even have breakfast?"

I shook my head.

"You're not right in the head," she said, plopping down in the living room.

"So you've told me since we were kids." I sat next to her. "Azrael's gone, Adrianne."

She straightened and turned toward me. "Gone? What do you mean?"

"We went to Claymore because we found Taiya. He's been holding her there all along," I said.

Her mouth fell open. "What? Why?"

I shrugged my shoulders. "I'm not sure. He said he did it to protect me. He also did it to use Taiya as bait so I'd come looking for her at Claymore."

"He's wanted you at Claymore since the beginning. Even enlisted me to try to convince you to go. He describes it like a fortress built to protect you."

"That much is true. A fortress is a good way to put it." I looked up at her. "And I'm going back to stay there for a while."

Her lips parted. "What about the wedding?"

"The wedding is still on…if I live till then," I added with a chuckle.

Adrianne wasn't amused. "When are you going?"

"As soon as we get settled in here, I guess. I'm afraid bad things are about to happen. It feels like I'm looking at blue sky when it's really only the eye of a hurricane about to blow me over."

"What kind of bad things?"

"It sounds like The Morning Star will launch a full-blown war to take my baby if he has to."

"And you think Azrael has known about this war the whole time?" she asked.

"The whole time," I echoed with a nod.

"But why wouldn't he tell you?"

"That's the million-dollar question."

"Is that why he left? Because you found out he was keeping it from you?" she asked.

I grimaced. "I think he left because I threatened to kill him."

"Sloan!"

I held my hands up in defense. "That's not the whole reason. He left a letter. He was planning to leave anyway."

She sank back in her seat. "He never said anything to me about leaving." Tears sparkled in her eyes, and I wanted to kill Azrael all over again.

I put my hand on her knee. "I'm really sorry."

"You called it. You tried to tell me," she said, sniffing back her emotions.

"That doesn't make it any easier."

She stood up and stretched her arms up over her head. "Nope, but I know what will make it better. Booze. Where's the liquor box, Sloan? I know you have one."

I looked at the time on my phone. "It's a little early, isn't it?"

She scowled. "Really?"

I pointed toward a box in front of the fridge. "I don't have much, but there's tequila and peach schnapps in that one. Warren has some whiskey stashed somewhere too."

"Tequila works," she said, crossing the kitchen.

"Shot glasses are in there as well." I got up to follow her.

She pulled the bottle from the box and unscrewed the cap. "Who needs a glass?" She turned the bottle up to her lips.

I laughed. "This is going to get interesting."

She winked a watery eye at me. "You'd better believe it."

By the time my dad showed up with dinner, Adrianne was passed out in my new bedroom. She never cried, but she cussed a lot. Warren drove her home after we ate, and I was in bed by the time he returned. His eyes were wide with bewilderment. "She's going to be in pain tomorrow."

I pulled the comforter down on his side of the bed. "Thank you for taking her."

"Of course." He stripped off his shirt, and for a second I forgot to breathe. Pausing by my side of the bed, he leaned and gently kissed my lips. "First night in our new house. Want to take a bath in our giant ass bathtub?"

I moaned with pleasure at the thought. "Absolutely." I looped my arms around his neck and kissed him again.

He smiled against my lips. "Give me five minutes to start the bath. Then I'll come back for you."

"Hurry," I whispered.

Across the room, he closed the bathroom door behind him. A second later, I heard the running water from the faucet. When he returned, he peeled the covers off me without a word and slipped an arm under my knees. The other arm he scooped behind my back. Effortlessly, he lifted me off the mattress and carried me to the bathroom. When he walked through the door, I laughed. "I think the tradition is carrying the lady across the threshold of the front door."

"Want me to take you outside and try again?" he asked, smiling.

I dropped my head back and laughed. "No way. The bathroom is much better."

Gently, he put my feet on the floor, then grasped the edge of his shirt I was wearing and pulled it up over my head. Bubbles were almost spilling over the edge of the tub that was lined with glittery votive candles. "Are those for the wedding?" I asked.

"Yes. Don't tell Adrianne."

"When did we get all these in here?" I asked, noting there were candles flickering all around the bathroom.

He slipped my cotton panties over my hips. "I hid a box up here this afternoon."

"Sneaky."

Taking my hand, he led me to the tub. I balanced on one foot and stuck my toes in. The water was perfect. I stepped fully inside as he slipped off the rest of his clothes. In the pit of my stomach, I felt a slight tingle. How could I not with the naked man standing before me?

But the tingle increased, effervescing like vinegar poured over baking soda. The sensation bubbled up, quickly rising to my brain, making the room spin out of control. I wavered, and Warren grasped my arms to steady me.

"Help me," I was able to say as my legs crumpled into the water.

Still standing outside the tub, he pulled me against him, my body trembling in his arms. He was shouting my name, but I couldn't respond. The trembling intensified to convulsions. It was a seizure. It had to be.

My spine arched and a scream rose from deep within me. Everything swirled out of focus then quickly snapped back together. Light exploded throughout the room in every direction, shattering the mirrors and windows, sending shards of glass slicing through the air.

Warren curled around me, a human shield against the spray. The sound of tinkling pieces against the marble countertops and the tile floor created an almost beautiful, deadly melody.

This was it.

This was the moment Azrael was waiting for.

The Vitamorte had risen.

CHAPTER NINETEEN

I EXPECTED TO lose consciousness. Wished for it even. But the sweet relief from the black abyss of a coma never came. On the contrary, my senses sharpened, burned my psyche, churned in my belly.

My eyes opened and saw Warren still curled around me. No longer a soulless void, his spirit was a brilliant white. He was not a human; he was an angel. And for the very first time, I could see him. All of him.

The shrill chime of Warren's cell phone reverberated off the bathroom walls, but he didn't move to answer it. Reuel's heavy footsteps approached our door. A bat flapped its wings somewhere outside the open window. My skin prickled against the cold breeze.

"Sloan?" Warren's voice echoed in my head. "Sloan, can you hear me?"

I blinked and nodded my head. "I hear *everything*."

A fist pounded against our door.

"Reuel, get in here!" Warren shouted, piercing my eardrums.

I winced.

Reuel rattled the locked door handle before striking it and

knocking the door open. A second later he was in the bathroom. His face turned bright red when he saw me. He quickly shielded his eyes with his hand. "I'm sorry. I thought you were in trouble," he said.

My face snapped up. "Whoa. You speak English now?"

"You can understand me?" he asked.

I looked at Warren. "What's he talking about?"

"He's not speaking English, Sloan."

"My God, it's happened," Reuel said, a note of wonder in his deep voice.

"Reuel, get the towels," Warren said. "Watch the glass. It's everywhere."

Reuel tiptoed across the floor, still using his hand as a blinder so he wouldn't see me naked. He picked up a towel, shook the glass from it, then tossed it to Warren. He quickly wrapped it around me. Reuel spread out other towels on the floor and Warren helped me out onto them.

"What happened?" Warren asked me.

With one hand, I held my towel. With the other, I gripped my forehead. "It's the baby. This is what Azrael was talking about. I don't know how to describe it, but it's like she just woke up or something."

Warren quickly pulled his boxer shorts back on, then took my arm and helped me back to the bedroom. Reuel was blowing out candles. I sat on the bed and Warren's phone rang again. "Answer it," I said.

When he turned toward the phone, I saw the red lines on his side, back, and shoulder where pieces of glass were embedded. I raised my hand toward him, power sizzling in my fingertips, and like iron being pulled to a magnet, the bloody glass fragments were plucked from his flesh and hung suspended in the air. He turned with wide eyes, and the pieces fell to the carpet.

He put the phone to his ear. "Hello?"

I could hear the whole conversation as clearly as if he'd used the speaker. It was Kane. "We've picked up some activity in the atmosphere. Are you OK?"

"Yes," Warren said. "I think the activity was Sloan, or the baby, rather." He was still staring at me, dumbfounded. "We're all right here, but I want a team at the house tonight and around the clock till we get back to Claymore."

"Roger that, sir," Kane said. "I'll send a unit now."

Warren ended the call. "That was Kane—"

I cut him off. "I heard every word."

"We need to get you back to Echo-10," he said. "We'll leave first thing in the morning."

I shook my head. "I want to leave tonight. Now."

He looked at the clock. It was already after ten. "We won't get there until morning at this rate. Are you sure you want to drive all night again?"

"Warren, I can warp there," I said.

His head snapped back. "Excuse me?"

"You heard me."

"How do you know?"

I shrugged. "I just do. I can cross the spirit line now."

Even from across the bedroom, I could see him gulp. "How is this possible?"

"It's like Azrael said. Our little girl is different. Very different." I stood and held my hand toward the dresser. The drawer slid open without me touching it. "Get dressed. We've got work to do."

I'd secretly hoped that crossing the spirit line and traveling unbound by time and space would be like flying, or maybe like moving at hyper speed aboard the Millennium Falcon.

It wasn't.

It was similar to stepping on and off a two-sided elevator. The doors closed in Asheville and re-opened in New Hope. We could travel inside the elevator shaft, but we couldn't cross through the doors on the other side. The whole process, from the time Warren took my hand in our bedroom to the moment we found ourselves at the doorstep of Echo-10, took about the length of slow blink.

Enzo was standing in the lobby when Warren scanned us into the building. "Kane called me." He pointed between us. "How did you get here so fast?"

"Aboard the Angel Express. Where's Lamal?" I asked.

He motioned to the elevator. "Floor four. I'll take you to him."

"Is Kane on his way here?" Warren asked as we rode up to the fourth floor.

Enzo nodded. "The whole crew is. Where's Reuel?"

"He stayed behind to board up our bathroom windows. He'll be here soon," Warren explained.

"Bathroom windows?" Enzo asked.

"My superpowers got a little messy tonight," I said.

The elevator dinged and we stepped off. We could have warped there faster. We followed Enzo down the hall to the door on the left. It opened to a college dorm style living area with a kitchen, bathroom, and four bedroom doors. He went to the second one on the right and knocked.

"Come in," Lamal called.

I paused, still taken back by my sudden understanding ear.

I looked at Enzo. "What did he say?"

Enzo shrugged. "I'm not sure, but I think he said we can come in."

"That wasn't English?" I asked, already knowing the answer.

Enzo looked at me like I'd grown a third eye. "No ma'am, and my Katavukai is limited."

I gripped my temples. "This is so weird."

We walked into the room and found Lamal reading on his bed. "A little late for house calls, isn't it?" he asked.

"I'm sorry for the time, but I came straight here," I said.

Lamal closed his book and swung his legs off the bed. He eyed me carefully as he slowly stood. "You comprehend what I'm saying?"

"I do."

"It's happened then," he said, walking over to me. "The Daughter of Zion awakens."

I turned my ear toward him. "The who?"

He put his hand on my stomach. "The child of the prophecy is here." The baby fluttered against his hand. "It's a miracle," he said softly.

"Are you ready to not be stuck here anymore?" I asked.

A hopeful smile spread across his face. "Yes, but we must do it in Chicago."

My head tilted. "Why?"

"It's the next part of Azrael's plan."

I gulped. Azrael had mentioned that in his letter, but he gave no explanation. "This is it then."

"This is what?" Warren asked.

I put my hands on my hips and looked at the floor. "This is the moment I have to decide if I trust Azrael or not."

Everyone stared at me.

I looked at Enzo. "How soon can we get the team in the air?"

He nodded. "Tonight, if we have to. They're ready."

"Tomorrow," I said. "Let everyone take their time in the morning, and we'll leave after lunch."

"Are you sure about this?" Warren asked.

I sighed. "No, but don't worry." I touched his arm and smiled. "I can handle it."

And I knew that I could.

"I want to see Taiya before we go to bed," I announced as we walked back to the elevator.

"She's been awake a couple of times in the past few days," Enzo said.

I smiled. "I know. I've kept in touch with Melinda."

We stopped at his floor and Enzo got off. "See you tomorrow," he said and stepped out of the way.

"Get some rest. We're all going to need it," Warren told him.

"You too, sir."

We rode to the first floor and walked down the dark hallway to the clinic. Inside, the nurse was working at her station and Melinda was asleep in the recliner by Taiya's bed. I looked at the nurse. "Does her mother sleep here every night or did something happen?"

"She sleeps here every night," the woman whispered.

I went to Taiya's bedside and took her hand. I squeezed her fingers gently and sent a small bump of my power into her. Her eyes fluttered open. They were no longer the brilliant blue I remembered. They had faded to a dull slate, the color of the sky before snow clouds roll in.

"*Praea.*"

My nerves prickled at the name given to me by my demon mother, but I was thankful for her voice nonetheless. "Good morning, sweet girl. You've been sleeping for a long time." I knew I was speaking to her in her common tongue, though I still didn't know how.

She smiled. "Praea is different."

"Quite different. You're different too. How do you feel?"

"Weak," she answered. "Tired."

I pushed a few loose strands of her red hair back off her face. "Rest. You've got nothing but time."

"I missed you, my sister."

My breath caught in my chest. "I missed you too."

Her eyes slowly closed again.

"You're back." Melinda's voice startled me. I turned as she straightened in her recliner.

"We're back," I said.

"I wasn't expectin' you for a few more days. Isn't today movin' day?" she asked.

I nodded. "It was. We finished and came back here." I pointed toward the door. "Why don't you let me sit with her tonight? You go upstairs and find a bed to sleep in."

She looked at Warren, then back at me. "Are you sure?"

"Positive. Go and get a good night's sleep."

Without protest, she got up and stretched her arms up over her head. She bent and kissed her daughter's forehead. "Come get me if you need me. I'm in unit two on the second floor."

"We'll be fine," I assured her.

"Goodnight," she said at the door as she left.

I looked at Warren. "You go on up to bed too. You've worked hard today."

"So have you, babe."

"I really am fine," I said. "I want to stay with her."

He tucked my hair behind my ear. "And I want to stay with you."

I pulled his hand to my lips and kissed it. I motioned to the bed in the other exam room. "At least go lie down."

He pressed a kiss into my hair. "I won't argue with that."

The recliner was even more comfortable than it looked, or maybe I was more tired than I'd realized. After replaying the events of the day in my head, the quiet *beep, beep, beep* of Taiya's heart monitor lulled me to sleep. But in my new state, even sleep was no longer the same. I closed my eyes to my world, but was very awake in a different one. I knew it wasn't a dream, but I also knew it wasn't reality. At least not the reality I was accustomed to.

I was seated at a bistro table with my back to the street. The sounds of people, their rolling suitcases, their bartering with vendors, was alive and loud behind me. The window of the cafe in front of me reflected the scene in fractals, but I couldn't turn in my chair to see it first-hand. Something was blocking me; I suspected it was the back of the recliner.

"Do you still hate me?" Azrael's voice perked my ears. I saw him on the other side of the glass in the cafe. He was drinking a beer from a frosted mug. I could see the bubbles rising to meet the foam that crested the top.

He held up his hand. "Never mind. Don't answer that. Do you at least believe me now?"

I shook my head. "I don't know what to believe. You've told so many lies."

He bowed his head in acceptance of my statement. "Yes. I have, but it's only ever been to protect you. To protect your daughter. To protect your world and mine."

"I don't know how to trust you," I said. "I certainly don't know how to forgive you."

"I don't need your forgiveness, Sloan, or even your trust. What I do need is for you to remember my words, whether you believe them or not."

A chill made me shudder.

"Remember my words," he said again. "Trust no one."

CHAPTER TWENTY

*E*CHO-10 WAS a flurry of activity when I awoke still in the recliner several hours later. I wondered if the sun was out, but there was no way to tell. I looked at my watch. Nope. It was five in the morning. I looked around the room, and Taiya was staring back at me. "Hello," she said in Katavukai.

I rubbed my eyes. "Good morning."

I looked through the glass wall into the other room. Warren was no longer on the bed.

"He said he would bring back breakfast," she said, causing me to wonder if she could read my mind.

"How are you feeling?" I sat forward, closing the footrest on the chair with a heavy thud.

She took a deep breath like she was testing the capacity of her lungs. "Very well, actually. I feel better when you're around."

I smiled. "I get that a lot."

Her face fell. "People used to be better around me too."

"I'm better around you. I've been very worried."

"What happened to me?" she asked.

Oh boy. This is a big conversation to jump into before coffee.

"Taiya, do you remember your father? Do you remember Ysha?" I asked.

With the mention of his name, I watched the blood drain from her face. She shuddered. "Yes."

"I killed him." I leaned forward in my seat. "Did you know that?"

She shook her head slightly.

"When he passed from this world, part of you died with him. We almost lost you," I said.

Her eyes darted around the room. "I'm no longer spirit, am I?"

I shook my head. "You're only human."

Tears spilled down her cheeks, and she buried her face in her hands. Swiftly, I moved beside her and put my arms around her shoulders. "I'm human," she wept into my lapel.

When she pulled back, I realized she was smiling.

I wasn't sure if I should apologize or not.

She gripped my biceps. Inside her forearm, my name was still scarred into her flesh. "I don't have to go back? He can't take me away again?"

I let out a deep sigh of relief. "No, sweet girl. He's gone forever. No one will ever take you away again."

A mixture of laughter and tears bubbled out of her. She hugged me again. "Thank you, Sloan. Thank you."

"Well, this is a pleasant sound very early in the morning. Laughter? Am I in the right building?" I turned as Nathan entered the room.

Warren was right behind him with a large Styrofoam cup and a plate of fruit with a bagel. He handed me the plate, then reached into his jacket pocket and pulled out two cartons of chocolate milk. "I love you," I said as I took them from him.

Nathan's head snapped back. "Geez, man. You said she'd changed, but this is terrifying."

I stuck up my middle finger. "Shut up, Nathan."

He winked at me. "That's more like it." He walked over to

Taiya's bedside. "Hello, young lady. It's good to see you up and smiling."

Taiya's cheeks tinged with pink and she scooted down in her bed, pulling the covers up to her chin.

I looked at Nathan. "I think she likes you."

"Ah, I like her too." He turned to me. "I would like to formally thank you for having another crisis and getting me out of drills today."

"You're coming with us?" I asked, surprised.

He nodded toward Warren. "By special request from the boss."

Warren shrugged and sipped his coffee. "We've had enough adventures without him lately."

"You're leaving?" Taiya sat up straight again. "You can't leave me."

I put my hand on her knee. "I won't be gone long. I have to go handle some business, but I'll be back."

She furiously shook her head. "No. No, you can't."

"It's going to be OK, Taiya. I'll return before you know it."

Nathan leaned toward Warren. "When did Sloan learn angel gibberish?"

Taiya dug her fingers into my arm. "Let me come. Let me come with you."

I peeled her grip off me. "I can't do that. It's too dangerous. Besides, your mother is here. You don't want to leave your mother, do you?"

Tears—this time, not happy ones—streaked her cheeks again. "Please, Sloan. Don't leave. They're going to kill you. They're going to kill you."

I cradled her face in my hands and brushed away her tears with my thumbs. "I'm not that easy to kill. I promise I'll be fine." But the fear in her watery eyes was truly unsettling. So unsettling that I had to change the subject. Fast. I held up a plump, red grape. "Want one?"

She shook her head.

"What's wrong with her?" Warren asked.

"She doesn't want me to leave. She's afraid."

"I don't blame her," Nathan said.

"Nobody does," Warren agreed.

Just then, Melinda entered the room wearing a bathrobe over her pink pajama pants and shirt. Her hair was matted on one side and she had pillow lines on her face. "What the hell is goin' on up in here? Why are so many people up at this ungodly hour?" Before I could answer, her eyes settled on her daughter. "Taiya?"

"*Ashta*," Taiya said. It was the Katavukaian word for *mother*.

"Taiya?" Melinda said again as she swept across the room. I stood and moved out of her way.

Warren nudged me with his arm as the two of them embraced. "Come on. Let's give them some privacy."

I nodded in agreement and followed him and Nathan out into the hall.

Melinda was right. It seemed half of Claymore was in the lobby or in the first meeting room. "Are all these people going with us?" I asked, drinking from my carton of milk.

"Enzo called an SF-12 all hands meeting," Warren said.

Nathan swiped a grape off my plate. "I'm counting a lot higher than twelve."

"Me too," I said as we passed the meeting room. "Do we need to be in there?"

Warren shook his head. "No. I talked to Enzo about it this morning."

"Do I have time to take a shower?" I asked.

"Sure," Warren said, gesturing to the elevator. "I promised Nate he could see the penthouse suite anyway." He pressed the button to call the elevator, and almost immediately the doors slid apart.

On the other side of them was Allison Fury.

Warren groaned.

Nathan tipped an imaginary hat.

And I let out a labored sigh as Fury brushed right past me,

purposefully knocking her shoulder against mine. I dropped my face back toward the ceiling. "Are you kidding me?" I asked no one in particular.

The three of us walked onto the elevator, and before the doors closed, I watched her walk into the SF-12 meeting. I pointed in that direction. "She's one of the twelve."

Warren shook his head. "You don't know that."

"Did you ask Enzo?" I asked.

He didn't answer.

Nathan leaned toward Warren. "She is one of the twelve, man. Hate to break it to you."

"And she's going with us today?" My voice was loud and squeaky.

Nathan nodded. "Between your luck and her talent, I'm sure that's a reasonable assumption."

I cursed under my breath.

Nathan looked at Warren. "I feel like all we need is Shannon Green here to complete the trifecta."

Warren chuckled.

I rolled my eyes. "Nathan McNamara, bite your tongue."

It was a two-and-a-half-hour flight from New Hope to Chicago aboard The Sentinel, Claymore's private jet. Nathan, Warren, Reuel, Lamal, Enzo, and I were gathered at a conference table in a semi-private cabin between the galley and the front of the plane where nine members of SF-12 were seated. Fury was among them.

I could see her through the crack in the dividing curtain. Her perfect head rested against the wall and earbuds were seated in her dainty ears. She was probably listening to music too cool for me to appreciate, like David Bowie or Depeche Mode.

Nathan leaned against my arm and lowered his voice in my ear. "If you stare at her any harder, I fear her hair might catch fire."

My lips spread into a smile. "One can hope, right?"

"Enzo, what's the plan when we land?" Warren asked.

"We will land at a small airport outside the city. Two passenger vans will be waiting to take us north to Uptown. If all goes well, Sloan will free Lamal and we'll drive right back to the airport and return to Claymore."

Nathan smirked. "That's a big *if*, my friend. You know things don't usually go well with us, so what's the real plan?"

"If there's trouble, we expect it to be from The Destroyer. As we understand it, there's a bounty on Lamal that Abaddon wants to collect. Right now, Sloan is like a blinking red dot on the radar of the universe, but once she taps her power to free Lamal, she'll go from a blinking red dot to a florescent red oil spill complete with smoke alarms and sirens. It will almost certainly stir up trouble."

Warren crossed his arms. "I'll bet that trouble doesn't wait for Sloan to use her power. I can feel the difference in her now. She's already an oil spill."

A brick dropped in the pit of my stomach.

"We need to get in and get out as quickly as possible," Enzo said.

"Abaddon will not come alone, especially since he expects Azrael to be there," Reuel said.

Everyone looked at me with questioning eyes.

"What?" I asked.

"Translate," Nathan said.

"Oh! I forgot," I said. "It really sounds no different to me. Um, he said Abaddon won't come alone because he expects Azrael to be there."

Enzo nodded. "We assumed as much."

Nathan crossed his arms and looked over at Reuel. "Why is it that you understand English, but you don't speak it?"

The looks on everyone's faces except for Reuel and Lamal made it clear we all wondered the same thing. Reuel and Lamal exchanged a puzzling glance. "Do we say?" Reuel asked him.

I leaned my elbows on the table. "Now you have to say."

Lamal was clearly worried. "Our language is the mark of our consecration. Speaking in a common tongue of this world means we have chosen to leave our home and become part of this one. Permanently."

I translated for the group.

Reuel cleared his throat nervously. "There is only one angel in our world permitted to speak other than Katavukai."

"He says only one angel in Heaven is allowed to speak our language," I said.

"Azrael," Warren answered.

Reuel slowly shook his head. "Samael."

The only sound was the roar of the engine of the plane.

"Are you saying...?" My voice faded away before I could even get all the words out.

"Azrael's one of the fallen?" Nathan asked.

Lamal looked at me. "The archangel forfeited his place with The Father when he aligned himself with The Morning Star."

I translated.

The boot Warren had crossed over one knee landed hard on the floor with a heavy thud. "He did what? How did I not know this?"

"Because he kept it from you, like he's kept everything else from us," I said.

Nathan pinched the bridge of his nose and squinted his eyes. "So he's working with Kasyade, the queen of evil, to use Sloan's kid to destroy the spirit line?"

"Azrael says his intentions are different. That he wants to protect Sloan," Reuel answered. "Which is why I agreed to help him."

My eyes narrowed. "Unfortunately, what he says is often very different from the truth."

Reuel didn't have a response.

"Lamal, you can see the future. What do you think?" I asked.

Lamal's eyes fell to the table. "I can only see the future from my world. Not this one." He looked back up at me. "For what it's worth, however, I do believe that though Azrael's methods are flawed, his intentions are not evil. I believe he wants to make amends with The Father and have his place in The Kingdom restored."

I sat back hard in my chair. "So best case scenario is he's going to use me and my daughter for his own salvation?"

Reuel and Lamal shrugged their shoulders in unison.

"What makes you so sure it's that and not world destruction?" I asked.

Lamal turned up his palms. "If he wanted to destroy the spirit line, wouldn't he have turned you over to The Morning Star already?"

I crossed my arms over my chest.

"Uh, Sloan?" Nathan asked, looking around the table. "We don't know what you guys are saying."

Just then, a blood-curdling scream came from the galley.

Warren and Enzo were on their feet before I could even register that someone might be in trouble. They pushed through the divider curtain and disappeared into the other compartment. I moved to get up, but Nathan blocked me with his arm.

I focused my attention on the other side of the wall and recognized one of the pleading voices immediately. It was Taiya. A moment later, Warren hauled her into the room by the arm with a startled flight attendant trailing behind them.

"Taiya, what are you doing here?" I asked, pushing my way past Nathan.

"I'm sorry. I couldn't let you leave me." She stumbled toward me and grabbed my arms. "I'm sorry. Forgive me. Please, forgive me, Praea."

I looked at Enzo who was behind the flight attendant. "How did this happen?"

He held up his hands. "I have no idea, unless she somehow hid in the cargo that was loaded beneath the plane."

"Remember we are talking about the master of prison breaks," Nathan said.

Taiya was still in her hospital gown. She wasn't even wearing shoes. I'd packed a bag of clothes from the closet that had been stocked for me at Echo-10, but none of my maternity wear would even come close to fitting Taiya. There was only one other female on board—apart from the staff and NAG, who was busy flying the plane.

I moved Taiya around me and put her in my chair, then I walked around the table and into the crew's cabin. I leaned across Kane who was seated next to Fury and tapped her on the shoulder. She slowly opened her eyes and turned to face me—no, scowl at me. "What?"

"I need your help," I said.

She blinked.

"I need to borrow some clothes."

She laughed. The bitch actually laughed. "My clothes won't fit you."

I gasped. "That's so mean."

Closing her eyes again, she leaned her head back against the wall. "No, honey, it's not mean. It's true."

"Hey!" My shock was replaced with anger. I almost ripped her out of her chair using my power, but I thought better of it.

She looked at me again.

"Why are you even here?" I asked her.

"Because this is my job," she said.

I leaned toward her. "Well, guess what, sweetheart. Your job is *me*. I'm your job. No one dislikes that more than I do, but right now I need your help. And if I have to ask for it again, it won't be nicely."

Her lips spread into a thin smile. "How may I help you?"

"I need clothes for another girl on the plane. I'm six months pregnant with Warren's daughter, so my clothes won't fit her. Otherwise, I wouldn't ask. Can we please borrow something for this poor girl to wear so she doesn't freeze to death?"

Her eyebrow rose in question. "Only six months?"

I lunged toward her, but someone from behind grabbed me around the waist. It was Warren.

"Can we all please calm the hell down?" he asked.

"What do you need, Warren?" she asked.

I'm going to kill her.

"You heard Sloan. We need clothes."

Without argument, she stood up from her seat and stepped over Kane. She opened the overhead bin and pulled out a black duffel bag, which she put on Kane's lap (he didn't object). From inside, she pulled out a pair of black pants and a black shirt. She handed them to Warren. "Bra and panties too?"

My fists balled at my sides.

He held up the clothes. "This is fine. Thank you."

Fury batted her lashes at him. "You're welcome anytime you want."

It was obvious this was all for my benefit; Fury clearly wasn't the flirting type. She got off on being on top, and I doubted it mattered who was beneath her.

"I want to throw her off the plane without a parachute," I muttered to Warren as we returned to the conference room.

"You don't have to deal with her," he said. "She's going to keep torturing you. It's what she does."

"She needs to know she doesn't intimidate me," I told him.

Nathan must have overheard because he laughed and pointed at me. "That's hilarious."

I ignored him and grabbed Taiya's hand to pull her out of my chair. "Enzo, where's the bathroom?"

"Back of the plane on the left," he said.

A few minutes later, Taiya walked out of the bathroom, carrying her gown. I frowned. She looked like an extra from Mad Max in Fury's black cargos and fitted Under Armor shirt. I shook my head and sighed.

"See if these will fit her," Enzo said behind me.

I turned to find him holding a pair of small black combat boots. "Thank you."

"We'll be landing soon, so you'll both need to buckle up."

"OK."

The three of us returned to the conference room. I put Taiya in a seat, then knelt to help her put on her shoes. "What are we going to do with her when we get there?" I asked, glancing around at everyone at the table.

Warren linked his fingers behind his head and leaned back. "I think it's pointless to expect her to stay here."

"We need one of those kid leashes," Nathan said.

It wasn't a bad idea. I tied her laces, then buckled her into the seat before sitting in my own.

After a few beats of silence, I realized everyone around the table was staring at Taiya. I didn't need to ask why. They were all thinking exactly what I was thinking: it wasn't a coincidence she showed up on the plane. Azrael said we couldn't trust her.

Looking around the table at my friends, I remembered his other warning: I couldn't trust any of them either.

"Where exactly are we going when we get there?" Warren asked Lamal, rattling me from my daze.

The wheels of the plane skidded along the runway as Lamal answered and I translated for him. "North of the city. A place called Watford Gardens."

"A cemetery? Are you kidding me?"

Lamal looked back at me from the passenger's seat of the van. "I'm surprised you haven't heard of it. It's quite famous. One of the most historic cemeteries in the United States."

"How on Earth would I have heard of it? That's not something they teach us in high school," I said with a smirk.

"I've heard of it," Warren said.

"You don't count. You lived here," I reminded him.

Nathan shrugged. "I've heard of it too. It was in that De Niro movie." He snapped his fingers. "Can't remember what it was called."

Warren nodded his head. "Oh yeah, I saw that."

"Something about the mafia, wasn't it?" Kane asked behind us.

I tossed my hands up. "OK, maybe I'm the only one who hasn't heard of it."

Warren patted my knee as Enzo drove through the cemetery gates and down the paved path.

"Which way?" Enzo asked when he stopped at a fork in the road.

Lamal pointed left.

Around the curve, the headstones and monuments made of stone and bronze were fractured and blackened with time. There were massive memorials, many guarded by marble statues that stood high in the gray sky. Private tombs lined the hillside with heavy iron and bronze gates that had soured to a dark green with the passing years.

Death was old in these grounds, calling up like a hollow echo from the deep, but it was everywhere.

Warren protectively curled his arm around me.

"Tell him this is far enough," Lamal said. "We should be far enough from the street to not attract too much attention."

"Lamal says you can stop here," I told Enzo.

He put the van in park and stretched his arm across the back of Lamal's seat to turn and look at us. "How are we doing on supernatural activity out there?"

I shook my head. "There's nothing."

"*Nanta,*" Reuel agreed.

"There are humans in the area," I said, "but it could be present company that I'm sensing."

Enzo picked up his radio to call the second van behind us. "Fury, I want eyes on the future before we get out."

"Roger that," she called back.

I sat upright. "She can see the future?"

Warren smiled. "That means she's going to scout the area. Make sure we're clear."

"Oh." I looked around the van but didn't see Fury anywhere. "Enzo, can she see us? Can she see like you do?"

"Yes, ma'am."

I looked at Warren.

He leaned toward Enzo's seat. "She wasn't in a special unit when I was here."

Enzo glanced back in the rearview mirror. "Not as far as you were aware. Azrael sent her to Iraq to recruit you here, sir."

Warren's gaze fell to the floor.

"She didn't tell you?" Enzo asked.

Warren shook his head. "She didn't tell me anything." He looked at me. "I always assumed it was a coincidence."

I rolled my eyes so hard it hurt.

The van was silent. After a second, Nathan leaned across Taiya toward me. "Well, this is awkward."

I pointed a finger at him. "Don't make it worse."

He smiled and sat back in his seat.

Fury's voice came over the radio. "There's a woman putting flowers on a grave over the hill, but other than that, we're alone."

"Should we wait for her to leave?" Warren asked.

Enzo shook his head. "I really think we should get out of here as quickly as possible."

"I agree," I said.

Warren looked at me. "You've got one shot at this. Are you ready?"

"I'm ready." And I was.

The cold air and the icy sensation of death took my breath when we stepped out of the warm van onto the cemetery grounds. There was nothing but stone statues, tombstones, and bare, gnarly trees as far as I could see. It was a proper setting for another supernatural showdown if it came to it. And if it did, it would prove that God, the universe, or whoever had a definite flair for the dramatic.

Lamal got out of the car and zipped up his coat all the way to his chin.

"Hold on." I held up a finger and walked behind Warren. I reached into his back pocket and pulled out a billfold. There was eighty-seven dollars inside it.

"What are you doing?" he asked.

I handed him the wallet and carried the money over to Lamal. I shoved it into Jesse's coat pocket. "It's the least we can do, right?"

Warren smiled and gave me a thumbs up.

I looked at Lamal. "You ready?"

He took a deep breath and nodded his head.

Stretching out my hand toward him, I searched until my gift honed in on Jesse's mortal soul. I gripped him with my power of life and held him.

Breathe in. Slowly exhale, and pull the trigger.

I aimed my left hand…

BOOM!

CHAPTER TWENTY-ONE

*L*IGHT DETONATED IN the center of the path. Jesse fell backward onto the grass. A nearby Celtic cross tumbled off its pedestal and crashed onto a grave marker. Taiya fell to her knees beside Nathan. Everyone covered their ears.

In the spot where Jesse had stood was an orb of light about ten inches in diameter, suspended five feet off the ground. I walked forward and realized I could see inside it. Lamal was there, smiling at me. He looked different, but I knew it was him. He was standing in the cemetery; the same statue of Mary was behind him that was in front of me. But everything was bright and golden. Leaves were on the trees, and I could feel the sun on my face through the orb. I was dizzy with happiness.

"You did it, Sloan," he said. "I'm so proud of you."

"You're home now?" It was both a question and a statement because I already knew he was.

He nodded. "I am. Thank you."

"What happens now?" I asked.

"Follow the path," he said. "You'll know the way." He held up his hand. "Until we see each other again."

I didn't want to say goodbye. I didn't want the window to disappear. I wanted to go with him.

But before I could touch the orb, it fizzled out, and the cold of the cemetery stung my skin again.

I shook my head to clear it, then looked around. Warren had hold of my arms from behind. Enzo and the other members of the team were searching the sky. Nathan and Reuel were kneeling beside Jesse. "Is he OK?" I asked.

"He's coming around now," Nathan said. "I don't think he's hurt."

About that time, Jesse's hand twitched. Then he flinched away from where Nathan was trying to take his pulse. Quickly, he scrambled across the grass, the same terrified look on his face that we'd seen on him before. He jumped to his feet, stumbled a few times, then took off at full speed down the path.

"Should we go after him?" Nathan asked.

I shook my head. "No. Let him go. We've done enough to that poor man."

"Where's Taiya?" Enzo asked.

I spun around and didn't see her anywhere. My heart pulsed with panic. "Taiya?" I called out.

"Over the hill, walking down the path to the east," Fury said over Enzo's radio.

Enzo's head whipped to the left, so I took off in that direction. When I reached the top of the slope, I saw her staggering along the road like she was drunk. "Taiya!" I called again.

She didn't stop.

Our whole group had caught up to me. SF-12 was on full alert, searching the horizon through the scopes of their M-4s. Everyone called her name.

She veered off to the right under an old, half-rotten tree. Then she stopped suddenly in front of a white marble angel. It stood at least ten feet tall and was pristine by comparison of every other monument in sight. She fell onto the grass in front of it.

"Taiya!" I yelled again.

Warren grabbed my arm and pulled me to a stop. "Wait. I feel like this is a trap."

He was right. Something was off. The stillness, the cold, the quiet...it was all unsettling. I closed my eyes and swept the area with my gift. "There are angels here that aren't accounted for."

"Still," he said. "We need to leave."

I nodded. "I have to get her."

I ran forward with Warren right beside me until we reached her. She was staring up at the angel. The rest of our group gathered around us. Nathan walked forward and used his sleeve to wipe the inscription on the pedestal beneath the angel's feet. He gasped as he took a step back.

I read it out loud in English even though it was written in Katavukai.

"Nadine Gravelle. An angel in human guise."

Warren pulled on my sleeve, tugging me back a few steps. His eyes searched the ground, and suddenly I realized what he felt.

Absolutely nothing.

The grave beneath the stone was empty.

"Warren?" A female's voice behind us chilled my soul.

We both turned slowly as a woman stepped onto the path from the other side of the road. She wore a long, dark emerald dress that swept down to her black boots. Her hair was black and straight past her shoulders. Her olive skin was pale like she was sick or even dead, but she was human. Of that, I was certain.

Enzo's fist was in the air signaling to Fury, wherever she was, to hold her fire.

"Warren?" the woman asked again. "Is that you?"

I'd seen her before. I covered my mouth with my hands. "It can't be. Nadine?"

Her face brightened. "Yes." She and Warren had the same smile.

Warren's arm came up protectively in front of me. He moved me slightly behind him.

"My son, I know this is confusing, but I need you to listen. You're in great danger here," she said, coming even closer.

He put up a hand to stop her. "That's close enough. I'm aware of the danger. My mother is dead."

She turned her palms up. "But I'm not. I'm here. Touch me. Put your hand in mine and see that I'm real."

Neither of us moved toward her. The breeze caught her hair and blew it across her face. I focused on her soul. It was pure, as beautiful as she was.

"Phenex knows you are here. This is a trick. You must leave this place at once," she said.

"How?" Warren asked.

"They all know you are here," she said, her strange eyes pleading. One was black, the other was the color of fire. "They are coming!"

No sooner had the words left her lips—a sonic boom shook the cemetery. Nadine rushed toward us as Phenex appeared. The devil child thrust a long knife at me, but Nadine lunged between us. My supersensitive ears could hear the blade rip open her green dress and slice through her guts.

I screamed.

The crack from a rifle echoed off the tombs, and Phenex floundered back and to the right a half step. When she swirled toward me again, her right eye and the surrounding bone was missing. There was no blood. "We should have known to find you here, Praea," she hissed, unhindered by the wound.

A second blast knocked Phenex to the ground. Fury had blown out her knee.

There was another boom, and suddenly Azrael was on top of Phenex. He threw her across the lawn, slamming her body into a statue of Mary. It crumbled into a thousand pieces. "Sloan, help Nadine!" he barked.

As I dropped to the ground over Nadine, there was another boom, and I looked up to see The Destroyer coming right at us.

Warren shoved me down and jumped over me, colliding midair with Abaddon. He unleashed his devastating power, flipping the angel back through the air and sending him through the front door of a sealed tomb. When Abaddon pulled himself from the rubble, SF-12 all fired at him at once. His body shook violently as it was riddled with bullets. Warren dove toward Taiya to shield her from the bullets.

"Sloan, now!" Azrael shouted as Phenex came at him.

I looked at Nadine. The knife was buried to the handle in her stomach, just below her sternum. Before I could send my healing power into her, I was knocked forward from behind. I slammed face first into the dirt before Phenex grabbed my hair and slung me across the grass. In my peripheral, I thought I saw Azrael flailing in the air, impaled on something jutting out from a statue. Maybe it was a spear.

When I hit the ground, I rolled and popped up on my knees. Phenex limped toward me, her knee almost completely healed. I stood and squared off with the demon, moving slowly in a wide arch, each of us silently daring the other to make a move. It was Nadine who caught us both by surprise. When Phenex was close enough, Nadine grabbed her leg, yanking her to the ground.

"Kill her, Sloan!" Nadine gurgled.

In a second, my hands were around the child's throat, and I sent every ounce of my killing power into her. Cracks of light splintered through Phenex's face before rupturing into the air. Her eyes were wild with terror—and then completely absent. I realized it was Maria now, lifeless at my fingertips as a shower of shimmery black ash rained down on top of us.

Azrael bellowed in pain, and I looked back as the statue that held him exploded by some unseen force. He fell to the ground and Nathan rushed to help him. Abaddon lurched forward, blood covering what had been a white shirt when he arrived. Reuel's heavy fist connected with Abaddon's face, knocking him sideways toward Warren. Warren blasted him with his power

again, and this time The Destroyer disappeared with a loud
crack!

Blood oozed from Nadine's mouth, but Maria's body was
between us. I used my power to lift the child off and gently place
her on the ground. Then I crawled back to Nadine.

I grasped the handle of the knife and pulled. Nadine lurched
forward in pain. Her eyes locked on mine and I heard Azrael's
voice in my head: "*Trust no one.*"

That's when I saw it.

The Morning Star stared back at me.

I recoiled, scrambling away from her.

From him.

An introduction wasn't necessary; his identity was branded on
his spirit. So was the evil that was synonymous with his many
names: The Morning Star. Lucifer. Satan. The Devil. Leviathan.

Even though I hadn't grown up in church, I'd heard of him my
whole life, but this was certainly not what I'd envisioned. There
was no tail, no horns, no pitchfork. Even beneath the polished,
feminine exterior that was Warren's mother, The Morning Star
was beautiful and aptly named. His spirit gleamed white, brighter
than any I'd ever seen before. Evil, however, radiated from his
being like an electromagnetic pulse. I could feel it. The baby could
feel it.

Azrael stood near me. "Do it now, Sloan! You have the power
to save her."

My chest heaved. I couldn't catch my breath. Realizing I was
still holding Phenex's bloody dagger, I pointed it at Azrael. "This
was you! This was your plan all along!"

The Morning Star rose from the ground, cackling with
laughter that prickled my spine and turned my stomach. "He did
well bringing us to this place, didn't he?" The smile on Nadine's

face was sickening. Her teeth were coated with blood. "It's a very poetic setting, Azrael."

"It's a good place for you to die, Leviathan," Azrael said with a sneer.

Nadine's head tilted. "Come, come. We both know that's not why we're here. I must say, I was beginning to wonder if you'd failed me, old friend. But here you are, delivering as promised."

"He delivers nothing!" I shouted. "You're not taking my daughter."

He spread out his hands. "I don't want to take your daughter from you, Sloan. To separate a child from its mother is cruel." He pointed to himself. "I am not cruel. I want to make this world a better place for all of us, and you have the opportunity to help me. Isn't that what you want? To use your gift to help others?"

My mind flashed back to images of Kayleigh Neeland, the first little girl I'd saved with Nathan.

Suddenly, The Morning Star was standing right in front of me.

"This could be a world free of its great oppressor. Sweet girl, aren't you tired of being a pawn in someone else's game?"

I threw the dagger down and laughed with heavy sarcasm. "Yes! Yours!"

He wagged a finger at me. "It's not my game, child. You and I are but similar pawns, only on opposing sides of the board. Make no mistake, I am no more the game master than you are." He extended his hand. "Join me, and we can end this together. Sloan, you can be free to govern your own existence, to make your own choices and live a life *you* want. Not to play a role which has been forced on you by an unseen tyrant."

"Sloan, look at me!" Azrael screamed. "Don't let him inside your head!"

I whirled toward him. "Should I let you inside my head instead? You're on the same side as he is, Azrael. I know the truth now." I gestured around to Warren, Nathan, and the rest of Azrael's crew. "We all know the truth about you!"

The Morning Star clasped his hands together. "She knows, then, about your fall from grace. And your son knows too."

Azrael held up his hands, pleading with me through his eyes. "Sloan, this isn't what it seems." He took a small step toward me. The front of his shirt was torn and bloody.

"I think it's exactly as it seems! 'Weak humans.' That's what you always call us, like this world would be better if we were in our rightful place beneath you. Or if we no longer existed at all. Even your own son. You said it. That Warren's better without the weaknesses of being human." I pointed to The Morning Star. "You're no different than he is. You lie, manipulate, and bend us to your will. Just like he does."

The Morning Star laughed again, this time at Azrael. "She makes a brilliant point. I like her."

"You," I hissed. "This is what I think of your plan to help the world." With a twist, I backhanded The Morning Star with my power, knocking him back a few steps.

With a smile, he wiped more blood from his mouth. "Are you certain, Sloan?"

I narrowed my eyes. "Go to hell."

He laughed, then slowly opened his arms as wide as he could stretch. When he threw his head back toward the sky, a wave of electric force blew me backward into Nathan and Reuel. I crashed into them, and the three of us toppled over like bowling pins falling in a painful heap onto the ground.

As I pushed myself up, I saw Azrael fire at The Morning Star, blowing him off his feet through the air. He skidded across the grass, spraying up rocks and dirt as his body dug a path along the graves until Nadine's skull connected with the face of a faded monument. Azrael pounced on top of him, but he was instantly overpowered. The Morning Star rolled and pinned him against the grass by the throat.

Azrael didn't seem to be fighting as hard as he could. It might have been because he was in cahoots with the demon, but if that were the case, why fight back at all? A flashbulb memory flickered to life in my brain: the image of my brand of toothpaste laying in the drawer of the Claymore penthouse bathroom.

Azrael was fighting for me. I was certain of it. And the only reason he was having trouble using his full power against the demon was because it carried the face of the woman he loved. I'd felt the same months before in my dream when Nathan had tried to choke me, and I had no choice but to use my power against him.

I needed to blast The Morning Star, but I feared Azrael would be caught in the crossfire.

Just then...

"Stayin' Alive" by the Bee Gees flooded the cemetery.

Azrael's ringtone caught us all by surprise, including The Morning Star. In that fraction of a second, Azrael threw a punch with his fist that connected with his face—with Nadine's face—and knocked the demon off him.

As The Morning Star flailed to regain his stance, I caught him with my power and jerked him up into the air, suspending him above us. I tightened my invisible grip until he squirmed against it in pain, then I lowered him to eye level with me. "I don't know how you took Warren's mother, and I don't care, but it ends here tonight. *You* end here tonight."

I searched his eyes and found Nadine while Barry Gibb crooned the "Stayin' Alive" hook in the background.

Holding her tight with my life force, I flung open my right hand and let death sizzle and crackle at my fingertips. I took a deep breath in. I blew it out slowly and released all my killing power into The Morning Star.

Burning pain sliced through my belly.

My concentration broke as my killing hand connected with The Morning Star...with Nadine.

A blast from Fury's rifle drowned out my scream.

Phenex's dagger clanged against a tombstone, splattering the marble with blood. My blood.

Nathan tackled Taiya.

She was screaming.

Azrael was screaming.

Nadine was silent.

I collapsed to my knees beside her lifeless body and covered my abdomen with my hands. Over her, suspended in the air, was the black rippled spirit of The Morning Star. It condensed into a tight sphere and came right at my face. When it collided with my head, a burning, liquid heat spread through my body as he filled me.

A quiet whisper spoke deep inside me. "This is only the beginning."

Everything went black.

CHAPTER TWENTY-TWO

*T*AIYA'S WAILS WERE the first thing I heard when I woke up. I wasn't sure how much time had passed. Warren's face appeared above me, shielding my eyes from the bright sunshine. "Lie still," he said, lifting my shirt gently.

"What happened?" I asked, trying to look around. All I could see was Reuel talking to Enzo a few feet away.

"Nadine is dead. The Morning Star is gone. Taiya is missing a few fingers, and you are going to need stitches. This cut is superficial, but it's deep."

"The Morning Star was in me."

"He what?"

I touched my forehead. "He was in me. Inside me. Are you sure he's gone?"

"Positive," he said. "He went up through the sky and parted the clouds. Look."

He moved so the sunlight blinded me.

I covered my eyes with my arm. "Why is Taiya missing fingers?"

"Because Fury shot her hand as she went to stab you again," he said. "Risky shot. Too risky."

"Taiya stabbed me?"

He gave a noncommittal shrug. "I guess stab isn't the right word. I think The Morning Star was trying to use her to cut the baby out of you."

I felt like I might vomit.

"Need a med kit?" Cooper asked, walking up behind Warren.

Warren looked back over his shoulder and nodded. Cooper handed him a canvas bag with a red first aid cross embroidered on the front. Warren unzipped it.

"I don't want stitches. Butterfly it or tape it closed as best you can so it won't scar as badly when it heals," I said.

He nodded and poured some kind of solution over my belly. It had to have been an antiseptic, but it burned like battery acid. Tears leaked back into my hair. "Enzo!" Warren yelled, digging through the bag.

Enzo left Reuel and came up on our right. "Sir?"

"Pinch the skin closed for me." Warren tore off pieces of medical tape with his teeth as Enzo dropped to his knees and put his hands on my stomach. I winced as he closed the wound.

"Get the team out of here and back to the airport before this place is crawling with cops," Warren said to him as he pulled my skin closed with the tape.

"What about the rest of you?" Enzo asked.

"We'll warp back and meet you at Claymore," he said. "Go. Now."

Enzo nodded and pushed himself off the ground.

Through her painful screams, Taiya was shouting, "Praea, forgive me," over and over again in Katavukai.

"Is she going to be OK?" I asked.

He nodded. "She won't go bowling ever again, but she'll live."

"She didn't mean to hurt me," I said.

"I know that. The Morning Star's power over her broke as soon as you forced him out. She's been screaming for you ever since."

"I need to help her."

"You'll have to hurry. She needs to leave with Enzo."

I held up my hand. "Help me up."

He hesitated, then hooked his arms under my armpits and lifted me so I didn't have to bend at the waist. As soon as I was vertical, the blood rushed to the wound, making me dizzy. I wavered, but he caught me. "You OK?"

"Yes," I said.

When the dizziness passed, I looked around the broken cemetery. The members of SF-12 were loading into the second van. I didn't see Fury anywhere. Azrael was behind us, slumped over Nadine's lifeless body. She was dead because of me. Warren caught my eye and shook his head. "Not now." He nudged me toward Nathan who was holding his jacket as a compress around Taiya's right hand.

We walked over and Warren helped me down next to them. Taiya shook and sobbed uncontrollably. "Praea, forgive me. Please forgive me."

I cupped her face in my hands. "Shh. I forgive you. You didn't do this. It wasn't your fault. Do you hear me?"

She nodded her head.

I looked at Nathan. "Let me see her hand."

He cringed. "It's really bad. Cooper gave her morphine."

She was missing a bit more than a few fingers. Half her hand was gone, part of it missing almost to her wrist. Only her pinky finger and part of her ring finger remained. "I don't know how I can fix this," I said.

"Do your best, but hurry," Warren said again.

I conjured a ball of light between my hands and Nathan held up her arm. The light was pliable like putty and I moved it around her mangled limb. She screamed even louder as the light cauterized the wound. As her screams faded, sirens intensified in the distance. My light fizzled out. The wounds had closed and the pain was gone, but her fingers were still missing and her hand was terribly deformed. I knew there was nothing else I could do.

The second van drove out of the cemetery. Enzo got in the first van and started the engine. Reuel got in the passenger's seat.

Warren pulled on Nathan's shoulder. "You have to go and take Taiya with you."

He nodded and stood up before pulling Taiya to her feet. When she was standing, she threw her arms around my neck. "Thank you, Sloan."

"You're welcome. Hurry and get in the van. I'll see you when we get back to Claymore."

"Do you promise?" she asked, tears dripping off her cheeks.

I kissed her forehead. "I promise. Stay with Nathan. He'll take care of you."

But it was too late. Blue lights bounced off the tombs and sirens blared as two city police cars came over the hill. They parked, and the officers got out with their weapons drawn, taking cover behind their doors. Nathan stepped protectively in front of me. Warren took my hand.

"Hands where we can see them!" someone shouted.

We obediently raised our hands into the air. In the van, Enzo's hands were on the steering wheel, Reuel's were on the dash. I couldn't see Azrael, but I doubted his compliance when the officer shouted again, "Get your hands up!"

Just then, to our right, an unmarked black SUV with flashing lights pulled in from the opposite fork in the path. And for the first time ever, I breathed a sigh of relief at the sight of Sharvell Silvers as she stepped out of the passenger's side, holding her badge up in one hand and waving with the other. "FBI, lower your weapons!"

She carefully crossed the lawn and approached one of the police cruisers.

Even from across the way, I could hear them talking. "This is part of an ongoing federal investigation of which I'm the lead investigator. I'm going to need your men to move out of here so my team can come in."

The officer argued. "We had reports of shots fired. It appears there are two dead bodies—"

She interrupted him. "I'll handle it from here, gentlemen. This is my crime scene and those are my men out there."

There was a lot of swearing as the officers retreated to their cars. Agent Silvers either didn't hear or she ignored them as she walked over to us.

"I never thought I'd be glad to see you," I said as she approached.

"Would you mind explaining what I'm doing here and why this cemetery looks like a war zone complete with dead bodies?" she asked.

I looped my arm through hers partly because I was so relieved she was there and partly because I needed a crutch. The cut on my stomach still burned enough to make my eyes water. "How did you know to come here?" I asked as I guided her to the small body lying near the pieces of the broken stone cross.

"I've been temporarily reassigned to Chicago while our investigation continues. Azrael called me this morning and said to keep an eye on this place today. We heard the reports come in over the scanners, so we responded." She stopped walking. "Is that Maria Juarez?"

I nodded. "That's her body, anyway."

"And the demon?"

"Destroyed."

She sighed with relief and looked around. She pointed to where Azrael was still holding Nadine. "Who's that?"

"That was Warren's mother." I took a deep breath. "I killed her."

Her arm went slack in mine.

"I'm still not sure how it happened, but I think you'll find prints or other evidence that ties her back to this somehow. I'd start with looking at the home in Los Angeles. The City of Angels seems an appropriate home for this one."

I heard her gulp next to me.

"Thanks for coming and saving us," I said.

She pulled her phone out of her pocket. "I'm going to call the coroner."

While she made the call, Warren came over and put his arm around me. "I think you should talk to him now."

I bit my lower lip and hugged my arms. "OK."

He tucked my hair behind my ear. "Maybe count to ten before you talk to him. He was right about a lot of things."

I nodded. "I know."

"I'm going to try to clean up some of this mess."

He walked off toward one of the demolished tombs, and I crept down the hill toward the fallen Angel of Death. "Azrael?"

He turned his face enough to acknowledge me. "I'm sorry I lied to you, Sloan."

"Why did you lie to me?" I asked.

"Honestly? I feared you'd crumble under the pressure of the truth."

"What is the truth?"

His shoulders rose with a heavy breath. "The Morning Star came to me in Chicago three decades ago, before Nadine gave birth to Warren. He wanted to use my son to breed the Vitamorte to destroy the spirit line. When I refused his offer of partnership, Phenex cut Warren out of Nadine's belly and left her there to die. I couldn't save her and get Warren back, so I made a deal with the devil. I pledged my allegiance to him if he saved her."

"And you were kicked out of Heaven," I said quietly.

He shook his head. "That wasn't the worst of it. The real evil was the method he used to save her." He stroked her face. "She was his insurance policy to secure my compliance."

"But you weren't planning on helping him?"

"Of course not. Life here would be slowly destroyed, and he

would have no need for Nadine and Warren when he was finished with them. They would die anyway."

"So instead you tried to keep me and Warren apart," I said.

"I tried to delay it for as long as possible, and in the meantime I built an army to protect you."

I didn't realize I was crying till my tears nearly froze to my cheeks. I sank onto the ground beside him and put my head on his shoulder. "I'm sorry I doubted you. Forgive me?"

He put his hand on the side of my face. "There's nothing to forgive. You had every reason to distrust me. And you were amazing here today. Exactly what this world needs you to be."

"I'm sorry I couldn't save her, Azrael."

"There was no way you could have. It would take too much to defeat The Morning Star. She probably wouldn't have survived either way. I made my peace with that many years ago."

"But then why the training with Lamal? You believed I could save her."

He shrugged. "I had foolish hopes, and I was wrong." His voice fell again. "There wasn't any way."

"Was that Nadine in the beginning who warned me about Phenex and it being a trap?" I asked.

"It was. The Morning Star was hidden at the point, giving Nadine control over her own mind." He smiled, but there was so much pain in it. "Even to the end, she was a fighter."

"I wish we could have known her," I said.

"Me too."

We both sat there in silence for a few minutes. "What happens now?" I finally asked. "I didn't destroy The Morning Star."

He looked up at the darkening sky. "No, but you certainly weakened him. It will be a long time before he's able to strike again." He turned to me. "And he will strike again. Maybe not in your lifetime, but this isn't over yet."

"No surprise there."

"Our priority now will be finding your mother," he said.

I shook my head. "Please don't call her that."

He put his hand on mine. "I apologize."

"Why is she the priority and not him?"

"Because Kasyade can procure another body in a moon cycle, which has already passed. It will take The Morning Star a solar year to do the same. The Vitamorte will be born by then."

"A whole year?"

He nodded. "It's part of his curse. He's also never allowed to cross the spirit line at all."

"So no warping for him?"

"Correct. He's actually quite limited in your world," Azrael said.

"What will happen with Nadine?" I asked.

"I want to bury her here. We used to take walks through these grounds when we were dating," he said.

"Az?"

"Yeah?"

"That's really creepy."

I felt his shoulders shake with laughter. "Perhaps a little." He reached into his jacket pocket and handed me his cell phone. The missed call that saved his life had been from Adrianne.

"She loves you," I said with a sigh.

He looked at me. "And I care for her very deeply. I hope now you understand."

I nodded. "I do."

"I'm going to make it right with her."

"I believe you."

We sat in quiet for a little while longer, then he gestured toward the tall marble angel that towered over us a few feet away. "I had this placed here over twenty years ago. It's beautiful, isn't it?"

"Very beautiful," I agreed.

Azrael leaned over and pressed a kiss to Nadine's frozen

mouth, then he gently placed her hands over her heart. "*Vara nai minta cantik, me anlo.*"

Until we meet again, my love.

While we waited in the freezing cold for the coroner to take Nadine and Maria away, Agent Silvers pulled me to the side. "Can we talk a second, Sloan?"

"Sure. What's up?"

"I thought you might like some good news in the midst of all this."

I sighed. "I'd love some good news."

"I found the other girls who were infected with the antibiotic-resistant Chlamydia strain."

My heart pounded with hope.

"Sofia Fuentes and Isabel Valenzuela have been at the Children's Research Institute in Dallas. When their medical team was informed that Amalia Acevedo, the girl you cured here, had recovered from the disease, they brought her to Texas to study the antibodies in her bloodstream. Because of that research, they've successfully developed a treatment for the disease that not only cured Sofia and Isabel, but it will also cure Ariana Padilla and anyone else who might have been infected that we don't know about."

I began to cry, and I covered my mouth with my hands. "That's the best news you could have given me." I hugged the agent. "Thank you so much."

She pulled back but held onto my arms. "No, Sloan. Thank you. None of this would have been possible without you."

I smiled and wiped my eyes.

"Go home and get some rest," she said. "You've certainly earned it."

"You too, Agent Silvers."

She winked at me. "Please, call me Sharvell."

Rather than warping back to Claymore, we took the jet with everyone else. Azrael stayed behind to take care of Nadine's arrangements. When we got on board the plane, Fury was in her seat, eyes closed and earbuds in place. I stopped beside her row, and Kane moved out of my way. I took his seat and tapped her arm.

She looked at me, readjusted in her chair, then closed her eyes again.

I plucked the speaker out of her ear. She was listening to the rock band Shinedown. I *loved* Shinedown.

She turned and glared at me. "May I help you?"

"I wanted to say thank you," I told her.

"Don't mention it," she said, taking her earbud out of my fingers.

I blocked her hand from stuffing it back in her ear. "I am mentioning it. You saved me out there today, and you saved Taiya rather than killing her. I wanted you to know I appreciate it."

Her head nodded slightly. "Then help me when we get back. Talk to Azrael. I want to be reassigned."

I blinked with surprise. "OK. I will."

She turned her face away from me and put the speaker back in her ear. I got up and walked back to the conference cabin. Enzo was filling out paperwork. Reuel appeared to be asleep. Nathan and Warren were quietly talking while Taiya studied the new form of her hand. Lamal's seat was empty.

Warren looked up at me. "Everything OK?"

I smiled. "Everything's great."

He got up and moved over a chair so I could sit between him and Nathan.

"So what do we do now?" Nathan asked.

Enzo pointed across the table at him. "You return to training."

Nathan's nose scrunched up.

"You've only got, what? A week left?" Warren asked.

Nathan nodded. "A week too long."

"I can't wait to tell Fury you said that," Enzo said with a grin.

I looked at Warren. "Speaking of—she wants out. She asked me to talk to Azrael about having her reassigned."

His eyes moved to the door to the room where she was. "That's probably best for everyone."

Nathan whimpered. "Say it ain't so…"

I shoved his shoulder and laughed.

The plane roared to life underneath us, and outside the window, the crew rolled the stairs away from the door. I leaned my head against Warren's shoulder. "Are you all right?" I asked, sliding my hand under his arm and threading my fingers through his. "A lot went down today."

He tightened his fingers against mine. "I'm still processing it. It's weird. I feel like I should have stayed with Azrael."

"He didn't want us to."

"I know. Still, it's my mom."

"I'm sorry for what I did and for what I couldn't do." My voice cracked as I stared at the table.

He reached across his body and put his hand under my chin to force my eyes up to meet his. "It wasn't your fault. You were abso-lutely amazing today."

"I'll second that," Enzo said.

"Most definitely," Nathan agreed. "Sloan, you were a badass."

"*Verta*," Reuel said with a nod.

Warren pulled our hands up and kissed my knuckles. "You need to focus on the positives. You destroyed Phenex and defeated The Morning Star. Our daughter is safe. And our wedding is in less than two weeks."

I rolled my head back against my headrest. "Oh geez. There's so much work to do."

He laughed. "And we took off without telling Adrianne we were leaving."

"Ugh. I'd better call her." I looked around for my bag that I'd left on the plane.

"Here," Nathan said, handing it to me.

I dug my phone out of the main pocket. There was, of course, two missed calls and a dozen text messages from Adrianne.

Enzo handed me a satellite phone. "Use this to call her. Yours won't work once we're in the air."

I hesitated. "Are you sure that's OK?"

He smiled. "Sloan, you own the plane."

Everyone at the table laughed.

I dialed Adrianne's phone number. As the phone rang, I prepared myself for a verbal lashing for not keeping her in the loop. She picked up after the third ring, but she didn't say hello.

"Adrianne?" I asked, plugging my free ear with my finger. "Hello? Can you hear me?"

The line was silent, but not dead.

"Adrianne?"

There was more silence, and then I finally heard her breathe on the other end of the line. Her words came out slowly, in a voice that didn't belong to my best friend.

"Hello, *Praea*."

THANK YOU FOR READING!

Please consider leaving a review! Reviews help indie authors like me find new readers and get advertising. If you enjoyed this book, please tell your friends!

REVIEW

GET THE NEXT BOOK
Book 5 - The Sacrifice
Order It Now!

Want more of your favorite detective?
THE DETECTIVE
A Nathan McNamara Story

Here's a FREE GIFT for you!
Download The Detective at
www.thesoulsummoner.com

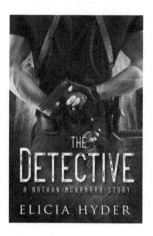

JOIN HYDERNATION

AUTHOR ELICIA HYDER

OFFICIAL FAN CLUB

★ Want leaked chapters of new books?
★ Want the first look at a new series I'm rolling out?
★ Want to win some awesome swag and prizes?

Join HYDERNATION, the official fan club of Elicia Hyder, for all that and more!

Join on Facebook

Join on EliciaHyder.com

OFFICIAL MERCHANDISE

Want Nathan's SWAT hoodie?

Want to start your own patch collection?

We've got you covered!

www.eliciahyder.com/shop

ALSO BY ELICIA HYDER

Be brave. Be strong. Be badass.

Roll into the exciting world of women's flat track roller derby, where the women are the heroes, and the men will make you weak in the kneepads.

A brand new romantic comedy series from Author Elicia Hyder.

ALSO BY ELICIA HYDER

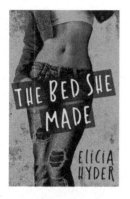

The Bed She Made

2015 Watty Award Winner for Best New Adult Romance

Journey Durant's father warned her that someday she'd have to lie in the bed she made. But she didn't believe him until her ex is released from prison and he threatens to bring her troubled past home with him.

To Be Her First

The Young Adult Prequel to The Bed She Made

At sixteen, Journey Durant hasn't yet experienced her first anything. No first boyfriend. No first date. No first kiss. But that's all about to change. Two boys at West Emerson High are vying for her attention: the MVP quarterback and the school's reigning bad boy.

ABOUT THE AUTHOR

In the dawning age of scrunchies and 'Hammer Pants', a small-town musician with big-city talent found out she was expecting her third child a staggering eleven years after her last one. From that moment on, Susie Waldrop referred to her daughter Elicia as a 'blessing' which is loosely translated as an accident, albeit a pleasant one.

In true youngest-sibling fashion, Elicia lived up to the birth order standard by being fun-loving, outgoing, self-centered, and rebellious throughout her formative years. She excelled academically–a feat her sister attributes to her being the only child who was breastfed–but abandoned her studies to live in a tent in the national forest with her dogs: a Rottweiler named Bodhisattva and a Pit Bull named Sativa. The ensuing months were very hazy.

In the late 90's, during a stint in rehab, Elicia was approached by a prophet who said, "Someday you will write a book."

She was right.

Now a firm believer in the prophetic word, Elicia Hyder is a full-time writer and freelance editor living in central Florida with her husband and five children. Eventually she did make it to college, and she studied literature and creative writing at the American Military University.

Her debut novel, **The Bed She Made**, is very loosely based on the stranger-than-fiction events of her life.

www.eliciahyder.com
elicia@eliciahyder.com

Made in United States
North Haven, CT
05 May 2022

18925290R00183